The Poetics of Passion

"A charming and sexy Victorian romance with a vibrant literary heroine and a swooning artist hero who go head to head. A captivating blend of witty banter, historical details and delightful characters, Ross's debut historical romance is definitely a novel that will enchant readers!"

   — ELIZA KNIGHT, *USA Today* bestselling author of *The Rebel Wears Plaid*

"Chock full of compelling characters, charm, and heartfelt emotion. I fell in love with Sebastian and Musa and their loyalty to their families above all else, even when their love was on the line."

   — HARPER ST. GEORGE, author of *The Duchess Takes a Husband*

"A story of hidden identities, secret longings, and the conflict of familial duty versus private pleasure, Delphine Ross conjures . . . the era with a master hand. A fascinating read!"

   — MIMI MATTHEWS, *USA Today* bestselling author of *The Belle of Belgrave Square*

"A passionate debut indeed, *The Poetics of Passion* combines the delicious elements of epistolary romance, artistic callings, secret identities and infamous scandals in high-stakes situations. An engaging love story with rich historical details and characters you can't help but root for."

— LEANNA RENEE HIEBER, award-winning author of the *Strangely Beautiful* and *Spectral City* series

∾

**Also included in this book:
an exclusive excerpt from
The Dance of Desire,
the next Muses of Scandal novel.**

The Poetics of Passion

A MUSES OF SCANDAL NOVEL

DELPHINE ROSS

MUSE PUBLICATIONS
NEW YORK

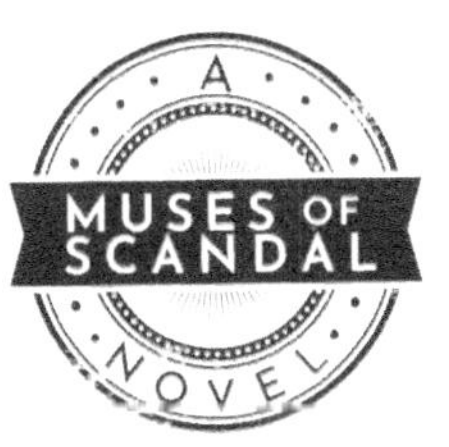

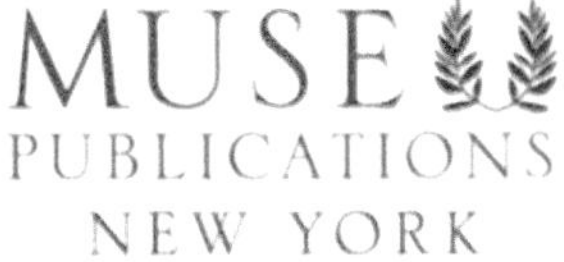

Books *that make you think.*

Books *that make you feel.*

Books *that inspire.*

First ebook and print publication July 2023. Updated February 2024.

For inquiries on bulk purchases, contact Muse Publications Special Sales: sales@readmuse.com

No AI was used to write this book.

Library of Congress Control Number: 2023906586

Trade softcover: ISBN 979-8-9853512-5-5
E-book: ISBN 979-8-9853512-6-2

Cover and interior design: Kris Waldherr

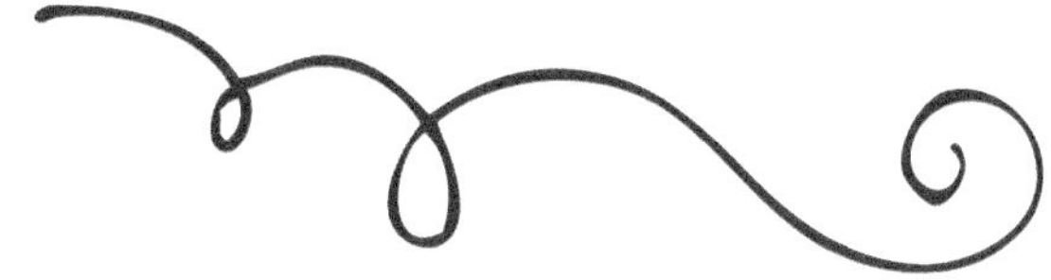

PROLOGUE
THE PAST

March 1845

THE FIRST TIME Musa Bartham's father saw the woman who'd become her mother, it was at a masked ball in Venice during Carnivale. The lady in question was the only one without a mask in a crowd of over a hundred. However, instead of standing out from a lack of sophistication, she glowed like a daffodil in a field of lavender. A falling star amid a cloudless night.

Later, Musa's father would tell his children this was the moment he knew he'd marry her.

He was not wrong. But it wouldn't be as simple as anticipated.

"Who is she?" he begged the ball's hostess, Lady Minerva Hadley. She was a widowed art collector with a palazzo on the Grand Canal in Venice.

"Neil Bartham? Is that you?" Lady Minerva retorted. "I must admit I hadn't expected your attendance! I thought you were too busy painting to mingle with society." She tapped his hand with her ivory fan. "You're interested in her?"

I'm not just interested, Neil thought. *I plan to wed her.* But this wasn't what one said, especially if one was an impoverished English artist in Venice.

While he considered the best way to reply to Lady Minerva's inquiry, he stole another look at the object of his marital ambitions.

The lady in question appeared only a year or two junior to his three and twenty. She wore no adornment save a slender choker of pearls and a cluster of pale gardenias pinned to her bodice. Necklace and flower were nearly the same shade as her silver-blonde hair, which hung in well-behaved curls to her waist. Her petite figure was set off in a simple ecru gown sewn of damask. A matching set of opera gloves covered her fingers, leaving Neil unable to tell whether she'd been claimed as someone's wife. This troubled him deeply.

But she's meant to be my *wife*, he thought madly and improbably.

And then her eyes met his. They widened as though she was struck by something wonderful yet terrifying. Her eyes were the same shade as cornflowers on an Alpine meadow. Not only were they beautiful, they bore kindness. An element of mercy. Even more so, he made out a spark of recognition in her eyes, as though they'd met before in another time and place.

This made no sense, but there it was.

"Well, Mr. Bartham?" Lady Minerva prodded. "Answer my question! Are you interested in her?"

"I-I'd like her to pose for me, my lady. Do you know her?"

Lady Minerva laughed. "Oh, I know her all right. She's my niece."

"What's your niece's name?"

Neil hadn't the self-control to play coy. By then he'd nicknamed Musa's future mother La Dame avec Merci, for she was as different from the La Dame sans Merci of Keat's poem as sugar from salt. As mad as it was, Neil sensed a thread tying him to his La Dame avec Merci—a thread that led all the way to his future, and his children's future, and beyond.

He saw his La Dame avec Merci seated beside him in his painting studio. He saw her in his future home, a mansion created by art and love. But, most of all, he saw four children tumbling about their feet, three girls and a boy, some bearing her light hair, others with his dark.

Before Lady Minerva could supply her niece's name, a rise of applause intervened. The guest of honor had arrived. Ethan Sutton, the powerful art critic who'd bankrolled Neil's travel from England to Venice and had insured his invitation to Lady Minerva's ball. Neil forced himself to turn from his *La Dame avec Merci* to acknowledge his benefactor. Besides, Neil hadn't seen Sutton in over six months, since the art critic's marriage to a woman whom Neil had yet to meet.

As for Neil's *La Dame avec Merci*, she approached Sutton. And then she was beside Sutton. Clutching Sutton's hand.

No. Neil was unable to think beyond that one panicked syllable.

"Here she is!" Sutton called to the crowd. "The former Miss Clio Hadley, now my bride!"

No, Neil thought again.

Neil awaited the thread he'd sensed to break, all those ripe scenes of artistic and domestic bliss scattering like beads from a broken necklace. The house, the children, the artistic renown. But, if anything, his desire was only renewed.

Even then, Neil knew this was not good. He didn't care.

"We're here on our honeymoon," Sutton continued. "But we're not without companions . . ." He pointed toward Neil, voice booming. "I see you, Bartham! Everyone, my protégé, Neil Bartham, the artist who will save British painting. Come, join us here!"

Somehow Neil set one foot in front of the other as he approached his benefactor. One step, another. And then he was before her, his *Dame avec Merci* who bore the unexpected name of Mrs. Clio Sutton.

The woman married to his benefactor.

The bride now on her honeymoon in Venice, the most romantic city in the world.

The muse who was meant to be *his* wife, not Sutton's.

"Good evening, Mr. Bartham," Clio said in a musical voice.

"The same to you, Mrs. Sutton," Neil replied.

And then Clio set her gloved hand in Neil's. The unexpected contact thrilled him beyond anything he'd ever experienced in his life.

Clio whispered, "Have we met before?"

"I was wondering the same, Mrs. Sutton," Neil whispered back. "I've never felt like this—"

He broke off, knowing he'd been madly forward. But, to his relief, a tremulous smile crowned her lips.

"I feel the exact same way, Mr. Bartham—I can't explain it." Then she pronounced the words that would seal their fates. "You must call on me tomorrow. I won't accept a refusal."

Ten minutes later, Clio and Neil were on an overly familiar first name basis.

Ten days later, they fled Venice together in the dead of night, winning Musa's future mother the snide nickname of the Muse of Scandal. The moniker was inspired by both circumstances and her namesake—Clio had been named after the Greek muse of history.

Ten months later, Clio and Neil returned to London. They wed after the Suttons' marriage was annulled for reasons Clio refused to reveal; her belly already swelled with child. The resulting scandal left the newlyweds exiled from polite society, but burnished Neil's artistic reputation to a fine sheen.

Ten years later, their four children, the first of whom was Musa, tumbled about their feet. Alas, as Musa and her siblings grew into adulthood, no one would receive them in society, leaving her sisters without marriage prospects, her brother shunned of opportunity. By the time Musa turned twenty, this realization led her father to undertake a desperate sacrifice—one which would have lasting repercussions for his family.

Neil gathered his paints and brushes. He kissed his beloved wife and children goodbye. Then he set off on a long and arduous pilgrimage for the Holy Land, where he planned to spend two years painting religious scenes of a treacle-hued sentimentality guaranteed to melt the heart of the frostiest London doyen. Through this act, Neil would rehabilitate the Bartham name into society's graces, thus restoring his children's futures and his wife's reputation.

He would never return.

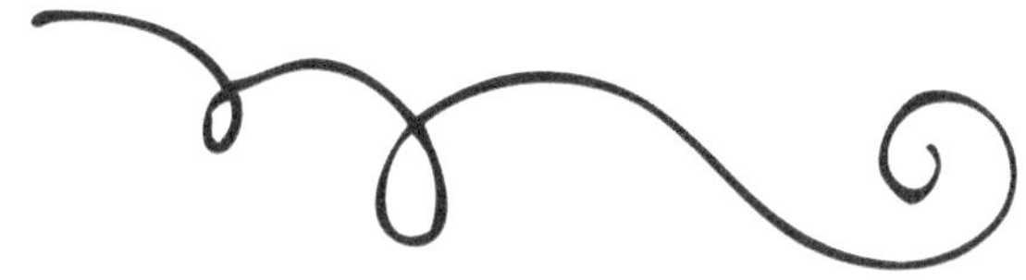

CHAPTER 1
THE PRESENT

In January of 1872, the inglorious Bartham family had been reduced from a West Kensington mansion of art to a shabby two-story townhouse in Brompton. This townhouse had been let only through the practical enterprises of Neil and Clio's eldest daughter, Musa. By then, Musa had reached the ripe age of twenty-six without an offer for her hand. This was in spite of her lustrous chestnut hair, willowy figure, and considerable intelligence—for the Barthams remained as outcast from society as they had prior to Neil's departure for the Holy Land.

For the best, Musa told herself. She didn't mind being a spinster. Unlike her tragically romantic parents, Musa bore a practical mind, the sort able to find solutions where others gave up. Thus, after a number of unsuccessful financial attempts, she'd taken upon herself to support her family through the means of poetry—and not just any poetry.

Poetry that dripped with florid emotion.

Poetry with rhyme schemes that brought flushes to cheeks and heat to groins.

Poetry that proved lucrative with gentlemen who yearned for forbidden encounters in nocturnal gardens scented with jasmine, and ladies who fantasized of kisses on chaise lounges hidden behind gilt-lacquered screens.

In other words, love poetry.

The irony that this love poetry was written by a young woman resolved never to wed was not lost on Musa, though her poems were shockingly passionate for one whose heart had never sped at the clandestine brush of a hand. But Musa had seen enough during the course of her life. She'd learned that grand passions, such as the one leading to her parents' marriage, led to grand scandals—and, if Musa were to have only one rule for her family, it would be no more scandals. To prevent further damage to their Bartham name, Musa's poetry books were written under the pen name of Felicity Vita.

Outside of her publisher, only Musa's sister Angela knew of Felicity's existence; their mother Clio remained too bereft to notice much beyond Neil's absence. She just assumed Musa found some way to monetize their father's art. Musa didn't dissuade her.

However, considerations of scandals were far from Musa's mind that winter morning. She thought only of providing for her family. Her father, for all his intentions, had left her mother with only enough income to survive for three years while he was off seeking respectability. Now, six years after his departure, they'd have been forced into the poorhouse had it not been for Musa's literary enterprises.

As Musa prepared to depart the Barthams' two-story townhouse to provide for her family, she'd just finished imbibing a warming second cup of tea. (No sugar, only lemon.) It was Friday, which was Musa's usual day to run errands. That day, she'd visit her publisher near Fleet Street with fair copies of poems for her next book, which was several weeks overdue, and collect mail addressed to her *nom de plume*. All necessary tasks to keep the Barthams fed and housed . . . though she did take a disconcerting amount of pleasure in the mail. Especially one gentleman's correspondence. A gentleman she'd never meet in person, alas.

Henry Whitney was his name. It was a good name. A solid

name. The name of a man who wrote the best letters she'd ever read in her life. Her editor advised not to answer, but Musa hadn't been able to resist. Henry's last letter pressed to meet her, but she'd regretfully declined. It was impossible. Anyway, love was better in letters than in real life—of this Musa was certain.

However, that Friday morning would not be like others. As Musa approached the front door, satchel in one hand, umbrella in the other—she'd noticed a gray cloud suggesting rain rather than snow—the doorbell clattered.

"I'll answer it!" Musa called to their overtaxed maid of all work, the only staff they could afford.

By the time Musa reached the door, the bell pull had been deployed four more times, evidence of their visitor's impatience.

She thrust the door open. "Aunt Minerva?"

Musa let her mouth gape. Her elderly dowager of a great-aunt was not expected. Nor was she particularly welcomed. Not after all that happened.

Musa had only met Lady Minerva Hadley once. Seven years earlier, Minerva had confronted the Barthams at the funeral of an ancient cousin—an encounter that ended with the dowager shouting about how Neil ruined her niece Clio's life "because he was ruled by his stiff John Thomas instead of his brain." Whether Minerva had communicated since with Clio in the intervening years Musa did not know. But Musa had attempted such. After Neil's disappearance, she'd written Aunt Minerva five times apprising her of Clio's distress and their financial difficulties. Minerva never responded. This did not win Musa's favor.

And now here she was, at the Barthams' door.

Without a word of welcome Aunt Minerva pushed her way inside, her sharp eyes scanning the dank hallway, the water-stained wallpaper, which was barely hidden behind her father's oil paintings and other works of art. She offered a silent shudder, her aquiline nose wrinkling as though she'd smelled something foul. Musa recalled they had fish the night before; she'd grown accustomed to the stench. On top of this, a sour chord drifted from the parlor amid raised voices. Her fifteen-year-old brother, Theo, arguing with his twin sister Lyra over the piano, which hadn't been tuned in ages. The two youngest Barthams got along like oil and water.

"Your family's situation is worse than I've been informed," Aunt Minerva greeted. "And it's all your father's fault."

"Good morning, Aunt." Musa did her best to keep her voice free of shock. She recalled to bob a curtsey, hoping her aunt had reconsidered Musa's requests for help.

"You're the eldest girl then? Musa, if I recall. What a ridiculous name!"

Musa flinched. "I like my name. It means 'inspiration' in Italian—"

"I *do* speak Italian, you know. Perhaps you've forgotten I've a palazzo in Venice along with a townhouse in Mayfair. How tall are you, miss?"

"Tall enough, ma'am."

Musa was statuesque like her father. Lady Minerva's comment had intended to insult.

Moving past the slight, Musa said in her most ingratiating voice, "You look healthy, Aunt."

"Spare the flattery, miss. I didn't want to come here. You should know this and be grateful."

Well, excuse me. Musa clutched her poems against her chest, that second cup of tea churning in her stomach. She should have taken it with milk instead of lemon.

"Is Mama expecting you?" she replied, more alarmed than she cared to show. Clio rarely wrote to anyone these days. For the most part, all she did was lie in bed when she wasn't sleeping or rereading old love letters from Neil. Occasionally she'd venture downstairs or into the garden as though to remind herself the world still existed beyond her room.

"No, miss. Where is your sister Angela?"

"Why do you ask?" Angela was the beauty of the family, or so people said. She most resembled the ethereal Clio, who'd been a great beauty in her day. Angela danced with a grace equal to the great Taglioni of earlier in the century. Angela was kind. Sweet. Of all the Barthams, she'd taken their fall from society's grace the hardest, though she rarely complained. Musa had confessed to Angela about her poetry to reassure their family's financial woes were addressed.

"Aren't you saucy? If you must know, she's written me." Her brow arched. "A desperate letter too!"

"She hadn't told me." Why hadn't Angela confided in her? Why would Aunt Minerva respond to Angela but not Musa?

Aunt Minerva's tone rose. "Again, where is Angela?"

"I don't know," Musa lied, knowing perfectly well her sister was still in the dining room. When Musa last spied Angela, she was dolloping cream on her porridge with a voluptuous sigh; cream was a luxury for their household.

Musa's spine prickled with a dread she couldn't quantify. Her dread combined with the urge to protect Angela. Surely Angela made a mistake writing Minerva.

Then it was too late.

The disturbance of Aunt Minerva's arrival drew Angela into the hallway, looking as lovely as ever though she wasn't dressed for visitors. Her silvery-blonde tresses dangled in graceful curls to her waist, much like Clio's as a young woman. Angela's petite beauty was only enhanced in that she was wearing one of Clio's Japanese silk kimonos over her nightdress, which Neil had used as a painting prop in the early days of their marriage. Angela appeared a nymph of the woods, a fairy of old. Beauty itself as well as kindness.

Musa frowned as Angela thrust herself into Minerva's arms with a too familiar air.

"Oh, Aunt, thank you *so* much for coming!" Angela fawned in an overly sweet tone. "You'll help me find a husband then?"

"Husband?" Musa's stomach turned even queasier. "What's this?"

"Shush, Musa!" Angela whispered, eyes darting. "Don't spoil things for me."

Musa answered in a low firm voice, "You've no need for a husband, Angela. You know why."

Because no one worthy of you will associate with our family.

Musa believed Angela to be as resolved to spinsterhood as she was. Yes, there'd been that flirtation when Angela was eighteen with a dancer visiting from Paris. But that had been a slip of the heart. Nothing at all like their parents.

Aunt Minerva extracted herself from Angela's arms. She smoothed her purple day suit as though wiping off a child's muddy handprints. "You're Angela, I presume?"

Angela curtsied prettily, batting her thick eyelashes. "Yes, ma'am. I'm so delighted you're here!"

Minerva peered at Angela through her gold-rimmed lunettes. "How old are you, miss?"

"Twenty-three come April, ma'am."

"You're a beauty though a bit long in the tooth. No inappropriate suitors to gossip?"

Angela flushed. "Just as I wrote, ma'am. None at all."

"Angela, what's going on?" Musa pressed, growing even more alarmed.

"Hush!" Aunt Minerva snapped. To Angela: "No other scandals I should be aware of, miss? Perhaps something someone else in your family has done?" A glare in Musa's direction. "Or your sister?"

Angela met Musa's eyes for the briefest moment.

Musa again sensed dread rising from her stomach. Or curdled tea.

She thought of Felicity Vita, the scandal should anyone discover the truth. She'd been so careful to cover her tracks. Writing her manuscript fair copies with her left hand so no one would recognize her handwriting—it helped that Musa was ambidextrous. Destroying all her drafts—it helped they'd scant servants. But Musa had never considered her sister a vulnerability.

"No, Aunt. Nothing," Angela responded.

Musa pressed in what she hoped was a reasonable tone, "Angela, please tell me what you wrote Aunt Minerva."

"Something wise regarding her future. Unlike your parents, or you for that matter," Minerva said dryly. "Very well, Angela. I'll introduce you to society—from there it'll be up to you to win a husband. Though you're pretty enough, I must warn you'll have a difficult time thanks to your parents' foolishness. But first, I should speak to your mother. Where is she?"

"In her bedroom. Upstairs!"

Angela grabbed her great-aunt's hand and pulled her from the hallway. Musa followed, imagining what they would find in Clio's room. Clio half-asleep in her rumpled negligee, clutching the last love letters Neil sent before his disappearance. A trail of crumpled handkerchiefs next to her pillows. Bottles of medication and various herbal teas and potions intended to calm nerves and heal any imagined illnesses.

Friday morning or no, Musa's publisher—and Felicity Vita—would have to wait.

CHAPTER 2

On the other side of London, Sebastian Atkinson was embracing a dark-haired temptress, one with whom he'd exchanged plenty of letters. Though they'd never met in person, that night she'd miraculously arrived at his door. Now she laid beside him in his bed, which was more than he'd ever dared to dream. The temptress was dressed in yards of pink silk and expensive lace; fabric fine enough that her glorious body shimmered beneath it, for she wore no chemise or stays. The translucent fabric allowed Seb to recognize the nubs of her nipples, the dark valley between her thighs.

Seb's fingers trailed along the swell of her hips. The curve of her breasts.

He murmured against her neck, "You agreed to see me after all."

She laughed, but it wasn't a laugh of ridicule. No, it was a kind laugh. A laugh akin to a caress.

"I've been waiting for your invitation, Seb. Why did you take so long?"

Seb groaned. "Why indeed."

She leaned over his reclining form, her graceful fingers tracing the muscles of his arms. Her nipples teased his chest as her mouth traced the seashell curve of his ear, whispering sweet verses.

Poetry.

Poetry that awakened his deepest yearnings.

Poetry that evoked his most tender emotions, as if the author herself could see inside his very soul.

Poetry written by the temptress now pressing her lips against his neck—a temptress who bore the all-too-enticing name of Felicity Vita.

Felicity Vita was the love poet all of London buzzed about, for everyone yearned to uncover her identity. Some said she was a noblewoman in disguise. Others ventured she was someone far less genteel. Felicity's first book, *Verses of Love Lost and Love Found,* aroused quite the rumpus, though it was ever so tasteful in its descriptions of sensuality. From there, the poetess published a volume of poetry every six months like clockwork, her latest being *The Poetics of Passion.* However, though no one could figure out the secret behind her *nom de plume,* somehow he, Sebastian Atkinson, a twenty-eight-year-old gentleman artist with few guineas to his name, had somehow lured Felicity Vita into his bed.

Sebastian sighed with impatience as Felicity raised the hem of his nightshirt. He wished he'd gone to bed naked to expedite their intimacies, but the January chill was too sharp in his attic. Nor had he anticipated Felicity would show up at his door. Hadn't her last letter informed him they must never meet?

But this no longer mattered. Not anymore. Felicity was there. In his bed. Beside him.

Seb was swiftly undressed by Felicity's eager hands, his muscled torso a swirl of shadows beneath her lace-covered figure. He strained to make out her features in the darkened room.

"Please, show me your face," he begged. "I'll light a candle."

She laughed again, a honey-warm sound. "I can see well enough. Come here . . ."

Soon he was flat on his back. She reclined above him, her kisses growing bolder. He wove his fingers into her long dark tresses.

"Let me see you, Felicity. I'm begging."

Again, that low honeyed laugh. "Beg away."

Alas, no matter how close she approached, Seb still couldn't make out her features. It was as though she was there yet nowhere. Nothing yet everything. An amalgam of ideals, all too wonderful to exist. Like true love itself. Like a dream.

All of a sudden, everything began to shake and shudder like an earthquake about Seb.

"Are you alright?" Felicity asked in a strange, deep voice before she turned her attention to places south. She kissed and stroked him until he thought he could take no more.

Sebastian answered her with a long moan. Her caresses were so able and eager. Real. He felt on the edge of losing himself to the most exquisite pleasure . . .

More shaking in his bed. A splash of cold water.

∼

"Seb! Wake up! Are you alright?"

Seb's eyes blinked open. He was soaking wet, still in his bed. Any lingering arousal deflated.

Only a dream. But oh, what a dream!

It was morning, not night. He was still dressed from the day before. And he was alone in his room save for his best friend, Lucas Ward, who was shaking his shoulder with one hand, clutching a water jug in his other.

"You threw water at me," Seb gritted out.

"You were having a nightmare," Luke explained, setting the emptied water jug on a mantel. "You were moaning and shaking! You wouldn't wake up. I was alarmed."

"So am I."

Seb drew a deep breath, barely noticing his soaked clothes in the wake of his pounding head. A harsh gray glare streamed rudely into his room, which laid up a precarious stairway in an attic aerie overlooking the whole of Spitalfields. It was an expansive room, large enough for Seb's needs as an artist—one wall featured his oils, another his drawings and watercolors. There was a skylight, an array of windows. A sandbag hanging from one beam for exercise. Most importantly, the attic was cheap, which allowed him to save money so he could provide for his two sisters, who remained in their family home back in Kent. He'd been forced into daily labor upon the unexpected deaths of his parents a year and a half earlier.

Cheap room or not, right now the attic felt far too large and far too light-filled for his liking. Everything was spinning.

He groaned. A hangover, that's what he had. A monster hangover. Worse, he still felt mildly drunk. How could this be after hours of sleep?

Seb pulled himself against his pillow, which was thankfully drier than his bed. He gestured for a towel, which Luke handed him—Luke who'd brought him home in his protective way, though Seb questioned how they'd arrived there. He seemed to recall running out of funds . . . and yet somehow they'd gotten back to Spitalfields all the way from Kensington.

Had Luke stiffed the hansom? He probably did.

As Seb mopped his hair, he tried to puzzle through everything that had occurred the previous evening. He and Luke went to the pub near the printing house where they both worked, Luke as a journalist, Seb as a pressman. Seb was upset. (Well, he wouldn't think *why* he'd been upset it was all too embarrassing in the context of his dream. Not until he'd gotten coffee into him, if his stomach allowed.) Luke was astute enough to notice Seb's distress. After all, they'd known each since they were boys in Kent. Luke even lived with Seb's family for a while, before making his way to London to seek his fortune as a writer. In an attempt to distract Seb from his emotions, Luke matched him glass for glass. Seb soon outpaced him, which led to them running out of money, which had probably encouraged Seb's all-too-intense dream.

Dreams of Felicity Vita, the poet.

Felicity Vita, his correspondent for the past year and a half.

Felicity, who sent intimate letters addressed to a postbox

bearing the name of Henry Whitney, a name Seb chose to protect his identity for reasons he couldn't quite explain.

Felicity, who'd written to him yesterday stating they could never meet in person, in response to a desperate letter Seb sent. *"Just meet me one time,"* he'd begged, *"though I hope it will lead to more than that."* He'd issued the invitation knowing he'd have to confess the truth that he was naught but an impoverished artist—but now this would never be.

The poet answered tersely in response:

> Darling Henry,
> Let us enjoy the communion of our Souls through our Words, not our Bodies. True Love is an Ideal only spoiled by the intrusion of Life—this is a Truth I know from personal experience.
> I look forward to your next letter!
> Yours in literature and affection,
> Felicity

Seb was devastated by her rejection, though he knew it was ridiculous. Who was he to presume so much of a famed poetess? To ask her to set her anonymity at risk? Anyway, they'd continue their correspondence. This would have to be enough.

It wasn't.

You can't love someone you never met, he lectured himself. *You've been swept away by your emotions. Again.*

"Sorry I threw water at you," Luke continued. "You were really—"

"Inebriated. I know."

Seb pulled on his boots in a quest to avoid the puddle of water beside his bed. He quickly changed into a dry shirt. It appeared fairly clean.

"You're too good to watch over me, Luke. About last night . . ."

"You weren't thinking straight," Luke finished, offering him a small glass of brandy for his hangover. "Don't worry about the hansom. He didn't mind us not paying."

Seb pulled a face at the brandy. "I don't believe that."

Luke offered a devil-may-care shrug, a gesture Seb recognized too well. "I told him you were deathly ill, and he'd be rewarded in heaven for his kindness."

"You never change. Next you'll tell me we did him a favor."

"Perhaps we did. What's better than the glow of a good deed?"

"The satisfaction of honesty." It was one thing to pull pranks, as they did while boys in Kent, quite another to skirt the law in London.

"Honesty . . ." Luke's blithe tone turned somber. "Very well then, I'll be honest with you."

Now it all came out, the conversation they'd avoided the previous evening. Not that Luke knew about Seb's correspondence with Felicity, which he kept locked away in his desk. Seb had simply confessed there was a woman who'd rejected him. Someone he thought he loved—Luke would have laughed at his moon-faced obsession with the anonymous love poet.

"Whoever you're enamored with," Luke said, wagging a finger, "it needs to stop. She's rejected you. Done. Move on."

Seb gagged down a sip of brandy before replying. "I know, I know. But the heart isn't so obedient."

"To be honest, I think you're still grieving your parents."

"Can't one grieve and also be infatuated?"

"I suppose you've a point. But here's something else to consider. You've barely painted in weeks." Luke pointed to Seb's latest painting, which was sketched in only sepia oil washes. "This looks like a pot of mud thrown at a canvas. What's it supposed to be?"

"Keats. La Dame sans Merci."

"Ah. Could have fooled me."

Seb gestured weakly. "I'm still in the early stages. Still figuring things out. Are you done criticizing me?"

"No," Luke replied. "You're distracted at work. Everyone's

noticed—you nearly incinerated a pile of newspapers, for god's sake! If nothing else, think of me. You're making me look bad since—"

"You recommended me for the job. And I do appreciate it, Luke, I really do."

"You can't continue like this, Seb. Whoever this woman may be, she must be trouble if you won't even confide to me who she is."

"I'm a gentleman," Seb protested, his face heating anew. "A gentleman never tells."

Luke scoffed. "Whenever you've taken a shine to someone in the past, I've always been the first person you told."

Another sip of brandy. "I've learned to be tactful."

"Tactful? You?" Luke laughed. "You're a waterfall of emotions. A seeping revelation of whatever hits your heart and soul. That makes you a great artist—yes, I do believe this—but also a terrible liar." He leaned in. "Tell the truth: are you involved with a married woman? Or a courtesan, though who knows how you'd pay for her? Is that why you're so secretive?"

Seb grimaced. "No! Nothing like that."

"Someone famous who refuses to be seen with you?"

This cut too close. "None of your business."

"Ooh feisty!"

"Anyway, it's over, Luke. Well, not exactly over—we're still friends. Just it won't progress further. She wrote as much to me. That's why I was so upset."

Though I desperately wish it wasn't so.

And here was the bitter kernel of Seb's obsession: writing to Felicity under the guise of Henry Whitney had allowed him to express truths he'd never dared admit even in the darkest hours of the night. Truths he didn't dare share with Luke or his two sisters.

Felicity was the only one who understood. Felicity was the only one who knew his true soul . . . though not enough to meet with him.

It was three weeks after his parents' unexpected deaths that Seb wrote Felicity Vita for the first time. It was a letter of appreciation, explaining how her poems offered comfort in the wake of his loss. He was shocked when she responded directly to his letter. *"I lost my father nearly five years ago,"* she'd answered in an elegant hand. *"I understand your sorrow—the loss weighs on one's Soul."* From there, their correspondence grew. In recent months, he found himself checking his postbox every day, rereading her letters over and over. All this had led him to issue his impetuous invitation to meet in person . . . and that dream.

Seb grew warm, recalling the dream's explicit quality. For all he knew, Felicity Vita was a fifty-year-old widow in Scotland with dozens of correspondents. She could even be a man.

Luckily, Luke didn't notice Seb's ruddy face. "Whatever's going on, let it go."

"I know I should. But I can't."

Luke led him toward the sandbag hanging from a corner beam. "Go! Punch it. Do whatever you can to get her out of your system."

"I've tried that many a time." Seb's muscles had become decidedly stronger in recent weeks.

"Try talking to her again. Convince her of your worth. You're talented, you've a manor house in Kent, damn it!"

"You mean a ramshackle house falling apart."

"It won't be once you make your fortune as an artist." Luke gestured at the canvas of *La Dame sans Merci.* "This could be good if you add other colors to it. You're not half bad looking either."

"Am I?" At that moment, Seb didn't feel half-bad looking with his queasy, pounding head. There'd been a time when he'd felt very handsome indeed, when the world glowed with sunlight and promise. This seemed a lifetime ago. Since his parents' death, he'd been so focused on providing for his sisters that he couldn't recall the last time he had a haircut or a decent meal. He'd grown distinctly lanky and overgrown, like an untended garden that no one bothered to visit . . . especially since his obsession with Felicity Vita had overtaken his life.

Luke responded, "You can be quite charming when you're not mooning over someone who doesn't reciprocate your affections."

"Thank you, I think. Have you finished?"

"No. Whatever's going on with you and this woman, fix it. I can't bear to see you this way."

Fix it. This sounded easy enough. But how to fix something when you couldn't reach the object of your affection?

Seb's gaze drifted toward Felicity's books. They were stacked in a neat pile on his drawing board. Besides *The Poetics of Passion*, whose purple binding really drew the eye, there was *Verses of Love Lost and Love Found*, *The Triumph of Eros*, and several others with similarly themed titles. Felicity's books were works of art. Books to appeal to artistic sensibilities. They were printed on heavy paper stock with black and white illustrations, though not as fine as what Seb could offer as an artist.

An idea began to formulate in Seb's hungover brain. An idea that surprised him, one he'd never considered before. Even if Felicity refused to meet with him, there *was* something else he could do.

Seb grabbed his copy of *The Poetics of Passion* and his portfolio. He gathered his coat and bowler and turned toward the door.

Luke called, "You're not going out? It looks like rain."

"I am."

"You'll frighten people. Seriously. At least comb your hair if you won't shave."

"No time!"

"Tell me where you're going, so I can find you when the police pick you up for disorderly assembly."

Seb threw a smile from the threshold. "To find a way to speak to her. Lock the door behind you when you leave. Oh, and don't steal anything!"

CHAPTER 3

"And your mother agreed to Angela seeking a husband?" Mary Nicholson, Musa's editor, asked, disbelief evident on her wide-open face. "I'm shocked. Shocked. Well, both at your mother and at Angela for wanting to wed."

Nearly two hours after great-aunt Minerva's unexpected arrival, Musa had arrived at the office of Persephone Press just before the rain began. Persephone Press was the publisher of Felicity Vita and other books written by women. (The publisher had a few gentlemen authors, but they'd agreed to publish as Anonymous. Only fair considering how many women were forced to publish as such over the years.) Mary was the brains behind the publishing house, which had been started by her father two decades earlier at the behest of her literary-minded mother. Indeed, Mary herself was named after Mary Wollstonecraft, the famed author and philosopher. When her mother passed on to her great reward, Mary took over running the press with her father's blessing; Mr. Nicholson was more interested in collecting fossils in Essex than publishing books in London.

Mary was a lanky woman of twenty-eight years of age with dun-brown hair and a manner some might consider blunt. Musa adored her for her honesty and intelligence along with her business acumen. She was also unmarried, though she was paired; Mary's companion Seraphina was away painting in Rome until summer. Nor was anyone else in the office, now that it was lunchtime. Usually Musa showed up then to avoid anyone associating her with Felicity Vita.

As Musa listened to Mary opine about Angela's matrimonial situation, she found herself unable to contain the emotions roiling inside her. She would have never expected the events of the morning to transpire between her favorite sister, her great-aunt, and her mother. Worst of all, she was having difficulties concentrating—especially after Mary passed Musa a new letter from Henry. Henry's letters were so delectable. It was a shame they'd never meet, but such was life as Felicity Vita.

"Angela is a fool," Musa finally responded. "A wonderful, lovely fool in this case. She claims she wants someone to love. A family. A husband."

"Marriage is a business arrangement," Mary said nervously—how strangely she was behaving this morning! "Capitalism at its worst. Women as products to be procured, only as good as their perceived value on the marriage market and the matches they make." Mary took a determined bite out of a biscuit before she continued. "Even in a best case where there's affection between husband and wife, it's complicated. It was fortunate for my mother that my father let her do as she wished. As for your family, look at your poor mother."

"I know!" Musa moaned in agreement. "Angela should know better."

"If it's any comfort, your sister's a beauty. This should grant her opportunities, but I worry she'll be propositioned for something less than love."

"That's my concern too."

Musa imagined a host of unsuitable suitors for Angela. Shallow heels only attracted by her appearance. Ancient widowers seeking to beget children. Scoundrels who understood Angela was compromised due to her family name. Worse, rakes who would offer illicit liaisons outside the bonds of matrimony. A townhouse on Grosvenor Square. Worth couture gowns. Glittering jewels made of paste. The gift of syphilis before they moved onto their next mistress.

What a mess it all was! Musa's father was charming, talented, and loving. But he hadn't been able to protect their family from society's scorn, and now he was gone. Nor had Musa been able to protect them—well, she provided food and a roof, but little else. That was the problem with love. It made you do foolish things, like elope with someone's wife and then take off to the Holy Land, abandoning your family.

Suddenly the weight of Musa's family and her responsibilities felt heavier than ever. How alone she felt.

"I don't know what to do!" Musa burst out. "Aunt Minerva can dress up Angela all she wants, but no one respectable is going to marry her. I'd thought I'd convinced her not to care about society. I've only delayed the inevitable. You can't shut out the world. You can only pretend it doesn't exist for a while."

"Too true," Mary agreed, reaching for the slice of cake hidden inside her desk. Her voice still possessed a strange tone. "You'll just have to watch over her the best you can."

A distant rumble of thunder.

Musa offered her friend a grateful glance. "You're very kind to listen. I appreciate it."

The rain began at last, a hiss of water against the windowpanes.

"I do consider myself more than your editor . . ." Mary said, studiously picking at her cake. "There's something I have to speak to you about."

"Is this about my new manuscript? I know I'm a little late—you've been so patient. Here."

After closing the blinds, Musa pulled from her satchel a manuscript containing her latest poems. She set the pages on Mary's desk as though offering something illicit.

To Musa's shock, Mary handed the manuscript back. "I-I can't accept this."

"Why not?" How strangely Mary was behaving.

"Oh, it's so hard to say, Musa."

"Is it about Henry?"

Mary pushed her cake away. "I only wish."

Musa prickled with nerves. "If you're unable to eat, there must be something seriously wrong."

All of a sudden Mary cried, "It's awful! I can't publish you any longer!"

"What?"

Mary grabbed a handkerchief from her pocket and pressed it against her eyes. "It's not you as much as I can't publish Felicity Vita."

This was a blow Musa did not expect. She pulled off her spectacles, surprised by a rush of panic. How to handle it? *Logic*, she told herself.

"Mary, I'm your bestselling author. You'd go out of business without my books."

Mary looked up from her handkerchief. "If only it was that!"

"What is it then?" Though Musa used her most "let's be reasonable" tone, she felt anything but.

"It's worse. I can't keep your books in print either." At last Mary met Musa's eyes. "I know I should have told you, but we've been hemorrhaging pounds for the past year. First, there was that plagiarized novel we published—still dealing with the lawsuit. Then the archeology book Papa published that cost more than expected, and those bankrupt bookstores owing us funds. Amid the worst of this, someone approached my father about investing funds into Persephone Press. To become a shadow partner, if you will. An American heiress. Papa assured she'd be amenable to all of my publishing plans, that she simply just wanted to play at being a publisher." A sob. "It turns out that's not what she had in mind at all."

Musa listened, stunned, as Mary laid out the worst possible outcome.

"From here on, she plans to only publish what she calls morally responsible books for children and ladies. Worse, she wants all of our backlist destroyed. Says she needs a fresh start. And I have no choice—Papa sold her 75% of the press, leaving us just enough to provide us with an income." Mary dabbed at her eyes anew. "She's not in London yet. Any day now, though. What a gorgon!"

Musa's heart sped like a metropolitan train pulling into Earl's Court. *Logic*, she reminded herself. It didn't help. "A fresh start? She'd have been better off starting her own press."

Mary sobbed, "I know, I know! If she'd confessed her plans, my father would never have agreed. She was ever so cagey until after the paperwork was signed. He thought he'd found us a savior. Instead, we made a deal with the devil. She was especially adamant about Felicity Vita's books. Says she doesn't want to risk scandal, being American and all. Papa had no choice but to agree."

Musa clutched Mary's hand, emotion spilling over her like an icy wave. She hated how out of control she felt. How frightened. She rapidly calculated the amount of money remaining in their bank account. *Two, maybe three months' worth of income.* Unfortunately, Felicity was more infamous than rich.

So many Barthams. So little income.

Musa choked out, "What am I to do? My family will starve!"

"I feel awful about this! But maybe not all is lost. I can loan you money, of course."

"I've no way to repay it. And you know I don't like debt." Musa had only just finished paying off the bills remaining from the pre-Felicity days.

"Let me think . . ." Mary pulled out a pencil and a piece of paper. "If you wrote something else, I'd be happy to publish it, though I doubt it'll sell like Felicity does. Here, let's make a list. Perhaps a book of aphorisms."

Mary wrote that down on the paper.

"But I write poetry—well, Felicity does," Musa countered.

Mary tapped the pencil against her temple. "You could write a children's book like Louisa May Alcott. *Little Women* is ever so popular though it's quite moral." The book had come out in two volumes just over a year earlier.

Children's books, Mary added to the list.

Musa rolled her eyes. "What, because there are four of us Barthams and my father's missing?" She prayed Papa remained alive. "Anyway, even if it sold as well as Felicity's books, writing about my family will only make things worse for Angela. Tongues will wag."

Mary looked up from her list. "A new *nom de plume?* Not for love poetry, of course."

"I simply don't have the heart for this. Not after all I've accomplished as Felicity."

Tap, tap, tap went Mary's pencil. "We'll release you from our contracts so you can publish Felicity's poems elsewhere. That's the easiest path."

Publish elsewhere went onto the list.

"But I'd have to trust another publisher not to reveal who I am." It was fortunate Mr. Nicholson had little interest in Felicity Vita's identity.

"Publish anonymously, like the Brontës?"

Musa shook her head, her eyes prickling like an illogical fool. "Still too much of a risk."

"I really am sorry, Musa—"

A clatter at the door interrupted Mary's apology. Musa pulled her spectacles on after giving her eyes an embarrassed wipe.

Despite the weather, a tall man paced back and forth before their door; hence, the clatter. He looked perhaps thirty years of age at most. His dark hair was particularly wild, with curls dashing in all directions beneath his bowler as the rain hardened. He wore a beard as rough around the edges as the man himself.

He appeared a better grade of beggar or someone worse: a gentleman fallen on hard times. Musa could tell his downward social trajectory by the quality of his clothes, which were rumpled but sewn of good broadcloth.

"You don't know him, do you?" Musa asked.

"Of course not! He's been out there for the past hour," Mary replied in a low voice. "I'd hope he'd take off once the rain started. I think he's waiting for someone—he seems desperate."

Musa frowned. She'd passed him when she'd entered the office, but she'd been so upset by her sister's news she'd barely taken note. "He looks inebriated."

Mary rose from her seat. "I'll order him to leave."

"And I'll back you up."

The gentleman abruptly opened the door, his steps uneven. If he wasn't drunk, he certainly appeared it. He was soaked to his skin. Musa glared at him. They might be the only two people in the office, but they weren't weak.

To her surprise, their eyes met.

His were shockingly blue, defiant with emotion. Mary was right: he did seem desperate, but not for drink. For something else. Someone to care for him. Something Felicity Vita would know how to handle; Musa had a sudden vision of Felicity soothing him. *"There, there,"* she'd say before leading him toward a much-needed bath.

But Felicity was kinder than Musa. Musa was protective. Harder. Logical, though she didn't feel such at the moment. She also felt threatened. Desperation made people do foolish things; Musa understood this all too well.

"We're not open to the public," Mary boomed, pulling herself up to her full height, which wasn't much over five feet. "You're dripping water all over my floor."

"Your door was unlocked," the man said, his voice full and brassy. "If it's unlocked, you're open, are you not?"

"A matter of semantics," Musa intercepted. Any sympathy she held fled. The man was pushier than anticipated. He clutched a portfolio and a book.

Decidedly a beggar.

Musa's stomach sank when she recognized the distinctive purple binding for Felicity's *The Poetics of Passion*. A literate beggar then.

Mary said, "I suspect you've been drinking. You should go."

"Not really! Please, I only need a moment . . ." He tucked his portfolio under his arm as he fumbled with the pages of *The Poetics of Passion*. "This is Persephone Press, yes? I'd like to speak to the publisher. Or editor. Whoever is responsible for Miss Vita's books."

"You needn't answer him, Mary," Musa began.

Mary held up a hand to silence Musa. "I'm her editor, so that would be me."

The beggar's bright blue eyes lit up. "Ah, you publish Felicity Vita, the love poet!"

Musa resisted the urge to laugh. Nerves, she told herself. She always felt this way whenever she encountered someone at Persephone Press seeking Felicity. It still amazed her how popular those poems were. Not that it mattered to the American heiress, she thought bitterly.

"If you've come to speak to Miss Vita," Mary said, cool as ever, "she's abroad at the moment. Paris. Venice too. Rome later this winter, I believe. She doesn't meet with anyone. Ever. Why, I've never even met her."

Musa piped up, "Miss Vita is quite the mystery. Rumor holds she's a noblewoman. An invalid. I've heard she's off to take the waters in Baden-Baden."

Mary added with a faux sigh, "It's all hearsay, alas. We consider ourselves fortunate Miss Vita entrusts us with her poems."

The beggar gentleman set his portfolio on Mary's desk with a determined slap. It coincided with a flash of lightning.

"I sense your distrust," he said in a low but determined voice. "Let me assure I'm not here to harass Miss Vita, or uncover her identity or location. I simply admire her books and wanted to introduce myself. I have something to offer her."

He fumbled with something under his portfolio. Something near the buttons of his trousers.

Mary rose, her fists tight. "Get out, you nasty man! Now!"

But, to Musa's surprise, he simply untied his portfolio to open it. That's what he was fumbling with. Not his trousers.

The beggar pointed to the open portfolio. "I simply want to offer my services as an illustrator to Miss Vita. Well, to your press really. Your books are works of art. I'm an artist. It's quite simple." He rifled through an indistinguishable array of drawings. "If you'd just take a moment to look. Please."

"We've illustrators here on staff," Mary said. This wasn't true—individual artists were hired by the book—but Musa wasn't going to correct her.

"I'm sure you do," he answered. "But if you could introduce me to Miss Vita so I could show her my art, I'd truly appreciate it."

Musa said firmly, "No one speaks to Miss Vita in person. Do you understand? Now go!"

He waved his arms in frustration. "Oh, I don't know why I bothered!"

The beggar broke for the door, abandoning his portfolio in his rush. The door slammed behind him, but not before letting in a splash of rain.

Mary shrugged. "I'm not going to chase him."

"Not in this storm," Musa agreed, thumbing through his drawings. There were ink sketches, charcoals, pencils. A few of models posing in Arthurian costume, but more featuring a child. A girl of about seven years of age. Her rabbit, or one appearing to belong to her, for the creature was dressed up in a bow and a small bonnet. Several kittens in a basket.

The compositions were charming rather than cloying. He was surprisingly talented, Musa decided. Growing up as the daughter of Neil Bartham had taught her to appreciate art even if she had little interest in creating it herself.

"Can't imagine these in a Felicity Vita book. You'd think he was a children's book illustrator or something," Mary muttered, tying the portfolio's leaves shut. "Oh well. Suppose he'll come back for this in time."

Musa glanced at Mary's list of publishing possibilities. *Children's books.*

The words jumped out at her. With this, Musa's innate pragmatism returned. She knew what to do.

She grabbed his portfolio and reached for the door.

CHAPTER 4

SEB RUSHED OUT of Persephone Press toward Fleet Street, rain pounding against his shoulders. He'd been impetuous to leave in the manner in which he had, but he'd felt too insulted. Yet again, he let his emotions get the best of him. And what had he thought speaking of Felicity Vita like that? He'd surely revealed his obsession in a way that made him seem crazed—and to Felicity's editor no less. No wonder they lied to him. He knew Felicity wasn't in Venice or Rome or anywhere outside London. She'd written Seb as much.

His portfolio. He'd left it on the desk in the office.

"Shit," he muttered. He flushed anew, recalling how the lady wearing spectacles grimaced when he'd forced his way into Persephone Press. She'd thought him drunk. It didn't please her at all, not one bit—he could tell by the way her nostrils flared. She'd even glared at him with narrowed eyes.

Yet there'd been something alluring about her despite her prim judgement and navy serge walking suit. Like she knew of his losses and might be sympathetic, if she'd only allow herself that luxury.

More fool me. And now his portfolio was gone. Well, he'd only stuffed some drawings in there.

Drawings of Jessica from the last day they'd been together before his parents took ill.

The day before everything changed for his family, leaving Seb in charge of his two sisters' fates.

And then Seb knew: he had no choice but to return for his portfolio.

He ran back toward the narrow alley where Persephone Press was located. The rain dashed against his face, but he welcomed it, for it reflected his sour mood. The weather seemed more akin to March than January, blustering with wind and water instead of snow. In his rush to leave home, he'd forgotten an umbrella—all he'd thought of was somehow finding Felicity, of uncovering her identity to put his obsession at rest.

Luke was right. I need to let her go.

Another rumble of thunder as the storm thickened.

Seb gritted his teeth and swiped at his eyes. Everything appeared a blur in the rain, like a French impressionist painting. The gentlemen on the street, their faces hidden beneath wide black umbrellas; the ladies with their oversized bonnets dripping with feathers and flowers; newsboys selling papers, eager hounds by their sides. The sounds, the colors. The overwhelming sense of loss, of disappointment that a rainy day always suggested to Seb.

Some feet ahead of him, a woman's voice floated his way. "Sir! You forgot something!"

Amid the miasma of rain-soaked humanity, he made out a feminine figure running toward him. The friend of the publisher, the dark-haired woman with the prim manner, the spectacles. Of course, she had an umbrella. Beneath it, she held his portfolio—he recognized the black rectangle clutched protectively against her chest.

Seb waved and felt himself begin to smile. The dark-haired woman drew close enough he could make out her spectacles. Not all was lost. Surely this was a sign his fortunes had somehow turned . . .

A slash of lightning so close the air flashed white.

The portfolio fell from her arms. Opened. Scattered. All those ink drawings into a puddle. Every last single one.

"Damn it!" Seb felt as though he'd been slapped by misfortune as he reached toward the puddle. He watched the ink bleed into the paper, Jessica fading into blotches of gray.

The dark-haired woman cried, "Let me help you! I don't suppose they can be saved?"

"They're gone." *Like my parents*, he thought, awash with sorrow and self-pity. *And Felicity.*

"I'm sorry, truly I am," she said, her eyes wide with contrition.

Seb grit out, "I am too."

He grabbed what remained from the puddle, nearly banging his head against her bonnet in his haste. And then he caught a whiff of her skin. Her chestnut-hued hair. She'd arranged the gleaming tresses in a series of severe plaits beneath her navy-hued bonnet. Her hair was scented with sandalwood. Civility. Suddenly he realized how much he reeked after his night out. Luke was right. He should have cleaned himself up before he'd rushed out.

No wonder the women treated me like a threat.

"They were lovely sketches too," she said, her tone suspiciously sweet. "They're of your daughter?"

"My youngest sister. It doesn't matter. I can draw more." This wasn't exactly true, but Seb wanted her to leave before he lost his temper.

"Really, I *am* sorry. Please, let me make it up to you, sir."

How polite she was. It disconcerted Seb.

Seb spat out the first request that came to mind. "The only way you can make it up to me is to introduce me to Felicity Vita. If that's not possible, let me illustrate a book of hers—perhaps then she'd agree to meet me. But you made it very clear this can't be. Plus you think me drunk. I'm not. I may have had a glass or two last night, but so would you if you had my day."

To his surprise, the dark-haired woman didn't criticize. "I can see you're upset, sir."

Seb laughed. "Upset? You only just realized this? For heaven's sake, we're standing here in a storm, and you're nattering on. It's ridiculous. Leave me be!"

The rain hardened. A boom of thunder. Seb ducked beneath an awning, expecting the dark-haired woman to depart in a huff. She didn't.

"A book." The two syllables fell from her lips. "That's a distinct possibility."

Her face turned coy beneath her umbrella. A prim calculation. Her pointed chin made her appear nearly fox-like. Cunning. Seb sensed there was more to her than she presented to the world. He wasn't sure how he felt about this.

"Yes, a book," he answered. "But only if I can meet Felicity."

"I can't guarantee this. But it's something we could discuss." She cocked her heard. "That is, if you haven't another appointment in town."

"No."

Seb was too taken aback by the loss of his sketches to lie out of pride. Plus there'd been the way she'd said those two words. *A book.* Two syllables suggesting an opening. An offering.

He couldn't turn away.

The dark-haired woman pointed down the block. "There's a tea shop a few steps from here. Their Victoria sponge cake is especially delicious. You look like you could use something to fill your stomach after your . . . indulgence."

Seb reluctantly followed her. "I'm not inebriated. Nor am I a beggar."

A soft laugh over her shoulder. "Of course you aren't."

"I don't care for your air of judgement."

"Well, I don't care for how you smell. Regardless, it's raining and you're without an umbrella and I've ruined your sketches. The least you can do is allow me to offer you tea so we can speak without being soaked by the heavens."

Seb swallowed his suspicions. "About a book?"

"Yes, a book. Ah, here we are!" She reached for a door painted a florid magenta and decorated in gold lettering. *The Pink Refuge*, it said. "Come! The cake won't wait."

CHAPTER 5

"Who are you?" Seb asked. "I'd like to know who I'm taking tea with."

The dark-haired woman threw him a taut smile from across the small table. "Let me assure you I'm not Felicity Vita."

He let out a short laugh. "I can't imagine you are! You're too . . . too . . ."

She raised an eyebrow. "Unattractive? Sharp-mannered? Unpleasant of aspect?"

Seb flushed. "I wasn't going to say that."

Well, she was hardly unattractive, if one cared for prim judgmental females.

"But you thought it, didn't you? Or some variation of it."

Seb's face grew warmer. He had the sense the dark-haired woman was provoking him for reasons he could only guess at. No doubt she felt his desperation, his yearning for Felicity. His inquiries had hardly been discreet.

It did not help his disquiet that he was the only male in the crowded tea shop; it seemed many had their same intention of taking shelter from the thunderstorm. He felt out of place, a wet hulk of a man amid a sea of femininity in beribboned bonnets and silks. Perhaps that was her plan for inviting him there. Even the wicker chair he balanced on felt too fragile for his form. He rubbed his palm against his rough chin, conscious of his unshaven state.

Still, the tea was hot and brought quickly, and the Victoria sponge cake did look delicious. He watched her reach for the pot, pour him a cup with a surprising grace. The tea cleared any remaining hangover from his brain.

"I simply meant Felicity Vita is probably older than you," Seb explained. "More experienced, judging by her poems."

She parried, "Well, I assume *you're* not Felicity Vita. For all I know, Miss Vita might be anyone. A gentleman even."

Clever. That's what she was.

Seb tried his best to sound airy and unaffected. "I admire her ability with a phrase. That's the only reason I want to meet her and offer my services as an illustrator."

"Then you've succumbed to the illusions of poetry," the dark-haired woman responded, avoiding his gaze as she wiped her spectacles. They'd fogged from the warmth of the tea shop.

"And you haven't?"

"No. Poetry fills heads with dreams that can never be fulfilled. I've a practical bent. After all, life is too short to waste time being fanciful." A tight smile. "Anyway, drink your tea—heaven knows you look like you need it!—and I'll explain my proposition."

As Seb sipped his tea, he allowed himself to take in the dark-haired woman at leisure. For some unfathomable reason, he felt he'd met her before. But it wasn't a logical memory, more of an inexplainable recognition.

The dark-haired woman sitting across from him had a pointed chin, a piquant beauty mark just south of her full lips. Though she presented as shockingly confident, he sensed a peculiar vulnerability about her, like she was playing at being an adult, though it wasn't that she looked like a child. She might have been anywhere from twenty to thirty years of age. He also sensed she was unmarried despite the gloves covering her fingers and her forwardness in inviting him to tea. A woman with a husband wouldn't be prowling around in a publishing house.

No, it was something else he couldn't quite name that gave him the sense he'd encountered her before. Yet to even mull this felt an odd disloyalty to Felicity Vita—or the Felicity Vita of his dreams.

She's rejected you, Seb. Move on.

"How old are you?" he asked, unable to hold back his blunt question.

The dark-haired woman didn't chastise him as expected. "I suppose you've earned the right to be forward since I destroyed your sketches." A graceful shrug. "Though to be fair, you did leave your portfolio behind. If I hadn't tried to return it, you'd still be without them."

Clever, he thought again.

"You didn't answer my question. And you still haven't told me your name."

She squeezed a second slice of lemon into her tea. "Nor do I know your name . . . unless you are lying about being Felicity Vita after all."

"Atkinson," he said, feeling as though he was trapped in a dream, one very different from the erotic affair that began his day. "Sebastian Atkinson. Previously of Bexley Heath, Kent. Now Spitalfields."

"Pleased to meet you, Mr. Atkinson of Spitalfields." She offered her hand. Her handshake was firm. "Miss Bartham at your service."

Bartham. Seb's mind roiled. "Your father can't possibly be—"

"Neil Bartham. The painter. Or the scoundrel, depending who you ask."

At last, she seemed caught off guard. Her cheeks even colored a ruddy hue beneath her bonnet.

Oh. That explained so much. The calculation he sensed in her wasn't calculation at all. It was desperation.

Everyone knew the history of the Bartham family. The love story of Neil and Clio, who'd gained the ruinous nickname of the "Muse of Scandal" decades earlier. The midwinter masquerade in Venice where the couple met, the middle of the night elopement. The numerous children born in quick succession—Seb heard numbers ranging from five to a dozen, all of whom lived estranged from society because they fit in nowhere. The daughters couldn't even get positions as governesses let alone husbands. As for the sons, their futures were similarly unpromising.

The Barthams weren't working class. Nor were they bourgeois or aristocracy. They weren't part of the Royal Academy set, or even the bohemian Pre-Raphaelites, who seemed to flirt with scandal for the spice it lent to life. Way back when Clio Bartham had been married to the famed art critic Ethan Sutton, who still held considerable sway in the art world. And now with Neil Bartham disappearing somewhere in the Holy Land . . . well, who knew how the family fared? Judging by Miss Bartham's unfashionable clothes, the family wasn't swimming in funds. Seb had even heard rumors Clio Bartham had gone soft in the head over her lost husband. Some whispered Bartham had run off with another woman, which only added to the turmoil surrounding the family.

As for Neil Bartham's art, Seb admired his early paintings, especially his *Ophelia* and his *Marianna in the Grange*. After Bartham's marriage, his art became prized by collectors who didn't mind a frisson of danger. Seb, however, noticed a sentimental quality began to colonize Bartham's art. Instead of Tennyson or Shakespeare, Bartham had taken to painting sweet-faced cherubs in church pews and other emotionally manipulative scenes.

"You're shocked," Miss Bartham said. "I suppose you'll want to leave before you're spied with me . . . though I suspect you've no one who'd care, given you're new to London."

How sharp she was! However, Miss Bartham was right: he had no true friend in London save for Luke. Still, for a moment, he imagined people looking at them. Whispering. But he was too curious about Miss Bartham to leave. He tried to recall her Christian name, the one she was rumored to have. Something Italian. Something fantastical and distinctly un-English. Something befitting a scandalous Bartham.

"You're the eldest daughter, I presume."

Miss Bartham nodded, staring intently at her tea as she swirled sugar into it, now using her left hand. She'd used her right hand earlier to lift the teapot. Ambidextrous. Another way she was outside the norm, like the rest of her family.

"Eldest of four, Mr. Atkinson. But I've something else to discuss."

"The book," Seb said too eagerly. "By Felicity Vita."

"Not by Miss Vita." She looked up from her tea. "Another one, now that I know you draw children and animals beautifully."

"The book requires illustrations?"

She took a thoughtful sip of her tea. "Yes. It's a book I'm writing, Mr. Atkinson—well, I haven't finished yet, but after seeing your art, I'm inspired."

"I'm honored," Seb said dryly.

"You should be. Persephone Press will publish it." She shrugged in the direction of his copy of *The Poetics of Passion* as though it was too vulgar to acknowledge. "As you already know, the press produces beautiful books, so it would be something for you to take pride in. However, your illustrations will have to be completed very quickly. The book must be available as soon as possible. Say, April. Before the Season."

Seb let out a long breath as he calculated, using his experience as a pressman. "That's an extremely tight timeline to publish a book, Miss Bartham. Four weeks, six at most, to afford time for printing." In addition, there was the matter of his new painting he aimed to finish that spring . . . a painting he'd hoped would make his reputation until he became so distracted by Felicity and her letters.

"I'll get the manuscript to you by tomorrow morning."

"How many illustrations?"

She rubbed her forefinger against the pout of her lower lip. "A dozen? Twenty?"

Seb let out a short laugh. "You haven't thought this through, have you?"

"Of course I have. Remember, I'm a writer, not an artist." She set down her teacup. "Let's see . . . Full page drawings. A dozen. Twenty half-page decorations. Not a lot of work."

"Work is work," Seb countered. "And your publisher will pay me—"

"In guineas, naturally. That's what my father would insist upon. I'd offer no less for you."

"How many guineas? And on what schedule?"

She took out a pad of paper and a pencil from her coat pocket. She marked a few rows of sums, explaining her rationale in quick words he couldn't follow. They quibbled over advances and money, all vulgar to Seb's mind, but she didn't seem to mind. Finally, she pushed the paper toward him as though it was a contract for labor, rather than a calculation.

She's a Bartham, he reminded himself. *She has no reputation to lose by being vulgar.*

"I'll send you a quarter payment up front, Mr. Atkinson, and half upon completion, remainder upon publication in April."

That was more than he'd anticipated. Still, he hid his excitement.

"One more thing. I want a share in the profits, so if the book does well, so will I."

She arched an eyebrow. "You drive a hard bargain."

He folded his arms before his chest. "It will encourage me to make my best work despite your ridiculous deadline."

Her mouth pursed; his eyes were drawn to that beauty mark below it.

After a long moment: "I assume a bank cheque is acceptable, Mr. Atkinson."

He challenged, "If your bank is such, Miss Bartham."

"Of course it is! But if you don't complete the drawings in time—"

"Oh, I'll complete them. If I don't, I'll return your payment— I'm an honorable man." A pause. "But I've one more requirement before I agree to your offer."

Her eyes widened, as though anticipating his demand. He waited.

Waited . . .

She let out a puff of breath. "You want to meet Felicity Vita."

"Yes, Miss Bartham. Be in the same room as her."

She blanched. "Breathe the same air, I presume?"

He nodded. "I promise not to reveal her identity to anyone, of course." He unsuccessfully tried to keep the desperation out of his tone.

She shook her head, mouth tight. "A meeting is impossible, Mr. Atkinson. I told you, I don't even know her! No one does."

"Then your illustration deadline is impossible, Miss Bartham."

She frowned. "For an indisposed man, you're very stubborn."

"This meeting is important to me for reasons I'm not at liberty to explain." Seb's voice rose despite his best efforts to remain calm. Again, he sensed ladies staring at them. Gossiping.

"You and many other readers," she countered. "How about this? If I can figure a way, I'll introduce you to Miss Vita. But you shan't be able to talk to her."

Seb pressed, "Would she speak to me?"

"No."

This was getting to be ridiculous. "How will I know it's her then?"

A sly smile. "Oh, you'll know. I've been told Miss Vita has a most singular presence. But no promises, Mr. Atkinson—everyone knows Miss Vita is a skittish sort." She offered her gloved hand. "If I can't convince her to meet with you, I'll double your advance against royalties. Deal?"

Unpleasant, that's what she was. And brusque.

Still, Seb accepted her hand—he could see no other way. He'd have to trust that, if Felicity saw him, she'd soften her resolution. And if she didn't . . . well, he'd put the matter of Felicity Vita to rest. Move on with his life. Finish his *La Dame sans Merci* painting to make his name known. Take care of his sisters and their ramshackle home in Kent.

"Deal," he answered.

They shook. He was again taken aback by the firmness of her

handshake, though this time he thought he sensed a subtle tremor in it.

She rose abruptly from the tea table. "I'll send you the manuscript tomorrow. Your address, if you please."

"My place of work is best. Chassen & Sons—here's their card. I'm a pressman there."

"A printer and an illustrator. How convenient." A hint of a nod. "Good day, Mr. Atkinson."

In her haste to depart, she nearly upset a teacup and glass with her skirts. Once she righted them, she turned for the door, umbrella in hand; the rain had slowed into docility.

Seb called out, "You still haven't told me what your book is about."

To his surprise, she flashed a bright smile; for once, her pleasure appeared unfeigned. "A children's book. One that will be filled with morality and righteous fortitude."

CHAPTER 6

ONCE SHE RETURNED HOME, Musa thoroughly washed her hands and face, using her strongest soap. She still sensed Atkinson's stench clinging to her skirts, as well as the desperation that led her to run after him like a common doxy. She again calculated the funds remaining in her bank account, recalling Mary's shocking news. She'd have to trust Mary to reimburse her for Atkinson's advance.

What have I done? I've entrusted a drunk with my family's future.

Once she'd seen Atkinson's sketches, Musa immediately envisioned the children's book she could write, one that could become popular enough to make up for the loss of Felicity's income. She'd been impulsive in approaching him, but she trusted her instincts. After all, her father had trained her eye from an early age. She'd even posed for him when he had need of a child model. Indisposed or no, Sebastian Atkinson was a gifted artist—this Musa could not deny.

And then it hit her anew: Felicity Vita's books really were no more. Whatever bound volumes been sent into the world would be the last of them.

No more royalties.

No more advances.

No more fan letters . . . well, she assumed Henry would continue writing her. To her relief, he'd taken her refusal to meet him with grace, though he'd clearly been disappointed. As for Atkinson's determination to meet Felicity Vita, she'd figure a way to evade her promise, even if she had to hire someone to impersonate the poetess.

I can fix this. I will fix this. All will be fine.

Still, Musa sank onto her bed, feeling as though she'd been pummeled in the stomach. She felt very alone.

Angela burst into her attic room. "There you are, lovely! I thought I heard you come in. Are you crying?"

"Of course not!" A nervous laugh. "Just tired, Angela. Long day. I only just returned from Persephone Press."

She wouldn't tell Angela about the changes there. No reason to worry her. Nor would Musa tell her about the children's book. She'd suspect something was off.

Angela's nose crinkled as she gave her sister a hug. "What's that smell on you?"

"Victoria sponge cake. Went to The Pink Refuge for tea."

"Is that all?" Without waiting for Musa's reply, Angela began to pirouette in the small room, too excited to remain still, her long pale curls falling from their pins as she twirled. "Oh, you missed so much this morning, Musa! It was such a beautiful scene—I do wish you hadn't rushed off! After you left, Aunt Minerva even apologized to Mama."

Musa's brow knit. "Whatever for?"

"Don't look so alarmed! It was over Papa. Aunt Minerva blames herself for not interceding when Papa met Mama in Venice years ago."

"What was she to do? Toss Papa into the Grand Canal?"

Angela leaped across the room, her arms graceful. "Aunt Minerva said she could tell Papa was obsessed with our mother from the start. That he planned to ruin her reputation, not caring she was wed to another."

Musa said dryly, "You forget her social ruin resulted in our births. I, for one, am grateful to be alive."

"True, but Aunt Minerva says such ruin is like death." Angela flushed. "Well, of a sort."

Musa grimaced. "I hadn't realized she considered us so irredeemable."

"Not me evidently. After all, she did agree to help me find a husband." Angela paused to worry a cuticle on her thumb. "But now all's well! She apologized to Mama, to me, even to the twins, who were very puzzled by it all." A pause. "If you were there, I'm sure she'd have apologized to you too . . . though it's strange she never acknowledged the letters you sent in the past."

Probably because I was conceived out of wedlock.

Musa said, "I'm surprised Mama agreed to speak to Aunt Minerva. She barely speaks to me most days."

An array of plies. "I was surprised too! Mama even spoke in complete sentences. Paragraphs! And then Mama wept copiously. It was like she'd come alive again, for you know how she's been."

"I do." *Too well.* "And then what happened?"

Another twirl. "Once Mama dried her tears, she thanked Aunt Minerva so prettily for taking an interest in my future. Oh, it was such a marvel, Musa! So touching!"

"Indeed."

Angela curtseyed with a reverence, marking the end of her dance. "Anyway, the main thing is I'm to stay with Aunt Minerva—"

"You're leaving home?" This Musa did not expect. Again she felt as though she'd a blow to her stomach.

Angela offered an excited nod, finally coming to a stand-still. "Just for the next few weeks. She thinks society will accept me more easily if I'm no longer living here."

Musa's voice dropped. "You do know finding a husband isn't the same as shopping for apples at a market."

"I know that. You needn't worry." Angela kissed her sister on her forehead. "I must go. Aunt Minerva's sending her carriage over."

Musa bit her tongue as Angela rushed from their room in a flurry of lace and determination. Anyway, Musa had a manuscript to write.

Tomorrow. I promised him a manuscript in one day's time. What was I thinking?

Well, she knew what she'd been thinking. Keeping a roof over her family's head.

She could do this. She'd written books under duress before. How hard could it be to write a children's book? She was desperate . . . and desperation was how Felicity Vita came into being in the first place.

Three years earlier, when it became clear her father would not be returning from the Holy Land as scheduled, Musa had fretted how to support her family. Unlike Neil, she possessed no facility for drawing, but she did have a way with words. She'd tried writing novels, improving tracks, and other forms of literature. But none of them stuck with her like Felicity's poetry had.

In the early days of Felicity Vita's existence, Musa had written a dossier of her alter ego's life, to help Musa shift into her *nom de plume* while she wrote. Felicity had taken multiple lovers over the years, all so grateful for her affections that they didn't dare gossip. She'd been married twice, both times to wealthy older men who'd died peacefully in their sleep; it was thanks to her husbands Felicity would never know want. Felicity possessed no extended family. Nor did she have children. She owned a palazzo in Venice and a Parisian *pied-à-terre* on the Île Saint-Louis. Felicity was ever so famous yet never seen in public—unlike Neil Bartham, whom everyone recognized as soon as he stepped foot somewhere, which made his disappearance all the more troubling.

Come home, Papa, Musa pleaded. *I wish you were here.* But she knew wishes were only that: wishes.

Time to get to work.

Musa unlocked her desk drawer, the one where she kept poetry drafts, fan letters to Felicity, and other papers. It astonished her Clio never questioned where the funds to run their home came from; such was her mother's state since her father's departure. Musa couldn't imagine loving something so deeply that you became so oblivious to reality. She'd never be such a fool. As for Angela . . .

But Angela does want to love. And so does Felicity Vita, damn her.

She wondered what Henry was doing at that moment. For a second, she wished she had accepted his invitation to meet, as unwise as it would have been.

"No tears," she whispered into the empty room. "Anyway, Musa Bartham has a children's book manuscript to write, not Felicity Vita. Get to it."

Musa pulled out a fresh sheet of paper. She emptied the contents of her satchel, searching for Mr. Atkinson's card. Chassen & Sons, near Kensington High Street. Next to the printer's card was her latest letter from Henry. It wasn't the same as having him there, but it would have to do.

A smile curled Musa's lips. With all the turmoil of the day, she'd pushed her correspondent's letter to the back of her mind. Now it awaited her like a treat from a chocolate shop.

Dearest Felicity, Henry had written:

> *I must admit I'm still pondering your decision for us not to meet. I must also admit it's a blow, though I understand your desire. A gifted poetess such as yourself requires privacy. Seclusion . . .*

Darling Henry. He was a true gentleman, as different from Atkinson as water from vinegar. How grateful she was to him for accepting the constraints of their relationship. Love truly was better on the page, wasn't it? Less complicated than in real life.

But she shouldn't be thinking of now. No, she should be writing the book.

Musa folded the letter away with a sigh. She picked up her pen to begin, using her right hand. She wrote with her left hand for Felicity's poems; Angela insisted upon this to protect her sister.

Musa paused over the inkwell. What to write? What did children even like to read? She hadn't considered this when she'd engaged Atkinson—she'd been too swept away by his art. Too confident of her ability to spin gold out of desperation.

All of a sudden she recalled those improving tracts she'd written way back when she was struggling for something to write. Why couldn't she rewrite them for children?

"That's it!" she cried. Instead of writing love poetry, she'd write poems with morals. Religious tracts. Lessons. Everything that was the opposite of what Felicity Vita would write. The American heiress who now owned most of Persephone Press would be pleased and so would society. Perhaps they'd even judge her parents more kindly.

Musa nearly clapped her hands with glee. This was going to be easier than she expected.

She dipped her pen and wrote boldly across a page:

Poems of Morality and Goodness
for Children to Abide
by Miss Musa Bartham

Something else was missing. Something to encourage her book's success. Atkinson's name. Though Persephone Press editions never acknowledged male authors, surely Mary would make an exception for an illustrator. Hopefully this would encourage Atkinson to do his best.

Musa took out a fresh sheet of paper and wrote at the top, 'The Parable of the Poisoned Biscuits.' That had a ring to it.

The words came quickly despite everything. Her years writing under the guise of Felicity Vita granted her discipline. Once she finished 'The Parable of the Poisoned Biscuit,' she began a sestina about the dangers of playing with farm animals, then an epic poem about a girl who refused to go to bed.

The hours passed. She was didn't stop writing when Angela returned from Grosvenor Square to collect clothes to bring to Aunt Minerva's.

Angela bit her lip with concern. "You're not being Felicity, are you?"

"No, someone better," Musa answered.

Musa was still writing when the dinner bell rang. She accepted a plate at her elbow from Clio, who actually ventured to the attic for the first time in months. Her mother was trailed by the twins, Lyra and Theo, both clutching Clio's hands as though they feared she'd dash back to her bed. For once, they weren't squabbling like the adolescents they were.

"What are you doing, sweetheart?" Clio asked, her tone shockingly bright.

"A present for our family, Mama," Musa assured. "Something wonderful, I promise!"

"That's nice of you, Musa," the twins chorused in their usual boisterous way.

Once it grew too dark to see, Musa lit another candle on her desk, shivering in the January chill. It was nearly dawn by the time she wrote *The End*. She made a fair copy for Atkinson to be safe.

But there was one piece missing in her manuscript, a detail to cement her children's book to society's purse strings. A heartfelt dedication.

To my beloved sister, Angela,
who is as pure of heart as she is of soul.

"There," Musa murmured, sliding her dedication behind the title page. "Let society stick it in their maw and buy it."

By then the first tawny tendrils of dawn were creeping across the gray-tiled roofs outside her window. Musa realized she'd been awake for nearly twenty-four hours. She'd close her eyes for an hour or so, then post the manuscript to Atkinson as promised. She wouldn't even undress fully, just to her chemise. Yet she couldn't sleep even after she wrote a rather saucy letter to Henry, one more explicit than she usually sent:

> *Dearest Henry,*
>
> *Forgive me for writing so intimately, but I must share this with you. I dreamt I'd pressed my fingers against your lips in order to commune with your gaze. To bring you to silence so we might better know each other's Souls.*
>
> *Your mouth was so soft against my fingers. So warm. But I wanted—no, needed—more. I opened the buttons lining my glove, baring the flesh of my palm for you to kiss . . .*
>
> *I feel so vulnerable confessing this. I trust you will forgive my forwardness—*
> *Your penitent*
> *Felicity*

She hadn't dreamed this exactly, but she'd fantasized it often enough to become a distraction. Was the letter too much? She reread it several times before addressing it, feeling as though Felicity had taken charge of her better judgement. Well, Henry would understand. He always did, though the writing of her fantasy hadn't lessened its hold on her imagination.

Release. That's what I need. Then I'll stop obsessing.

Musa closed her eyes, trying to imagine her dear Henry beside her. He'd written he had dark hair and was tall, but little else save that he cared deeply for his family, who lived apart from him. For some reason, Sebastian Atkinson's face floated through her mind, with his dark hair and blue eyes.

Annoyed, she turned onto her side and pulled the blanket up to her neck.

Ridiculous. He's nothing like Atkinson.

Henry had brown eyes, she decided. An aquiline nose. Strong brow. Perhaps a hint of sun across his cheeks from long constitutionals taken along the Thames.

Once Henry's face settled in her mind, Musa wiggled deeper beneath her blankets. She envisioned herself as Felicity greeting him in her boudoir, a lacy peignoir barely covering her soft flesh. She imagined Henry's warm lips against hers. First they'd be gentle, then punishing in their lusty need. He'd lead her to her bed, brushing butterfly kisses along her length of her arm. All this would raise Felicity's desire to a fever pitch.

"Take me," Felicity would cry without coyness. *"Make me yours, Henry!"*

And he would.

Henry would be scented with expensive cologne, not alcohol like you-know-who. (How annoying Atkinson was, even if he was a gifted artist. The deals one made to provide for one's family!) Henry would be god-like perfection. So was his long muscular body lying beside hers in her huge, silk-strewn bed.

Musa sighed, a luxurious warmth flooding her limbs. She let her hand drift beneath her chemise. As she caressed herself with an expert touch, she imagined Henry doing all the things she'd never even imagined until she found herself required to research the acts of love for Felicity's poems . . . though of course Felicity never wrote about such acts directly, only through insinuation.

"Ah, Felicity," Henry cried in her imaginings. *"I adore only you!"*

Musa felt her climax build like a rain-swollen river overflowing a dam. No longer able to hold back, she gave way to the pleasure coursing through her. She shuddered, muffling a soft gasp against her pillow.

Afterward, she smiled, pleased with herself. She could take care of everything, even her need for passion. Her body was a mechanism, one she could contain and control, along with her emotions. Unlike her sister, with her yearnings for marriage, and her mother, with her devotion to her father, Musa didn't need anyone. Not really.

As for her correspondent. . . well, Henry truly was ideal in every way. He wrote wonderful letters. He inflamed her imagination to a place where she was able to achieve bodily release on her own. They'd never meet. He'd freed her of the need for an actual lover. Worse, a husband.

Or so Musa told herself before she drifted into slumber.

CHAPTER 7

SEB FOLDED AWAY the terse letter accompanying Miss Bartham's cheque and book manuscript. Just as she'd promised during their tea, a thick envelope had arrived at Chassen & Sons in the morning post. Miss Bartham's package bore no return address save for the Persephone Press imprint on the stationary. She hadn't even trusted him with her own address.

But there was something else calling to Seb's attention. Something he didn't expect to find so enticing.

Musa. That was Miss Bartham's first name, which she'd set on her letter and the cover page of her manuscript.

Musa. Like music, which Seb used to enjoy before the death of his parents. He recalled attending concerts and singing songs, the pleasure those offered.

Musa. A variant of society's nickname for Miss Bartham's mother, Clio Bartham, the Muse of Scandal.

Seb shook his head. Try as he might he couldn't equate the name Musa with the woman who'd dropped his drawings of Jessica in the rain, insisted on having tea with him at that ridiculous pink tea shop, and sent such an imperious note with her manuscript.

Musa was a beautiful name. Not a name suitable for the woman who'd hired him to illustrate a children's book that, from the looks of it, was more lecture than literature.

Her manuscript bore the foreboding title of *Poems of Morality and Goodness for Children to Abide.* Who was going to read this? But, on the other hand, she'd marked his name below the title as illustrator, a consideration he hadn't expected. It filled him with hope.

He had a book that would be published with his name on the cover. Perhaps Felicity would notice the book when she next visited Persephone Press, though he'd yet to figure out how she would connect his art to Henry Whitney. Maybe he could insinuate such in a letter . . .

Stop, Seb. Let it go.

"I will," he muttered into the air. "Once I meet her."

After all, wasn't that why he'd agreed to illustrate Musa Bartham's tome in the first place?

Seb set the manuscript on his worktable and stretched. He'd just finished the overnight shift, was about to go home to sleep for a few hours before heading out to Kent to visit his family. The following day was Sunday, which was his day off. He'd begin planning Miss Bartham's illustrations for her book then.

And my book too, he thought with a start. After all, the more books sold, the more money he'd earn. Didn't that make him essentially a partner in the book?

"You look pleased with yourself, Seb. Much better than when I last saw you," Luke said; he'd slipped in without Seb's notice. Chassen & Sons printed *The Greater London Gazette*, the newspaper Luke wrote for, which offered the friends ample opportunity to visit. "Did you manage to talk sense into your La Dame sans Merci?"

"Not exactly," Seb replied. "But I made progress."

"Ah, that's good news." Luke pointed to the manuscript on Seb's desk. "What's this?"

"Book illustrations. A commission I took."

Luke's brow crinkled. "I thought you were going to work on your Keats painting, find a patron and all that."

"I am, but I couldn't turn down the job." He gestured weakly, seeking an excuse to avoid confiding about Felicity Vita and his bargain with Musa Bartham. "My sisters . . ."

"Yes, I know. Your sisters, the ramshackle house in Kent."

On safer ground, Seb explained, "It's a tight schedule. I've a week to get sketches to the author, the final book due in March."

"I suppose you won't be sleeping much," Luke said wryly. "Who hired you?"

"An author at Persephone Press."

"Don't they publish Felicity Vita, the love poet?"

Seb laughed nervously. "She's not the author whose book I'm illustrating."

Luke shrugged. "It's hardly the same as selling a painting to a wealthy collector. But if it helps pay the bills . . ." And he sighed.

It was then Seb noticed his usually sharply dressed friend appeared less turned out than usual. Not only was his customary flower in his buttonhole wilted, his usual brightly colored linens were a drab ecru.

Luke so woebegone that Seb felt obliged to ask, "What's wrong?"

Luke said in a low voice, "Between you and me, there's rumors of a layoff at the *Gazette*. I need to prove my worth with an article that'll get some attention. To tell the truth, I haven't had anything in weeks—it's very distressing." Another sigh. "If only I could locate a good story. A fresh angle."

Seb thought of Musa Bartham and her family. Yes, she'd irritated him, but Seb wasn't a gossip. Plus she'd hired him. Surely that meant he owed her some consideration.

Still, maybe . . .

Seb leaned in. "I've a story for you, but it's in confidence. Miss Musa Bartham—"

"Bartham? Of the 'Muse of Scandal' Bartham family?" Luke's brow raised toward his receding hairline.

Seb nodded. "She wrote the book I'm illustrating."

Luke cocked his head. "That *is* interesting. What's she like?"

Seb flushed. "I didn't notice."

But he had. He recalled the warm scent of her skin when she nearly bumped heads with him after dropping his sketches in the rain. (Was she perfumed with sandalwood? Or amber?) Her tightly plaited hair, as though she intended to control her life by controlling her body. If Seb was to be honest, he supposed Musa Bartham could be considered attractive, but nothing like he imagined Felicity to be. Miss Bartham was all hard angles and sharp words and distrust. As for her clothes, they were nondescript at best, even a bit shabby . . . though they did show off her comely figure.

Luke replied, "So she's not a stunner like her mother was reputed to be back in the day. Have no idea what Clio Bartham is like now. No one's seen her in public for years. Not since the husband supposedly ran off to the Holy Land."

"Miss Bartham has chestnut-colored hair, I'd say. Large brown eyes. Soulful. Creamy complexion with pink cheeks. Slender figure. Tall."

"Then you did notice her." Luke cocked his head with interest. "What about her book? Is there anything I could use? Is it a memoir about her mother? Or an exposé of her father, now that he's presumed dead?"

"Believe it or not, a collection of children's poems! I haven't read the manuscript yet. It only just arrived in the post. Here, take a look."

Seb handed Luke the manuscript.

"Poems of Morality and Goodness for Children to Abide," Luke pronounced. "My, that's a mouthful. I suppose I could present it as the story of a family's redemption, if I get desperate enough. 'Daughter of Scandalous Barthams Begs Forgiveness from Society.' But this seems a bit much even for a slow news day."

"Perhaps with my illustrations?" Seb asked hopefully.

Luke paged through the manuscript. "Maybe if you drew her weeping and dressed in mourning, making amends for her parents' sins. Or throwing herself into the Thames, like something from a penny dreadful."

Try as he might, Seb couldn't imagine Musa Bartham showing any sort of emotion, let alone drowning herself out of passion.

"Unlikely," Seb replied. "But maybe there's something else you could use?"

Luke shuffled the manuscript pages back into order. "There's nothing here worth writing about, though I can arrange for a book review, if that's a help. Well, I should leave you to it."

Luke left, looking so disconsolate that Seb wished he could make up something for him to write about. After everything Luke had done to help him and his sisters, it was the least Seb could do. Anyway, Luke would figure something out, though Seb hoped he wouldn't try anything disreputable. As for Miss Bartham, for all her unpleasantness, she'd been more than proper in her interactions. Boring even, just as her manuscript appeared to be. Musa Bartham was decidedly cut from a different cloth than her parents.

Perhaps that's how children were, Seb thought. They grew in reaction to their parents, though Seb hadn't felt that way about his. He'd been fortunate to have the most loving mother and father imaginable. As for his sisters, he'd see them in a few hours.

With this, Seb tucked Miss Bartham's manuscript and cheque into his satchel and departed. His anticipation rose as he thought of his journey to Kent. He'd be there in time for Saturday dinner, trains willing.

To read on the train, he'd brought his latest letter from Felicity. He hoped it would be akin to the ones she'd sent before he'd foolishly asked to meet her. This would set his mind at ease.

Her letter was that . . . and so much more.

Dearest Henry, he read:

> *Forgive me for writing so intimately, but I must share this with you. I dreamt I'd pressed my fingers against your lips in order to commune with your gaze. To bring you to silence so we might better know each other's Souls . . .*

He reread the letter more times than he could count, unable to separate his relief at the letter's welcoming tone from the flush of lust stupefying his brain.

"Sir, are you well?" an elderly man seated in his train compartment inquired. "You turned quite red."

Seb folded away the letter in a nervous rush. "Perfectly well, thank you."

And then the train pulled into the station, and there was no more time for Seb to obsess over letters and Felicity Vita and fingers and lips and souls. There was only his family and his eagerness to see them.

CHAPTER 8

"Sebbie! You're here! I missed you so!"

Seb's sister Jessica launched herself at him as soon as he'd opened the door to his family home. He gathered his little sister into his arms. How lanky she'd grown! Children at her age seemed to change from week to week, and he hadn't seen her in a month. Such had been his preoccupation between his job at Chassen & Sons, his *La Dame sans Merci* painting, and Felicity's letters; he flushed anew at the memory of her latest. And now a children's book on top of this. How would he get it all done?

I have no choice. But for today, I'll try not to worry.

Seb beamed as he set Jessica down on the worn Persian carpet covering their entryway.

"You've learned to fly since my last visit, elfling," he teased, relishing everything about her seven-year-old self: her sweet smile, dishwater blonde plaits, and rosy cheeks. Jessica's birth had been a midlife surprise for his parents, which made her all the more precious to Seb. She looked somewhat healthier than when he'd last seen her, when she'd been in the embrace of yet another winter cold. Ever since the death of their parents a year and a half earlier, Jessica's health was fragile, a result of the scarlet fever she thankfully survived. Unlike his parents.

As though to reassure himself of her presence, he gave her another hug.

Jessica giggled. "You're squeezing me!"

"That's because you've grown too big for my arms! Did you lose more teeth?"

"Two," she cried out, opening her mouth wide for examination. "I've a big one coming in here. Look!"

Seb heard footsteps from the dining room just as the grandfather clock chimed three. As though propelled by the clock, his other sister Daphne approached with her arms open, her lips spread into a warm smile of welcome. Daphne was only a scant two years younger than Seb. She resembled her brother, with her thick dark curls and blue eyes. Seb always found her calm ways deeply soothing.

"So glad you're here," she exclaimed, embracing Seb.

Seb's heart swelled with warmth and affection. How lonely he'd felt so far from his sisters, despite Luke's loyal friendship. He noticed an air of strain across Daphne's forehead he didn't recall from his last visit. He'd ask whether she was overtaxed when they were out of Jessica's earshot. Now that he had additional funds from Musa Bartham's book, perhaps he could arrange for a maid-of-all-work to come more regularly.

Jessica tugged at his hand. "Look, I've a present for you!"

She offered a bright red scarf, which, judging by its slipped stitches and uneven length, she'd made with her own hands.

Seb wrapped it around his neck. "Ooh, so soft!"

Daphne explained, "She's been watching at the window for the past hour for you. You should come more often. It would do you good." She squeezed her brother's other hand. "You look a bit pale beneath that straggly beard of yours. And your hair is wild with curls, but I think I like it! Is this the new artistic fashion?"

"Only until I have time to find a barber." Seb kissed Daphne's cheek. "Sorry I've been away for so long. My schedule . . ."

"I know, I know. You're busy working." A nervous smile. Again,

Seb sensed worry weighing her. "I appreciate all you do for us, but you should at least get some sunshine on your cheeks."

"Night shift means I sleep during the day," he explained. "But I've good news! I've been hired to illustrate a book for children." He bent down to Jessica's height. He set his palms on her shoulders. "If the author will let me, I'll ask for your name to be printed on the dedication page. In time for your eighth birthday, if I can manage it."

Jessica giggled. "For Jessica Elizabeth Atkinson. I like that!"

Daphne's eyes widened with reproach. "I thought you were going to focus on getting a patron through a gallery. You said that was the best way to make your reputation. Is this wise on top of your job at the printer?"

Seb let out a defensive laugh. "The more irons in the fire the better, wouldn't you agree?"

"I suppose," Daphne said, avoiding his eyes again. "I just don't want you to take ill from overwork. Is Luke keeping you out late?"

"Not really," Seb evaded. "He's actually watching out for me in his way."

"I can only imagine," Daphne said, shaking her head. "If it's like when you were boys—"

"Stop worrying, Daphne!" Jessica piped up. "Seb's here! Let's enjoy ourselves."

"Wise advice from someone so young," Seb agreed.

Daphne laughed and linked her arm into his. "Come, brother. Let's catch up over food—I was about to set dinner on the table. I managed to find a decent chicken, roast some vegetables."

"My favorites," Seb breathed. He couldn't recall the last time he'd enjoyed a home cooked meal.

Jessica added, "We've an apple tart from the last of the apples in the orchard. With fresh cream!"

"I want to hear more about this book," Daphne pronounced, smiling at last. "I suppose it's good news after all."

And his sisters pulled him into the home where they'd spent all their lives as though no time had passed.

Amid his family's *oohhhs* and *ahhs* as the three Atkinsons laughed and ate and teased each other in their old way, Seb explained all that led to his children's book commission, omitting it would be published in April—Daphne would be alarmed at the tight deadline. Nor did he mention Felicity Vita and her letters. Best not to worry her.

Anyway, he was home with his sisters now. That's all that mattered. He hadn't realized how weary he was until he'd arrived. A day off was definitely called for—and better yet, a day with those he loved.

While the three of them ate and caught up on their lives, Seb looked around the ancient dining room, which appeared to have sprung a leak on one wall, judging by a dark stain of moisture marring the lime-washed plaster. Bexley Manor dated from the sixteenth century and had once been the center of a lively farming community. Seb's parents purchased Bexley Manor before his birth, intending to bring it to modern standards, but they'd never been able to afford such. That was the problem with an old house. There was always a leak to repair, termites to banish.

Still, the Atkinsons loved Bexley Manor, and with their parents gone, their devotion had only grown. The house personified their past. Their shared history. The house was large enough that Seb had plans for it once he made his reputation. Plans he'd yet to share with Daphne.

"Will you stay over?" Daphne asked once Jessica finally—and reluctantly—went to bed after they'd played several rounds of snap. "You look exhausted. Plus it's so cold out tonight."

The two Atkinson siblings were seated in the sitting room before the fire, which was satisfyingly warm, especially when contrasted against the January wind howling outside. Daphne bent over a large embroidery hoop, stitching a brilliantly colored floral bed cover—she often took on commissions—while Seb sketched absentmindedly in the journal he always carried. More sketches of Jessica, but this time for his children's book.

"I suppose," Seb agreed. "I'd have to rush to make the last train back. Unless I want to walk back to London." He grinned as he stretched out his long legs. "Which I don't."

Daphne offered a half-smile. "You can visit with Jessica in the morning then. She talks about you all the time, Seb."

"I'm sorry I've been away for so long."

"I know, I know. You're busy." Daphne bit off a length of floss. Seb's anxiety prickled again. There was something in her gesture that troubled him. That tension in the air he'd sensed earlier . . .

"Something's happened, hasn't it?"

Daphne set down her embroidery hoop. "I didn't want to write you. Wanted to tell you in person."

Now Seb's nerves were really tingling. He closed his journal. "What is it?"

"It's hard to speak of . . ." A long breath. "Jessica's heart. Her lungs. They're still quite weak."

Seb reached over to drape his arm around her shoulders. "But she looks better. Her cheeks are rosy."

Daphne shook her head ruefully. "The rosy cheeks are part of it. They're related to the scarlet fever—she's never fully recovered. When she fainted a few weeks ago, I brought her to see Dr. Trimmings." Dr. Trimmings had been the Atkinsons' physician since birth. "He said her heart might be weakened, which could have long-term ramifications for her health." She swiped at her eyes with her palms. "I don't want to believe him, of course."

"Has she fainted since then?"

"Once, after skipping rope. I know I should have warned her, but she's such an active thing."

"Did he have any recommendations?"

"Only the name of a Harley Street physician who specialized in pediatric coronary disease. But he's in great demand. To even consult with him would cost more than you send us each month."

Daphne's voice broke. "I didn't want to burden you with this. You already do so much."

Seb squeezed his sister's shoulder. "I'll gain the funds. I promise. In the meantime, I'll send what I have."

First thing in the morning, he'd head home and begin those book illustrations. He'd do everything he could to shape *Poems of Morality and Goodness for Children to Abide* into a success. After all, the more books sold, the more money he'd make.

He had to for Jessica's sake. And quickly.

CHAPTER 9

MUSA TAPPED her foot as she sat in the rather shabby lobby of Chassen & Sons Printing in Kensington. Before her, a gray-haired, pouch-bellied gentleman addressed her with an air of confusion. Mr. Chassen himself.

"I've no idea where Atkinson is," Mr. Chassen admitted, pushing back his mop of white hair from his pince-nez before his eyes. "What did you say your name was again, miss?"

"He should be expecting me—we had an appointment today at 9:15. I'm Miss Bartham."

Musa waited for the air of astonishment that inevitably followed recognition of her family name. None came; she supposed Mr. Chassen was too harried to care.

The hallways of Chassen & Sons buzzed with activity and noise. The building was larger than she'd expected, a cave of brick and iron and industry. She saw men in shirtsleeves and braces running back and forth on the floor, their voices rising with instructions. The acrid scent of ink and sweat.

Chassen glanced at his pocket watch. "It's 9:30 now. Haven't seen him all morning, but he often works the overnight—he may have left early. Are you certain he said he'd be meeting you?"

"Quite." Musa rushed with annoyance, though to be fair Atkinson hadn't exactly agreed or refused. He never responded to the letter she'd sent with the manuscript for *Poems of Morality and Goodness for Children to Abide*. Nor had he sent returned the signed contract for their book.

She recalled Sebastian Atkinson's appearance when they'd first met. His untamed curls, bearded cheeks, the stench of whiskey on his clothes.

More fool me.

She prayed Atkinson hadn't gone off drinking with her cheque. In retrospect, she should have sought another illustrator, one more reliable. But then again, if she hadn't seen his art, she wouldn't have been inspired to write *Poems of Morality and Goodness for Children to Abide*.

"I'll look for him, Miss Bartham. In the meantime, pray take a seat."

Mr. Chassen pointed to a much battered oak bench with an apologetic half-smile.

Musa perched on it, her spine rigid to avoid brushing the ink-stained wall. Her posture was aided in that she'd asked Lyra to lace her stays extra tight for the day suit she wore. It was one altered from Angela's cast offs—Aunt Minerva had deigned to upgrade her sister's wardrobe for her society launch once she realized Angela hadn't had a new dress in years. The day suit was a fine navy wool suitable for a winter morning, to which Musa added lace cuffs. She appeared business-like and authoritative, she hoped. Nothing like what Felicity Vita would wear—Felicity, who in Musa's ripe imaginings, would lounge around on a wicker daybed adorned in a lacy pink tea gown while she rejected a queue of lovers until her Henry arrived.

As Musa envisioned this, she suppressed a tickle of laughter in her throat, a hint of a smile. A warmth across the pool of her belly.

Henry had responded to her daring letter about her unbuttoned glove with an even more delicious reply. And then she remembered: she'd brought his latest with her for fortitude on an unpleasant task. The letter had awaited her at Persephone Press when she checked that morning; she'd gone there first in case Atkinson had written.

Musa tucked her hand inside her skirt pocket, where she'd hidden the folded sheet of paper. She imagined Henry's hands against the paper as he addressed her. The curve of his fingers caressing his pen. She'd already memorized what he'd written:

> *Dear Felicitous One, how greatly I admire your forti-tude of spirit! (Forgive the alliteration—felicitous, forti-tude. Ah, let me add a third: friend, for that is how I think of you. See how frivolous you make me?) Your most recent letter arrived at a moment when I was in need of cheer.*
>
> *As to that letter, you are unlike all other women, for you boldly express your desires. And unbutton your glove to woo its will.*

Henry understood her, appreciated her. But this was not the time to be thinking of romantic letters. This was the time to be thinking of her family and her book. Musa would lay a bet Atkinson hadn't even started the illustrations yet.

Her mouth tightened. She tapped her foot beneath her skirt. She glanced up at the large round clock on the brick wall above the glass entryway.

The clock showed 9:35.

Where was Atkinson?

Now that she'd grown accustomed to it, Chassen & Sons wasn't an unpleasant environment, but it was noisy. The presses were running, the metal plates clanging, insistent. Their rhythm mimicked the beat of her heart. Nerves.

What if I've made a mistake hiring him? What will I do then?

The big hand ticked toward 9:40.

Well, you now have a manuscript at the least.

9:45.

Simply find another illustrator, that's all. Though he won't be as good . . .

"Miss Bartham?"

The rich male voice came from a direction Musa hadn't anticipated: standing beside her. She let out a short yelp. A gentleman had approached without her knowledge amid the hubbub.

A gentleman neatly dressed in a suit sewn of herringbone wool, crisp white collar.

"I'm sorry, Miss Bartham. I didn't mean to startle. Are you well?"

Musa's lips parted, her cheeks flushed. She blinked, her brain sideways.

Who are you?

Whoever he was, he was dark-haired, his thick curls oiled and coifed. Clean-shaven save for longish sideburns that gave his mien a sensitive air. Eyes as blue as she imagined the Adriatic Sea to be, though she noticed dusky circles beneath his eyes. A sharp nose over a soft mouth, with lips that were full like an angel in a painting. Chiseled jaw above a thickly corded neck. Yes, an ideal of masculinity itself. The sort of masculinity Musa imagined someone like Felicity Vita would reward with an afternoon of lustful attention in her boudoir.

Musa tried to look away from those deep blue eyes but found she couldn't. She could drown in them, though this was something Felicity would do. Not Musa. Musa wouldn't drown in anything, especially someone's eyes, no matter how pretty their hue.

"I startled you, didn't I?" the gentleman asked, his tone apologetic. "It's the noise in here—it's hard to hear. I should have written to suggest we meet elsewhere, but didn't dare presume."

Musa blinked again, her spine regaining its rigidity against the wooden bench. That voice. She knew it.

"Mr. Atkinson?" It couldn't be.

"The same."

Sebastian Atkinson offered a lopsided grin, the corners of his eyes crinkling. *Now* she recognized him. What a difference a shave and a haircut could do, along with not being indisposed from drink. But she'd never confess this to him. No, it would be rude to remind him of such, especially now that he looked so . . . altered.

Yes, that was the word for how he appeared. Not handsome. Not masculine.

"Good morning," she sputtered.

Another quick grin. "And good morning to you, Miss Bartham. I apologize for keeping you waiting. I'd gotten carried away drawing and lost track of the time." He presented her with a folded set of papers. "Your contract signed."

"Thank you." She tucked the contract inside her bag.

"If you'll accompany me, Mr. Chassen has offered his office for our meeting. It's more conducive for viewing art. Better light."

He stretched out a hand to help her from the bench. She avoided his touch, still startled. She stood, smoothed her skirt.

"As you wish, Mr. Atkinson."

As Musa followed Sebastian Atkinson past the print floor, her heart pounded like a fool.

He's a pretty face, that's all. Use him for inspiration. A poem. Perhaps a sonnet by Felicity. And then she recalled. Felicity Vita was no longer publishable. That was why Musa was at Chassen & Sons in the first place.

She pushed away a surge of panic.

What have I done?

"This way," Atkinson said. "I promise I'm not leading you astray."

"I didn't think you were, Mr. Atkinson."

"We'll be going upstairs, Miss Bartham."

They ambulated past printing plates, books, and flat files, the floors cluttered with stacks of newspapers and paper. She forced herself to look at the bricked walls, the timbered ceiling. Toward anywhere but the languid silhouette of the gentleman before her. The gentleman with dark curls and wide shoulders and blue eyes and . . . and . . .

Stop it, Musa. She pinched her palm. *He startled you. That's all.*

Atkinson must not have noticed Musa's distraction, for he continued speaking over his shoulder as though all was it should be.

"Nearly there, Miss Bartham. The office is in the quietest part of the building."

Musa trilled with nervous laughter like a ninny.

Contain yourself, you idiot.

"I appreciate that, Mr. Atkinson. I'm eager to see what you've created thus far for my book."

Atkinson offered another glance over his broad shoulder. There was an odd cast to his expression. Something she couldn't quite identify. Perhaps he was tired. That would explain the dark circles.

"I'm equally eager to show you, Miss Bartham. Your manuscript was . . . interesting."

Musa's tone was brisk. "I trust you found it edifying, Mr. Atkinson. Inspiring."

He must not have heard her words, for he did not respond. Instead:

"Up the circular stairway, if you please. Take care with your step, Miss Bartham- the ironwork can be treacherous. Are you certain you don't require assistance? No? Ah, here we are!"

Some twenty-six steps later—yes, Musa counted them—they emerged into a large open room crowned with skylights and floor-to-ceiling windows. Wide-open, airy but warm. There was a stout wood stove set in the center of the room along with a fireplace on one wall. Beyond the windows, an expansive view of Kensington High Street. Golden rays of sunlight flooded the room, suggesting a brighter day ahead along with the promise of spring.

Musa let out a breath, resisting the urge to twirl like a child in the enormous space. That wouldn't do. Instead, she gazed at Atkinson, still surprised by how nicely he'd cleaned up. He inclined his head toward a long table where the light was brightest.

It was there she made out at least a dozen drawings, each laid on the oak table at a precise distance from each other.

She nearly clapped her hands with glee.

CHAPTER 10

"Here they are, Miss Bartham," Seb invited, willing his voice even. He'd laid his preliminary sketches across the breadth of the table, aiming to overwhelm her with quantity before she'd start quibbling over quality.

Now that Musa Bartham was before him again, he sensed an unexpected vulnerability in her, one he didn't notice during the tea. He suppressed a yawn. On top of that, he was fighting a cold. His throat was a little sore, nose congested. Too many late nights. Not enough sleep.

But this wasn't the only reason he felt so off that morning.

It was Musa Bartham. She was more attractive than he remembered from their one and only meeting. He hadn't noticed how her chestnut hair curled against her wide forehead, granting her face a rather inquisitive air, like the world was too full of interesting possibilities to be ignored. This aspect softened her tight mouth, though her bottom lip was fuller than he recalled. Rosier too, though he couldn't imagine her using carmine. He'd forgotten about the fetching beauty mark below that lip, which approached the left side of her chin.

Musa Bartham still appeared rather fox-like . . . but foxes could be alluring.

Not that it mattered: Seb had no interest in her. No, his heart was for Felicity. That last letter she'd sent, the one about the glove—he couldn't resist answering it. As a result, he had yet another erotic dream about Felicity. This time they were lying entwined on a bed covered in opera-length gloves sewn of deep red silk. The memory invited a hint of arousal, distracting him from his scratchy throat.

Calm yourself, Seb.

"Ah, you've completed so many!" Miss Bartham's stern mouth relaxed at last; her beauty mark shifted ever so slightly. Her skin was luminous, though all he took was an artist's aesthetic interest. That's all.

He shook himself back into attention, banishing thoughts of red silk gloves. "So many what?"

A low laugh. "So many drawings for my book. I must admit I'm relieved, Mr. Atkinson."

He forced his gaze from her full bottom lip, which she nibbling in an aspect of befuddlement.

"Yes, my drawings . . ." As for her book . . . that was another story.

He'd despised every word she'd written.

She leaned over the table to better examine the art, her spine a graceful curve. Her warm amber eyes darted back and forth across his drawings, reminding him of an anxious bird he'd once seen in Brighton, instead of a fox.

Again, her small perfect teeth nibbled her bottom lip. Her mouth tugged down, pulling her beauty mark alongside it. She clasped her hands, her gloves wrinkling tight on her knuckles. Gray kid. Not red silk. But still . . .

Against Seb's will, his dream returned. Felicity's bared body splayed across those gloves. The curve of her breasts as she reached for him . . .

Not now, Seb.

Musa Bartham's expression grew taut. Seb rushed with anxiety, but not because of an erotic dream. She was trying to contain her anger, for that's what she did. Well, he'd anticipated she'd be upset once she saw his art. He had no choice, not if he wanted their book to be successful.

Seb waited for her to speak.

One second. Two. Three.

"Mr. Atkinson," she said, her tone cool. "I'm confused."

"Confused?" Seb willed his expression innocent. He resisted a sneeze.

Miss Bartham's mouth tightened. "It's this, Mr. Atkinson. Your drawings are fine—yes, more than fine! The compositions are inviting, the anatomy graceful . . ."

Of course the daughter of Neil Bartham would mention such, Seb thought.

"Then what is the problem, Miss Bartham?"

She jabbed at the table with a forefinger, where each illustration offered something *very* different than Seb knew Miss Bartham expected.

"But! Your drawings! Have nothing to do with my manuscript!" She drew a deep breath. "Forgive me, but it's as though you illustrated another book." Her voice dropped. "A disreputable book."

"Oh," Seb breathed. "Perhaps we should discuss your manuscript."

She shook her head vehemently. "Mr. Atkinson, you were paid to illustrate *my* manuscript—"

"I *did* illustrate it, Miss Bartham." He coughed. "Or how I believe it should be illustrated."

Her brow creased. "*Should* be illustrated? I'm confused. Care to clarify, sir?"

More feigning of innocence. "I'd assumed your manuscript had yet to be edited."

"You presumed, you mean." She grabbed one drawing, then another. Seb flinched at the sight of his art being pulled here and there.

"Let me explain, sir." She jabbed at an ink sketch. "Here, I see a picture of a little girl, her clothes soiled from play, instead of neat and tidy as specified in my poem. What is edifying about that?"

Seb flinched again, resisting another cough. He'd anticipated her resistance, but it was still difficult to hold back his emotion. He'd drawn Jessica from memory after Daphne told him the truth about her heart. Jessica as she'd been before she'd taken ill. It had been like resurrecting his youngest sister from the past, when both his parents still lived.

Seb willed his tone even. "That's why they're drawings, not engravings, Miss Bartham. We've time for changes before finalizing them for printing. Is this your only complaint?"

"No." Another finger jab. "Here you've drawn a little boy chasing a chicken. Is that one meant to accompany my poem about avoiding farmyard animals? And this one shows the child stealing a biscuit from a kitchen." She fell back into the chair nearest the work table as though overcome by annoyance. "How does this illustrate the dangers of not following the commandments of our Lord?"

This time, instead of coughing, a corner of Seb's mouth twitched. He sometimes had the embarrassing fault of laughing when anxious. Again, he'd thought of Jessica while he'd drawn these, how her eyes would gleam with mischief, her delight in sugary treats.

"Perhaps it illustrates something else," he admitted, finally giving way to a sneeze. He wiped his nose with his handkerchief.

Miss Bartham didn't even offer a "Bless you" before she launched into the next part of her rant. "And then this drawing— oh, I don't know where to begin! There are no good children here. No tiny angels in the house. Nothing to edify or inspire."

Miss Bartham's eyes met his squarely. Anger. Frustration. Well, he understood. Any urge to laugh or sneeze or cough fled.

"Perhaps children don't care to be preached to," he countered, his tone steely. "Perhaps that's the problem with your manuscript."

"This isn't for you to judge. You, sir, are my hired hand!"

"And you, miss, forget I'm as invested in your book's success as you are—if it doesn't sell, I lose money too. A relationship between an author and an illustrator requires compromise. Give and take. That's what ensures the success of a book, the union of art and words. Look at Edward Moxon's illustrated edition of Lord Tennyson's poems."

The Moxon Tennyson had been published five years earlier to public acclaim. It was filled with stunning engravings drawn by John Millais, Dante Gabriel Rossetti, and others—artists who came to fame years before Seb had ever picked up a brush.

She countered, "But the Moxon is for collectors of fine art. Mine is for children and their caretakers."

Seb frowned. "If that's your intent, I cannot see how you hope to gain a child's interest. You've written a collection of dry lectures. No wit. No cleverness. No warmth."

"They have warmth!"

"Really? A verse entitled 'Be Good or Fear the Reaper'?"

She fluttered her lashes with what Seb perceived to be faux modesty. "I didn't mean the *literal* reaper. I meant not to play with farm tools—"

"Farm tools?" Seb's tone was incredulous.

She pursed her lips. "It's a metaphor. One you apparently did not have the sophistication to comprehend."

Seb shook his head, surprised by the hurt he felt. He suppressed another sneeze. "As an artist, I have no interest in tormenting children with such pablum."

"As the author, I would suggest I know more what would win a child's approval." She set her arms akimbo. "What do you know of children, sir?"

"For one, my youngest sister posed for these drawings."

"She's the best thing about them, despite your lack of respect for my manuscript."

"Your manuscript doesn't deserve respect. It's not good." He indicated his drawings with a sweep of his arm. "I've worked hard to imbue these drawings with charm. A sense of mischief so children might identify and take pleasure while they learn. Delight."

"Delight? What does that have to do with a children's book?"

The words Seb tried to contain spilled forth. He couldn't have stopped himself even if he tried. "There is no delight in your manuscript. No invitation to joy. No sense of pleasure." His voice dropped. "Do you know of pleasure, Miss Bartham? It appears you don't, in your insistence on lectures and morality and warnings."

"I-I know of pleasure." She stamped her foot, setting her straw bonnet awry on her neat head. "Our collaboration is at an end, Mr. Atkinson."

"I dare say it is, Miss Bartham!"

"I'll void our contract. I must ask you to return your advance when you are able, unless you've already wasted it on drink."

He thrust a bank note at her from his pocket. "I only used a small portion to purchase art supplies. Here's what's left over—I'll forward the remainder as soon as I am able."

"I'd like my book manuscript too."

"I fear I marked up the one you gave me with annotations, which I'm sure would displease your moral sensibilities." Seb cocked his head. "Perhaps I should burn it instead?"

"Unnecessary. I'll take it."

He pointed. "Over there, on the end of the table."

He watched her tuck the manuscript inside her satchel. He watched her slender figure retreat down the circular staircase. He listened to the tap of her heels against the ironwork steps.

Once he could no longer hear her step, Seb curled his head into his palms. He'd been too invested in the book. Too invested for Jessica's sake. That was the problem with caring. It left your heart too vulnerable.

There's only one person who would understand, he decided. *I must write Felicity.*

Mindful of the time, Seb took out another sheet of paper, some ink, and a pen. He'd write her a quick letter before he going downstairs to the press.

He'd only written two words—*Darling Friend*—before he heard tentative steps behind him. A throat clearing.

Seb glanced over his shoulder.

Musa Bartham had returned. She appeared to have set her bonnet straight on her head, though her cheeks remained flushed with anger. His jaw tightened. It wasn't enough for her to insult his work. She'd come back for more.

She was clutching her manuscript, the one he'd written his notes on, as she approached.

He kept his tone level as he turned to address her. "I thought we'd finished with our business, Miss Bartham."

"I'd thought so too, Mr. Atkinson . . ."

A step toward him.

"Then I realized we weren't."

He met her eyes. They pooled with moisture, to his astonishment. Tears. Seb instinctively reached for his handkerchief before he stopped himself. Tears were trickier to deal with than anger. Only one thing to do: take the offensive.

But before Seb could speak a single word, Musa Bartham threw his annotated manuscript at him. The pages flew hither and thither before settling at his feet.

He felt as startled as if she'd dumped a bucket of cold water over his head.

"Farewell, Mr. Atkinson. We shall not meet again."

She marched down the circular staircase without a glance back.

CHAPTER 11

In all of Musa Bartham's contained and controlled life, she'd never felt so agitated. And it was all Sebastian Atkinson's fault.

She fled Chassen & Sons as though she feared Atkinson might chase her, as ridiculous as the prospect was. The further along Kensington High Street she rushed, the more furious her steps became. She wished she hadn't had Lyra lace her so tightly that morning.

Well, everything had ended as she expected with Atkinson. The only aspect surprising her about their blow up was her inability to recognize him since he was sober. (The nerve of him!) But Musa was smart. Musa had planned ahead, anticipating what might happen.

First, she'd go home to collect her copy of the manuscript. After that, to Persephone Press. Surely Mary knew of another illustrator who could work under such time constraints. Anyway, it was a bright morning, the clouds lifting, the sun shining. The exercise would do her good. Really it would, though her eyes were stinging from the cold.

Not tears, she told herself. No, the only time she ever wept was when Papa was pronounced missing. And she'd begun the day with such optimistic anticipation too. Now all she felt was anger. Fury.

Damn him, she thought, jaw tight. *How dare he!*

But what upset her most wasn't Atkinson's slandering of her book, or his presumption in editing her words. It was that she'd lost her temper. Musa Bartham never lost her temper, not since she was a small child. She hadn't intended to throw her manuscript, but it seemed better than slapping him, which had been her first inclination.

For this alone, she despised Atkinson. He'd spurred her into throwing a manuscript, something that had never even entered her mind before. Not Musa Bartham, with her practical, contained ways. Musa Bartham, who was as different from her mother and father as chalk from cheese. Unlike her parents, she didn't have a passionate lack of concern for how one's actions affected those around you. She was responsible, damn it.

It's all Atkinson's fault, she thought again.

When she'd first seen him, her heart actually panged the tiniest bit. He'd shaven, cleaned himself up, and was dressed impressively. She even felt a sense of achievement. *Look at what my employment encouraged,* she thought, awash in pleasure. (See, she did feel pleasure!) He was more handsome than she expected. Taller and more masculine, with those blue eyes. It didn't matter. He was just as unpleasant and stubborn as she judged.

She'd been wrong to hire him. She'd let herself be swayed by talent, but talent only took you so far. To be successful, one needed moral rectitude. Consistency. Like what she had . . . or so she believed until she threw that manuscript at Atkinson.

"A momentary aberration," she told herself. "I shan't lose my temper again."

Again, she swiped at her eyes. Such a cold wind!

By then Musa was approaching her home in Brompton, which appeared more forlorn than usual because a dazzlingly grand brougham was set in front of it. The contrast between the shiny black carriage and their shabby house did not grant the Barthams any advantage.

Musa forgot about Atkinson as she hurried toward the front

door. Whose carriage was it? What had happened in the two hours since she'd left that morning?

The door opened before Musa reached the first step. Lyra, who resembled Neil as Musa did with her dark chestnut hair and lanky build, popped her head out.

"Thank goodness you're back!" Lyra cried, pulling Musa inside. "We had no idea where you'd gone!"

Musa shrugged off her coat. "Whose brougham is that?"

Lyra flailed with excitement. "You're not going to believe this. Angela is here with Aunt Minerva. So is Sunny—that's his brougham."

Musa's eyes widened as she untied her bonnet. "Sunny? Really?"

Lyra nodded. "Really. He arrived alone."

"But it's not Papa's birthday."

"I know! I have no idea what to make of it. Go—they're in the drawing room with Mama. And she's up and dressed!"

Sunny—the nickname of Virgil Sydenham, Viscount of Sunderland—was the only son of the Earl of Sunderland, Neil Bartham's most loyal art patron. Sunny had taken a liking to the Bartham children, who found themselves amusing him when his father paid contemplative visits to Neil's studio in the years before his disappearance. There'd been a time when Clio actually wondered out loud whether Sunny entertained a *tendresse* for Angela, though that had been quickly dispelled. After all, there was no way the Earl of Sunderland was going to let his heir marry a scandalous Bartham, genius artist father or no.

Still, Musa was impressed by their loyalty. In the six years since her father's disappearance, Sunny visited the Bartham family exactly once a year, on the anniversary of Neil's birthday in August, and always accompanied by his father dressed in black as though Clio was already a widow.

Never any other time, though. Until today.

Musa was about to burst into the drawing room when she stopped herself. She took a deep breath, smoothed her hair.

Contained. Calm. Nothing like my parents. That's what I am, damn it.

She forced a serene smile across her lips. She opened the drawing room door.

Inside, all was as Lyra reported. Sunny, her mother, Angela, Aunt Minerva, and Clio were seated in a circle near the fire, which blazed anemically for a January morning. Angela looked fluffed up like a bird in a new gown replete with lavender lace unfurling from the neckline. Clio frowned as though she had yet another headache coming on. However, she was dressed for visitors in a pretty silver-gray tea gown, one Musa knew was a favorite of her father. Only Aunt Minerva appeared as she always did, with her thin-lipped mouth a resolute line of judgement.

"And who have we here?" Musa called out in her most pleasant tones as she approached the group. She bobbed a curtsey in Sunny's direction. "My lord, what an unexpected pleasure!"

Sunny rose from his seat, the one nearest the fire. He'd gained in girth since Musa had last seen him; his impeccably tailored jacket couldn't hide the curve of his belly. His red hair was shaggier than she recalled, surrounding a rather round face with pleasant but indistinct features. His cheeks were ruddy as though he'd been out riding to the hounds beneath too sharp a wind.

"No need to be formal, Musa." Sunny gave her a quick handshake before flushing and stumbling back to his seat in his usual way. What Sunny offered in kindness he lacked in polish, to his parents' chagrin. "I've come as a friend to your family—"

"Which we appreciate ever so much," Musa said.

"Indeed, he arrived here at nine sharp," Clio began, tugging at a lock of hair that had loosened from her temple. "I was taken unaware."

"Then he sent his carriage to bring me and Aunt Minerva here," Angela added, biting her lip. "We've been waiting since ten for you, Musa."

"I appreciate your patience," Musa replied, her pulse speeding. Something had happened. Something bad.

Not Papa, she prayed. *Please, let him be safe.*

Sunny flushed in his awkward way. "I simply had no choice, Musa. My father would want as much—" he flushed again "—though I'm sorry he can't be here. Had something to do, I forget what."

"It's my father, isn't it?" Musa asked, her eyes stinging anew. "You've word of him. Something bad."

"No, no!" Sunny reassured. "My apologies! I hadn't thought how this would appear to your delicate sensibilities, Musa. I've no news of Mr. Bartham, rest his soul—"

Clio let out a wail. "He can't be dead! I know he's not. I can still sense his soul entwined with mine, even if I don't know where he is."

"Get on it with already," Aunt Minerva snapped with exasperation. "Just tell the girl! She must know."

Musa sank into a seat. "Know what?"

Angela blinked, her chin wobbling. She was about to cry, Musa was certain.

Sunny began, "It would be remiss of me not to inform you of news that has come to my attention." His voice dropped. "Someone saw you at The Pink Refuge with a disreputable looking man. Unchaperoned. In conversation."

"You mean your mother saw them, boy," Aunt Minerva interjected.

Sunny offered an embarrassed nod. "Mama was present with the Vicomtesse of Avalon and told me of it. She said you and the man appeared overly familiar, like you were plotting something."

Musa let out a long breath, uncertain whether to laugh or cry.

Relief. That's what I feel. Relief Papa is as he had been. Lost, but not dead.

As for Lady Sunderland, she was a remorseless gossip, one who did not share her husband and son's fondness for the Barthams. The few times Musa encountered her at one of Papa's exhibitions, she'd treated Musa like her family was tainted with leprosy.

Musa forced an uneasy laugh. "Oh, I can explain! I bought him tea because he was down on his luck. I felt sorry for him, that's all. He's an artist—"

"Artist? You mean a *beggar*, if you're buying him a meal. I wasn't aware your family possessed funds for philanthropy." Aunt Minerva's left brow raised along with the pitch of her voice. "Did you find this *artist* on the street?"

"No, Aunt."

"Wherever did you meet him then?"

"At a publisher. Persephone Press."

As soon as the words came out from her mouth and Angela's eyes widened, Musa realized she'd made a massive mistake.

"Why were you *there* of all places, miss?" Aunt Minerva demanded, tapping her fan against her knee. "Persephone Press—I can't even begin to enumerate how damaging this could be! First off, if you care at all about your sister's reputation, you shouldn't be tarrying in trade."

"I'm not tarrying in trade," Musa lied. "Not exactly."

"Secondly, Persephone Press only publishes books by women. Scandalous females. Oh, I know it's owned by that Nicholson chap, but everyone knows he's addled in the brain. They publish seditious essays like those by Mary Wollstone-whatever her name. Tasteless rubbish." Minerva fluttered her fan as though she was about to bat someone with it. "How dare you go there, miss, with Angela about to be launched—"

"Launched?" Sunny interrupted, a baleful expression infusing his plain features. "Angela? Out in society? For courtship?"

"Well, not a Season, but I intend to sponsor her in society. Introduce her to those with influence."

"The marriage market," Sunny breathed, appearing shaken. "You want to find a husband for her."

"Impossible, I know," Minerva rejoined. "My sense was swayed by sentiment."

Now Angela was weeping outright. She threw herself into Clio's arms. "Oh Mama, what shall become of me?"

"There, there, beautiful!" Clio soothed, weeping herself. "You can stay with me forever! We can go to the seaside even. Some place far from London where no one will ever bother us."

"But I want a husband, not a seaside resort. A family of my own," Angela sobbed. "Not that I don't love you, Mama."

"Wait! The publisher, the tea, and the artist aren't what you think," Musa interrupted. "Let me explain."

"Explain away," Aunt Minerva demanded.

A nervous smile. "You see, I'd meant a surprise for Angela."

"Oh, this is a surprise all right," Clio said, sharper than Musa expected of her mother.

"No, a *nice* surprise, Mama," Musa promised. "A good surprise. I wrote a book—"

"Musa, shush!" Angela blanched, no doubt thinking of Felicity Vita and her poems.

Musa reassured her sister, "A book for children, not adults."

"Thank goodness," Angela muttered beneath her breath.

"Only fools write books. Or men," Minerva snapped.

"I've written something moral and good, which is hardly foolish," Musa rejoined. "You see, I'd met with that artist at The Pink Refuge because he's going to illustrate the children's book for me. That's why I bought him tea."

Aunt Minerva's eyes narrowed. "I thought you said you felt sorry for him, miss."

"That too, Aunt. You know artists."

Clio snapped, "Your father is an artist! How can you speak of him in such a way?"

Aunt Minerva held up a hand to silence Clio. She addressed Musa. "And what was your artist's name? I'll be checking, miss."

Musa pronounced in a tone more confident than she felt, "Mr. Sebastian Atkinson. He specializes in drawing children. Lovely ink drawings suitable for fine books. Persephone Press offered to publish the book. Mr. Nicholson is an old friend of Papa's and agreed as a special favor."

This wasn't true, but neither Mr. Nicholson nor Neil were available to contradict Musa.

"My book will be out in April. Here, let me get my manuscript. You'll believe me then."

Musa took the steps two at a time toward her room. She gathered her manuscript draft from her locked drawer.

When she returned to the drawing room, Angela was upright in a chair clutching smelling salts, surrounded by Sunny, Aunt Minerva, and Clio in a tight circle, their voices rising and competing with Angela's sobs, unaware of Musa's return.

Musa watched, her stomach clenching.

Clio to Angela: "There, there, beautiful!"

Sunny: "A children's book is a good idea, I say. Can only help, what with Bartham gone and all, eh?"

Aunt Minerva: "Only if it's a *proper* sort of children's book."

Angela, amidst more sobs: "I-I suppose? But why take tea in public with a strange man, and especially when I'm to be launched? That's not proper at all!"

Aunt Minerva: "Because your sister is a fool like your father. Good thing she's not male. Think what trouble she'd get into if she had a John Thomas instead of a—"

Clio, shocked: "Don't you dare speak of my daughter or my husband that way!"

Musa cleared her throat. All four turned as one toward her.

She shyly slid the pages of her children's manuscript across the sideboard.

"Come look! See? All very proper. Educational. I'd simply thought to make some pin money for the household, that's all. And look, I've dedicated it to Angela—that's my surprise. Go ahead, read it!"

Sunny lifted the top page. "*Poems of Morality and Goodness for Children to Abide.* Hmmm, I suppose that's . . . that's . . . upstanding for the name of a children's book. Though it's hardly *Little Women*. I adored that novel!"

"You read children's books?" Aunt Minerva scoffed.

Sunny flushed. "Only for my youngest cousin's sake."

Clio examined another page. "Why is there a rhyme about a reaper, Musa?"

Angela peered over her mother's shoulder. "And it's titled 'Be Good or Fear the Reaper' too! That's a bit lacking in pleasure, don't you think?"

Musa offered a nervous giggle. To her dismay, memories of Atkinson's reaction returned. *"There is no delight in your manuscript. No invitation to joy. No sense of pleasure. Do you know of pleasure, Miss Bartham?"*

"Oh, funny you should mention that poem," Musa blustered. "It's a metaphor. Reaper as in farm tools, rather than the Grim Reaper. Though I suppose it can be understood either way."

"Fancy, aren't we?" Aunt Minerva said. "However, I *do* like the sound of it. One cannot lecture children too soon on the precarious state of their souls!" She propped her lunettes on the edge of her nose. "I also like this one, 'The Parable of the Poisoned Biscuit.' Children should learn not to steal sweets from the kitchen. They must be treated with suspicion, as though they're tiny criminals in waiting, plotting all the time. Why, if they could, I wager they'd steal the sugar from my tea!"

"Ridiculous," Angela pronounced, swiping at her cheeks. "What child is going to want to read this?"

"It's for their parents, really," Musa protested lamely. "A book of instruction and morality."

"Let's get another opinion." Angela opened the door and called upstairs, "Lyra, Theo! Come see what your sister's written!"

"That's not necessary. Anyway, I've yet to edit it," Musa evaded, grabbing the pages before the twins arrived; again, Atkinson's disapproving face rushed before her. "Really, I must leave. Immediately."

"But you just came home!" Clio protested, reaching for her eldest daughter. "I want to know more about your book, sweetheart. I didn't say I thought it was a bad idea."

"I've an appointment, Mama. I simply stopped by to collect my manuscript."

Musa rushed toward for the door, clutching the pages against her chest. Before she could make her escape, Aunt Minerva grasped her wrist. The dowager was surprisingly strong for a septuagenarian.

"If you care about your sister, you best introduce me to your Mr. Atkinson, miss," she ordered in a low tone. "The sooner the better, so I can vouch for his respectability. Tea next Sunday—I'll invite Lady Sunderland.

CHAPTER 12

Aunt Minerva's words reverberated in Musa's brain as she approached Chassen & Sons for the second time in less than four hours. *"If you care about your sister, you best introduce me to your Mr. Atkinson . . . Tea next Sunday . . ."*

It was impossible. Improbable, though she understood her great-aunt's reasoning—Atkinson's appearance in her drawing room would prove all was as Musa claimed. And now here she was, before the door of the printer prepared to present Aunt Minerva's demand to Atkinson. But there was another reason for Musa's return beyond the need to squelch Lady Sunderland's malicious gossip: her family's reaction to her children's book manuscript.

Atkinson was right. She'd written unappealing, incomprehensible pablum.

Shame flooded Musa's chest. What an idiot she'd been. Naive. How could she have been so wrong about her book? It was more than humiliating. It was horrifying, as though she'd discovered spinach on her teeth after a private audience with Queen Victoria.

Well, there was only one thing to do. Apologize. If necessary, grovel. Pray that Atkinson would agree to continue with her book, and be willing to suffer through a tea with her great-aunt and Lady

Sunderland. It was a lot to ask of someone she'd insulted. Heavens, Musa didn't want to take tea with them herself.

It's for Angela's sake, her conscience reminded. If Angela wanted to truss herself up in feathers and silk to become someone's wife, Musa would support her folly. She loved her sister even if she didn't understand her sometimes.

Yet Musa found herself unable to go inside the printer. To approach Atkinson . . . especially since, as she left her home, a boy messenger arrived with a letter from the artist. Besides returning the remainder of the advance for her book, Atkinson included a terse note. *"I trust this brings an end to an unfortunate episode."* No signature. She'd squinted at the page for more time than it took to read. His elegant hand reminded her of someone else she knew, though she couldn't recall who.

And here she was, prepared to swallow her pride. Worse, apologize. Musa Bartham never apologized save for small breeches of courtesy. Musa Bartham never had any reason, for her judgement was always correct.

Until now.

"Time's a-wasting," Musa muttered into the air.

She drew a deep breath. The entrance to Chassen & Sons appeared to have grown in size since her last visit. Taller than she recalled. Bigger and heavier in its oak and iron structure. She began to pace, her anxiety getting the better of her. Perhaps if she practiced her apology first.

"Dear Mr. Atkinson, I am so sorry. I was mistaken in my—no, that's not right—"

"Miss Bartham?"

Musa whirled. The man himself. Atkinson had approached from Chassen & Sons while she was mid-pace. He didn't appear quite as sharp as when she'd seen him that morning, when he'd stunned her so. But then again, neither did she, she suspected. Not after dashing back and forth around town all day.

She forced what she hoped was a rueful smile. "Mr. Atkinson! Just the gentleman I seek."

"Go away!" In his quest to avoid Musa, Atkinson stumbled over his feet, but recovered. He pulled out a handkerchief and blew his nose loudly. "If you're looking for the remainder of the money I owe you, I already sent it."

"Yes, yes, I know," she said, chasing after him. "Please! Grant me a minute!"

He stopped short, nearly colliding with her skirts.

"Miss Bartham, I should warn that if you've returned to torment me anew, I've just completed a twelve-hour shift, I'm fighting a cold, and I can't remember the last time I slept more than three hours. On top of that, I was up all night drawing your illustrations, which you promptly insulted. And then you threw your manuscript in my face! My nose got a paper cut."

"Oh, I am so sorry! I-I now understand I was unkind."

"Unkind . . ." He flailed his arms as though to invoke the elements. "Is that all you have to say? What is it with you and throwing papers around? First you dump my drawings into a puddle, then you toss your manuscript at me. I know you believe yourself slighted, Miss Bartham, and think I've been forward in editing your work. Well, children aren't as you believe—I know this from personal experience! I understand you have an artistic vision for your book, but—"

"Shush," she said.

She set her gloved fingers against his lips, effectively silencing him. A forward gesture to be sure, but she couldn't think what else to do to halt his torrent of words.

Atkinson blinked, meeting her gaze. How blue his eyes were! She felt his mouth shift against her hand. His struggle to calm his temper.

"Mr. Atkinson, I'm asking you to commune with me. Please?"

He nodded. Yet Musa found she didn't want to move her hand from his mouth. Perhaps it was the realization she'd never before touched a man this way. Ever.

The gesture felt shocking. Intoxicating. Yet strangely familiar, as though she'd done this before. But why? And what was she thinking using a pretentious word like "commune"?

Because you just wrote such in your last letter to Henry, you ninny, she realized with a start. She let her hand drop from his lips.

"I'll give you exactly a minute," Atkinson said; he appeared as disquieted as she felt. "Nothing more."

To underscore his words, he dangled his pocket watch.

"You may begin, Miss Bartham."

"Thank you," she said primly. "I'll be quick as I can—I can tell you feel poorly. Mr. Atkinson, I know you dislike me, and well, I'd felt likewise toward you—I'm sorry if this sounds rude, but I'm not one to lie. Well, not really. Not much. However, now I realize I was wrong to insult you. I also understand I was wrong about my book—I know that now!" A deep breath. "I can be rigid and stubborn, but this book is very important to me. More important than I can say. I can't tell you why, but you would understand if I told you my reasons. Besides my family, which I need to support without a father at home, there's my sister. You've a sister and you must care about her since you drew her so beautifully." She flung out her hands. "You see, I also care about my sister more than the world itself, but . . . oh never mind! No time to speak of this now! The main thing is if you forgive me, I'd like to—"

"Time!" Atkinson called, holding up his pocket watch. "And you're right: I do dislike you, Miss Bartham. But I'll grant you another thirty seconds."

Was there amusement in his deep blue gaze? He was enjoying her humiliation. This didn't bode well.

Musa softened her tone to gain pity. "I don't need thirty seconds, Mr. Atkinson. Only ten. I'm asking you to illustrate my book again. No, begging you. Even if we can't be friends, I think we can work together to create something beautiful, uplifting, and wise. That's all."

With this, Musa clamped her mouth shut. She wouldn't mention her great-aunt's tea invitation, nor the gossip from The Pink Refuge. Not yet. One mountain at a time.

Before Atkinson could respond to her groveling, a gentleman about their age approached. Beneath his mustard-yellow bowler, he had a receding hairline and a sandy beard, a sharpness in his warm brown eyes. A rather stylish appearance complete with a limp rosebud in his buttonhole. He clutched a black leather case, which appeared heavy.

A journalist, she suspected. Scourge of her family.

"Seb, you ready?" The gentleman acknowledged Musa with a glance, his brow furrowing as though to ask *Who's this?*

"Not yet, Luke," Atkinson replied, waving him off. "I'll catch up with you."

"The Churchill Arms. Don't be long!"

Once the sandy bearded gentleman left, Atkinson gave Musa a terse nod. "Begging suits you."

"Only if it's successful," Musa countered, anxious.

Atkinson offered a slight smile. Or was it a grimace?

"Tomorrow. 9:15. Here. We'll start over—oh, excuse me!" A hearty sneeze; he refused her handkerchief. "But you'll need to completely rewrite your manuscript, Miss Bartham. No more poisoned biscuits or reapers. Understood?"

"Understood, Mr. Atkinson," she said, gratitude coloring her words. "And thank you!"

Seb felt shaken as he headed toward the Churchill Arms, not daring to look behind—and not just because of the cold he was fighting. He'd left Musa Bartham standing on the sidewalk in front of Chassen & Sons' doorway, an expression of forlorn relief on her sharp, fox-like face. He was grateful Luke had interrupted so he could extract himself from her presence. He'd eat and go home. Hopefully, after good night's sleep, he'd feel better.

Seb and Luke were joined inside the public house by three other workers from Chassen & Sons. They were lively and loud, to Seb's relief. It distracted him from recalling Musa Bartham and her fingers on his lips. He'd been so shocked by her forward gesture that he found himself unable to turn from her. More shocking was her appearance. Her chestnut hair had loosened from her plaits beneath her bonnet, long silky tendrils curling around her pointed chin. Her tailored navy suit looked decidedly less crisp than it had several hours earlier.

She appeared softer. Vulnerable. Desperate.

"Who was the lady were you speaking to?" Luke asked once Seb slid across the table at the public house; Luke was in the midst of ordering a steak and kidney pie. "Not your La Dame sans Merci?"

Seb forced a laugh. "Heavens, no."

"Then the infamous Miss Bartham, I presume."

"The same."

"What's this?" Joe, their friend who worked in copyedits, interjected.

"Oh, I found Atkinson chatting up a lady," Luke answered in his joking way. "A Bartham."

"A Bartham? Really?" His colleagues leaned in, brows collectively raised.

"Not important," Seb countered. "A business proposition. That's all."

Again, he thought of her gloved fingers against his lips, how their eyes had met. Hers were a rich amber color behind her wire spectacles. A lovely color—if she was an oil painting, he'd mix yellow ochre with sepia to match the hue, with perhaps a hint of moss green. To his shock, he'd felt the allure of attraction. He understood Miss Bartham's too intimate gesture was intended to silence him, not elicit a sensual response.

It's because you don't feel well you're fixating on this. Eat and go home, Seb. Get some rest.

"She's prettier than I expected," Luke commented after taking another swig of beer. "You made her sound like a gorgon of the highest order."

Seb wiped at his nose before taking a sip of hot tea. "She is a gorgon! To her credit, she admits as much—that's why she was here." He forced a laugh. "She came back to apologize. After she insulted and fired me, no less."

Joseph addressed Seb. "You've a Bartham who's a lady friend?"

"No, no! Most definitely not a friend. An author—well, she thinks she's one. She hired me to make drawings for her children's book."

And then Seb related the entire story of *Poems of Morality and Goodness for Children to Abide* to general amusement and laughter: how he'd met Miss Bartham in the rain, that she'd destroyed his drawings of his sister but insisted on taking him out to tea. Her offer for him to illustrate her book. His agreeing despite the book being unbelievably god-awful.

"She wrote a poem to a child about the Grim Reaper, for heaven's sake! Can you believe it?"

Yet he couldn't shake the memory of her touching his lips. How warm her flesh had felt through her gloves. To his surprise, he found he wanted to take her hand into his and unbutton the pearly buttons, exposing the creamy expanse of flesh hidden behind the prim gray kid. He'd kiss her fingers one at a time before sucking them into his mouth, wrapping his tongue around them. This, despite their overt dislike of each other.

The unexpected desire stunned Seb. It seemed like something he once experienced with another woman, though he hadn't. He'd definitely recall if he had. And then she'd gone and asked him to *commune* with her, as though he was a spirit at a séance instead of a man standing next to her on the street. What sort of person used such a word in regular conversation? Yet it all felt so familiar.

I've read of this. But where?

It struck him like a splash of cold water: Felicity. She'd written him such in the last letter she'd sent, the one that delighted him with its forwardness. He'd since memorized every word of it. *"Forgive me for writing so intimately, but I must share this with you. I dreamt I'd pressed my fingers against your lips in order to commune with your gaze . . ."*

Luke shook Seb's shoulders. "What is it? You look like you've been struck by lightning."

Seb blinked as though he was shaking off a dream. "I feel as much."

Luke leaned in across the table. "Is it your Miss Bartham?"

"No. I mean yes." Seb threw out his hands. "I don't believe it!"

"If you tell me, I'll decide whether you should believe or not."

"I will . . . but I need to collect my thoughts first."

Surely Seb was imagining this. He must be. It was a coincidence. Nothing more. And then there was Seb's head, which was starting to pound, his scratchy throat.

Before Luke could press further, Joseph interrupted with a convoluted story about his brother, which Seb couldn't follow though he nodded and laughed in the appropriate places. Tall Bob from the pressroom countered with another tale Seb hardly noticed. His mind was still swept up recalling Musa Bartham's fingers against his lips. That letter from Felicity. *"Mr. Atkinson, I'm asking you to commune with me . . ."*

It cannot be, he told himself.

Every so often, Luke glanced across the table, his head cocked. His curiosity was his defining trait as a reporter. This was a story Seb knew would stun his friend, if it was true.

"I should leave," Seb said, interrupting Tall Bob's monologue. "I need sleep."

"Oh, must you?" his coworkers chorused.

"I really should."

"You can't leave without telling me your Miss Bartham story," Luke insisted in a low enough voice that the others didn't notice. "I forbid it."

"Okay. In a minute," Seb whispered back.

Again, he heard Musa Bartham's voice ring in his memory. *"Mr. Atkinson, I'm asking you to commune with me . . ."* He stared into his lukewarm tea, still barely noticing the conversation about him, still filled with disbelief, still feeling like the devil was tormenting his mind and his body.

Luke will think me mad. Hell, I think I'm mad.

But if he couldn't confide his suspicions to his oldest friend, who could he? In the past, Luke was always there for him, just as Seb had been for him. If it hadn't been for Luke, Seb had no idea how he would have survived those first painful months after his parents' passing.

Despite his burgeoning cold, Seb waited to tell Luke until after their coworkers' departure, as though he feared setting off a firearm in a public place. Then he waited until those in the surrounding tables left.

"I'm probably completely mistaken about this," Seb said at last. "But I suspect Musa Bartham may be Felicity Vita."

"Show me your proof," Luke demanded. "Now!"

Just over an hour after Seb's shocking supposition about Felicity Vita, the two men arrived at Seb's attic studio in Spitalfields. Luke had insisted on accompanying him home despite Seb's attempt to beg off, using his cold and exhaustion as an excuse. Such was Luke's excitement that he even paid for the hansom cab instead of stiffing him.

"I don't care if you're dying," Luke said. "I refuse to leave you alone until you tell me more."

"I told you I don't have proof," Seb protested.

Except for that letter. But it wasn't proof. Not really.

"I don't believe you," Luke countered. "Your expression says otherwise."

Seb sneezed. Once he recovered he muttered, "I shouldn't have said anything."

"But you *did* say something, Seb. And if you're right, what a story this would be! My editor would go mad for it. Can you imagine? Felicity Vita the secret identity of Musa Bartham, daughter of the infamous Muse of Scandal! I can see it plastered on newspapers across London."

This Seb had not considered. He should have known better

than to confide in a journalist, even if the journalist was his oldest friend. As unpleasant as he found Musa Bartham, he had no interest in ruining her life.

And yet, if she was Felicity, he'd feel furious. Vulnerable. Humiliated, especially as he recalled how he begged Musa to introduce him to the love poet. If Musa was truly Felicity Vita, she'd led him on a merry chase this past week.

"Mr. Atkinson, I'm asking you to commune with me . . ."

He thought of all those letters he'd sent Felicity, where he'd spilled out parts of his soul he'd never shared with another human. They were too precious to show anyone. Especially a journalist.

"Felicity Vita isn't a story to be sold, Luke," Seb said in his loftiest tone. "She's simply someone who interests me."

"And why would that be?"

"Reasons I shan't speak of." Seb wiped his nose anew. "And now will you please leave me in misery?"

"I've never known you to be so coy. So circumspect. Hmmm . . ." Luke took a slow turn around the attic. "Maybe there's something here to serve as proof."

"You should go. I feel ill." Well, not ill as much as sick to his stomach over what he'd said, though his head was starting to pound. Why had he told him? That stupid letter with the fingers and the glove had bedazzled him. He should have kept his suspicions to himself.

"You protest too much, my friend." Luke pointed at Seb's easel. "Does her identity have to do with your art? Tell me if I'm getting warmer."

"I'm not playing a children's game. I was wrong to say anything."

Luke met his friend's eyes. "Now I *know* you're hiding something."

Seb sputtered, "Really, you should go."

Luke spread his arms in front of him as though sleepwalking. "Am I getting hotter? Or colder? Come on, give me a clue!"

"No." Seb folded his arms before his chest. Suddenly his stomach dropped.

Did I leave out Felicity's letters?

Before he could stop himself, his eyes darted toward his worktable. To his relief, no letters, only his usual pile of drawings . . . and his usual stack of Felicity's poetry volumes.

Luke's gaze met his. He raised an eyebrow.

"The worktable! There's something there—I know it!"

"No!"

Before Seb could stop him, Luke rushed over to the worktable to the stack of Felicity's books. He grabbed them. Clutching the books against his chest, Luke pivoted toward the half-finished painting of *La Dame sans Merci*. And then:

"Sebastian Henry Atkinson, there's a connection between Felicity Vita and your La Dame sans Merci. I know it! And I won't leave until you tell me what."

With this, Seb gave up protesting.

"All right, but you must keep this to yourself—I haven't told this to a living soul. Swear on our friendship."

"I swear!"

Seb said in a low voice, "Felicity Vita has been exchanging letters with me for the past year and a half."

Luke let out a long whistle. "Damn. That's quite the secret. I truly had no idea."

In for a penny, in for a pound.

Seb unlocked his desk drawer and pulled out a stack of letters. They were tied with a thick red ribbon several times over.

"Here are her letters. No, you can't read them! They're private."

Luke fell into the chair before Seb's worktable, eyes wide with disbelief.

"Private? After you informed me these are supposedly penned by Felicity Vita, the infamous love poet? And you've been corre-spondents with her for over a year? And that Felicity Vita is the *nom de plume* of the woman who's been tormenting you for the past week, who happens to be one of the scandalous Barthams?"

"I know, I know! I must be mistaken."

Seb couldn't reconcile that the woman who'd written the god-awful *Poems of Morality and Goodness for Children to Abide* was also the author of *The Poetics of Passion*. It made no sense. Why would Musa Bartham do this? Was it only for money? Or another reason? Nor could he reconcile her prim figure with his florid dreams of Felicity Vita and her decidedly sensual letters.

"You should leave," Seb said, blowing his nose anew.

Luke grabbed his friend by his shoulders. "Not until you let me read the letters!"

Seb resolutely shook his head.

"What did this Musa-Felicity write you? Erotic fantasies?"

"Nothing improper. Not really."

Seb flushed as the memory of Musa's fingers against his lips returned. Her fragrance. Her warmth.

Coincidence, he thought again, feeling feverish.

Luke let out a short laugh. "As a journalist, I'm sure I've read worse."

"I'm sharing this with you because you're my closest friend, not because you're a journalist."

"And as your closest friend, I want to help you," Luke said. "Show me her letters. Let me judge whether you're mistaken or not. Come on! It'll set your mind at ease."

A long moment passed, one in which Seb felt caught between his morals and his hunger for the truth.

"You promise not to tell anyone?" he asked, feeling nearly as vulnerable as when he'd first written to Felicity over a year earlier.

Luke set his hands against his heart. "I swear on my mother's grave."

"Your mother's alive."

"If she had a grave," Luke sidestepped. "You can trust me, Seb. Really."

"Truly?"

"You know I only have your best interest in mind."

I'm going to regret this. But Seb couldn't turn back. He needed to tell someone, to prove to himself he'd imagined it all. That it was only a fever-dream borne of exhaustion and yearning. But now that he thought of it, he supposed it was possible the apple didn't fall far from the family tree—even if the apple in this case wore wire spectacles and modest navy suits and penned moralistic children's books.

Seb untied the ribbon around the letters and pulled out the top one.

"Okay then. Here's the first letter she sent. You can see it's dated October 1870, which is when we began writing each other."

"'Dear Mr. Whitney,'" Luke read aloud over Seb's shoulder. "Who's he?"

Seb glanced up from the letter. "A name I made up. Henry Whitney. Don't smirk at me that way! It's not every day one writes a famed poetess. I felt shy."

"Henry's your middle name. But why Whitney? Here, let me take a closer look."

"My mother's maiden name," Seb explained, reluctantly letting Luke take the letter. "Be careful!"

"I know, it's precious." Luke took out a pince-nez to better examine the letter. "Pretty handwriting. Slight scent of perfume. A female wrote this, or someone who wants you to believe they're female." He looked up from the letter. "Let me make sure I understand this correctly. She has a *nom de plume*. As do you."

Seb cocked his head. "I never thought of it like that. But yes."

"She sends letters here?"

"No, I've a postbox—mail delivery is dodgy here. However, I mail mine to her via Persephone Press. That's how I ended up illustrating her children's book. I'd gone to Persephone Press because Felicity refused to meet me in person—I'd written to ask."

Well, begged, if Seb was to be honest.

Luke hooted with disbelief. "*That's* why you were so upset the night you were foxed."

Seb offered a reluctant nod. "I'm not proud. But yes."

"You're in love with Felicity Vita!"

Seb flushed. "Not love. Obsessed. Infatuated. Humiliated."

"To think I had no idea . . ." Luke handed the letter back. "But here's the part of your claim my brain refuses to comprehend: why would Felicity Vita write you, Seb? Why would a poet famed for her anonymity send you letters, of everyone in the world?"

Why indeed. Looking back, Seb was astonished too.

And so he found himself telling Luke the story of how he discovered Felicity's poetry soon after his parents' untimely passing, when all felt so lost. Her verses had spoken to his heart so deeply that he was moved to write to an author for the first time in his life. Instead of receiving a formal response from her publisher as expected, an envelope arrived from Felicity herself.

"It contained the kindest letter I'd ever received. The loveliest. The next thing I knew we were exchanging letters maybe once a week, then more often. She wrote about her poems, ones she'd yet to publish. Soon I had no doubt she really was Felicity Vita. Then she began to take over my imagination. My dreams. My art. And now . . ."

Seb gestured to his oil painting of *La Dame sans Merci,* a painting he started with Felicity in mind, hoping to come to peace with his obsession. A painting he scarcely touched in recent weeks because he'd grown so preoccupied with Felicity's letters—and at a time when he should have been thinking of his sisters. Their future.

"You don't know what it's been like, Luke, how crazed I've been! That morning when I rushed off to Persephone Press, I'd hoped to somehow to put an end to it."

"And that's when you met Musa Bartham."

Seb nodded. "I only agreed to illustrate her children's book because she promised to introduce me to Felicity Vita, though she was ever so evasive about it. Well, I *did* need the money from the job, but that's another story."

He wouldn't speak of Jessica and her health woes. Not now. If he got into that, he'd truly lose his mind.

"So you've been a lovesick fool. But not as much a fool as Musa Bartham, if she is Felicity Vita—I know, I know, you may be mistaken. The Barthams have bad judgement, but for a daughter to be writing love poetry . . ." Luke waved his arms. "It belies the imagination!"

"Another reason Felicity Vita can't be Musa Bartham," Seb agreed.

"Yet you suspect her. Why?"

Seb evaded, "Something Miss Bartham did. It was similar to something Felicity wrote about in a letter. Similar language."

"What was it?"

Seb wiped at his nose anew. "Something a gentleman shouldn't share."

"Okay then, Gentleman Seb. Do you have a sample of Musa Bartham's handwriting we can compare to Felicity's letters?"

Seb set Musa's manuscript for *Poems of Morality and Goodness for Children to Abide* on his worktable next to the letter Luke had read.

"See, the handwriting isn't the same." Seb wasn't sure if he felt relieved or disappointed.

"Let me take a closer look." Luke held the two pages side by side. "Same stock paper—look at the watermark! Same color ink too. But you're right. Not the same hand."

Seb's pulse began to speed. "I just recalled something. I think Musa Bartham may be ambidextrous—I noticed this when we took tea."

Luke met Seb's eyes. "And you met her at Persephone Press. Same publisher as Felicity Vita."

"But Miss Bartham was there about her children's book. Not proof."

Or was it? Seb didn't know what to think; now his heart was really pounding. He felt raw with emotion, off kilter, betrayed, on top of his cold. How could a woman he disliked so much also be the poetess he cared for? A woman he did want to *commune* with, damn it?

Luke said, "Proof or not, here's what I think. Whether Musa Bartham is slumming as Felicity Vita or Felicity Vita is a mudlark with a literary bent—" he set his palm on Seb's pile of letters "—you have letters from Felicity Vita. Or someone who claims to be her. If your Felicity is Musa Bartham, do you think she suspects you're her correspondent?"

"No." It was a good thing she'd thrown his annotated manuscript back at Seb. What if she recognized his handwriting?

Luke let out a long breath. "That's excellent news. Makes it easier."

"Easier to what?"

"To investigate her, of course!"

Seb wiped his hand against his forehead, lightheaded. "There's no need for an investigation—you promised you'd look at this as a friend. I was just so stunned. I needed to tell someone. I felt like I was going mad!"

"But you didn't tell any friend, Seb. You told me, your closest friend, who happens to be a reporter in need of a good story." Luke's voice grew low and insistent. "I know I promised not to push you, but do you know how many people yearn to know who Felicity Vita *really* is? What a newspaper would pay for this story? How many people would clamor for it? They would adore nothing more than to read her secret love letters." He rubbed his hands together. "This could change your life more than an illustrated book or an oil painting."

Jessica, Seb thought all of a sudden. *The doctor. This would cover it.* But it wouldn't be right.

"I don't want to harm Musa Bartham. I'm not in the business of upending women's lives. Besides, we're working on a book together —I really need the money for my sisters."

"This is a far easier way to gain money."

Seb folded his arms across his chest. "It wouldn't be right."

"But Felicity Vita is a fantasy—a fantasy that's beguiled you, Seb. Kept you from living a real life. Tell the truth, when's the last time you kissed someone? Had an intimate encounter with some-thing other than the palm of your hand?"

"That's not the point." Indeed, it was over a year since—well, Seb didn't want to think about that.

Luke urged, "Come back to reality. Make your fortune. Make mine."

"What, so you can buy more fancy clothes? Pay for cabs?"

"She's a Bartham. She's accustomed to scandal."

"Go away! I've a book to illustrate."

"A book by Musa Bartham," Luke taunted. "Or is it by Felicity Vita?"

"Go!" And then Seb let out a long sneeze and a cough. Now his throat really felt scratchy. "I shouldn't have said anything. I imagined it all."

"But what if you haven't?"

Once Luke left, Seb glanced at Musa's children's book manuscript. Could it be the woman he'd so desperately sought was before him all along? Was the touch of a hand against his mouth enough to prove this? The choice of a word?

You're ill. That's all.

Again, he recalled Musa's fingers against his lips. Worse, he kept thinking of their first encounter, that tea at The Pink Refuge when he begged her to introduce him to Felicity. She was probably laughing to herself the entire time.

"You want to meet Felicity Vita," she'd said.

"Yes. Be in the same room as her."

"Breath the same air, I presume . . . A meeting is impossible, Mr. Atkinson. I told you, I don't even know her. No one does . . ."

He shook his head in an effort to dispel the memory. It didn't work. He felt feverish. Deranged. He should rest. After all, he had to be back at Chassen & Sons in the morning, cold or no. Musa Bartham would be there at 9:15 with her revised manuscript. He should be focusing on his art. For Jessica and Daphne's sake. Especially Jessica's.

"She's not Felicity," he muttered. "Impossible."

He retied the thick red ribbon around the letters, throwing them back on his desk beside Felicity's books. He tried to recall the last time he'd taken a day off. Or even slept a full night outside of his drunken outing a week earlier. He'd been working so hard at everything save his *La Dame sans Merci* painting. As for that canvas . . .

I'll paint for a little while. It'll help me feel better.

Seb lit an additional oil lamp to illuminate his canvas. He changed from his good suit into his painting clothes. He pulled out his palette and brushes, refreshed his paints. For some reason, he painted his figure of La Dame sans Merci with dark curls and a knowing smile, though he'd only roughed it out in sepia washes. If he didn't know better, he'd think it was Musa Bartham taunting him instead of Felicity Vita.

Impossible, he told himself again.

Only one thing to do. He rolled up his shirt sleeves. He loaded his brush with paint.

He'd paint for an hour or so, then rest. The act of setting color against canvas would distract him. He wouldn't allow a cold to get the better of him. There was too much to do.

CHAPTER 14

THE FOLLOWING MORNING, Musa reluctantly wound her way through the narrow streets of Spitalfields—and it was all because of Atkinson. He wasn't at Chassen & Sons when she'd arrived. She'd thought all to be settled with him, that they'd arrived at an accord after her apology. She'd even felt confident enough she'd considered how to best present her great-aunt's invitation to tea.

She'd supposed wrong.

"He didn't come into work today," a gentleman with a receding hairline and sandy hair explained when she arrived at Chassen & Sons. Musa assumed he was a journalist; she recalled him from when she apologized to Atkinson. "You're Miss Bartham, are you not?"

Once she nodded, he provided her with Atkinson's studio address.

"He'll be expecting you," he said too eagerly for Musa's liking. "Tell him his friend Luke sends greetings. You should hurry."

And so Musa had hurried off to Spitalfields, clutching her revised children's book manuscript against her chest. As independent as she prided herself to be, Spitalfields was nowhere near Kensington High Street. She ended up purchasing a map along the way to avoid becoming completely lost.

Once she got off the omnibus, she passed Petticoat Lane, Brick Lane, the Market, places she'd never trod before in her years. Nor had she ever desired to do so. East London's reputation preceded itself. For all of the Barthams' scandals, her family was downright aristocratic compared to what Musa witnessed in Spitalfields.

Despite the frosty morning, a scantily clad woman reclined on a stoop with a cup of tea in her hand. Two child beggars on a corner squabbled over a basket of apples, which looked rotten. On another corner, a cluster of crones jeered at her. And then there'd been a pack of men outside a public house, gaping at Musa as though she were a lamb chop dripping with mint jelly. "Hoy, girl with the papers!" they shouted. "Come write about us! We'll make it worth your while."

Damn you, Atkinson, she thought. Wandering around the wilds of east London was not on her list of tasks for today. Or any day, for that matter.

A few wrong turns later, Musa found herself on Folgate Street in front of Atkinson's door. She was relieved to find his address in better repair than others she'd passed. He lived in a solid red brick building set next to a small but clean shop selling sundries. Even his landlady appeared less threatening than the other denizens of Spitalfields. She was a rather round middle-aged woman with a kind smile; she emerged from the shop after Musa pulled the bell.

"You're here to model for the artist, miss?"

"If you mean Mr. Atkinson, yes. But not to pose," Musa answered. "I've business regarding a book." She felt defensive after the situation with Sunny's mother, though there was scant chance the countess would ever step foot near Spitalfields.

His landlady didn't blink an eye. "Top floor, miss. Only door on the landing."

Four flights later, Musa knocked at Atkinson's door. It swung open at her rap.

Unlocked.

For all of Luke's assurances, it appeared Atkinson wasn't expecting anyone, judging by the silence greeting her. She prayed he hadn't returned to drink. Her anxiety overtook her irritation. Her heart began to thud, accompanying her clenched stomach in an unholy duet.

She forced herself to venture inside, clutching her manuscript like a shield.

She discovered a wide open room with walls that sloped high. Skylights let in the cloudy sky. A wall of windows offered an unobstructed view of the roofs surrounding Spitalfields Market. The other walls were covered in art: watercolors, charcoals, and oil paintings. At first glance, the room appeared to be empty of humanity, though she made out a long work table cluttered with paint tubes and brushes and journals. On a desk, a pile of her books—well, Felicity's books.

Musa flared with unexpected pleasure at the sight of them. It was so rare for her to see her books out in the open in someone's home. The purple binding of *The Poetics of Passion* poked out beneath *Verses of Love Lost and Love Found* among others. Such was her cautious nature that she hid her printed copies at the bottom of her closet under a stack of blankets. Next to the books, she saw a photograph of a handsome older couple clutching hands; the gentleman resembled Atkinson but with gray hair. *His parents?* How strange to think of Atkinson having a family. She wondered what they made of him living in such an environment.

Before Musa could further mull this, a tall pile of letters drew her attention. They were secured with a ribbon the color of poppies, arranged in such a way so no writing showed.

She forced herself to look away. Ladies didn't read gentlemen's correspondence. Still, her curiosity prickled.

No one ties their regular correspondence with a pretty ribbon. They must be love letters.

Musa set her manuscript beside the letter pile, uncertain if she was amused or put off Atkinson had a lady friend. What would she make of Atkinson's obsession with Felicity Vita? Anyway, it was none of Musa's business. She had no interest in him outside of their book. None at all.

In another corner, a heavy sandbag hung from a beam. *So Mr. Atkinson is a pugilist of sorts.* This didn't surprise her, given how combative he could be. On the far wall, an easel held a long, life-sized painting of a woman. La Dame sans Merci, judging by the composition. Though the canvas was sketched only in rough sepia paint and splotches of color, it was easy to make out a haughtiness in the tilt of the fairy woman's head, a half-smile below her wild eyes.

Atkinson's version of *La Dame sans Merci* was a conundrum: prideful, amused, appealing. The woman bore a full mouth, a pointed chin, thick dark hair. Statuesque. If Musa didn't know better, she'd think he'd based the figure on her.

A coincidence, she told herself.

Suddenly a snore sounded from the furthest corner of the attic, where the shadows lay deepest. She nearly let out a yelp.

Sebastian Atkinson. He'd been there all along.

He lay sprawled on a large mattress, deep asleep. He appeared to be dressed still from the day before. He wore trousers, but his shirt was untucked and his braces pulled from his shoulders. He'd removed his collar, leaving the flesh at the base of his neck bared. His sleeves were rolled up, revealing nicely muscled forearms coated with fine ebony hair.

Her annoyance returned. For all of her apologies and entreaties, he was as unreliable as she suspected he'd be—and now here she was, miles from home alone in a strange man's domicile in an area of London she never thought she'd step foot near.

Was he drunk again? She approached him cautiously and sniffed.

He didn't reek of alcohol. No, he smelled mildly sour from linseed oil, turpentine.

"What a reprobate," she muttered. Only one thing to do: wake him up. The only question was whether she should shout at him or drop a book on the floor.

But then Musa stole a second look at Atkinson's sleeping form . . . and found herself unable to move.

Sebastian Atkinson appeared like an angel from one of her father's books of Italian frescoes. A disreputable angel to be sure, but one who would have won the approval of anyone with an appreciation for beauty. And that's what he was: a beautiful man. His face was relaxed, with a half-smile caressing his lips. His rich mahogany hair curled about his sharp jawline. And his hands, oh his hands! They were more calloused than she'd expect for an artist. They appeared strong, like they were accustomed to manual labor. She recalled her father's hands, which were long and sensitive. Delicate even.

Atkinson let out a little cough and settled onto his back before he began to snore. Now she could make out the entirety of his body. His long legs. Slender torso. His wool twill trousers fit him nicely, she decided, and were a fashionable plaid, though they were stained with small splatters of paint.

Her eyes flicked toward his crotch before she flushed and forced her gaze to his mouth—the mouth she'd touched like a madwoman. What had she been thinking? It was all because of that insouciant letter she sent Henry. She'd been so forward. So ridiculous. Thankfully, Henry had responded kindly, which made Musa wish all the more she dared to meet him.

Enough already. Do what you came here to do.

Musa pulled up a stool next to Atkinson's mattress and folded herself onto it. She cleared her throat, curious to see how long it would take him to notice her presence.

Instead of waking, Atkinson's mouth widened into a smile more seductive than she imagined possible.

"You," he murmured in a caress of a voice, still asleep. He stretched his arms in her direction.

He's dreaming of his lady friend, Musa thought. *That's all.*

"Come," he whispered, eyes still closed. "Closer. Commune with me."

And then something gripped Musa, a force she couldn't quite explain. It was more than annoyance. More than a desire to shock him into alertness.

She sidled beside him on his mattress, her heart pounding. *Madness. I shouldn't do this.*

Atkinson's arms wrapped around her. He felt warm, strong. He pulled her next to him on the mattress though he still slept. Musa didn't resist, though she couldn't explain why. Anything could happen. Something that shouldn't.

Curiosity, she told herself. *That's all.* She'd never been so near a man before under such circumstances. Never been kissed or embraced or even held hands. Who knew if she'd ever have this opportunity again?

"See what you've done to me," he murmured in a honey-thick voice, eyes still shut. "I know who you are, what you've done. Yet I desire you . . ."

Musa's blood grew warm. Her response shocked her. No, stunned her.

I should stop this. Wake him.

Still within his arms, Musa carefully brushed his lush hair from his brow. He still didn't wake. His forehead felt clammy beneath her touch. No, sweaty. Whether he was drunk or not, she couldn't seem to turn away.

His embrace tightened, yet he was gentle. She was close enough she could make out a small pale scar above his right eyebrow. Close enough she could press her lips against his if she dared . . .

Atkinson's eyes sprang open.

"Miss Bartham," he sputtered, his color high. "What the hell?"

What was I thinking?

With this, whatever spell she'd sensed broke. His smile turned to a grimace as he jumped from her. She jumped too, knocking over the small pine table next to his mattress in the process. A sketch book and his pocket watch fell to the floor, a clatter of accusation.

Atkinson broke their gaze, grabbed his boots. "Why are you here?"

His voice was rougher than usual, his breathing uneven. His eyes appeared glassy too.

"Your colleague gave me your address. Luke," she answered, regaining her facilities. "He said you expected me here. I brought my revised manuscript."

"A misunderstanding, Miss Bartham. My apologies."

Atkinson picked up his pocket watch from the floor, muttering a curse. There was something vaguely off about his movements, as though he still wasn't fully awake. He scrambled to his feet, tucking his shirt into his trousers, his braces over his shoulders.

"It's eleven in the morning! I must have overslept. I'm so sorry!"

Musa suddenly realized it wasn't linseed oil he smelled of. Something else. Perspiration, perhaps. Or . . .

She pressed her hand against his forehead. Hot. Burning.

"You've a fever, Mr. Atkinson," she announced, alarmed. She'd been wrong to judge him drunk.

"Only a cold. Exhaustion." He pointed to his canvas. "Besides your book, my job, I've my painting. Busy. So very busy."

Musa rose for the door. "I'm going for a doctor."

He grabbed her arm. "Don't, I beg you!"

"You're obviously ill, Mr. Atkinson."

"I-I only need rest, Miss Bartham. A few minutes, that's all. Please. We'll go over your manuscript then."

Before Musa could insist otherwise, he sank back onto his mattress and began to snore. She couldn't bear to disturb him.

CHAPTER 15

WHEN SEB NEXT OPENED his eyes, his attic was awash in a low golden light. Candles. Two candles, to be precise. One on the fireplace mantel and another on his desk. Someone had extinguished his oil lamp in favor of softer illumination. *How long have I been asleep?* He couldn't tell, though a glance toward the skylight revealed a deep cobalt sky with a crescent moon.

The hiss of words drew his attention to the other side of the attic. Someone was whispering. Someone female.

Across the room, two women were seated at his worktable, one with silvery blonde hair, the other with chestnut curls that had escaped their pins. He immediately recognized the latter as Musa Bartham; he recalled the shock of discovering her beside him before he'd given way to exhaustion anew.

The woman accompanying Musa was older, middle-aged. She was beautiful, from what Seb could make out amid the candlelight. Delicate of bone structure. Ethereal. She wore a pale blue gown simple in its construction, like something he imagined a Pre-Raphaelite muse might have donned for posing. Her voice was silvery too.

The two women leaned toward each other, revealing a

surprising intimacy. Seb silenced a cough, eager to listen to them for as long as he could. To uncover their secrets.

"You have to ask him," the older woman murmured in that otherworldly voice. "You have no choice, sweetheart."

"He's sick."

"His fever broke. He'll be fine by Sunday."

Sunday? What was this about?

Seb squinted at the two, as though he could sharpen his hearing by sharpening his eyesight.

"I suppose," Musa answered, her tone flat. "But it's a lot to ask of someone, Mama."

Mama. Seb was in the presence of the Muse of Scandal herself, Clio Bartham, née Hadley, the former wife of Ethan Sutton, art critic extraordinaire of the London art world. Clio Bartham, who hadn't been seen in public in years. Not since the disappearance of her husband several years earlier.

The shock of this realization must have registered on Seb in some physical form, for the two women turned as one toward him.

"Mr. Atkinson," Musa said, rushing to his side. Her skin was scented with an exotic fragrance. Her usual sandalwood. "You're awake."

A second later, she was joined by her mother, who set a gentle hand against his forehead.

"Definitely cooler." Mrs. Bartham offered him a mug containing something that smelled rancid. "Drink."

He refused the mug with what he hoped was a polite grimace.

"Please, Mr. Atkinson. It's herbal tea—well, with a few other ingredients I shan't divulge. Best while it's hot. It'll taste worse cold. Trust me, this will help you improve."

The tea was as foul as he expected. He sipped at it, trying not to gag. It was disgusting: some sort of fetid broth combined with bitter herbs. Perhaps something decaying.

As soon as the tea hit his tongue, a memory flashed. He'd tasted it before. He recalled Mrs. Bartham supporting his head to help him drink the warm liquid. Musa's worried expression as she pressed a cool washcloth against his forehead. *"God-willing, his fever should break soon, Mama. I think he's more exhausted than anything . . ."*

Mrs. Bartham took the mug away once he'd drunk enough to her satisfaction. "Better?"

To Seb's surprise, he *did* feel better—his sinuses clearer, his throat soothed. Or perhaps it was the relief of no longer drinking the tea.

"How long have you been here, Mrs. Bartham?"

"Long enough. It's nearly five of the morning."

Overnight. He tried to recall exactly what happened after he awakened with Musa near him on his mattress. He couldn't. Nor could he remember much before.

He flushed, too aware of Musa's presence. Her scent. Had anything happened between them? He assumed not, if her mother was here.

He said, "I'm very grateful to the two of you for watching over me. As well as very embarrassed to have been such a burden."

Mrs. Bartham replied, "You gave my daughter quite the scare. She sent a note about your illness—"

"Well, I sent it to my sister Lyra," Musa protested. "You had a fever, Mr. Atkinson. I didn't feel right leaving you alone, but didn't want my family to worry where I was. Luckily, your landlady's son was able to act as my messenger."

She stayed with me. He recalled refusing the doctor to save money. He'd assumed she'd leave. She hadn't.

"Lyra showed me the note," Clio Bartham added in a firm voice. "As she should have. I came to help."

"I could have taken care of him, Mama," Musa protested. To Seb, "I'd written my sister to send belladonna, food. There was nothing in your pantry."

Seb flushed. He hadn't a chance to shop. Plus he was watching his budget.

Clio glared at Musa, jaw squared. "You should have written me, not Lyra."

Musa stood, her mouth a thin line. Shoulders taut. He supposed their relationship was complicated, given their family history.

Suddenly it hit him anew: Clio Bartham was in his attic. Clio Bartham, the Muse of Scandal herself. Clio, who'd been named after the muse of history. A goddess. How different she was from her daughter, yet similar! He sensed the two women were strong in their ways, stubborn. He supposed they needed to be, with Neil Bartham gone so long.

And then he recalled Luke had sent Musa Bartham to his address—Luke, to whom he'd confided his belief Musa was Felicity Vita.

You're supposing a lot, Seb. You've no proof really.

"I feel much better, Mrs. Bartham, Miss Bartham. You're very kind to take care of me."

Clio Bartham offered a wry smile. "I understand you're illustrating my daughter's children's book. You might say we've a vested interest in your health."

Musa pointed toward his desk. "I brought my new manuscript —that's why I'm here."

The pages laid there next to Felicity's letters, which he'd taken out from their locked drawer to show Luke. He hadn't put them away.

Shit.

He rose to his feet, dizzy, rushed over to the desk. The red ribbon he'd used to secure them appeared as he recalled. Untouched thankfully. He slammed the letters into the drawer, which he locked.

"I'm grateful to you both," he said. "But you should leave. I'm fine. Really."

Well, not entirely. Though his fever and cold felt better, his heart continued to gallop.

"If you insist," Musa replied. "Send a note once you're ready to discuss the manuscript." A raised brow. "I trust you'll edit it for me again?"

"No, no, that won't do—I wouldn't presume to write on your manuscript. I've learned my lesson." He wouldn't risk revealing his handwriting.

She countered slyly, "Then how shall I know your thoughts?"

"I-I shall have to tell you. Let's say a week from today. Wednesday next. Chassen & Sons."

She nodded. "9:15 again?"

Seb agreed. He felt as though he couldn't breathe, but not from illness. Nor could he turn from her warm amber eyes.

Mrs. Bartham ordered, "Musa, leave Mr. Atkinson to rest. Come."

However, once mother and daughter reached the door, Seb couldn't resist taking Musa's hands in his to thank her. He needed to touch her. Needed somehow to uncover whether she was Felicity, as though the warmth of her flesh intersecting with his would reveal such a secret.

Before he could think twice, his thumb caressed the back of her hand. She didn't pull away.

Oh.

He released Musa's hand, feeling as though he'd been scalded.

"Thank you," Seb said, flustered. "Truly. You both cared enough to remain here with me, to make sure I was better. I appreciate it. One day I hope to return the favor—not to nurse you through a fever, mind. But to help in another way. Well, beyond illustrating books and such. Well, you understand."

Stop babbling. You're making an ass of yourself.

Clio Bartham exchanged a look with her daughter before she said something he did not expect.

"That's lovely to hear, Mr. Atkinson. You see, I do have a favor to ask you." A bright smile. "Will you come to tea this Sunday afternoon? That is, if you've recovered enough. It's a tricky situation involving my aunt and Musa . . ." a rise of color along her neck ". . . too much to explain now."

Seb recalled what he'd overheard while half-asleep. *"It's a lot to ask of someone."*

"Would you like me to attend, Miss Bartham?"

Their eyes met. There was a warmth in hers he didn't expect.

"If you please," was all Musa said. "I'll send a note with the particulars."

She turned away, but not before she exchanged another long look with him. Then she was gone along with her mother.

Downstairs, Musa felt very fortunate her mother managed to locate a hackney cab almost immediately. After a night of sleepless watch over Atkinson, she just wanted to get home and into bed. What a strange, long night it had been! She didn't know what to think. The sight of Atkinson's squalid living arrangements disturbed her more than she wished. They also won her sympathy, to her surprise.

How on earth did he end up there? Atkinson was educated, talented and—Musa had to admit—handsome. He'd mentioned having family, friends and employment. He had parents he obviously loved and a sweetheart whose letters he cherished. She didn't think it was drink; she hadn't spied a single bottle in the attic. Yes, he was an artist, and artists were often impoverished. But the worst place Neil Bartham ever lived in was a bedsit in Earl's Court before he gained success.

But it wasn't only Atkinson's poverty that disturbed Musa. There'd been his painting of *La Dame sans Merci*, with the figure so closely resembling her. Atkinson's thumb caressing her hand as he bid farewell. His arms reaching for her in his sleep. Worse, the awareness she'd desired him in that moment. It felt like a spell overtaking her senses. Dangerous. Foolish. Illogical. Would she have resisted his attentions if he hadn't awakened?

I shouldn't have encouraged him.

No doubt Atkinson had mistaken her for his sweetheart—curiosity or no, she had no right. Anyway, her correspondent Henry should be romance enough, not a starving artist she was beholden to for the success of a book. As for her promise to introduce

Atkinson to Felicity Vita, that was another complication she'd solve in time.

If he has a sweetheart, perhaps meeting Felicity doesn't matter as much as you think, Musa told herself. She didn't quite believe this, given how insistent he'd been when they'd made their agreement at The Pink Refuge.

"You're deep in thought, Musa," Clio Bartham said as the hackney pulled away. "Is all well?"

"Just exhausted, Mama."

"Look, the sun's coming up." Clio pointed out the window toward the sky. "I don't think I've watched a sunrise in years. Your father used to insist on waking me up to view them with him. Said a sunrise was always prettier than a sunset. Purer colors." A pause. "He was right, sweetheart . . . but I couldn't bear to watch one without him beside me."

Musa took her mother's hand and squeezed it.

Clio dabbed at her eyes. "I know he's not coming back. I've lied to myself these three years, for all my chatter about his soul entwined with mine. I'd wanted to believe this so much—"

"Papa may still be alive," Musa interrupted, her throat tight. "We need to hope."

The horses let out a whinny. The cobblestones seemed especially bumpy in this corner of London. Or perhaps Musa was sensitive after a long night without sleep.

"Perhaps," Clio answered. "But our family can't continue as we have. Or, I should say, *I* mustn't. Angela has awakened me to this, with her desire to wed, and you, with your children's book. I have no idea how you've made ends meet for us these past three years. I'm afraid to ask."

"I managed," Musa said, shocked by a rush of sorrow. She bit back tears.

I'm tired, that's all.

"I feel so badly. I saw you so weighed down by worry, but I was too filled with sorrow to intervene. Too self-involved. All I knew was there was coal in the scuttle, food on my plate." Clio's hand tightened on Musa's. "Tell me, how did you support us? You didn't borrow money, did you?"

Musa swallowed hard. "I-I found ways. I wrote a few things."

"My clever girl! Other children's books?"

Musa laughed, uneasy. "Not exactly."

"Well, whatever you wrote, I'm sure it was wonderful." Clio kissed Musa's cheek. "You'll show me, won't you?"

"Nothing really," Musa evaded. "Only some articles here and there."

"You're so modest. I know you'll be the one to restore our family name with your children's book. Oh, I know there was that trouble with Sunny's mother, but Aunt Minerva's tea will smooth things over. You'll accomplish for your siblings what your father couldn't, bless his soul. I'm so proud of you, sweetheart! Doesn't Angela look so happy these days?"

Musa turned toward the carriage window, staring at the sun rising, too troubled to respond. In that moment, she swore to herself her mother must never learn of Felicity Vita. Nor could anyone else.

When she got home, she'd throw out her poem drafts. As for Henry, she knew she should stop writing to him. But she couldn't bear to.

CHAPTER 16

Dear Mr. Atkinson:

I trust your health has improved enough that you've returned to your place of employment; hence, I have addressed this letter to Chassen & Sons instead of your studio. If you remain able to attend my great-aunt's tea this Sunday at 4, it would be remiss of me not to explain the circumstances surrounding it, which are complicated at best. They unfortunately involve my dear sister, Angela, and the tea you and I'd taken at The Pink Refuge when we'd met.

But first, here is my great-aunt's address . . .

THAT SUNDAY, Seb prepared to take tea with Lady Minerva Hadley and the Barthams as though he going into battle. He dressed in his finest clothes: his only frock coat, a stiffly starched collar, and a dark green waistcoat Daphne embroidered with delicate *fleurs de lys*. He shaved carefully, oiled his hair, and set his drawings in his best portfolio.

To his surprise, he was more anxious than he could recall.

When he agreed to the tea invitation, he had no idea he and Musa provoked gossip that day at The Pink Refuge. Nor was he aware Musa's sister Angela was about to be launched into society, and that this tea was intended to smooth over any additional scandals. He'd since learned his attendance was to prove he truly was illustrating a book written by Musa Bartham—a book that would be edifying and moralistic for children. It would also serve as evidence the Barthams had turned over a new leaf.

Perhaps the real reason for your anxiety isn't due to the tea.

Even now, two days after waking to discover Clio Bartham nursing him, Seb remained stunned by his suspicions regarding Musa and Felicity Vita. He'd nearly convinced himself he was imagining things until he received a new letter from Felicity. In it, she mentioned she was taking a break from poetry to write something else. *"I shan't confess any details about my new book here, darling Henry, but it will be very different from my previous ones. Instead of poems, I shall be writing something more upstanding. I must admit I am feeling rather trepidatious about this new enterprise—forgive me for my secrecy!"* He'd folded away the letter fixating anew about Musa's hand against his lips, Musa's children's book manuscript, and so on in an unruly merry-go-round of torturous rumination about Felicity Vita.

You're imagining things, Seb. Coincidence, that's all.

As Seb walked toward Mayfair that cold Sunday morning, his mind continued swaying back and forth on the Musa-Felicity Conundrum, as he'd grown to think of the situation. All too soon he arrived at the grand Grosvenor Square townhouse Lady Minerva Hadley called home. For once, he was early; he considered strolling around the square to take up time, but decided he'd find no joy in it.

He drew a deep breath and pulled the bell.

"I'm Mr. Atkinson. Lady Hadley expects me for tea," he announced to the formally suited butler, hoping he didn't sound as unsettled as he felt.

The butler brought him into the drawing room, advising him to wait.

Lady Hadley's townhouse was surprisingly tasteful for someone with wealth. Seb was occasionally called to Mayfair to run errands for Chassen; most of these houses took pride in their excess of gilded decoration and heavily upholstered furniture. Lady Hadley's contained few items for such a large drawing room. There was a grand piano set in one corner, a card table in another. In the center of the room, a delicate looking round light-wooded table, about which several wicker chairs were placed in anticipation. Next to a wall of tall windows overlooking the square, a long chaise lounge covered in pale pink damask.

The walls were hung with a variety of paintings newer than expected for someone of her lineage. Seb made out an early Millais oil, a Burne-Jones watercolor, a number of Whistler decorations in muted hues, and several historical subjects painted in a modern fashion. Her ladyship had an eye, Seb decided.

"You approve of my art?"

The owner of the voice sounded sharp as a whip and old as the sands.

Seb turned. An elderly dowager addressed him from the doorway, dressed in a plum-hued loosely draped Aesthetic-style tea gown and diamonds. She could only be Lady Hadley—such a display of jewels could be considered vulgar for daytime. But the wearer had the authority to pull them off.

"I do, my lady," he answered. He bowed with all the grace he could muster.

"Mr. Atkinson, I presume. You're on time."

"I'm relieved to hear such. I feared I was early, which is as rude as tardiness."

Lady Hadley was unable to offer a response, for the drawing room suddenly flooded with guests, many more than Seb anticipated. He'd expected the presence of only Musa, her mother, her great-aunt, and Lady Sunderland, who'd spied him with Musa at The Pink Refuge. Not so. Next to Musa, he made out an exquisitely beautiful young woman with pale blonde hair—she resembled a younger version of Clio Bartham—and a gawky male and female bearing the same chestnut hair and lanky build as Musa. They appeared to be edging toward adulthood. Four Barthams in total. In addition, there were half a dozen servants, who brought in a seemingly endless array of tea implements and trays. No sign of Lady Sunderland, whom Musa had described as formidable in her letter. Nor did he see Clio Bartham, but then again, the Muse of Scandal was never seen out in society.

Musa approached. She was dressed in a dark green velvet gown with three-quarter sleeves. It was a few years old, judging by the lack of bustle. Seb found himself unable to tear his gaze away.

"Mama is sorry she couldn't attend," she said in a low voice. "It wouldn't do. Not with Lady Sunderland being present."

"I understand, Miss Bartham."

Yet I understand nothing at all. He felt time slow, the air thicken as the Musa-Felicity Conundrum swirled anew inside him.

"My three siblings, Mr. Atkinson," Musa introduced, gesturing toward them. "Theo and Lyra are the youngest. They recently turned fifteen."

"Twins!" they exclaimed as one. Seb had the sense they'd explained such many times before.

"And my sister, Miss Angela Bartham."

The silvery-blonde lady offered a pretty nod. "I thank you, Mr. Atkinson, for coming to tea. I believe my sister wrote you of our delicate situation." Her tone wavered with nerves.

Seb replied, "I shall do my best to smooth over any difficulties."

And then it was too late: the butler arrived anew. "The Countess of Sunderland and her son, my lady."

"Quick, places!" Musa hissed.

The four Bartham siblings stood in a line before the door. Seb took a spot beside them, feeling as though he was being presented at court instead of attending a Sunday tea.

A heavy-set *grande dame* draped in even more diamonds than Lady Hadley staggered into the room—Seb presumed her to be Lady Sunderland. She clutched the arm of a rather full-figured young man. His pleasant but bland features were topped by a shock of reddish hair that appeared untamable, though it shined with pomade. Both bore distinctive overbites and weak chins, marking them as mother and son.

The *grande dame* screwed her mouth sideways as she took in the room's inhabitants.

"Let's be quick about this then," Lady Sunderland said in a brash voice. "I know who you are. You know who I am. We don't need to go through the rigmarole of a tea, do we?"

"As charming as ever, Eliza," Lady Hadley said, calmer than Seb expected. "We appreciate your visit regardless. I wish you'd brought Lord Sunderland. It would have been lovely to see him after so long."

"He's responsibilities, Minerva. As have I."

Lady Hadley's brow arched. "Such as eavesdropping at The Pink Refuge on innocent young women?"

Lady Sunderland sputtered, "Minerva, I know why you've called me here. You can fancy up Miss Angela Bartham all you like, but she's still mutton dressed as veal."

"Now now, Mama," the flame-haired gentleman intervened, granting a soft look in Angela Bartham's direction. "It's unfair to blame the children for the actions of the parents—"

"Silence, Virgil! I'll decide what's kind or not. I *know* what I saw at The Pink Refuge." Lady Sunderland pointed to Musa. "You. Eldest daughter, am I correct?"

Musa curtseyed. "Miss Musa Bartham, my lady."

"You're the one I saw at The Pink Refuge. Is it true your mother's gone mad over your father's death?"

Musa clutched her hands, the only sign revealing her distress. "My lady, I don't believe he's passed—"

"And this also makes you mad in the head, correct? Fruit from the tree and all that, which is why you were out in public with—" she pointed to Seb "—*this* man."

Seb exchanged a look with Musa, who for once appeared cowed by another's presence. He fought his temper. Anger. Frustration. Emotion, as usual.

"Sebastian Atkinson at your service, my lady," he gritted out.

Lady Sunderland turned his way. "I know you've cleaned yourself up, but I recognize a vagabond when I see one."

Not trusting himself to speak, Seb drew out his portfolio. He set the drawings across the fragile tea table, hoping art would distract Lady Sunderland from her tirade.

"We're publishing a book. A children's book," he said in clipped tones. "Miss Bartham has written it and I am illustrating it. I must admit to being puzzled. I'm uncertain what's disreputable about a children's book, my lady. Yes, we met for tea at The Pink Refuge to discuss her book, for she hired me to illustrate it. Since it was a business meeting, we didn't think it required a chaperone. However, I must confess I wasn't at my best, for I had unfortunate news—"

"News?" Lady Sunderland interrupted, her hooded eyes glittering with salacious interest.

Seb blurted, "My parents passed away."

No need to explain it was a year and a half earlier. A collective gasp rang about the room. Seb felt mildly guilty but continued.

"I was greatly distressed by this news, for their unexpected deaths left my youngest sister without a mother and a father—she's but seven. I've another sister closer to my age, but she's also been affected by the loss of our parents."

Despite himself, his words caught in his throat. He considered divulging about Jessica's health issues. Too private, too manipulative, even in this instance. In addition, he prayed their family doctor was wrong about Jessica—to say anything felt like tempting fate. Jessica would be meeting later in the week with the Harley Street pediatric cardiologist. Seb's remaining funds from *Poems of Morality and Goodness for Children to Abide* were promptly allotted toward the first part of the payment. The remainder would have to be paid on credit.

"So sad!" Angela Bartham cried out in a tremulous voice; perhaps she was recalling her missing father.

"Yes, very sad, Miss Angela," Seb agreed. "However, in the interest of professionalism, I'd insisted on meeting with Miss

Bartham to share the progress I made on her book. She noticed I looked poorly. Therefore, she insisted on taking me to tea as a restorative measure, caring less for gossip than she did for my well-being." Seb met the Countess of Sunderland's sharp little eyes. "If kindness is disreputable, Miss Bartham is guilty as judged. I hoped a civilized society would be more tolerant."

He gestured to the array of drawings across the tea table. "Now, if you'd like to examine these, my lady, you'll find proof of my account."

Lady Sunderland's thin mouth screwed anew. "I needn't see your drawings, young man. I don't care for art as my husband does." Then, "Minerva, I do hope you've Earl Grey. I could use something restorative."

CHAPTER 17

MUSA OBSERVED the remainder of the tea with unease. Something was bothering her, though she knew she should feel relief at Lady Sunderland's surrender. Something important, though she couldn't decide what it could be. Her pragmatic and logical mind clicked away without coming upon anything definitive. This bothered her greatly.

After Atkinson recited his family history to Lady Sunderland—a history that astonished Musa, for she'd no idea about the death of his parents—everyone chatted companionably as though they hadn't gathered to discuss yet another Bartham scandal without Clio's presence. Lady Sunderland settled on the settee beside Aunt Minerva like they were the closest of friends. Angela sighed with approval as she examined Atkinson's drawings, which really *were* lovely.

Once the last tea sandwich was nibbled into polite oblivion, the twins made their way to the grand piano to play a four-handed Chopin duet from memory. Angela accompanied them by dancing a graceful minuet to the pleasure of all.

"She appears like a fairy," Lyra said, smiling adoringly at her sister from the keyboard.

"Indeed she does," Lady Sunderland replied in a dry tone. "Your family has many talents."

Including a talent for trouble, Musa thought, skin still prickling.

It wasn't the absence of her mother that bothered Musa. Clio was never invited to any functions involving society. Nor was it the evident ease in which Atkinson ingratiated himself into her family's goodwill, as though he was a gentleman of leisure, not a starving artist. She was relieved he appeared fully recovered from illness. She stole an approving look at how well his jacket fit across his broad shoulders. Not to mention the luster of his neatly combed dark brown hair and his deep blue eyes. She'd misjudged him.

Every so often his intent gaze met hers. She found herself flushing like a maiden, recalling how they'd nearly embraced in his sleep. (What had she been thinking?) But that wasn't what was needling her.

Musa searched the room for the source of her discomfort, her mouth tight. For all of Mr. Atkinson's attempt to mend fences, she trusted Lady Sunderland as far as she could throw her. Nor did it help that Sunny's eyes remained fixed on Angela as though he was a starving man and she was a buttered crumpet. Musa prayed the countess didn't notice.

"Now that all has been resolved," Aunt Minerva said once the twins finished their piano duet, "I have news. Something I've been mulling ever since our dear Musa announced her children's book with Mr. Atkinson's charming drawings. Angela, will you do the honors?"

Angela clapped her hands like an overly excited seal.

"We're going to have a ball here! One to mark the publication of your book, Musa, and to introduce me to society!"

"And not just any ball," Aunt Minerva added with a superior air. "A costume ball!"

Musa sat up straight. This was bad. *Very* bad, though she couldn't explain why a costume ball bothered her so much beyond the mingling of trade and society, which was uncommon at best. (What *had* gotten into her great-aunt?) Was it because her parents met at such a ball? Or because Aunt Minerva was holding the ball before the start of the Season, as though to offer Angela an advantage in a horse race? Or perhaps it was the way in which Atkinson was staring at her? (Did she have frosting on her nose? Or something else?)

The answer arrived inside Musa like a thunderbolt.

Felicity. If anyone were to find out, Angela's chances would be ruined.

But no one knew who Felicity Vita was—no one who would betray her. Certainly not Mary nor Angela, both whom Musa would trust with her life. Certainly not Atkinson, who had no idea of her *nom de plume* even if he was obsessed with the poet. Nor Henry, who'd been loyal for the past year. Anyway, Felicity's career was at an end. Over. Done.

Her great-aunt's ball was good news for her children's book. Really. The more copies it sold, the sooner she'd forget about Felicity. Truly.

Atkinson smiled as though he'd been offered a sack of guineas. "This is such a wonderful surprise. Thank you, my lady. Don't you agree, Miss Bartham?"

"Thank you, Aunt," Musa said, forcing an enthusiasm she didn't feel. "It's very generous of you."

"What a marvelous idea, Lady Hadley!" Sunny cried. "I trust her ladyship and I will be invited?"

"Uncouth," Lady Sunderland opined. "Especially if you're selling books."

"It'll only be uncouth if I say so," Aunt Minerva replied in an ingratiating manner. "And you'll be the guest of honor. That is besides Angela and her sister, of course, and the book, and Mr. Atkinson, who illustrated it—"

"I understand," Lady Sunderland said tartly; Musa had the sense she'd thrown up her hands in resignation.

"We can attend, yes?" Theo asked, Lyra agreeing energetically.

"Of course, of course," Aunt Minerva answered impatiently. "It *is* an event for a children's book, is it not? Families will be invited.

Parents and children as well as young people." She glanced at Musa and said *sotto voce*, "Though not your mother."

Musa bit her lip, troubled by the sacrifices her mother made to marry her father . . . and continued to make. A twinge pinged her chest as she recalled Henry and his letters. How easy he made it for her to swear off any thought of romance in real life. What would she do without him?

"Lady Hadley, I'd like to bring my sisters to the ball, if you don't mind," Atkinson asked, a warm grin lighting up his too handsome face. "My youngest sister especially."

"It shall be quite the soirée!" Angela wrapped her arms around herself with excitement. "I'm so happy!"

Lady Sunderland stood abruptly from the chaise.

"It's all very thrilling," she said in a tone that suggested anything but. She gestured toward the window. "Look, it's starting to snow. Forgive us for bringing your tea to a close, but we must leave posthaste. Come, Virgil!"

Once the countess departed with her son, Angela offered Atkinson a bright smile. "I do appreciate your attendance, Mr. Atkinson. And your illustrations—they're lovely!"

"My pleasure, Miss Angela," Atkinson replied, offering a polite bow. "Your praise means much coming from a daughter of Neil Bartham." He nodded in Musa's direction. "Until we next meet, Miss Bartham."

Atkinson turned toward the door, portfolio in hand, shoulders squared in anticipation of the weather. Musa felt a sense of loss she couldn't decipher for all her trying.

"You're not going to let him go like that?" Angela whispered. "After how kind he was?"

"I'll see him soon enough."

Angela shook her head at her sister. "It's snowing out, for heaven's sake." She called out before Musa could stop her, "Mr. Atkinson! We'd like to invite you to share my family's carriage." Aunt Minerva had loaned them her clarence, which seated four, for the day. "They'll be heading toward Kensington."

Lyra agreed, "We've plenty of room without Angela."

"He doesn't live anywhere near us," Musa replied.

"We can take him part of the way," Theo said. To Atkinson: "Especially since you've been ill."

"I'm fully recovered now," Atkinson demurred. "I'll be fine."

"Even so, a carriage part of the way is better than none of the way, yes?" Lyra piped up. "What say you, Mr. Atkinson?"

To Musa's disquiet, he agreed.

CHAPTER 18

Outside Lady Hadley's townhouse, the snow was as lovely as Seb anticipated. Bracing after the warmth of the drawing room. Serene. He'd felt well enough to walk home, hoping to gain clarity on all he'd learned about the Musa-Felicity Conundrum. Yet, though the snow wasn't *that* heavy and Seb lived in the opposite direction, he'd accepted Angela Bartham's offer before he could think twice.

And then Seb realized: he hadn't been able to refuse because he wanted more time with the Barthams. He'd known of Neil Bartham's family for as long as he could recall—anyone interested in art couldn't avoid their soiled history. But now that Seb was there with them, he felt strangely at home in a manner he hadn't since his parents' death.

However, it was more than this.

He glanced across the crowded carriage at Musa, whose eyes met his.

She turned away, busying herself by wiping her spectacles with a handkerchief.

"Tell me, Mr. Atkinson," Lyra Bartham began in a jovial tone, "is your wife also of the artistic persuasion?"

Musa looked up from her furious spectacle cleaning.

"I'm unwed," he answered, tucking his portfolio to the side of the carriage.

"A sweetheart?" Musa asked, her voice odd.

He shook his head. "I'd hoped to settle my situation before tying myself to another." This wasn't fully true; it was more that he wished to attend to his home, which desperately needed repair, as well as take care of his sisters. Now, with Jessica's health being what it was, his priorities had changed.

Don't think of this. Just trust the doctor will have reassuring news.

Lyra's cheeks prickled pink beneath her chestnut curls. "But your fortune will surely be made soon, yes?"

"Artists and fortunes are a complicated matter," he evaded. "I'm sure Miss Bartham's book will be an assist. I do have a large oil painting underway, which I hope will make my reputation. It would reassure my sisters."

"Ah, yes, your sisters!" Theo Bartham piped up; Seb sensed he was the more serious one of the twins. "Tell us of them, Mr. Atkinson."

"My youngest one is Jessica." His smile rose as he indicated the red scarf wrapped around his neck. "She knit this for me."

Musa said tartly, "We should stop badgering Mr. Atkinson about his situation. It's impolite to ask so many questions."

"Don't be a spoilsport, Musa," Lyra teased. "Mr. Atkinson is perfectly able to answer for himself."

"He certainly is," Theo agreed. "Look at how quickly he silenced Lady Sunderland! I've never seen that before." To Seb: "We're not being rude, are we?"

"Not at all," Seb assured, enjoying the banter between the twins. "I enjoy talking about Jessica. It's almost like having her here with me. My other sister's name is Daphne. She's exquisitely talented at embroidery. They reside in Kent in our family home."

"Yet you're here in London," Lyra said. "Not with them."

"I've employment as a pressman at a printer. One must make a living."

"Is this why you live as you do in that attic in Spitalfields?" Musa asked.

"I don't understand what you mean, Miss Bartham." But he did. It had been one thing for Luke to visit him there, who comprehended the sacrifices he made on behalf of his sisters, another for Musa and her mother. They must have judged him little better than a pauper.

Suddenly it all seemed too much to speak of. Between his ambitions for his art, his fears for his sisters and his home, his work to support them all, he felt overcome by responsibility. Well, no need to inflict his mood on the Barthams, not after that surprisingly pleasant tea.

"Ah, here's where I should depart," he called out, knocking on the roof to bring the carriage to a halt. "I can walk from here. You've all been very kind."

Once the carriage came to a stop, Seb staggered out toward the entrance of Green Park. The park was beautiful. White. Pristine. Unlike his emotions. Why had they suddenly hit him with the force of a slap?

Because you spent time with another family. You miss your own.

Seb offered a half-hearted wave to the Barthams. Then he headed into Green Park with a determined air, staring at the snow dancing around him.

He'd scarcely taken four steps when he heard someone yell his name. He turned.

Musa Bartham was running toward him from the carriage. Musa of the musical name and the Musa-Felicity Conundrum. Yet again, she was clutching his portfolio. Yet again, he'd left it behind in his rush to flee her.

When she reached him, this time she didn't drop his portfolio when she handed it to him. Not that it mattered—the snow had scarcely accumulated on the grass.

"I fear my returning your portfolio is becoming a ritual of ours," she said, breathless.

"I hope for the last time." He clutched his portfolio and bowed. "Thank you, Miss Bartham. I'll be more mindful in the future."

He waited for her to leave, to retreat to the carriage bearing her family. She didn't. She stood there, her prim suit covered by a dark wool cloak dappled with ice crystals. How bright her eyes were behind her spectacles. Again, she reminded him of an inquisitive fox.

The moment dangled between them. He heard the carriage horses whinny with impatience.

She burst out, "I want to apologize for the twins, Mr. Atkinson. I could tell they upset you with their prying."

"They didn't upset me, Miss Bartham. Not at all."

Under the guise of Henry Whitney, he'd written Felicity Vita so many things. Intimate things. Yet he'd neglected to share details that might leave him vulnerable . . . and now he felt more vulnerable than ever, Musa-Felicity Conundrum or no.

"You should go," he muttered. "Your carriage awaits."

"Yes, I should. You're quite right . . ."

Still, she didn't move. Nor did he. He stood there before her, his portfolio clasped against his chest, the snow falling about them. He half-expected the twins to run to fetch her. But then, to his surprise, the carriage lurched into motion, abandoning Musa in Green Park.

By the time Seb decided the gentlemanly thing to do would be to chase after the carriage, it was too far away.

"Hang my siblings. Hang their schemes," Musa cried out. "They think to pair us off, the minxes! I'm so sorry, Mr. Atkinson—I know you dislike me."

"I don't. Not anymore," he confessed, the blunt words springing from his lips. "You're shivering."

Without thinking, he wrapped Jessica's scarf around her neck to keep her warm. She didn't remove it. The color suited her, Seb decided. Red like a fox. Red like her cheeks in the cold, framed by her chestnut tresses.

"I'll walk you home," he said. "I don't mind."

And he didn't. He took in the snow still falling about them.

White. Swirling. Beautiful. Magical. This woman he suspected to be Felicity Vita. He wasn't ready to leave her . . . or this moment. To his surprise, he wanted the moment to linger. To expand. He even recalled his painting of *La Dame sans Merci* back in his rooms, wishing Musa could pose for it just as she appeared beneath the snow with her warm amber eyes, her rosy cheeks, so he could hold the memory forever. Yet he sensed a weight about her today. A mournfulness. Why?

"I can walk by myself. You've been ill," she said, tightening the red scarf about her neck. "The important thing is you have your portfolio. Again, I appreciate your smoothing over the situation with my great-aunt and the Countess of Sunderland. All is well."

"Are you well though?" He drew a deep breath. "You seem so alone."

"Alone?" To Seb's surprise, her amber eyes gleamed with emotion. "Is that how I appear?"

"You seem to bear so much responsibility, Musa—I mean, Miss Bartham." The familiarity slipped out without thinking.

"Miss Bartham," she agreed, flushing. "You didn't answer my question, Mr. Atkinson. Do I seem so very alone?"

"Very well, since you asked . . ." How to parse this? "Today at tea, I noticed how your family relies on you. Your sister Angela, for example. It's obvious how much she looks up to you—I suspect you wrote your children's book to help launch her into society."

"I hadn't intended it that way," Musa protested, eyes still moist. "Not at first. The children's book was simply a way to provide for my family."

"Still, it's helped her reputation. I sincerely doubt Lady Sunderland would have given her a second chance if not for that book."

"You and your art were a help," she countered. "You handled her brilliantly."

"It's not only that, Miss Bartham. There's the rest of your family too. It's clear the twins see you as the head of your family. I also noticed your great-aunt didn't lift a finger on behalf of you and your book save to propose a ball, and it's really for your sister's benefit, not yours. And then there's the matter of your mother, who wasn't able to accompany you today for reasons I shan't enumerate. So, yes, I think you're alone."

As Seb spoke, he realized how deeply he respected Musa Bartham. Like him, she loved and protected her family. Like him, she'd do anything to take care of them.

We're more alike than not, he suddenly thought. This stunned him. Since his first meeting with Musa Bartham, he'd been so focused on disdaining her for her rigid priggishness. What if her behavior was her way of taking charge of a difficult situation? If so, it wasn't that different from the choice he made to live in a down-trodden part of town to save money.

Perhaps that's why she'd written those love poems.

With this realization, the Musa-Felicity Conundrum reared anew inside Seb like a bucking stallion. And then he found himself staring at her. Specifically her mouth, which was pink and luscious with that fetching beauty mark just below her lips.

He wondered what it would be like to kiss her, whether this kiss would somehow reveal the truth of her identity.

He wondered whether her lips would be warmer than he'd expect on such a cold day. He imagined the snow on her cheeks. Melting against his mouth.

He wondered whether she'd taste of Earl Grey and tea cakes, of vanilla and fondant. Sweetness.

Seb drew a shuddering breath. He'd never forced a kiss on a woman before—he'd never needed to. There'd been the model who was more than eager once they were alone, the Belgian friend of Daphne's who eventually married a banker, the sister of a coworker at Chassen & Sons, and a few others he couldn't seem to recall in that moment. If Musa resisted his advances, he would have let her be; he would bow, apologize, and set off on his way. He would even understand should she choose to slap him for his forwardness.

A short kiss, he decided. A kiss to test how she'd respond. A kiss as though he could unearth her secret identity by the merest brush of their lips.

Before he could reconsider, he leaned toward her mouth. He managed to avoid her spectacles. Beneath her bonnet, her hair was scented with lush promise . . .

Before their lips touched, she pulled away as though his attempt at a kiss never occurred.

"I-I must go," she said, touching her mouth as though it was a new country.

"Yes, I suppose you should," Seb said, feeling more upset than he had any right.

"Farewell, Mr. Atkinson."

"The same to you, Miss Bartham."

They stood there in the snow, their eyes locked. Their breath pluming in the air. His red scarf wrapped around her neck.

"I'm leaving now. Really. Again, thank you for being so understanding, Mr. Atkinson."

Seb bowed. He hadn't the heart to ask for his scarf back. How strange and awkward it all was!

At last, she took a step away, her eyes still locked with his. A second step. He turned east, toward Spitalfields. Soon she'd be lost inside Green Park amid the snow. He told himself by the time he arrived home, she would have forgotten his attempt to kiss her. That when they next saw each other at Chassen & Sons, all would be as it had but without acrimony.

Suddenly she called out, "I'm not alone, Mr. Atkinson."

Seb turned, not trusting his ears. "Excuse me?"

Musa approached anew. Seb sensed an air of desperation roiling her brow.

"I said I'm not alone. Not truly." An uncharacteristic giggle. "I-I have someone courting me. Someone wonderful. A gentleman."

Seb's stomach dropped. "Who is he?" Rude as it was, he had to ask.

"He's kind. Intelligent. A gentleman." An uncharacteristic giggle. "I haven't even told Angela about him. It's a very peculiar tale how we came to meet each other, one I can't share—oh I'm sure you would think it strange!"

Now Seb's heart was truly pounding.

"Do you send each other letters?"

Her eyes widened. "How did you know?"

Shit, Seb thought. *If you're not Felicity Vita, I'll eat my hat.*

CHAPTER 19

How strangely Atkinson is behaving! Musa thought after she confessed about Henry. *Yet how surprising he'd guessed at our correspondence.* But there had been little about the day that wasn't surprising, if Musa was to be honest—and if there was one thing Musa prided herself on, it was her ability to see a situation for what it truly was.

First Atkinson had attempted to kiss her—the very first romantic kiss anyone ever offered her; a kiss she nearly given way to. The remembrance of this possibility weakened her knees. She had no choice but to pretend it hadn't happened. If only she could have included a description of the near-kiss in one of Felicity's poems! It would have made a lovely sonnet: the snow falling about them, the warmth of his cheek, his nose almost smudging her spectacles before she'd turned away. But it wouldn't have been loyal to Henry. Anyway, she had no interest in Atkinson.

Yet what surprised her most was her compassion for Atkinson. He'd lost his parents. He'd chosen to live in poverty to provide for his sisters. He loved them, wanted to take care of them, just as she did for her family. Art wasn't the easiest way to make a living—she knew this all too well, for all her father's success.

Now Atkinson was peering at her as though she'd sprouted

tentacles and wings. Not that it mattered . . . but why had she told him she was being courted?

She supposed it was the shock of him attempting to kiss her. That was all.

"I shouldn't have spoken of my correspondent," she said. "I've been indiscreet."

"No, no. I appreciate your honesty, Miss Bartham." How strangely his words came, like he had a pebble in his shoe. "Nor should I ask about your correspondent, though I must admit I'm curious." An uneasy laugh. "I've never met anyone being courted with letters before. Do you plan to meet him one day?"

"I-I'd rather not speak of this. The important point is I'm not alone. Not really." She offered a brave smile, or tried to.

"I'm reassured on your behalf." He set his hands in his pockets. "It's grown colder, don't you think?"

"I can walk by myself, Mr. Atkinson. You must be eager to head home."

"It's nearly dark—I insist on accompanying you to your door."

By then, the snow had slowed and the sky cleared. As they walked through Green Park, he turned silent, though he stole glances at her as they made their way. His expression was one she couldn't comprehend; she wondered if she'd somehow caused offense. Still, she chattered, no doubt out of nerves.

She spoke of their children's book, his illustrations, her frustrations in rewriting it, keeping her tone light.

"Did you read my latest draft, Mr. Atkinson? You haven't mentioned it, so I assume you still disapprove."

His expression finally relaxed. "I was going to wait until Tuesday to speak of it. No need to mix business with pleasure, Miss Bartham."

Was this pleasure? Well, it certainly wasn't business. Thus far, they'd been set up by her siblings who'd abandoned her in Green Park, he'd tried to kiss her, then she'd nearly wept like a ninny when he'd mentioned she'd seemed alone, and she'd confessed about Henry. Oh, and it was freezing cold in the snow.

She said after a moment of thought, "If this is business, we must make the most of our time together, now that my great-aunt is invested in our book's success."

"Business then." A sly smile. "In regard to your children's book, I think you'll still require my help . . . and not just for the illustrations."

To Musa's surprise, she actually laughed at his teasing. As she laughed, she sensed the sound shimmering up toward the sky, which had deepened into a pure cobalt. By then, they were nearly to Musa's home.

"Like a sapphire shining," she said without thinking.

"What is?" He stole another one of those peculiar glances at her, like she was a curiosity from the London Zoo.

"That's what my father always called the sky when it turned this shade of blue. See, being a Bartham isn't all scandals and sorrow." She pointed down the block. "There's my house. Looks like my brother's waiting on the steps for me."

"Ah, I'll leave you then."

She returned his sister's scarf to him. "Thank you, Mr. Atkinson. Really. And not only for the use of your scarf. You're kinder than I gave you credit. A true gentleman. You performed a service for my family."

"Well, you nursed me from a fever." He draped the fluffy red scarf around his neck. It was still warm from her skin. "Please, call me Sebastian. Or Seb, as my friends do."

Musa stared down at her clasped hands. "I don't think we can consider ourselves friends, though I'm relieved you no longer dislike me. Comrades-in-arms for our sisters, perhaps. Book collaborators."

"Book collaborators then. At least until we finish."

"Until we finish . . ."

She half-expected him to bring up Felicity Vita, and her promise to introduce him to her. He didn't. He took a step closer. For a moment, she thought he might try to kiss her again. Her traitorous heart even leaped in anticipation.

He only reached out to tuck a strand of her hair behind her ear.

"There," he said. "I've been itching to do that all afternoon." And then: "I'll see you Tuesday at Chassen & Sons at 9:15."

"Until then," Musa rejoined, feeling oddly disappointed.

He bowed, a graceful snap of his waist, before turning to walk in the opposite direction. Toward Spitalfields, where he lived in squalor for the sake of his sisters and his art.

She watched him for longer than she cared to admit. Longer than she wished she wanted to.

How strange his life is!

Musa felt an unexpected pang in her chest, a stinging behind her eyes. If she were a sentimental sort, she'd weep at the romanticism of it all, the orphaned artist with the sweet little sister and family to support. She'd already shown too much emotion that afternoon.

Don't be ridiculous, Musa. Tears are the provenance of Felicity, not you. Anyway, Felicity doesn't exist. Not anymore.

She forced herself to look away, to head home. Mary was scheduled to stop by for a visit. Social, not business. Musa welcomed the distraction.

Musa waved toward her brother on the steps. However, as she approached her home, she made out it wasn't Theo waiting there after all. Thunderous piano music spilled out from their house, indicating he and Lyra were cooperating in tormenting a Liszt sonata into oblivion.

Musa squinted behind her spectacles, which were fogged from the cold. It was difficult to tell exactly who was seated there—the cobalt sky had deepened to Prussian blue. Whoever he might be, it was clear he was a gentleman from his stylish yellow bowler hat and thick beaver fur coat.

For a moment, Musa panicked he could be a bill collector. *We're up to date*, she reminded herself. Still, who was he? And on a Sunday night too?

She called out, "May I help you, sir?"

The gentleman stood. He greeted in a friendly tone, "I've been ringing the bell, but no one answered. Must be the piano." A toothy grin beneath his bowler. "Surely you recall meeting me, Miss Bartham. From Chassen & Sons?"

Musa let out a breath. "Oh, you're Mr. Atkinson's friend! Now I recognize you."

"Yes, Luke Ward with *The Greater London Gazette.* If you don't mind, I have a few questions to ask."

Musa wrinkled her brow. "Not about my father, I trust." Even now, years after Neil Bartham's disappearance, reporters still occasionally showed up eager for gossip.

"No, I'd never presume! Questions about your children's book, Miss Bartham."

Musa laughed, a shrill nervous sound. "Ah, Mr. Atkinson must have confided in you."

Mr. Ward nodded, his deep brown eyes glinting beneath the gas lamps. "Yes, he mentioned he was illustrating it. I'd like to write an article about your book, if you don't mind. I think our readers would be most fascinated. No doubt many of them are parents with children."

Musa's suspicions dropped away. Tick, tick, tick went her brain.

"An article is a marvelous idea, Mr. Ward! Your timing is advantageous. My editor has promised me a visit tonight—"

Musa's words were interrupted by a man shouting from the road. Someone running her way—she made out the slap of his footfall, a flash of red scarf in the twilight.

Sebastian Atkinson had returned.

CHAPTER 20

"How unexpected you're here! But fortunate too," Luke said to Seb after Musa led them into the Barthams' drawing room; she'd stepped away to stop her siblings from banging on the piano. "I'd anticipated only having Miss Bartham and her editor to interview."

"How fortunate indeed," Seb answered, glaring at his friend. He'd been nearly to the end of the block when he turned, wanting a last glimpse of Musa. No, *needing* a last glimpse, if he was to be honest. His heart skipped a beat—and it wasn't because of Musa. Even in the twilight he recognized Luke's mustard-yellow bowler hat, one of his friend's dandyish affectations.

Shit, he thought anew before running their way. There was no good reason for Luke to be there. Again, Seb regretted confiding his suspicions to him about Musa and Felicity Vita, for all of Luke's promises. And now . . . well, Seb was more convinced than ever he was right.

"I'm sure Miss Nicholson, our editor at Persephone Press, will arrive soon," Musa said, cheeks pink with excitement. "She'll be so excited to speak to you, Mr. Ward! However, I should tell you it's my dear sister Angela who inspired our book."

Luke said smoothly, "Ah, what a touching story! Sisterly devotion—our readers will be enthralled." He leaned forward, briefly touching Musa's hand; Seb was shocked by the unreasonable urge to punch his friend in his smug face. "I have no doubt your book will gain much popularity like *Little Women*."

"How kind of you to say so, Mr. Ward! I can only hope to gain a modicum of Miss Alcott's success."

The doorbell rang more politely than Seb expected, given the rather downtrodden state of the Barthams' house. Upon his arrival, a glance had given him the sense the household was run on string and spit, with Musa doing everything possible to keep things together. Just as he'd suspected.

Musa excused herself, leaving Seb alone with Luke in the drawing room.

"I know why you're here," Seb whispered in a rush. "She's not Felicity Vita—I was mistaken." He wouldn't let Luke expose her, not for all the money in the world.

Luke raised a brow. "Really? Take a look at what I found in their trash bin earlier today."

Luke pulled out from his pocket a handful of poem drafts. Seb grew cold, recognizing Felicity's familiar swirls and dashes, the blue ink on the paper stock.

Oh Musa. How could you be so careless? Yet his heart leaped at the proof—he'd been right all along. But there was no time to rejoice.

"You have no proof she wrote it!"

"It's damn compelling, if you ask me," Luke rejoined. "I spoke to my editor—"

"You promised me you wouldn't!"

Luke whispered furiously, "Believe it or not, I'm trying to help you—you've got bills, the ramshackle house, your sisters and so on. You stand to make a lot of tin, if she's truly you-know-who."

"As would you, so spare me your altruism. Anyway, that's not Felicity's handwriting—I'd recognize it anywhere."

"You've always been a poor liar. Look."

Luke drew out a letter from his pocket—the same letter Seb had shown him at his studio several days earlier. Not only that, it appeared he'd taken at least a dozen others. Seb must have been too ill to notice.

Seb reached for the letters, but Luke tucked them back in his pocket, too swift to be stopped. "You stole those!"

"Stole what, gentlemen?" Musa returned with Miss Nicholson in tow, whose eyes sparkled with excitement. "What did I miss?"

Luke said in a world-weary voice, "Oh, Mr. Atkinson is concerned I might steal inspiration that should be set toward your book, Miss Bartham. I assured him you seem the sort who has ideas to spare."

"Oh, I would agree! Miss Bartham is ever so gifted," Miss Nicholson said, offering Seb a firm handshake; her hand was still cold from the outside. "Forgive me, I didn't recognize you at first, Mr. Atkinson. You appear so different from when we last met." To Luke: "This is such exciting news for my press! We'd be delighted to be interviewed." A nervous laugh. "We have a new publisher. It's quite the transition for my father. A Miss Amanda Seeley of Boston. She recently arrived in London."

Musa's mouth tightened. "Already?"

Mary nodded. "Two days ago. She'll be extremely pleased. An interview is such good news!"

Luke ventured slyly, "Well, it's hardly an interview with Felicity Vita. Now *that* would be a coup."

Musa and Miss Nicholson exchanged an anxious look and blanched. Seb again resisted the urge to punch Luke, though he had only himself to blame. He should have kept his suspicions to himself.

How can I fix this?

Alas, no answer came, none that wouldn't make Seb a duplicitous, irresponsible fool. Not only would his confession leave Musa distressed he'd deceived her about Henry, she'd be furious he divulged his supposition with a member of the press. The only possibility was to limit the damage.

Seb hastily disagreed. "I don't think an article is a good idea. It's best to let our book speak for itself when it's published. A review, but by someone with knowledge of children's literature."

Musa shook her head firmly. "I beg to differ. The more people who know of our book and its wholesome message, the better." She quickly explained about her great-aunt's plan to launch the book with a costume ball in April. "So you see there's also a society aspect to write about as well as a literary, Mr. Ward."

The costume ball. Why did Musa have to mention it? The event would only heighten the potential for something to go very wrong.

"Is this prudent?" Seb interjected, unable to keep panic from infusing his tone. "It's a private ball, is it not?"

"Private or not, all this is most newsworthy! I quite agree as editor," Miss Nicholson said, her voice pitched high with excitement. "Sorry, Mr. Atkinson, you're overruled."

Luke grinned like a fool. "I assume I'll be invited to this costume ball to write about it, Miss Bartham? It could be part of a series of articles about your children's book."

"I'm sure my great-aunt will be amenable to your request," Musa said, more agreeable than Seb had ever witnessed.

Miss Nicholson said, "No time like the present to begin. Mr. Ward, what do you require of us for your articles?"

Luke screwed up his face as though thinking; Seb knew what was *really* going through his mind. Newspaper headlines. Felicity Vita. Worse.

"Well, interviews, of course. I could also follow your progress as you publish the book." A rakish grin. "I'd love to see any manuscript drafts you have, Miss Bartham."

Don't show him, Musa! Seb wanted to shout. He settled for a far milder, "I don't believe that's necessary."

"I don't mind," Musa said. "I've nothing to hide, though I should warn Mr. Ward we're still editing the manuscript. Mr. Atkinson has been so helpful on that front." A warm glance toward Seb that made his heart pang. "The book has taken on a much different tone than it originally had. Kinder. Gentler. More appropriate for children's tender minds."

"Wonderful news," Luke said. To Seb: "I'd also like to see your sketches, of course. I know those will appeal to our readers."

"Oh, what a marvelous idea to include art in your article!" Miss Nicholson exclaimed, Musa agreeing. "You see, Mr. Atkinson? This will be marvelous publicity! Look, you even have your portfolio here—how fortunate for us. Shall we begin?"

An hour later, the interviews were finished to Seb's relief. He immediately rushed to leave before he'd say something he'd regret. Or worse, *do* something he'd regret, especially when he considered Luke in possession of those letters and poem drafts. However, there was one action he could take to protect Musa. He could write to warn her—it was the least he could do.

As soon as he returned home, Seb pulled out his paper and pen. *"Dearest darling Felicity,"* he began.

How strange to write Felicity knowing Musa would read his words. Definitely not something he ever expected. He stared at the words for far longer than it had taken him to write them.

Dearest darling.

Well, that's how he'd thought of Felicity. But now there was no need to be so effusive. Not anymore, though he again imagined how Musa might have felt crushed against him in the snow had they kissed. The soft warmth of her lips opening beneath his . . .

An unexpected thought arrived.

I nearly kissed Felicity Vita.

Against his will, he felt himself stir against the fall of his trousers. Damn it, knowing Musa Bartham was Felicity Vita should reduce his arousal, not increase it. It was because of those blasted erotic dreams of Felicity. All their fault.

Seb balled the letter and threw it into the fire. He splashed cold water on his face. He punched the sandbag until his knuckles felt chaffed. He jumped up and down, hoping the tailor who lived below him wouldn't pound on the ceiling.

He sat down and began anew.

"My dear Felicity," he wrote. There, that was better. Warm but not overly familiar.

He continued: *"What I am about to write may distress you, but I pray you pay mind . . ."*

Seb wrote the rest of the letter quickly, before he lost his nerve. Or worse, before he became aroused again. He kept the letter short to avoid revealing anything he shouldn't, but not so terse Musa would think something was wrong.

While he wrote, he realized there was an air of finality to his missive. A sense of leave-taking, now that he knew Felicity's true identity though he hadn't intended such.

The gentlemanly thing to do would be to end their correspondence, make some excuse. It would be for the best. Really. Truly . . . especially since she cared for Henry. How would she react if she learned he'd deceived her as to his identity? She'd hate him, feel humiliated.

And yet he couldn't stop.

The thing was he *loved* Felicity's letters. Cherished them. They'd offered him comfort when he most needed it.

Once he and Musa finished the children's book, he'd find a way to drift gracefully out of her life. After the costume ball. He'd make up some excuse for Henry. Perhaps Henry could head off to India or take a position in South America, something to render their correspondence impractical. Anyway, Seb should be focusing on the children's book and other opportunities to make money for Jessica's sake. Nothing that would betray Musa.

He stood abruptly and reached for his sandbag anew. Two punches. Another. A third. Whatever it took to tire himself out.

"What a mess," he muttered.

CHAPTER 21

BARTHAM DAUGHTER PENS
CHILDREN'S BOOK

The Greater London Gazette, 7 February 1872: Miss Musa Bartham has announced the impending publication of Poems of Morality and Goodness for Children to Abide *this coming April. The children's book will be illustrated by Mr. Sebastian Atkinson and published by Persephone Press, which is under new American management.*

Inquiring minds might be questioning the newsworthiness of this announcement. The author of Poems of Morality and Goodness for Children to Abide *is the eldest daughter of painter Neil Bartham whose elopement with Mrs. Ethan Sutton in 1845 drew much outrage—yes, London's very own 'Muse of Scandal.' In 1866, Mr. Bartham disappeared whilst traveling to Jerusalem, which most assume has led to an untimely demise.*

With the publication of Poems of Morality and Goodness for Children to Abide, *we presume the new generation of Barthams seeks to turn over a fresh—and less scandalous—leaf.*

Lucas Ward was as good as his word. Within three days of his unexpected appearance at the Barthams' home, a short article about Musa and Atkinson's book was published in the society section of *The Greater London Gazette* for all of society to read. The article was hidden beneath the fold, but it was there regardless.

Musa learned about the article when she arrived at Chassen & Sons Tuesday morning. Though she was a few minutes early in her usual way, she discovered Atkinson waiting for her in the lobby. The mention of her parents' history in the article didn't upset her as it might once have—she was too distracted by Atkinson's presence.

Her head grew light as she recalled their near-kiss in Green Park. And then she'd gone and ruined things by telling him about Henry . . . Henry, who'd sent a most alarming letter a day earlier:

> Dearest Felicity,
> What I am about to write may distress you, but I pray you pay mind. Today, I overheard a gentleman speak of you in a manner I found deeply concerning. He intends to uncover the truth behind your nom de plume in order to profit from it. I know you have laughed in the past at such attempts to unmask you. However, there was a measure of determination in this gentleman's tone that left me anxious on your behalf.
> Felicity, I beg you take great care. I couldn't bear for anything to happen to your precious self.
> Yours always,
> Henry

Musa told herself it didn't matter, now that Felicity would no longer be publishing. Still, she'd been disturbed. And now here she was with Atkinson, whom she'd promised to introduce to Felicity Vita upon the publication of their book. He hadn't mentioned their agreement in some days, but she was certain he was biding his time.

What a mess.

"Look!" Atkinson shyly offered the newspaper like it was a bouquet of roses. "I hope you'll be pleased, Miss Bartham."

Miss Bartham. As though he hadn't tried to kiss me. She felt deflated. Disappointed.

What did you expect? You're book collaborators, not friends. As for her siblings and their matchmaking, Musa made sure to disavow them of *that.*

Still, she sensed a new awkwardness between her and Atkinson while she read the article. Perhaps he was thinking of that near-kiss too. Best to continue pretending nothing occurred. Yes, that's what she would do.

"I thought you weren't in favor of Mr. Ward writing about our book," she said once she'd finished reading, folding away the newspaper with as much fanfare as she could muster.

"I wasn't, Miss Bartham. But once I reconsidered, I realized it would be useful after all." Another bashful smile. "The newspaper's already received several inquiries from readers about our book."

"Really?" She was astonished by a surge of optimism.

"Really." He pointed down the hall. "After you, Miss Bartham. We've much to do if we're to get this book to press quickly. We'll use Mr. Chassen's office again."

Mr. Chassen was occupying his office, just as Seb planned. His employer was seated in his favorite oversized chair, feet up on his desk while he perused what appeared to be some sort of ledger. Seb had made the unusual request of requesting his employer's presence the day earlier, offering some cockamamie story about the press room being too noisy and Miss Bartham suddenly requiring a chaperone for propriety's sake.

The truth was Seb feared being alone with Musa. Feared what he might reveal now that he'd proof she was Felicity Vita. Or worse, what he might do. When she'd arrived that morning, he was alarmed at how his stomach flocked with what felt like large butter-flies. No, hummingbirds, he decided.

Musa was dressed in the same prim navy serge suit she'd worn the first time they'd met at Chassen & Sons, which now seemed the most alluring outfit he could imagine. All those buttons along the bodice, along her wrists—he imagined her nimble fingers fastening them while she dressed. The form-fitting tailoring caressing her trim form, all the way down to the gray kid gloves. The fabric against her flesh. Seb felt as overcome as though she were Felicity Vita herself. Which she was.

This isn't going to be easy.

"Ah, Mr. Chassen," Seb called out, his voice high with nerves. "I promise we won't take long. This is Miss Bartham, the author of—"

"Yes, yes, I know," Chassen interrupted without shifting from his semi-prone position. "Not a problem at all, Atkinson. I'm intrigued by your children's book." To Musa: "Forgive me for not standing to greet you. I recall you some weeks ago, Miss Bartham. You were quite distressed. Pleased to see all worked out with you and Atkinson."

Musa answered, "As am I."

Seb and Musa's eyes met before she dropped her gaze toward her hem.

Chassen continued, "Just ignore me as you will—" a short laugh "—and I'll ignore you." He turned back to his ledger after letting out a soft grunt of dismissal.

"Shall we?" Musa said in a low voice.

Seb led her over to the long table where they'd sparred during their first meeting, setting her most recent draft on it. Then he took out his drawing kit and a new sketchpad.

He asked, "In the interest of saving time, what do you suggest?"

"Well, as book collaborators, it would be most logical to work through the manuscript sequentially." Her mouth skewed in an aspect of puzzlement. "I must admit I'm surprised you haven't marked any edits. I thought you wouldn't be able to resist."

A nervous laugh. "Why don't you mark them, Miss Bartham? My handwriting is illegible."

He offered her a pencil from his drawing kit, one he'd just sharpened. He felt a warm shiver as her fingers brushed his.

She took a seat, all business. "Very well. We'll start at the beginning. You tell me what you plan to draw, and I'll edit accordingly."

He opened his sketchpad. "Here, I'll draw as we go."

"A good plan."

She turned to the first page of her manuscript. He opened to a blank page of his sketchpad.

She said, "As you can see, I've decided not to include 'The Parable of the Poisoned Biscuits.'"

"Ah, but that one was my favorite," Seb teased. "What did you substitute?"

"'The Tale of the Talented Cat.'"

"I did like that story, but thought it needed more refining. Does the mouse really need to be punished for its transgression?"

"Look, already fixed!" She held up the manuscript page, which she'd covered in edits. "Now the mouse doesn't get eaten by the calico after all."

"Much better," Seb agreed, "even if the mouse shouldn't have gone into the garden to visit the cats in the first place."

"Well, I decided the mouse deserved a chance, even if he'd made a mistake."

Seb gave himself a mental shake. *If only life was so simple.*

"Here, let me try something . . ."

His pencil danced across the page. Three cats beneath moonlight, a calico, a tabby, and a tuxedo. A small mouse watching from a distance, safely hidden in the knot of a tree. A whole story told in pictures, expanding on her verse. It was easy. Charming. Sweet. Jessica would adore this.

"I like that!" Musa said. "But maybe make the calico wear a bell around her neck, so there's narrative tension."

Seb glanced up at her. "How so?"

"Well, the calico hates the bell, which adds another layer to the story. She needs to prove herself stealthy. Hence her desire to catch the mouse, but the mouse is far too clever to be caught."

A few pencil strokes created the bell, a small triangle tied to a ribbon.

"Next one?"

Musa pointed to a page that looked freshly drafted. "I thought we'd work on the story about the farm tools. Change it a bit."

Seb couldn't resist the grin falling across his lips. "You mean no reaper?"

"No reaper," she agreed, her hand cupping her chin. Seb's breath caught. How winsome she appeared! Delectable. Several tendrils of her chestnut hair escaped from her pins. He resisted the urge to twine his fingers into its length. He'd yearned to do so in Green Park—and much more than he dared admit.

Don't think of this, Seb.

"Have you another idea?" he asked.

"Yes! Instead, I'd thought a watering can. The children could use it to mimic spring rain, splashing in puddles and such. For art, the seasons perhaps, one scene to a page? We'd start with spring showers, then summer, and so on. What do you think?"

"I like it," Seb said, surprised. He knew Musa was intelligent, but not in this manner. She was a quick study. Flexible. Inventive. "Here, let me try something."

At her command, he drew a flock of rosy-cheeked children chasing each other around a garden. Each child held a watering can and grinned with mischief beneath a sunny sky. In the final panel, the watering can was frozen with ice as a little girl resembling Jessica played nearby with a shaggy dog in the snow.

Time passed without notice. Drawings became pages. Sentences became poems. He heard Chassen come and go, then return; he'd barely taken notice. How easy it was to work with Musa, how delightful! She was cooperating as a good collaborator should, eager to offer input, but open to new directions. Encouraging of his talent, yet precise in her instructions.

"These are good," Musa said, offering Seb a warm look of appreciation as she pointed at the sketches across the table. "Very good."

"No, you're good," Seb answered. Flustered, he added, "You're good at revising, that is. The manuscript—it's good!"

He looked down. Somehow they'd grasped each other's hands. And then what he most feared happened. He found himself yearning to kiss her again. Desperately.

He imagined the warmth of his breath against her cheek. The scent of her hair. How it would feel to twine his fingers into that hair . . . and more. Yes, to commune with her.

Silence fell between the two of them. It felt weighted with unanswered questions, Seb would later think.

"Musa," he began, his voice a low rumble of invitation.

Before he could continue, the gruff sound of snoring rattled. Chassen. He'd fallen asleep—Seb hadn't noticed. To be honest, he'd been so involved—no, *engrossed*—with Musa he'd forgotten they weren't alone.

"We should leave," Musa murmured, their hands still entwined. "I'd hate to disturb him."

"No, no, he won't remember a thing when he wakes." Seb didn't know if this was true, but he couldn't bear for them to depart this enchanted space of art and companionship.

Her lace cuff brushed against his wrist. Her fingers caressed his palm. Or was he caressing hers?

"You tried to kiss me in Green Park," she whispered, flushing. "And now you're holding my hand."

How to respond?

"I did try to kiss you," he admitted at last. "And yes, we're holding hands."

Seb sensed her mind clicking away, computing. Confusion. But she didn't release his hand.

"Oh." She bit the soft of her lip. "Do you want to kiss me now?"

Seb swallowed hard.

"Very much so." A beat of the clock. "May I?"

Before she could answer, Chassen began to mumble and cough as he roused back to consciousness. "Ah, where am I? Oh, sorry Atkinson—you're still here? Forgive me for dozing off on you!"

Musa let go of Seb's hands as though she'd been caught shoplifting. She sprang to her feet, brushing her gown of invisible wrinkles.

"I was just leaving, Mr. Chassen! Thank you for the use of your office. Very kind of you!"

"Yes, yes! We've done enough for today," Seb agreed, collecting his sketches into a pile. "Here, take your manuscript, Miss Bartham. I'm sure you want to make a fair copy of it."

And then she rushed off with a flustered farewell, leaving Seb in a puddle of lust and frustration.

Oh Musa-Felicity, what am I to do about you?

CHAPTER 22

THE TALL GRANDFATHER clock in the hall was chiming five as Musa arrived home. How had a full day passed at Chassen & Sons? It felt like only an hour or two. All had gone so well with Atkinson. Better than well, really. Beautifully. She couldn't believe how lovely his drawings were, and how easily they'd worked together. *Poems of Morality and Goodness for Children to Abide* would truly be something special. She was certain Atkinson arranged for the presence of Mr. Chassen to avoid any awkwardness after their near-kiss in Green Park. She was grateful for his consideration . . . until she wasn't.

"Do you want to kiss me?" she'd asked Atkinson. What had she been thinking? It was lucky Chassen awakened when he did. Who knew what might have happened otherwise?

I should be happy we didn't kiss, Musa thought as she took off her bonnet. *Why aren't I?*

Henry. She hadn't thought of him once all those hours while she'd been with Atkinson. Instead, she'd found herself staring at Atkinson's hands as he'd sketched. His long fingers curled along his pencil, so sensitive and skilled. To her horror, she'd felt a warm curl of arousal rise from her stomach even before he'd asked to kiss her. She'd imagined him caressing her body. Sensitive. Skilled . . .

"Musa? Is that you?"

Her mother's voice drifted from the dining room, accompanied by the rise of laughter and chatter. Beyond it, Musa made out the clatter of meal preparation from the kitchen. The scent of lamb, potatoes roasting. Her stomach growled in response.

Nearly time for dinner. She and Atkinson hadn't paused for even a cup of tea.

"Here, Mama!" Musa called, hanging up her coat.

Inside the dining room, Musa found her entire family assembled around the table. Great-aunt Minerva had brought Angela to visit—Angela, who looked lovelier than ever. Hope suited her, Musa decided. Next to Angela, the twins were playing a tapping game with spoons as though they were still children, not adolescents of fifteen. Clio sat majestically at the head of the table, dressed elegantly in a simple blue gown adorned with a strand of amber beads.

Save for the presence of Aunt Minerva, everything appeared as it might have been before Papa's disappearance.

Clio rose from her seat to embrace Musa. "I'm so glad you're home! We're celebrating the article about your children's book. We'll even have cake! Though I do wish the article could have been kinder about Papa—"

"It's the best news you could have hoped for, Clio," Aunt Minerva cut in. "What can you expect, given the situation? Best to acknowledge the scandal, get it out of the way." To Musa: "I assume you read it, miss?"

"I did, Aunt," Musa replied, forcing a smile into her voice she didn't feel. "Good news indeed! I'll be right back."

She needed to be alone for a moment, to catch her breath. To quiet her thoughts. Her emotions; if she wasn't careful, she'd end up a slave to them, like her parents.

What about Henry? Again, she thought of the letter he'd sent warning of gossip about Felicity. He cared about her. Deeply. But he was nothing but a voice in her head, words on a page. He wasn't flesh and blood in any real way . . . at least not yet. Atkinson was.

All the more reason for Musa to watch herself around him. She didn't need that sort of distraction, especially now.

The steps toward her room felt particularly steep. Once inside, Musa closed her door. She drew out Henry's letters. There were dozens. No, over a hundred letters. Letters filled with passion, humor, and kindness. Letters that flirted with her and professed devotion. Letters that gave Musa a sense of connection to another human, a man she claimed was courting her. A man she cared for, though they'd never met beyond the page.

A man she'd probably hurt when she'd refused to meet him.

It really wasn't right. Either she should meet with Henry and entrust him with the truth about Felicity Vita, or she should let him go so he could love someone else. Someone real.

I can't bear to think of losing Henry.

Musa wiped at her eyes. It was all Atkinson's fault. The artist was a distraction, nothing more. Again, she wondered how his mouth might have felt if they'd kissed, whether his tongue would have laced with hers—

Stop thinking of this!

She shoved Henry's letters away, splashed cold water on her face. Perhaps writing him a letter would help her feel less terrible. She'd have to be quick—it was nearly dinner time.

Dearest Henry, she began. *What a long day I've had! My new book is off to a brilliant start. I've been told there's press interest in it, which will help gain readers. I only wish I could tell you more details—*

A knock on her door. Her mother. "Musa?"

"Just a moment! I'll come to dinner." She set down her pen.

"It's not dinner, sweetheart. May I come in?"

"Of course!" Musa answered, hiding her letter beneath her blotter. Why had her mother come up?

Clio slid into the room. She clutched something in the folds of her gown.

"Is all well?" Musa asked, unsettled.

Her mother perched on the edge of the bed. "I wanted to ask

you about your other writings, the ones you've been supporting us with. There's nothing to cause problems for Angela? You'd warn me if there was, wouldn't you?"

Musa flesh prickled. "No, Mama. Not really."

"I'm glad." Clio cleared her throat. "You do seem to write a lot of letters."

"Well, it's necessary."

Musa's tone was sharper than intended. Hopefully it would end any discourse.

Clio let out a long sigh. "You're not making this easy."

Musa's stomach tightened. "Easy? I'm uncertain what you mean."

"Very well."

Clio pulled out a copy of *The Poetics of Passion*. She set the book on Musa's desk with a thud. Its eye-catching purple binding seemed to radiate accusations.

Merde. Musa's heart pounded like a drum. *What to do?*

A ready answer arrived: *Lie as though to save your life.*

"Whatever it is, it's not what you think, Mama. Really it isn't! I don't know anything about this book. Or the author, whoever she—or he—is. Truly."

"I'm sure. But explain this." Clio opened *The Poetics of Passion* to its title page. "Aunt Minerva informed me Persephone Press also publishes Felicity Vita. Is this true?"

Musa offered an uneasy laugh. "Oh, is that all?"

Clio shook her head. "It's more than all! This is a *very* big deal, Musa—that's why Aunt Minerva brought it up."

"And why would Aunt Minerva own a book by Felicity Vita?" Musa deflected, anxiety rushing through her veins.

"Because she's protecting us! Once you'd mentioned Persephone Press was publishing your children's book, she felt it her duty to learn more." Clio's tone turned steely. "Musa, Angela can't have a hint of impropriety. Not now. This is her future. Her life."

"I'd never injure Angela!"

"Not intentionally, I'm sure. But this book . . . why, I had no idea it came from the same publisher as yours!"

Musa quickly reassured, "You needn't worry. Persephone Press has a new owner. Mary—I mean Miss Nicholson—her father sold it."

"And who is Miss Nicholson exactly? I knew you were friends with her, but not that she was involved with this Felicity Vita author. I'd heard murmurings about her scandalous poetry, but I never expected to find her connected to my children."

"It no longer matters," Musa choked out. "Felicity Vita is no more."

Clio's voice dropped. "Did she die?"

"No, no! Not that. She's no longer writing poetry. Not anymore." Musa felt a catch at the back of her throat. A pang. "You see, Persephone Press will no longer publish Felicity Vita's books. The new owner wants to publish less scandalous subjects. That's why Miss Nicholson approached me to write a children's book for them."

Clio's brow creased. "It's all very strange. Suspicious."

"Mama, I assure you Persephone Press only publishes morally upright books now. Nothing that would cause a scandal for anyone. Especially Angela."

"Good." Clio let out a long breath. "I'm relieved. You can't imagine the shock I felt when Aunt Minerva showed me that book!"

Musa girded herself for more questions. More prodding. Thankfully, Clio rose to her feet with an apologetic smile. However, she left the volume of *The Poetics of Passion* on Musa's desk like it was too foul to be handled.

Clio embraced Musa. "I know these past few years haven't been easy for you, sweetheart. I've been so absent. I'm doing my best to make amends, to be more responsible." She caressed Musa's cheek and offered an anxious smile. "Forgive me if I overstep some-times. We'll need to find a new way without . . . without . . ."

"Papa. Yes, I know."

Clio bit her lip. "Well, I won't keep you any longer. Dinner should be ready any minute."

"I'm not hungry after all."

Once Clio was gone, Musa returned to her letter, feeling far more turbulent than when she'd started it.

Felicity really was no more.

Though Musa understood this intellectually, the events of the day brought them home to her: the arrival of the American heiress, the interviews with Mr. Ward, even her mother's warning about Angela's prospects. Deep in the back of her mind, Musa had half-expected Mary to announce she'd been mistaken, that all would be as it was. And what of Henry? Was she really going to continue writing him, now that Felicity was no more? The risk was too high.

Now she really did feel alone.

She tossed out the start to her letter to Henry and began anew.

> *Dear Henry,*
>
> *I fear the time has come for us to bring our correspondence to an end. Circumstances in my life have shifted such that it behooves me to lead a more discreet existence.*
>
> *Please know how grateful I am for your many kindnesses. Your letters have brought me more joy and comfort than you can ever imagine.*
>
> *Yours in true friendship—*
> *Felicity Vita*

To Musa's dismay, a single tear dropped onto the letter. She ignored it.

"You'll mail this first thing in the morning," she told herself, folding the letter into an envelope. "You have no choice. Not if you care about your sister."

She sat there on her bed, staring at the addressed envelope, thinking of Henry. Thinking of his love letters, how cherished they'd made her feel.

Only one last thing to do.

She took out every single letter of Henry's from their locked drawer. Read them one last time. Then she forced herself to burn them all, ignoring the tremble of her bottom lip, the wobble in her heart.

Goodbye Henry, she thought. *Forgive me, dearest.*

Had she really loved him? Or did she simply love his letters? Well, now she'd never know.

CHAPTER 23

THAT NIGHT, Musa tossed and turned beneath her blankets for hours. How would Henry react to her letter? Would he feel abandoned? Sorrowful? Would he mourn her? Though she didn't want to cause him pain, she selfishly hoped he'd be as affected as she was . . . and yet who would he really be mourning? Certainly not Musa Bartham. Henry wouldn't even know her if he tripped over her on Oxford Street. Then again, neither would she know him.

Atkinson was right. I really am alone.

For the first time since she'd invented her *nom de plume* to save her family, Musa wished she could shed Felicity's identity as though removing a coat. To be herself in full, not divided into two women. To be loved for who she was by Henry, not because he believed her to be an infamous poetess.

When does a secret identity become a trap?

Musa's question remained unanswered as she struggled to sleep. And yet, try as she might, her thoughts returned to the yearning in Atkinson's face before she'd left Chassen & Sons so abruptly that afternoon. The desire she sensed coming from him, especially after their near-kiss in the snow.

A desire he'd admitted.

A desire she'd felt as well.

You're only trying to distract yourself from Henry. That's all.

If it had been any other night, Musa would have taken care of herself until she forgot her worries in sensual release. But it wasn't any other night. It was a night after she'd promised her mother to never put Angela at risk because of Felicity Vita or Persephone Press. It was a night when she burned every love letter she'd ever received in her life in order to reduce that risk. A night after a day when she'd spent time with a man who'd admitted he wanted to kiss her.

Someone real. Someone who wasn't a name dashed at the bottom of a piece of paper.

Felicity Vita would know what to do about this. She'd write Henry hundreds of letters, unconcerned with who found them. She'd lounge around dressed in a revealing tea gown without stays, wearing nothing but a chemise beneath yards of translucent pink lace. If Sebastian Atkinson had said he wanted to kiss Felicity, she would have led Atkinson from Chassen & Sons to her luxurious mansion nearby. Once inside her boudoir, they'd tear each other's clothes from their bodies, not caring when buttons spilled onto the floor and . . .

Stop it, Musa! You're not Felicity—and that's the problem. You need to accept she's gone.

All of a sudden it came to Musa. There was one way to free herself of Felicity, to bid farewell to her . . . as well as to rid herself of her ridiculous yearning for Sebastian Atkinson.

She'd become Felicity.

Musa sat up straight in her bed, shocked.

I can't be Felicity Vita, she told herself. *Not in actuality.* However, a wicked answer came her way:

If you can't embody Felicity, who can?

"This is how I shall let her go," Musa whispered into her empty room. "I'll be her tonight."

The idea was madness. Unwise. But once she'd said those words aloud, she couldn't turn back.

Musa dressed quickly before she changed her mind. Quietly

enough that no one might hear her despite the late hour. She chose a pale pink lace tea gown several years out of fashion, but suitably opulent for Felicity's needs. It was constructed in such a way that it didn't require stays. She pulled it over her chemise, aware of the tender press of her nipples against the fabric, the caress of the lace against her stomach.

Downstairs she crept, boots in hand, after leaving a note on her bed explaining she'd gone out in case anyone sought her. She wrapped her cloak around herself. How strange she felt! How possessed! She told herself she was acting in a perfectly rational fashion. If one has a problem, the best thing was to deal with it instead of pretending it didn't exist.

Outside, the pavement was covered in a thin crust of frost, gleaming beneath the starry sky, which had cleared of clouds. The air was crisp, glorious, brilliant. Musa inhaled, feeling like she was breathing champagne. Everything was bright and bubbling and sharp. When had she last gone outside without wearing stays? Twelve years? More? Without stays, it was easy to run. Easy to be free. Easy to be wild.

Easy to be Felicity.

She found herself running toward where Brompton Road met Fulham, where there was a cab stand. First, she stopped at a post-box. She forced herself to drop the letter to Henry inside it.

No turning back.

A block away, a hackney carriage lingered, the horses at rest, a pair of gray dappled nuzzling each other over their feed bag. The driver, an older man with a generous paunch, widened his eyes at Musa's appearance. His gaze swept over her chestnut hair, which was tangled and loose. Undressed, just as Felicity Vita would wear when rushing to a lover.

"I'm in a hurry," Musa announced, staring back at the cab driver with as much hauteur as she could summon. "Spitalfields, Folgate Street. Now!"

～

Seb was sleeping when a knock sounded on his door. No, a pounding. He staggered toward the door after wrapping his dressing gown about him and pulling on his trousers. "Just a minute," he shouted. One thing Seb had learned in his twenty-eight years was that nothing good ever happened late at night. It couldn't be Luke, not now. Had something happened to Jessica? His heart thudded. His sister was to consult with the Harley Street doctor in a few days.

Seb lit a candle and opened the door.

"You," he breathed.

Musa Bartham stood on his landing—but it was a Musa Bartham he'd never encountered before. He rubbed his eyes, disbelieving what he saw.

Her hair was loose about her shoulders. Her dress beneath her cloak draped strangely. No petticoats; the lacy hem appeared bedraggled like it had been dragged in the street. Most unusually, he sensed an air of desperation in her expression, as though she were caught between tears and laughter. Perhaps even anger. Had she somehow found out about Luke's snooping? Or worse, that he was Henry?

"Yes, me," she answered.

Before Seb could react, Musa pushed into his rooms. Too shocked to stop her, Seb glanced around quickly. Had he left anything out to betray his knowledge of her secret identity?

Her letters.

He found them out on his worktable beside his pile of books by Felicity Vita—he'd been looking through the letters to ascertain which Luke had stolen.

Seb rushed over to his worktable to lock them inside his desk drawer. And just in time: she approached the worktable and chose the top-most volume—*The Poetics of Passion* of course—and paged through it. Was she going to confess her identity? Or read him a poem?

"Miss Bartham, this is most unexpected."

She set the book down and approached. She pressed her fingers against his lips.

"Shush," she said.

Seb's eyes widened. Arousal rushed from his mouth. Down his neck. Across his body and . . .

Sweet heaven help me.

Her fingers were ungloved. Cold from the outside. Cold against his soft lips. She must have rushed over without preparation for the weather. Beneath his trousers, he felt himself grow stiff. How could it not? There she was, her hand against his mouth yet again, dressed like an erotic dream. He was afraid to move lest he wake and she disappear.

He desired her.

He wanted her.

God help him, he adored her—or at least the version of herself she'd presented as Felicity Vita in all those letters they'd exchanged.

He fought the urge to warm her hands in his, slowly kiss each finger. Taking them into his mouth, just as he fantasized when he'd first realized the truth about her secret identity. Yet at the same time, he knew he should command her to go home. This was insane. Irresponsible. Scandalous. He didn't. He felt as though he never wanted her hand to leave his lips. To dwell in this place of possibility and potential, where Musa Bartham and Felicity Vita blurred together as one.

"I want you to listen, Mr. Atkinson. Will you?"

He nodded, swallowing hard.

At last, she removed her hand from his mouth. She slowly removed her spectacles. Set them on his table. She spoke, her voice as lush as velvet.

"You said you wanted to kiss me earlier."

He nodded again. His head felt light with lust.

"I know this makes no sense, but I want you to pretend I'm Felicity."

He grew even more aroused, if such a thing was possible. He

was grateful he had the presence of mind to throw on those trousers.

"Why would I do that?" His voice was oddly pitched, he decided. All the blood running south.

She set her mouth close to his ear. "It's this, Mr. Atkinson. You like Felicity's poetry, yes?"

He nodded. Now he was sweating despite the cool night air.

"Well, she inspires me too. And I require inspiration."

"Inspiration for what, Miss Bartham?"

"Inspiration for editing our children's book."

A nervous gulp. "You seem very inspired to me."

She closed the distance between them. Set her hands on his chest where his heart was speeding.

"I could always use more." Her voice dropped. "So I'll be Felicity tonight. That'll help me write better."

His mouth felt dry. He knew he should tell her to leave. But he couldn't bear to say as much. Nor could he address her as Felicity out of fear he'd end up revealing all he knew.

He stepped away, yearning for distance between them. He didn't trust himself not to grab her, throw her onto the bed and take her as though she were a common doxy.

"I thought you didn't like poetry. Anyway, a children's book isn't the same as a love poem."

"I lied, Mr. Atkinson. I do like poetry."

And then she recited his favorite poem by Felicity—or the start of it, before he silenced her with a soft kiss.

A testing kiss, like the one he nearly set on her in Green Park.

A kiss that would be easy for her to deflect, should she change her mind.

She didn't. She leaned into him. Against him. Still, Seb's conscience tugged. He'd known Musa Bartham for less than a month, but Felicity Vita he'd known for far longer. What she appeared to be proposing wasn't something a rational woman, even a Bartham, should offer.

Was she drunk? Drugged? Or . . . ?

He inhaled the air about her. He smelled nothing but the warm scent of her skin, her perfumed hair. Sandalwood again.

He set his hands on her shoulders. "This isn't wise. Are you certain you want to be here? And what of your—"

Letter writing friend, he was about to say. But he had no chance to speak. No, he couldn't speak.

She shrugged her cloak off.

Beneath it, she wore nothing but her chemise beneath her gown, which was a lacy pink tea confection of a mode a few years earlier. Regardless, it suited her, both the color and the style. No stays. Nothing to disguise her nipples from pressing against the thin fabric. He resisted the urge to cup her breasts in his hands.

She breathed into his ear, "I think you know what to do, Mr. Atkinson."

Seb could no longer contain himself. He wrapped his arms around her. She gave a little exhale, a soft moan. And then he realized there they were, standing there with his door still open.

He shut the door.

He reached for her hand.

CHAPTER 24

"You're trembling," Sebastian Atkinson said. Well, perhaps Musa should address him as Seb from here on. She glanced toward the closed door—the door setting them off from the rest of the world, from her home, where no one even knew she'd left her bed in the middle of the night. A surge of panic rose.

What have I done?

Her mind replied, *It's not what you've done. It's Felicity.*

Well, if she was going to be Felicity, so be it.

"I hadn't noticed I was trembling," she answered, defiant. Brazen.

Once you get this out of your system, you'll be freed. Do it.

Seb tenderly brushed the line of her jaw with his fingers. "If you haven't noticed, perhaps I shouldn't either."

With this, he tipped her mouth toward his.

As his arms tightened against her, Musa let her body melt against him as though he was the sun and she was ice. She felt soft, malleable in ways she'd never expected. Her breasts pressed against his chest, her skirts against his limbs like she belonged there.

In short, kissing him felt like arriving home on a cold winter day.

"Oh," she said when he came up for air.

Oh indeed.

As wonderful as their kiss had been, she'd felt uncertain at first. Awkward, even. She wondered whether he could tell she'd never been kissed before. But he said nothing. He only stood there before her, clutching her hands.

She sensed he was waiting for some sign from her. A nod. A smile.

"Again," she whispered.

This time when they kissed, there was no one to spy them like in Chassen's office, no reason for him to be tentative or cautious. And so his kiss became demanding. Hungrier. Desperate. She was caught by surprise, and even more surprisingly, curiosity. She found herself pressing against him, slipping her hands inside the folds of his worn flannel dressing gown, the first time she'd ever touched a man in such a fashion. To her amazement, she felt his nipples pucker as she explored his broad expanse of lightly furred chest, which was oh-so-warm. Inviting.

He let out a small groan from the back of his throat, fervently pressing his lips against her shoulders, her cheek. His tongue tracked the length of her lovely neck beneath her hair.

He slid his trousered thighs between hers. A hardness pressed against her hip. Arousal. She'd read of such in the male of her species, but never expected to experience this in her life. She felt an odd sense of accomplishment. She'd encouraged this in him. She, Musa Bartham, a woman who'd never been kissed until several minutes earlier, whose pulse had never before raced in the presence of another.

Well, her pulse was racing plenty now.

It's Felicity Vita he desires. Not you.

It all felt natural between them. Expected, like they'd done this before. A strange familiarity, though she'd only known him weeks. She supposed such was the madness of attraction—her father described feeling this when he met her mother so many years ago in Venice. Yet, instead of giving way to sensation, something prickled at the back of Musa's neck. Something where she knew all wasn't as it should be in his studio.

Once they'd broken away, she glanced around. Everything appeared as she recalled from her previous visit. She made out her book manuscript on his work table, an array of sketches, the photograph of his parents. However, no pile of letters tied with a ribbon—perhaps they had been from his sisters after all. On another table, there were his paints, brushes, and palette . . .

That painting of *La Dame sans Merci*. That's what was different. He'd turned it against the wall, though all of his other art remained where she'd last seen it. She wondered if it still resembled her.

"What are you looking at?" he asked, setting another kiss against her neck.

"I want to see your *La Dame sans Merci* painting," she demanded. "Show me."

He lifted his head from her, his pupils dark with arousal. "Really? *Now?*"

"No time like the present."

"What is this, some sort of art exhibit to prove I'm worthy of kissing the daughter of Neil Bartham?"

"I didn't say that." Another endlessly decadent kiss. "Anyway, remember—"

He winced. "Yes, I know. You're Felicity Vita tonight, not Musa Bartham."

"That's right," she said in a tone more confident than she felt. "Show me your painting."

"Musa or Felicity or whoever the hell you are, you're the most infuriating woman I've ever met. Yet I can't stop kissing you. I can't even think straight now, let alone discuss art."

And then his mouth clamped over hers anew. This time, she felt his tongue flicking against her, testing. Patient, gentle. She parted open for him, welcoming his taste, his warmth.

Then she stopped thinking. Or tried to, anyway.

Somehow while they'd kissed, they'd ended up standing beside his bed, or rather the sorry mattress that stood in for a bed. It was set in the darkest corner of his room. They collapsed onto it as one. Musa's elbow panged sharply as it met with the wall. She forgot the pain as he kissed it, rubbing the discomfort away.

Warmth spread across her body. She felt something else open within her. Something comprised of desire and yearning. Something she'd never experienced save in her private encounters when she pleasured herself alone in her room.

"You can leave anytime you'd like," he said, inching toward the foot of the bed. "But I hope you won't, Felicity or whatever the hell your name is."

"I-I wouldn't dream of it."

Felicity. What would she do? Then it became a question of what Musa *wouldn't* do, especially now that Seb had reached beneath the hem of her dress. Ever so tenderly he removed each of her boots, freeing her feet. He brushed his lips against her stockinged ankle. How sensitive her flesh felt! He looked up, his blue eyes locking with hers. She sensed a query within their depths. A daring.

Whatever he was about to do, it should be enough to bid farewell to Felicity, shouldn't it?

After what seemed like a long moment, she murmured, "Only this one night. Only that."

A hint of a smile. "If that's what you want."

"I do."

"Very well . . ."

He oh-so-gently reached beneath her chemise toward her garters. After he untied them with a slow precision, he rolled each stocking down until her legs were bared, the better to set his mouth against the inside of her calves.

"I want to bring you pleasure. May I?"

His tone was gentle. Inviting. Felicity would say yes without a second thought. However, Musa couldn't seem to speak. She settled for a terse nod.

He slid beneath her chemise. Hidden by yards of fabric, all she felt were his hands on her hips. She let out a low moan as he set a line of kisses up along the inside of her thighs, toward where her drawers split. Once he reached there, he gently caressed the delta of dark curls. His warm breath brought her desire to a fever pitch as his mouth nuzzled the folds of her ripe pink cleft open. Testing. Teasing . . .

She gasped as his tongue wrapped around her bud.

Though she'd read of such acts in her research for Felicity's poems, she never expected to experience this. Not in her life. These acts were not performed by polite people—well, not that she knew of. But then again, if she was Felicity Vita, Felicity would have had such experiences, wouldn't she?

Any shame or unease she felt fled in her curiosity. Her desire.

As he licked, sucked, and nuzzled her, her pleasure grew in a way that was keening. Overwhelming. Despite the sensual intensity of the act, she couldn't let go. Couldn't release. It was painful how close she was, like struggling with a door that wouldn't unlock.

He continued kissing and caressing her, his mouth hot against her mons. She grew too aware of the tick of the clock, her inability to climax. Then she considered the strange situation she'd set them in when she'd shown up at his door in the middle of the night insisting he call her Felicity. How awkward it all was. Especially now.

"Stop!" she cried out. "I-I can't."

"Can't what?" He crawled out from beneath her skirts. "You don't like what I'm doing? Because *I* like what I'm doing."

"It's not that, Seb . . ."

How could she explain what she barely understood herself? How she needed to have control? That she couldn't let others give to her without feeling vulnerable? Wasn't that what her act of being Felicity Vita was about? A way for her to gain dominance, to let go of Musa, who was proper and practical and prim. Everything Felicity was not.

"It feels unfair," she said at last. "Uneven."

This wasn't exactly true, but close enough.

He hoisted himself beside her on the mattress. She heard him let out a long sigh in the dark.

"Uneven . . . Let me assure that I crave to make love to you, for all the craziness of this evening, which has me more puzzled than I've ever been yet strangely delighted. It's not often a man has a beautiful woman show up at his door in the middle of the night, especially after confessing his desire to kiss her! But I wouldn't take such a risk. That would be decidedly unfair, since we're speaking of such matters, not including the usual reasons of chastity outside of marriage and fear of pregnancy and that I suspect you're a virgin and—oh, I feel awkward even saying such! And yet I can't turn you away . . . especially since you've informed me I shall only have you in my bed this one night."

"Oh," Musa said. She waited for him to continue speaking. And he did.

"But here I am with you by my side, which definitely was *not* on the list of activities I expected to take place this evening . . . well, now can you understand my confusion, Musa—I mean, Felicity. I'm not complaining. Not at all! Anyway, the thing is I'd intended to bring you pleasure in a way that every woman I've ever been with— not that there have been so *many*, mind—always assured me was enjoyable—"

"And you did bring me pleasure. You did!" Musa interrupted, humiliation thick in her throat. "But I-I . . . oh, I can't speak of it! It's not so much the unevenness as . . . as . . ."

Seb laid back, staring up at the ceiling. Silent.

"I understand," he said at last. "I think I know what to do."

He rolled over to kiss her. Then he blew out the candle, throwing them into pitch darkness. He set his head against her neck. Near her ear.

"I want you to close your eyes," he said in a soft voice. "And listen to me, if you can allow yourself such."

The words he offered were kind. Gentle. Forgiving. Inviting. The sort of words someone would say to a person in need of soothing rather than arousal.

As he spoke, she felt tension leave her body. Her fingers. Her toes. To her surprise, she even grew mildly sleepy.

"Imagine you're dreaming, Musa—I mean, Felicity. Oh, I know you're not dreaming, but think of what you'd dream if you were to do so."

He took her hand in his and gently set it over her lap, near where his mouth had tasted her only moments earlier.

"I want you to dream of what happens when you touch yourself. I assume you do this, given that you didn't seem that surprised by what I was doing to you."

Her eyes sprang open. He was leaning over, watching her, his gaze bright in the shadows.

"Why?"

The syllable sounded vulnerable rising from her. Shameful.

Seb's voice felt like heat in the room. "I want to know the best way to touch you. To learn from you, especially if we're to only have this one night."

Whatever mad spell that had pushed Musa into fleeing her home broke. She wasn't Felicity. She was only a pretentious, desperate woman, one who'd betrayed the gentleman who'd loyally written her affectionate letters all these months. A woman who might be undermining her most beloved sister's chances at future happiness. Yet she couldn't find the will to leave Seb's bed.

She burst out, "I can't say that."

"You don't need to tell me . . ." He brushed his warm lips against her neck. "Show me."

Show me.

Two words. Two syllables.

Too much.

She squirmed in his arms. "But it's so dark!"

"I can see enough," he murmured, his tone caressing. "If this was a dream, what would a lover do to you?"

A dream. That she could imagine, couldn't she?

Musa shut her eyes anew. Again, she thought of Henry and her fantasies involving him all those times, alone in her room. She wasn't alone now. Nor was she in her room.

"Show me," he said again. "How would you want a lover to touch you?"

After what felt like a long moment, she set her palm against the curve of her pubic bone. Though it remained covered by her lace gown and chemise, she sensed heat rising from where Seb had tasted of her.

"Show me," he asked again.

He slid his hand over hers.

His hand. Her hand.

Her vision of Henry mingled with Seb's warm body beside hers. And then it was only Seb's body.

Her body. His body. Their bodies.

She wiggled her hips, raising her skirt and chemise until her thighs were bared. The curls cresting her delta, the ripe pink flesh hidden beneath.

She showed him exactly what she would do. How she would do it. As she touched herself, his hand followed her lead. Gently. Surely.

And then it was only his hand on her, caressing her. Touching her.

And it was fine. More than fine.

She let her pleasure reach toward the ceiling, like a series of hosannahs.

Afterward, she laid in his arms. He settled the bed linens over them, tucking the worn quilt around her shoulders with a care that surprised her. Almost as though he loved her.

"Better?" he asked.

She nodded, feeling surprisingly emotional. Was this how it felt to be cherished? To be cared for? She hadn't known.

"We should sleep," he said, his voice a low caress in the dark. "That is, unless your family is worrying where you are."

"I left them a note."

"Good." He kissed her on her forehead and nestled his head against her shoulder. Again, almost as if he loved her.

She couldn't sleep. She was still too shocked by what had just occurred between them. How he'd somehow managed to understand her needs. Part of her thought she should reciprocate in some way, or at least apologize for bursting in on him in the middle of the night. Uneven, she thought anew. For all her research as Felicity Vita, reading about sexual acts was *very* different from experiencing them.

She settled for taking his hand in hers. His hands felt strong. Calloused, probably from press work.

And then she said something that shocked her. Something she never planned on revealing to anyone save her sister and editor.

"I really am Felicity Vita."

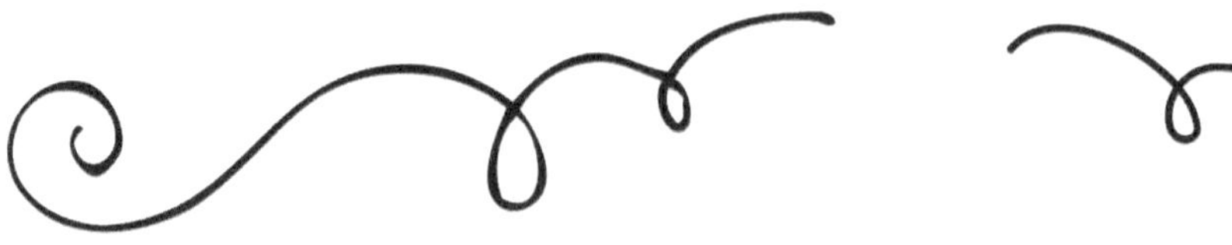

CHAPTER 25

"You're Felicity Vita."

Seb said the words as a statement, not a question. He knew he should act surprised, profess amazement. Alas, he'd never been a good liar save on the page. He felt blood drain from his face, thinking of all those letters he'd sent her under the guise of Henry Whitney, especially the last one where he warned her to protect herself . . . and here she was, entrusting him with her most dangerous secret.

His mouth grew dry as he searched for what to say next. To his relief, she filled the yawning silence between them.

"I wasn't just pretending to be Felicity when I came here. She's my pen name. *Nom de plume,* if you will."

He let out a long breath. "That's quite a confession."

Dare he confess he'd been writing to her as Henry all these months? Would she feel betrayed? Or made a fool?

No. She doesn't love you. Not yet. Whoever she imagined Henry to be, that's who she desired as she'd laid in his bed beside him. Ironic at best. Heartbreaking at worst.

To his relief, she didn't notice his discomfort, for she began to speak in a rush he wouldn't have been able to interrupt even if he tried.

"I know this sounds mad, Seb! And it *was* mad, but you must understand how destitute we were after Papa's disappearance. You see, he left us only enough funds for three years—he thought he'd be back in eighteen months, two years at most." She laughed in a manner that sounded akin to a sob. "But he didn't return, and no one could find him anywhere. It was so awful! There were bill collectors at all hours, and Mama wouldn't come out of her room. No one would help us. As for my sisters and my brother, how could I let them be so shamed?"

"Shamed by what?"

"We'd already moved from Kensington to Brompton to save money. My siblings didn't complain, but I could tell it bothered Angela. She's ever so conscious of status, though no one expects anything of us because we're the scandalous Barthams. Fortunately, the twins were too young to notice much. As for Mama, let's just say she hasn't been in this world ever since Papa left, for she loved him so. Though lately—well, you've met her, Seb. She's improved."

Seb managed to interject, "So you searched for a way to provide for your family."

A vehement nod in the dark. "You must believe I'd tried everything before I turned to poetry as Felicity Vita. Mary—Miss Nicholson, that is—gave me manuscripts to edit, for I've always been clever with words. She suggested I publish a novel, but I couldn't concentrate enough to write one, I was in such a panic. Next, I tried sensation stories, but I hadn't the imagination for those. Too bloodthirsty. Finally, I wrote improving lectures to be sold as pamphlets." Another sob-laugh. "After reading my children's book, you can imagine how well those went."

"But love poetry?" Though Seb had known she was Felicity Vita, the story of Musa Bartham's transformation into the love poet still astonished him.

"I know, I know, it's ridiculous! Me, Musa Bartham, writing love poetry. A virgin, as you surmised correctly. A woman who'd never even been kissed, for all those letters Henry sent me. Though for all I know, he could be a blackguard."

"I'm sure he isn't a blackguard," Seb inserted hastily. "Your correspondent's name is definitely Henry?"

He still couldn't believe it. *I should tell her the truth. What a coward I am!*

She nodded in affirmation. "Not that it matters any more . . ." Her voice dropped as though the effort of speaking caused physical pain. "I just sent him a letter to break things off. Too much of a risk. Not with my sister about to be launched."

"Did you love Henry?" Seb had to know.

She avoided his question, which gave him all the answer he needed.

"It no longer matters," she said at last. "I hope he will forgive me for hurting him . . . just as I hope you will forgive me for using you to satisfy my carnal curiosity."

Seb's heart twinged. *Carnal curiosity. That's all I was to her.*

"I forgive you, though there is nothing to forgive. I was a very willing participant, in case you hadn't noticed."

He had to force the conversation onto safer ground, for the longer she spoke of Henry, the more he feared he'd confess the truth. She'd feel betrayed. Devastated. Humiliated.

"How did you end up writing those poems?"

"It's a complicated story, Seb. They came to me after Miss Nicholson mentioned erotica sold well, though she hadn't published it. One night when I was sitting with Mama, I found letters Papa wrote her before he disappeared. I knew I shouldn't read them, but I was so curious. So eager to understand how they loved each other enough to defy the world. The letters weren't explicit, but they were certainly as you'd expect. Mama had written responses to his words along the paper margins, almost like a poem. I set them down on a fresh page, taking the loveliest parts and changing the phrasing so even Mama couldn't recognize them."

She broke off, overcome by emotion. He squeezed her hand, yearning to offer comfort. She didn't pull away.

When she was able to continue, she said, "It now seems so ridiculous, how it all came together. But you must understand how desperate I was! When I showed the poems to Miss Nicholson, she said she thought they'd sell, for I was careful to keep my language tasteful enough that I wouldn't get into trouble. I never expected they'd become so popular, though they certainly haven't made me rich."

"Weren't you afraid of being caught?"

"All the time! Another scandal was the last thing my family could survive. I did everything I could to protect myself. Beside my *nom de plume,* I wrote the poems with my left hand, so no one would recognize my writing."

"Ambidextrous," Seb said. He'd been right.

She nodded. "Eventually I ran out of Mama's love letters to use for my poems, so I began researching . . . well, *reading* erotica really. To educate myself, though some of it was rather shocking. I mean, I don't have any personal experience, as you could probably tell."

Seb was uncertain whether he wanted to laugh or weep. The image of Musa perusing pornography for the sake of providing for her family . . . it really was too much.

"But soon it became more than that, Seb. The thing is, I *liked* being Felicity Vita. Somehow by impersonating her, I felt freed of my worries. Lighter. After all, *felicity vita*—'happy life'—was all I wanted for my family and myself."

"And that's how Felicity Vita came into being," he said, moved by her confession. After all, didn't everyone want a happy life?

"Yes." Her voice caught. "But it's over now. You heard what Miss Nicholson said about the new publisher. You don't know the worst! She's taken Felicity out of print. No more books from her. Ever. That's why I wrote a children's book."

This filled Seb with a strange sorrow. He'd loved Felicity Vita's poems. They'd truly spoken to his soul, for all of Musa's commercial intent.

"I admire your fortitude, Musa. No, I admire *you.*" And he did.

"I don't know how admirable it is. The truth is I've been selling tasteful smut."

"They were beautiful poems. Touching poems. I went to Persephone Press because I loved them so."

"And because you wanted to meet Felicity Vita. Now you have."

A long moment passed between the two of them. A moment in which Seb was seized by the urge to reach for Musa anew. She was so close, lying beside him in his bed. It would be so easy. Natural, even. He didn't.

Instead, he countered, "I suppose our bargain has been fulfilled, or at least your part of it."

"Yes, you've met Felicity Vita!" An awkward laugh. "Now you only have to illustrate my children's book." She met his eyes. "You promise not to tell anyone?"

"I promise." He'd convince Luke to remain silent. He had no choice.

"Thank you. You're a true gentleman, Sebastian Atkinson. A rarity."

"I-I don't know about that." Again, he thought of Luke, how unwise he'd been to confide in him, those stolen letters.

I'll find a way to fix it. I must.

Musa released his hand and yawned. He waited for her to leave his bed, to go home. She remained beside him, her eyes closing. And, a moment later, she appeared to sleep; he watched her shoulders rise and fall in a gentle rhythm. She even snored. He remained awake, more troubled than he'd expected possible.

He thought of Luke circling about Musa, those articles he offered to write about their children's book. He thought of Angela with her hunger for respectability so she might wed, and Musa's determination to protect her. Him with his lies about Henry, Musa's letter to break things off. (How would he handle this?) He even thought of his sisters, and Jessica's illness and his need for funds to provide for them. But all of these thoughts didn't compare to the most shocking one of all.

He now knew he loved Musa Bartham in all her complex, duplicitous glory.

She doesn't love you, Seb. She loves Henry. And you can never tell her the truth.

CHAPTER 26

When Seb awakened, morning had arrived and his bed was empty. For a moment he considered whether he'd dreamed of Musa arriving at his door. The warm scent of coffee offered reassurance all had happened as he remembered. But where was she?

He searched his attic. The sky was a cool blue on the other side of his windows, so bright it made his eyes smart. He didn't see her cloak. Nor did he spy her worn leather boots, the ones he'd removed from her before they'd . . . well, he wouldn't think of that now. The more important question was whether she'd left.

The door to his attic opened—and there was Musa, her thick wool cloak concealing the revealing pink lacy dress she'd shown up wearing.

"I went out in search of breakfast," she said, handing him a Chelsea bun wrapped in brown paper. "You were sleeping so peacefully I couldn't bear to wake you."

Seb nodded his thanks, overcome by relief at her return. The Chelsea bun was still warm, but he didn't eat it. Not yet.

I'm here with Felicity Vita, he thought. *I mean Musa Bartham. Musa-Felicity. And I'm in love with her. But she's in love with Henry. And she's broken off with him.*

For all of his suspicions as to Musa's identity, her confession had stunned him . . . along with the night they'd shared. He recalled her cry of surprise as she'd climaxed. The memory of it went straight to his groin. He shifted, hoping she wouldn't notice his erection; fortunately he was still wearing trousers. He tightened the sash of his dressing gown.

He watched her putter about his spirit stove. Her movements were certain as she heated up the coffee. Domestic.

"Coffee's ready," she said in a cheerful tone, offering him an earthenware mug. He resisted the temptation to pull her back into his bed—especially once she slipped her cloak off. She'd wrapped a shawl around her bodice, hiding the most revealing parts of that lacy pink gown. "I noticed you only had used tea leaves in your pantry."

Seb's arousal fled as reality returned with a slap. He'd taken to reusing tea out of economy.

"Coffee's fine. Aren't you having some?"

"I had mine earlier." She sat beside him on the bed, casting a shy glance his way. "You're not eating. Don't you like Chelsea buns?"

"I-I do. Very much. Thank you."

The Chelsea bun was ripe with the scent of cinnamon, lemon zest, and butter; Musa must have purchased them from his land-lady, who baked them fresh every morning. As Seb ate, he tried to disregard her warm presence beside him, the remnants of fragrance lingering in her hair. She ate also, her delicate pink tongue licking the creamy icing off her fingers, as though to savor every bite.

"These are so good," she moaned. "I hadn't realized how hungry I was! I didn't eat any dinner last night."

Seb found himself speechless. Besides being in love with her, Musa Bartham was the most adorable, desirable woman he'd ever met—and the sounds she was now making only reminded him of this.

I am in so much trouble.

To distract himself, he glanced across the room toward his *La Dame sans Merci* painting, which he'd revised to resemble Musa more closely. It was fortunate he'd set the oil canvas against the wall to give his eyes a rest. He'd have felt vulnerable if she'd spied it.

She must have sensed his thoughts, for she tilted her chin at the canvas. "Show me what you're working on."

Seb forced a lightness into his voice he didn't feel. "Are we really going to argue over this again?"

She offered a sly smile. "Very well. If there's one thing I've learned in my years, it's better to beg forgiveness than to ask permission."

Before Seb could stop her, she rushed toward the canvas. "Don't look!" he yelled. "Please, no!"

Too late.

Seb's painting was far more developed than it had been even a week earlier. Instead of appearing akin to a pot of mud splashed on a canvas, the beautiful young woman in the center of his composition now bore color. She was gowned in gold and silver, her thick chestnut hair long and tangled about her bared shoulders. However, the expression in her somber eyes was sly in its allure. Seductive yet cruel. Unavailable.

Musa inhaled sharply. "It's me, isn't it? *La Dame sans Merci.*"

Seb nodded, again unable to speak.

"I noticed she resembled me when you were ill . . . but not like this." Musa's tone was odd, Seb thought. "Did you change the painting after I threw my manuscript at you? Or after I'd apologized?"

His hands shook as he took another sip of the coffee, which had gone cold. He stole a glance at her profile, which was fine and piquant and sharp and clever. Fox-like.

Foxes had always been his favorite animal, he decided.

"Before and after," he admitted, finally daring to meet her gaze. "I started the painting weeks before I'd met you, intending it to be a portrait of Felicity Vita . . . and this is how I imagined she appeared."

A subtle flush rose across Musa's cheeks. "Like me?"

"Like you . . . and then when I met you, I revised it to more closely resemble you."

"When?" Her tone was demanding. Startled.

"After I tried to kiss you in Green Park," he said.

"Oh."

She let out a long breath. The sound seemed to echo in the attic as Seb awaited further reaction to his confession.

She brushed her palms against face, her eyes gleaming. Was she weeping? No, this couldn't be.

"But she's not you," Seb hastily reassured. "You're not like her. Not really."

"I'm relieved to hear that." She gestured toward the canvas. "She does appear rather unkind."

And then without another word, she draped herself on the chair nearest the canvas.

"Paint me," she said.

Seb drew a deep breath, his heart pounding against his ribcage. How much longer could he handle being alone with her? He was another breath away from sweeping her back into her arms. A step away from confessing he was Henry. Yet he couldn't bear for her to leave.

He answered, "I'd be honored if you posed for her, Musa. But I'd rather draw you, if you don't mind. Sketches are more practical for my needs. Quicker too."

"Do it then."

She set her spectacles on her lap. She tilted her head in the same position as the figure of La Dame sans Merci in his painting.

"Like this?" she asked.

Seb nodded. He put down his coffee. He reached for his sketchbook and pencils.

One sketch led to another. A close up of her eyes, how they flashed with intelligence and wit. A study of her profile, the way her neck led to her jaw. The piquant beauty mark just below the full of her lips—lips he hadn't kissed enough for his liking.

As he drew Musa, he was grateful for the opportunity to look at her for as long as he wished without excuse. To give form to her face on the page, as though these would allow him to express the tenderness—no, the admiration—he felt for her. He yearned for her. He loved her. Musa was more than her beauty, more than her grace, more than her poems written under Felicity's guise.

And yet there was something else weighing on him. Something that made him want to slow his hand as he drew: the knowledge that once she departed, their one night together would be over. Never to be repeated. It would become nothing more than a memory to torment him in his darkest moments . . . along with the awareness he loved her, but she loved someone who wasn't him.

And it was all his fault.

If only he'd been honest from the start about Henry. Confessed the truth, as difficult as it would have been. Now it was all too late, too far gone. She'd feel played for a fool once she learned he'd deceived her about his letters. She'd view their relationship as uneven, to use her word.

The pain of Seb's regret felt nearly physical. A weight. A loss, especially as he recalled her face as she climaxed against him, how her lips had parted with pleasure, her eyes clenched, the little gasp she'd given. How wet his fingers had become while he touched her, revealing her desire for him, her trust. The shudder overtaking her body before she collapsed against him with a languid sigh of satisfaction. "*Better?*" he'd whispered . . .

"Better?" she asked.

"I'm sorry?"

"I was asking you whether this is better?" She pointed to her profile. "I tilted my chin slightly."

"I think I have all I need for now." He laid his sketches across the floor, a gallery of Musas.

Musa put on her spectacles and rose from the chair, smoothing her skirts. "They're beautiful, but I sense something's preoccupying your thoughts. I've been presumptuous, bursting in here as I did."

He stood to meet her eye-to-eye.

"Perhaps I'm thinking of our book," he lied. "I will finish up those illustrations as soon as I can for you." He added tenderly, "You've fulfilled your part of the bargain, after all."

She blanched. "Don't tell anyone about Felicity. Promise me."

"I'll protect you." This, at least, wasn't a lie.

But what of the other ways you've misled her?

His stomach twisted, the Chelsea bun he'd eaten heavy in it.

Tell her the truth, an insistent voice whispered. *Even if she despises you, she deserves to know.*

He took her hand in his. A bead of sweat across his forehead.

"If I'm to be honest," he began, still clutching her hand, his words tight with anxiety, "I keep thinking of last night. About what you'd confided about your . . . correspondent. Perhaps the situation is different than you believe."

She cocked an eyebrow behind her spectacles. "How so?"

How best to phrase this? Perhaps if he presented the truth from her perspective.

"How do you think Henry would feel if he discovered Felicity Vita didn't really exist—well, she *does* exist—but what if he learned she was only a name on a page?"

Musa offered a blank stare. Heavens, this wasn't going well.

He cleared his throat and tried again. "I mean, what I'm trying to say is—"

A sharp knock on the door. Musa pulled her hand from his. Seb's landlady called from the hallway, her tone urgent.

"A lady's here for you, Mr. Atkinson. Your sister."

Seb exchanged glances with Musa, whose cheeks turned as rosy as her revealing pink lace gown.

"I wasn't expecting anyone," he explained, unlocking the door. He was uncertain who he felt more protective of: Musa, who he'd never seen so vulnerable with embarrassment, or Daphne, who appeared breathless with distress as she approached his threshold.

And then he knew. Something happened. Something bad. Daphne never came to his rooms without notice, especially not without Jessica accompanying her.

Before Seb could decide what to do or say, Musa grabbed her cloak and fled after muttering the tersest farewell he'd ever heard.

"Who was that?" Daphne asked, her eyes wide.

"No one you know," he evaded. *Only the woman I love.* His pulse sped. "Where's Jessica? Who's with her?"

In lieu of an answer, Daphne embraced her brother and began to sob.

CHAPTER 27

COSTUME BALL PLANNED
FOR BARTHAM BOOK

The Greater London Gazette, 23 February 1872: Lady Minerva Hadley has announced a costume ball to mark the publication of Poems of Morality and Goodness for Children, *a children's book written by Miss Musa Bartham and illustrated by Mr. Sebastian Atkinson. The event will take place this April at her Grosvenor Square mansion.*

Miss Bartham is a distant relation to Lady Hadley as well as the eldest daughter of famed painter Neil Bartham, whose disappearance whilst traveling to Jerusalem remains unresolved. In a recent interview conducted by the Gazette, Miss Bartham said: "I was inspired to write Poems of Morality and Goodness for Children to Abide *to offer an oasis of godliness during these troubled times. However, I would be remiss not to mention that my beloved sister Angela served as inspiration."*

Coincidentally, rumors have been building for some weeks that Lady Hadley will be sponsoring Miss Angela Bartham this Season, marking the Bartham family's return to society in over two decades. Whether or not these rumors are proven true, Lady

> *Hadley's costume ball is certain to win attention from both the*
> *Ton and the literary world.*

Two WEEKS after Musa spent the night with Seb, a second article was published about their book. This time, the article was placed front and center in the society section of *The Greater London Gazette*. It was accompanied by one of Seb's charming illustrations and a flattering portrait of Angela; Seb must have drawn it sometime after that tea.

Seb, whom Musa hadn't seen since that night when she'd shown up at his door like a lust-filled madwoman.

Seb, who'd been more intimate with her body than anyone in her life.

Seb, who'd treated her as though he'd cherished her even after her confession about Henry. As for Henry, he'd sent the kindest note imaginable acknowledging her final letter: *"I bear you only the warmest thoughts, darling Felicity, and wish you the happiest of lives."* She'd read his words with tears in her eyes, feeling as though she'd betrayed him as much as she'd used Seb.

Since that night, Seb had understandably avoided her, though he sent a bouquet of roses soon after. The flowers were gorgeous ones, with petals the deepest red she'd ever seen. Their rich perfume seemed to follow Musa throughout the house. The bouquet astonished her, especially when she considered the twice-washed tea leaves in his pantry.

Seb's note accompanying the roses mentioned nothing of his sister's arrival that morning or Musa's abrupt departure. *"I've family business to attend to and will be away for the next week or so,"* he'd written in peculiar block letters. *"I will continue to work on the drawings for our book and appreciate your willingness to model for my canvas."* Though Musa sent thank you notes to both his place of employment and studio, he did not reply.

Seb's silence bothered her more than she cared to admit. She suspected it was because of what happened with his sister Daphne. Even if she remained unaware of how Musa had essentially thrown herself at Seb, the situation was untoward. Perhaps Seb had also been unsettled by her confession about Felicity Vita—it must be disconcerting to learn the poetess you idealized was all too mortal.

As the days passed, Musa found herself thinking of Seb at odd moments. When she was staring out the window, lost in reverie, she'd recall his lopsided grin when something amused him. While making her bed, she'd imagine what it would be like to find him there. At the bakery, a tray of Chelsea buns made her feel ridiculously like swooning. Even her father's art reminded her of Seb and how intimate it felt to pose for him before his sister's sudden arrival.

All this made Musa's heart pang in a manner that was decidedly impractical.

It's for the best I'm alone, she told herself. *What a mess I'd make if someone really loved me.*

"Musa, did you see this?" Angela shrieked once Luke Ward's article made its way to her across the Barthams' breakfast table; she'd taken to visiting from Aunt Minerva's early in the morning before society stirred. "I didn't expect a second article, along with an illustration of me. This is wonderful! I wonder what Mr. Atkinson will think. He's all but famous!"

"I'm sure he'll be pleased," Musa answered. She glanced toward the sideboard, where Seb's roses miraculously still bore life well over a week after their delivery.

"How are his drawings going, sweetheart?" Clio asked. Since rejoining the living, she'd gone overboard in displays of attention to her children. She offered Musa milk for her tea, which Musa promptly declined. "Oh I forgot! Lemon only."

"It's fine, Mama. As for Mr. Atkinson, I'm sure he'll make the book deadline."

The doorbell jangled. "That's Aunt Minerva with her carriage," Angela said, clapping her hands. "I can't wait to show her the article. And look happier for goodness' sake, Musa. This is good news!"

"Do I look so mournful?" She thought she'd hid it well.

"I can tell you're thinking of Mr. Atkinson," Angela accused. "You've been decidedly distracted since he sent those flowers."

"No, no. Just a lot on my mind these days," Musa said weakly, yearning for a Chelsea bun.

Before Angela could counter Musa's claim, Aunt Minerva entered the dining room in a rush of cold air and strong *eau de parfum.*

"I saw the newspaper article," she said in a flat tone. "Vulgar, but it'll do."

"How can you say the article is vulgar, Aunt?" Angela cried. "The engraving made me look beautiful!"

"The article mentions your father's disappearance. By now, I'd hoped for *that* to be swept under the proverbial rug, miss, along with his other foolishness."

Here we go, Musa thought, glancing across the table at her mother, who'd grimaced at her great-aunt's pronouncement. *Please don't insult my father's penis again.*

Alas, Aunt Minerva couldn't resist. "After all, if it wasn't for Neil Bartham and his stiff John—"

"You do know I'm here, yes?" Clio interrupted, her brow furrowed. "And that your words are unkind to the man I love most in the whole entire world!"

"You mean the scoundrel who ruined you and your children's prospects?"

Clio folded her arms before her chest. "My children wouldn't be here without him!"

"Oh hush, you two!" Angela cooed. "Let's celebrate good news instead of delving into the past again. Aunt, you of all people know I've plenty of prospects. I think the article is well played."

"And I think it's wonderful," Musa added, determined to distract her family as well as herself.

"I've more good news to relate," Angela said. "My new wardrobe is to be delivered today. Thank you so much, Aunt!"

"Aunt, you're too generous," Clio protested, her expression softening. "Angela isn't having a season, just being introduced."

"I won't have my family humiliated by society," Aunt Minerva grumbled with a warm gleam in her eyes.

"I think it's more than that," Angela teased. "I've never seen you so excited as during my fittings."

Her aunt let out a small shrug. "I have exquisite taste. And you, miss, are exquisite."

"I *do* adore you, Aunt!"

Musa watched, astonished, as Angela offered Aunt Minerva a warm embrace. Even now, weeks since Aunt Minerva had agreed to sponsor Angela, Musa still couldn't fathom how quickly everything changed. Instead of a soiled past, the Barthams had a promising future . . . or so it seemed.

Just then the door rang anew. A moment later, the maid-of-all-work announced, "Flowers for Miss Angela. Sent by a Mr. Carles. They're ever so beautiful, miss!"

"Oh, how wonderful!" Angela rushed to the hall to claim her prize.

Clio's furrowed brow returned. "Who's this Carles fellow, Aunt? Why's he sending flowers here, instead of to you?"

"He's one of several callers Angela met at my home several days ago. Not noble, but has a small estate in Surrey and a decent per annum," Aunt Minerva answered in a matter-of-fact tone. "I suspect he's anxious to make sure Angela receives the flowers. Lady Sunderland couldn't help but speak of Angela when she was at The Pink Refuge earlier this week."

"The Pink Refuge again? She must live there," Musa said, her skin prickling.

"No matter. Word's out about our beautiful Angela. Blame it on the Bartham name, miss." Aunt Minerva's tone dropped. "Or that Lady Sunderland is determined for Angela not to marry her son."

"Ah, so she's noticed." Musa had wondered as much. Sunny had spent most of that Sunday tea offering moist glances in Angela's direction.

Aunt Minerva glanced over her shoulder in case of Angela's return. She whispered, "He made it rather obvious."

"Sunny's always had a soft spot for her," Clio observed wistfully, no doubt thinking of what might have been had circumstances been different. "His father's been very kind to our family."

Aunt Minerva shrugged. "Better to marry Angela off to someone else's son than her own. All for the best really. It's wiser for a woman to be paired in the world than not—paired with a respectable man, that is," she clarified, tossing a pointed glance at Clio.

Musa was again prevented from defending her father's honor by Angela's return. Her sister's arms were filled with pink tulips surrounded by lacy green fronds. "Oh, isn't it wonderful!"

Aunt Minerva replied, "They're all angling for an invitation to the costume ball, I'd wager." She folded the *Gazette*, setting it on the table with an emphatic gesture. "Mark my words, miss."

All because of Musa's book," Angela said, ever loyal. She blew a kiss in Musa's direction. "You're such a wonderful sister!"

Angela's show of affection warmed Musa's heart. But then she glanced over at the newspaper on the breakfast table. A smaller headline popped out, partly obscured by the paper fold:

POETESS'S LOVE RE—

Merde. Musa's stomach felt as though it had been invaded by some sort of winged creature. She reached for the newspaper, but not before Clio picked it up and began to page lazily through it. Musa rapidly ran through a list of possible headlines, each worse than the last. POETESS'S LOVE REVEALED! Or even POETESS'S LOVE REUNITED.

"Mama?" A nervous laugh. "May I have the newspaper? I want to save the article."

Clio offered a wide smile. "You should, sweetheart! Such wonderful news!" She kissed Musa on both her cheeks. "I'm so proud of my clever daughter."

Newspaper in hand, Musa bounded up the steps to her room. Once inside, she slammed the door shut, her hands shaking. She opened the *Gazette* to reveal the article in full.

Fortunately, the article was a short piece of only three paragraphs. It was set beside a rather lurid advertisement for mercury pills, which hopefully would draw attention away from it.

Unfortunately, the article was exactly what she feared.

POETESS'S LOVE REVELATIONS!

The infamous love poet Felicity Vita has been known for her reclusive ways. But no longer! It turns out the poet has been sending love letters to a mysterious gentleman—letters that The Greater London Gazette gained possession of through a series of surprising events.

Last night, six of these letters were discovered in Green Park tucked behind a brick beneath a park bench. The Gazette was alerted to their presence from an anonymous message delivered to our office.

What will Miss Vita's letters reveal? In the meantime, our experts are examining the documents to ascertain their provenance and any legalities regarding their publication. If these letters were written by the elusive poet, their content may prove to be more popular than her books.

Musa paced back and forth in her room, her panic rising.

Henry wouldn't do this, not because I'd ceased our correspondence. His last letter was so kind.

A dark voice inside her answered, *He already knew someone stole the letters. That's why he wrote to warn me.*

Her anxious pacing was interrupted by a sharp rap at her door.

"Go away," she called out; she didn't trust herself not to reveal her distress to her family. They mustn't know, especially Angela.

"I'm . . . sick. Breakfast disagreed with me." She made a number of gagging sounds more unnatural than alarming.

Another knock. "It's me, Mary. I know you're not ill. Let me in!"

Musa unlocked her door. "You saw the article?"

Mary nodded. "I came as soon as I could. Oh lord, what a mess!"

She opened her arms. Musa stepped into them, shaking.

Be practical, Musa, she told herself. *There must be something you can do.*

Then it came to her: Sebastian Atkinson. He worked at Chassen & Sons, the same printer for *The Greater London Gazette.* She knew this now, given that his friend Luke had written the article about their book.

Seb was the only person who knew about Felicity Vita outside of Angela and Mary . . . and he'd promised to protect her.

But he doesn't want to see me. Not anymore.

Her mind countered, *But what choice do you have?*

Musa extracted herself from Mary's arms. "I have an idea," was all she said as she rushed for the stairs. "Keep your fingers crossed!"

CHAPTER 28

Musa found Seb in the second place she looked: the South Kensington Museum.

She discovered him alone in the gallery displaying drawings by Raphael—Raphael, whose art had won the disdain of the Pre-Raphaelites a generation earlier, which had granted the group of artists their name. It figured Seb would go against the grain in seeking out Raphael's art, just as her father had years ago.

No one else was in the huge gallery where Musa found Seb, not even a guard. Her heart leaped as she took in his dark, tall form. Seb wore his customary brown greatcoat with his customary red knit scarf around his neck. He appeared as though he'd barely slept, for he was unshaven, his hair unruly. Not that dissimilar of appearance to when she'd first met him at Persephone Press weeks earlier . . . but now everything was different.

She watched Seb for longer than she should, given the urgency of her situation. *If he's disappointed to see me, I don't think I can bear it.* And so she waited for him to notice her first. It took him a good five minutes—five minutes in which she flooded with everything she felt for him. Emotions she refused to name out of practicality and fear, especially now that her relationship with Henry was finished.

Once Seb caught sight of Musa, he approached slowly. His expression was such she couldn't tell what he was thinking. Or feeling. How vulnerable she felt!

"Musa? Why are you here?"

She sensed an air of wonder in his tone, though she couldn't decide whether it was born of anxiety or surprise.

"Looking for you." For what more could be said?

He ran his fingers through his thick, dark hair. "No one knows I come here. How did you find me?"

The explanation Musa could have offered Seb was too complicated to offer, as well as too personal. She first searched for him at Chassen & Sons; she assumed he'd returned to his usual schedule since his last letter to her. When she didn't find Seb at work, she thought to try the South Kensington Museum before heading to Spitalfields. Her father often visited the museum when he required serenity—and she sensed the same need in Seb, though she couldn't explain why.

Neil especially loved this particular gallery, with its twelve-foot Raphael drawings extending toward the crowned ceilings. If Musa closed her eyes, she could recollect him explaining their history when she was a child. *"There are hundreds of pieces of paper to make up that big drawing,"* he told her. *"Drawn in chalk and then painted in tempura. And then the big drawing was sent all the way from Rome to Brussels to make a huge tapestry. That tapestry is now in the Sistine Chapel in Rome."*

"How did he do that, Papa?"

"Because he had lots of help, little one. No one works alone. Not even me . . ."

Musa blinked and the memory scattered . . . and there she was alone in the South Kensington Museum with Sebastian Atkinson. Seb, who was her only hope in fixing her mess of a life . . . and whom she'd grown to care for despite all her attempts to guard her heart.

"How did I find you?" she repeated slowly. "I guessed you'd be here."

A hint of a smile. "Clever girl."

She took encouragement from his praise. "Artists like museums. The South Kensington isn't far from Chassen & Sons."

"And here I am."

She nodded. Her mouth felt dry. A pool of warmth flooded her limbs. Her heart. The memory of how he'd felt curled against her that night after her confession about Felicity Vita. She resisted the urge to throw her arms about him, as though to recapture the tenderness he'd shown her then. The compassion.

He took a step in her direction. "I'm so glad you found me, Musa. I have something for you."

Another step. She didn't dare meet his eyes. Didn't dare trust herself. He smelled of soap tinged with lemon verbena and something else. Something she only knew as his scent: the hint of perspiration, linseed oil.

He set a small black cardboard portfolio into her hands. Musa didn't need to open it to know what it contained.

"You finished the illustrations for our book."

He nodded. "Ahead of schedule too. I was going to bring them to Persephone Press this afternoon. But since you're here, you can give them to Miss Nicholson. However, I don't think that's why you came looking for me."

Musa gave up any show of composure. "Two weeks ago you offered to protect me. I desperately wish to accept your offer. I don't know what else to do—I feel so alone!"

He closed the distance between them in the empty gallery. "Tell me what's happened."

She burst out, "I've been betrayed!"

He blanched at the vehemence of her words. But he didn't pull away. Nor did he reject her.

"I promise I'll do whatever I can to help."

She pulled out the newspaper section, jabbing at the headline of *POETESS'S LOVE REVELATIONS!*, which remained as shocking as it was when she first read it. She quickly explained about the article. She also confessed how, after she'd written her farewell to Henry, he'd sent a letter warning her of gossip.

"Henry must have suspected this might happen, Seb. Someone must have stolen his letters. It must be that—I can't believe he'd betray me. I knew it was a risk to write him, but I never expected this. And before you ask, no I haven't written him regarding the article. No time, and anyway it's too late. Here, you must read it!"

"I believe you," Seb answered.

And so he didn't read the article. Nor did he question her account. This reassured her. He trusted her enough to believe there was a problem, and her reaction was appropriate.

Encouraged by his response, she added furiously, "If I ever find out who stole those letters, I'll never forgive them. They're a blackguard of the worst degree. They deserve to be ostracized. Hated. If it's anyone I know, I'll never speak to them again!"

Seb blanched at the vehemence of her words. Yet he couldn't look away from her, or so it seemed to Musa. He tucked a loose tendril of hair behind her ear, beneath her bonnet. She knew she should draw his attention back to the article, tell him exactly what she needed—after all, time was wasting. But there they stood surrounded by those glorious Raphael drawings, and it suddenly felt so insignificant.

His eyes met hers. There was a gleam of moisture on his thick, dark lashes. Was he holding back tears?

"You're sad," she said; now it was her turn to express wonder. "Why?"

"I-I missed you, Musa," he said at last. "So very much. I didn't think I'd see you again." A soft sigh. "This has been the longest two weeks of my life."

Despite her distress, she felt a surge of joy at his confession. "Because you finished the illustrations?"

His mouth twisted in an odd fashion. "Among other reasons."

She still didn't understand, but there was no place or time to ask, for she launched herself into his arms, letting that damned newspaper fall to the marble floor of the gallery along with his precious portfolio.

Seb's arms felt strong, muscled beneath his greatcoat. Protective, which was exactly what Musa needed.

Her embrace tightened about him. She didn't plan to kiss him, just to hold him. To comfort him—or so she told herself. After all, he was vulnerable with emotion. So she didn't kiss him, though the act of not kissing Sebastian Atkinson took more willpower than Musa knew she possessed. Nor did he kiss her, which was as frustrating. If he had, she'd have no excuse not to give way to her yearning in such a public arena.

For some reason, this choice not to kiss felt the most transgressive act she could imagine. It brought her desire for him to a fever pitch. The anticipation. The ache. Her mouth felt swollen. Her body aching for something she could not name despite all those lustful, sensual poems she'd written under the guise of Felicity Vita. All these were emotions that were illogical and impractical . . . but emotions she could not ignore.

How different this was from what she felt for Henry all those months during their correspondence. For all the beauty of his letters, their graceful turns of phrases, she now understood he'd been a chimera she'd never wanted to catch.

As for what she now felt for Sebastian Atkinson . . .

If I didn't know better, I'd think I was in love with him.

A guard entered the gallery, his shoes tapping against the marble floor. Seb pulled away, causing her additional distress. Was he going to abandon her in the middle of the museum in her time of need? No, he was picking up the newspaper and portfolio from the floor.

"Come with me, Musa," Seb said, a razor-edge of anxiety in his voice. He tucked the newspaper section into his coat pocket, still not bothering to read it. "I'm begging you."

CHAPTER 29

THE TRAIN from London was swaying as it made its way into Kent, toward where Seb told Musa his family home was. "I need you to see it, so you'll understand who I am," he said. "I promise to have you back before dinner so your family won't worry." She'd agreed to accompany him, though she remained puzzled by his insistence. On top of that, he'd yet to read that *Gazette* article. Nor had he responded to her request for help.

But there was something else weighing her.

"You planned not to see me again," she said in a low voice, too conscious of the crowded second-class carriage. Fortunately, an elderly lady placed a rather large shopping bag on the seat beside them, granting them a small measure of privacy. "That's why you were going to bring the illustrations directly to Miss Nicholson."

She didn't dare tell him how this tore at her heart. She didn't fully understand it herself. Again, she felt a mass of emotions and yearning. Illogical. Impractical.

His answer was delayed as the train went around a bend, throwing her against him in the compartment. She let her body linger a second too long, relishing the pressure of his shoulder against hers. His masculine scent.

He said at last, "I thought it prudent. Business, not pleasure."

"As my book collaborator, this seems rather abrupt of you."

Another awkward pause as the train settled on the track.

He whispered, "It's safe to say we're more than collaborators, Musa. Especially now that I know your pen name."

"I-I suppose."

She clutched his portfolio all the tighter against her chest.

"I'd intended to stay far from you, thinking you had enough trouble already. After the other night . . . well, I thought you preferred not to see me. You rushed out so quickly in the morning."

"Because of your sister."

Still whispering, Seb added, "You said we'd only have that one night. It led me to believe . . ."

His words drifted into silence as he avoided her gaze.

"Is that why you sent the roses with the note?" she asked. "To bid farewell?"

At last, he looked her square in the eye. "Among other reasons."

She flushed, feeling a strange guilt. She reconsidered how her behavior might have appeared to his sister that morning, when she'd darted off like a fugitive. A new thought emerged. Was he bringing Musa to his family home to meet his sister? To somehow smooth things over?

Another sway of the train. Two more stops passed. The carriage remained fuller than Musa would have liked, for it held her back from saying the thoughts crowding her mind. Even the few sentences they'd exchanged seemed wrung reluctantly from his lips. Fortunately, the elderly lady seated near them appeared hard of hearing.

Everything is different now because of that night and his knowledge of Felicity.

She glanced up at Seb. His gaze awaited hers.

"Come," he said, offering his red scarf to protect her from the cold. "Our station is next."

～

Seb's house was but a short distance from the train station, a walk Musa was glad for. The coolness of the late February air distracted her from the nerves she felt, along with the bright sun. She was also soothed by his red scarf around her neck, the warmth it offered, for the further they walked, the more disquieted she grew. What would she find when they arrived? She imagined a small farmhouse surrounded by a picket fence, a trellis draped with nascent grapevines. His sister Daphne bustling out the door once she spied Seb from the window overlooking the garden. As for his youngest sister, Musa envisioned her looking as she did in Seb's illustrations for their book: bonny cheeked, dark hair in pigtails as she giggled and played.

I want you to understand who I am, he'd said. Why? She should be pressing him for help, explain what she needed him to do at Chassen & Sons. Yet she couldn't seem to.

She glanced toward Seb, whose expression was more serious than she'd ever witnessed. Anxious, though his eyes no longer gleamed with emotion like they had in the Raphael gallery. He remained silent as they walked.

He led her down a long country lane lined on both sides by tall cypress trees. Small brown sparrows sang despite the cold, chirping as they flickered from branch to branch covered in hoar-frost. The scene was bucolic and serene, as unlike London as tar from honey.

"There," he said at last. "This is where I grew up."

They'd come to a halt before a Tudor era manor house larger than she'd expected, but one that had clearly seen better days, judging by the peeling paint on its timbers and the ragged shingles on the north side, where presumably the wind blew strongest. A few of the windows were shuttered; Musa was uncertain whether this was due to the season or broken windows. No smoke rose from the chimney. Nor did she sense any sign of life inside the house; the curtains were closed.

"No one's home," she said.

Seb shook his head. "Not now. I'll explain more shortly." He opened the gate, offering Musa his hand to avoid an icy patch. "I promise we won't stay long."

He unlocked the door with a thick ancient key. The turn of the cylinders was a clank of metallic promise.

"There," he said.

Musa was surprised. The shadow-filled house was cozier inside than expected, given how large it appeared from the lane. Warmer too, though this made no sense for there was no cozy fireplace to offer heat. She untied her bonnet and set it atop a coat rack. The air ruffled the tiny hairs at the base of her neck, where she'd coiled her hair up into a tight knot that morning. She placed his portfolio on the table beneath the coat rack.

Seb opened a set of heavy velvet curtains with a swipe of his arms. Sunlight spilled in from a high window, illuminating a tidy entryway. The walls were covered with art. Watercolors, charcoals, oils. Seb's art, or so Musa assumed.

He offered a quick bow. "Welcome to Bexley Manor—or so my parents used to call our home."

"It's lovely . . ."

"But ramshackle, I know."

"I was going to comment on your art."

"Ah, those are early pieces." A rueful smile. "I hide them here."

He led her into the drawing room, where an ancient mantel clock ticked the hour. The room was dwarfed by a large stone fireplace taking up much of one wall. An embroidery hoop rested on a wooden stool. In another corner, a stuffed doll dressed in a gingham apron.

Evidence of his sisters, Musa decided.

As though anticipating her thoughts, Seb said, "I wish you could meet Jessica and Daphne, but alas, they're away."

Musa picked up the doll, which appeared well-loved. "They live here though."

"Yes . . . but both are now traveling south toward Nice."

"That sounds lovely."

"It would be under different circumstances."

Different circumstances. What does that mean?

Musa was tempted to question further, but Seb had already moved deeper into the house.

"This way, if you please . . ."

She followed him. The drawing room lead into a dining room. He pointed to a darkened corner of the lime-washed wall. "You can see where the plaster is water-logged. Every time it rains or snows . . . well, you can imagine what happens."

"I understand. We have similar problems in our home."

"The joys of strained finances," he said, his face clouding. "My parents . . . let's just say they didn't leave as much as we'd expected when they passed. But that matters naught compared to other losses. It was quite a blow when they passed. We were close." A pause. "Scarlet fever. It was very sudden."

"How awful. I'm sorry." She'd known his parents had died, but not the cause. What a shock it must have been!

He stared out the window, a faraway air to his gaze. "As awful as it was, it could have been worse. My youngest sister Jessica . . . she nearly died of it."

"She's better now?"

He didn't answer her question. Instead: "This way is the kitchen. You can see it hasn't changed in probably a century. The oven especially is a terror to use. My sister Daphne—"

"The one I nearly met."

"Or would have if you hadn't rushed out." At last, a teasing tone returned to his voice. "If it's an assurance to you, I told her you were my book collaborator, not my lover."

Lover. No one had ever referred to Musa as such in her life. "How did she respond?"

"She said you looked formidable and smart. I told her she was correct." He pointed to the stove. "Anyway, Daphne thinks we should remove it, that it's a danger to humanity . . . but I'm tarrying. I did mean it when I promised I'd have you home by dinner, Musa. Come, there's more over here."

The kitchen led to a small windowless chamber that appeared

used for laundry, which in turn led to another wing that was wide and open and full of light. It was empty save for a small standing loom and more of Seb's art along the walls. Musa wondered if the wing had been a barn of some sort centuries earlier.

She approached one wall, which displayed a series of richly colored watercolors depicting medieval scenes. *How talented he is. Different from Papa. More emotional in a way.* For all of Neil's technical facility, his art dazzled the eye rather than moved the heart. This was true even in the later years of her father's career when he chose sentimental subjects for the sake of the family finances. There was a purity about Seb's art. A directness.

Seb said, "This room wasn't always so empty. It's where my mother used to weave. She had several looms, a standing one and a flat loom—they took up a fair amount of space. She and my sister were—well, in my sister's case, *are*—talented in the textile arts."

"Is that what Daphne does?"

"Yes. She's a gifted embroideress. She never wed—well, hasn't wed yet—because she wanted to devote herself to her craft. She's even taken on commissions from churches and manor houses. As for my mother, she made tapestries. There's a stunning set she wove for their four-poster bed. I wish I could show you them."

"Where are they now?"

"Gone." A rueful sigh. "We needed the money, as you probably surmised. The looms save for that one went first. Daphne insisted. I'd wanted to wait, but she's less sentimental than I am. Then the tapestries, though there's still a few upstairs we were too attached to let go of."

"I'm sorry."

Another sigh. "So am I. I work and I work—"

"And it's never enough," she finished.

He offered a half-smile. "You're probably the only person I'd admit this to."

"Likewise," Musa rejoined. "Families. Sisters. Houses."

"The joys of life. The responsibilities of life."

"And then there's art."

"Yes, art . . ." Seb pointed toward the high lime-washed ceiling, beyond where his paintings hung. "If you look closely, you'll see where I tried to decorate a corner in an attempt to recreate a medieval fresco. I didn't understand the correct proportion of plaster to pigment, so it faded over time."

"If I squint, I can make out some of it," Musa answered.

"I always wanted to turn this wing into a studio-gallery. A refuge for the arts, like Morris did with his Red House down the road. I considered this after my parents passed, but it wasn't possible." Seb's voice dropped. "I've never told Daphne of my dream. She'd say I was impractical, I expect, though she'd be sympathetic. I had a fantasy that if I made my reputation with my *La Dame sans Merci* canvas . . ."

"Which is why you came to London," Musa finished. "As well as to find employment on behalf of your sisters."

He nodded ruefully. "Money and art. A tricky mix." His voice grew low, urgent. "I'm the only painter in my family. My parents were puzzled by my predilection though supportive. As for my parents, once upon a time my father planned to create some sort of school. He was a scholar of classics. Taught at a public school until my birth . . . and then my parents fell in love with Bexley Manor, which they decided was suitable for a growing family."

Musa responded, "My mother's father was also a classics scholar, though he didn't teach. Greek classics especially. He spent a lot of time traveling to the islands seeking artifacts. He taught my mother the ancient languages and brought her on some of his travels, where she learned about herbs and history." A pause. "She was a very different woman before my father left for Jerusalem."

Seb took a step toward her. Close enough to touch her.

"Ah, that explains all the names in your family. Lyra, Theo, Clio. Though what of Angela?"

"Angela was christened Allegra. Her name shifted because, well, she looks like an angel." Musa rushed with warmth as Seb's eyes sought hers. "As for myself . . ."

"I know. Your name is Italian for inspiration." He brushed her hair back from her face, adjusting his red scarf about the slender column of her neck. "That's who you are, Musa-Felicity or whatever you want to call yourself. Inspiration. Cleverness. Brilliance."

His words made her throat clot with emotion. "Outside of my family, no one's ever known that in all the years of my life. Never. They've always accused me of having a frivolous name. Silly. You're the first."

He was so close now. Close enough that she could see where he'd nicked his chin shaving. Close enough that she could smell the shaving lotion he'd used. Close enough that she made out the myriad shades of blue comprising the color of his eyes. The pale scar over his brow. The pulse of his heart in the hollow of his jaw.

Seb shook his head slowly. "More fool them."

She didn't stop him when he gently pulled her spectacles off, setting them safely on a window ledge. Nor did she stop him when he unfurled the red scarf from her neck, letting it drop to the floor. He set a tentative kiss against the newly bared flesh at the base of her clavicle, as though asking permission to continue.

She knew she should remind him of the newspaper article and her purloined letters, tell him how he could help before something worse occurred. *Later,* she told herself, for now there was only Seb and his kisses and a yearning that made her bones feel liquid and her heart expand beyond her body.

"Please," she said softly.

At last his mouth took possession of hers.

CHAPTER 30

You should not be kissing her, Seb scolded himself. *You should be offering help in regards to that blasted article. Reassurance.* Worse, her tirade still rang in his ears. *"If I ever find out who stole those letters, I'll never forgive them . . . If it's anyone I know, I'll never speak to them again . . ."*

But there he was with Musa Bartham in his arms and she smelled so good, tasted so good, felt so good, God save him. Like she belonged there forever with him. And she was willing. Oh so willing. Her mouth opened beneath his, their tongues lacing and tasting each other as though they'd devour each other if they could.

When he'd brought her to his home, he'd never intended this to occur . . . but he should have known better. He loved her, though he doubted she felt likewise. He desired her—those two weeks they'd been separated had seemed the longest of his life. He'd been a fool to think he could bring her somewhere far from the rest of the world and wouldn't be tempted to touch her.

She let out a long sigh of wonder, shifting in his arms as they broke away. She offered a shy crooked smile. Nervous, that's what she was. He was too.

"Do you feel like you're kissing Felicity Vita?" she asked, caressing his cheek.

He pressed his lips against the heart of her palm. "I'm not thinking of her now. Only of you, Musa of the inspiration."

And that was the truth . . . though the truth was more complicated than she had any idea.

Tell her, he commanded himself. *Before you lose courage.*

After all, he'd wanted her to see the life he led, so she'd understand the situation he found himself entrapped within. Wasn't this why he'd brought her to Bexley Manor in the first place? But then her arms curled around him and he found himself lifting her warm body against his—he'd grown strong in his months working at Chassen & Sons—and he couldn't confess the truth. Not yet. He wanted her so badly. Desperately.

This is so wrong. Yet it feels so right.

How luxurious she felt against him. Glorious. Beautiful.

She was trembling. So was he.

"Why have you brought me here?" she asked, her voice low and insistent. "You said it was to understand you, but I sense there's more. Something that will distress me. Does it have to do with that article? My letters?"

He inhaled deeply to calm himself. He couldn't speak of those. Not yet. But he would. He had to.

"I'm going away, Musa. Leaving London."

"For good?" The color drained from her cheeks. She blinked. Her eyes were misty in that dear, sharp face of hers. That face that haunted his art. His dreams.

"For now. It all depends."

"Depends on what?"

His eyes stung, damn them. "I can't speak fully of this yet."

She struggled from his arms. All the better to meet his gaze.

"But what of our book?"

"I can't be at your great-aunt's ball, if that's what you mean. But you have the final illustrations, so that's settled. You'll have your book to support your family."

"Oh. So much for being book collaborators." Her tone was bitter.

"Well, we are collaborators. Or, I should say, *were* now the book is finished."

She found her way to the wooden bench nearest them as though she had a blow. As she settled onto the bench, her skirts crinkled about her ankles. Even here in private, there was a primness about her . . . but he knew better.

"Was it something I did, Seb? Because I came to you like a madwoman that night?"

He couldn't bear it. Didn't she realize this had been the most wonderful night of his life, for all its peculiarity? "It's my sisters. Well, my sister, Jessica . . ."

And then he told her the reason Daphne had unexpectedly shown at his door that day—a reason he could barely vocalize out of fear.

Jessica had taken ill anew shortly before they had a chance to consult with the pediatric cardiologist. She ended up in hospital, where the pediatric cardiologist finally examined her; Seb had been stunned how frail his youngest sister looked, though she'd tried to put a good face on it. Once her condition stabilized, the cardiologist urged they send Jessica to recover by the sea for six months or longer. Someplace in the south of France, where the sun remained warm and the breezes gentle.

Someplace that cost far more money than Seb was able to scrap together from his scant savings, the advance payments for their children's book, and the few paintings he managed to sell on such short notice.

He didn't tell Musa where the rest of the money for Jessica's travels came from: he'd sold six letters to the newspaper. Felicity's letters. Only a small fraction out of those Luke had stolen—Seb had chosen the least damning and personal ones.

When Seb agreed to the deal, Luke assured Seb he'd use the scrap of poetry he found to authenticate the letters as Felicity's; this would protect Musa from exposure. Luke also promised to never reveal Musa's connection to the poetess of love. This offered Seb scant comfort, but what choice did he have?

His sister's life for a heart. Musa's heart.

"Will your sister improve?" Musa asked, her eyes wide with concern. To his relief, she hadn't asked how he'd obtained the funds to pay for the travels; if she had, he'd have no choice but to reveal the truth.

"I've been assured she will, but it may take some months. Daphne is traveling with Jessica to Nice now. It's best I join them until she improves. I couldn't stand if anything were to happen and I wasn't there."

"I understand," was all Musa said. "And now I understand you."

But you don't understand everything. Once he told her the truth about the letters, she'd know no one else could harm her. That she was protected, or as much as she could possibly be under such circumstances. Perhaps this would bring her peace of mind even if she hated him for his betrayal . . . especially once she learned he'd written to her under the guise of Henry Whitney.

She'll never forgive me.

"So this is the last time we'll see each other," she said, her voice catching.

"At least for some months, I expect."

In the distance, he heard a bluejay. A crow.

Tell her, Seb. Tell her everything.

He couldn't. Not yet. He wanted this moment, this hour, to stretch into eternity. This one perfect memory before everything was blasted between them.

"If we've only this one day," she said in a quavering voice, "I want you to show me the rest of your house." A long breath. "Upstairs."

Seb forced himself to say, "Musa, if I take you upstairs, I suspect you're not interested in viewing what remains of my mother's tapestries."

She stepped into his arms. "We only have this one day, Seb."

Seb's mind reeled, understanding her implication. "But we were to share only one night together. Wasn't that what you said?"

"That was a night with Felicity Vita. Now you need a day with me."

She kissed his jaw, her breath warm against his ear. In response, he felt himself thicken, god help him. Stiffen. She must have sensed as much, for she shifted in his arms.

"Oh," she whispered, eyes wide. "You're aroused."

He swallowed hard. "Painfully so. In case you didn't realize it, you're an extremely desirable woman."

A woman I love beyond all others. A woman I've undermined in ways I can't confess. Not yet.

"And you are an extremely desirable man, Sebastian Atkinson. I know this seems sudden. I can't explain it, but I feel as though I've known you for so much longer than I have." She gave a little laugh. "When my mother and father met, that's how they felt. Strange, isn't it?"

"Not so strange." This, at least, was not a lie.

She nodded in the direction of the stairway. "Take me upstairs."

"Are you certain?"

She offered a slow smile. A nervous smile. She was anxious. He was too. But she nodded.

Seb's mouth grew dry. His heart pounded. "I must tell you something first, Musa—"

She set her fingers against his lips, as she had that morning outside Chassen & Sons only two weeks earlier.

"Shush," she said.

This time her hands were ungloved, just as he'd fantasized after reading her letter. Her skin was warm despite the cool air, for they'd still not lit a fire in that abandoned ramshackle house that held all of Seb's losses and memories and hopes.

Before he could think twice, he found himself drawing her fingers one at a time into his mouth just as he'd yearned to so many times. Licking them. Sucking them as though they were the most delectable meal he'd ever tasted. And she *was* delectable. Didn't he already know this from when they'd slept together?

She shuddered. Her eyes widened as she let out a long breath. That beauty mark, the one just below her bottom lip, lifted as her smile widened. He always found it particularly fetching.

She took his hand in hers. Set his fingers against her mouth.

Her tongue flashed between her ripe, red lips as she licked his thumb.

His knees buckled. Desire. That's all he was made of. It felt like light, dazzling brilliance, rushing through his veins. His muscles. Toward his extremities . . . most of all, toward the one between his thighs.

All of a sudden any anxiety he'd sensed in her appeared to flee. And then they were racing up the stairs, him after her—or as fast as he could with a swollen cock. Her teasing laughter floated above him, leading him forward.

"Catch me!" she called. "This way!"

The stairway twisted and turned toward the landing. She was so swift. So eager.

He found her in the first bedroom past the top of the stairs. A room that hadn't been used since his parents' death; the room his parents had shared as husband and wife all those years. How different the room now appeared, stripped of everything but a solitary bed curtained in damask and draped in white linens—Daphne had removed anything that might have given it individuality.

It could have been any bed anywhere. Not a bed from Seb's past . . . for it was now a bed where Musa Bartham lay, appearing like a goddess to his besotted eyes.

Musa of the musical, inspiring name; Musa, who'd written him all those letters under the guise of Felicity Vita.

Musa, whom he loved beyond reason.

Musa, whom he'd betrayed.

CHAPTER 31

Musa awaited him on the bed with her arms wide open. Seb settled beside her, his heart still pounding like a drum. The sheets were scented with lavender. Fresh. New. Cool from the winter air despite the sun spilling along their ivory surface. He had the sense the bed was waiting for him, for her, for their bodies. A place of sanctuary apart from the rest of the world.

She reached for him, pulling him down beside her, laughing. Then she settled on top of him, squatting across his lap. In control, as he knew she liked to be.

A mischievous smile spread across her lips.

"That's better. You're exactly where I want you, Sebastian Atkinson."

"Am I?" he teased in return. However, the voice in the back of his head was far less blithe.

I should not be doing this. He should lead her from the bed, return her downstairs, continue to explain why he'd brought her to his family home, where his sisters were absent because they were traveling to a place where the sun still reigned. He couldn't. Not yet, especially as he took in her smile taunting him to kiss her again.

And again . . .

As they kissed, she slid herself between his thighs, the skirts of her simple blue wool gown surrounding his legs. All her petticoats and folds and yards of fabric. He resisted the urge to rub his erection against her like a lust-filled animal. To take his pleasure despite the layers of clothing separating their bodies from each other.

I'm going to be damned for this unless we stop.

He pulled away. "I think we've gone as far as we should."

She kissed his forehead as though she was bestowing a benediction. "You look so serious!"

"This is very serious," he murmured, drawing a breath in an attempt to control his arousal. "You do know that?"

"I know." She swallowed hard, her eyes meeting his. "This is the most impractical thing I've ever done. Unwise."

"The same for me . . . and we should stop." Another kiss, one he couldn't bear to end. How alluring she felt! How delectable!

"Don't stop," she breathed.

God help me, I can't resist her.

In a ragged voice, he proclaimed, "If we only have this one day, I shall make it perfect for you."

And then he silenced the voices within him. Or tried to.

He strained to kiss her neck. The base of her chin, below her beauty mark. The tender flesh of her ear, which he bit gently before releasing it.

When he pulled away at last, she offered a gasp of yearning.

"More," she murmured. "Now."

She raised her hips against his hand, pressing against him despite the layers of skirts, petticoats. Sighing and making sweet little moaning sounds. He couldn't bear it. She began to untie his cravat. Unbutton his shirt. He shivered in the cool air, but didn't dare stop her. His skin prickled with gooseflesh.

She swept a warm hand over him. Caressing him. She set a line of butterfly kisses along his chest.

Once she'd reached his neck, she tugged his shirt from his shoulders. Her eyes were dark with desire. So trusting. So eager.

"I want to see you, Seb. All of you."

Another surge of guilt pulled at him, but he was too far gone.

"Are you certain?"

She nodded, catching the soft flesh of her lip between her teeth.

He'd never undressed so quickly in all his life. He slid from the bed, removing his boots, unbuttoning the fall of his trousers, letting the garments drop to the floor. There was no art to his undressing, no teasing. Just pure need to fulfill whatever she requested. Perhaps he feared she'd change her mind. Or perhaps he feared he'd change his.

He watched her eyes widen. The long breath she emitted.

"I had no idea, for all my research. I mean, I've seen illustrations but . . . Are they all like that?"

Seb laughed, startled. "I wouldn't know personally."

"Nor I." She tilted her head, looking rather wicked as she contemplated him. "Can I touch it?"

He let out another burst of laughter. Surprise. "I'd be delighted."

"It's my turn to bring you pleasure," she murmured, meeting his eyes. "As you did for me that night. Please?"

A tentative caress. Then bolder. Her soft fingers explored the ridge cresting his arousal, the sack beneath it. Soon he was pressing against her palm. Rocking. And then . . .

"I think that's enough, Musa of the inspiration. Unless you want me to come right now."

"I am quite curious about that. But no, not yet." Another mischievous grin. "Unless that's what you'd like."

He let out a shaky breath. "I'd rather wait, if I can. Rather take care of you first . . . that is, if you're willing to let me."

A subtle flush rose along her chest, toward her face. She slid off him, settled on the edge of the bed, offering the back of her bodice. She offered a nervous glance over her shoulder his way. An invitation.

He accepted her invitation by brushing his lips against the nape of her neck. She bent over, affording him access to the buttons lining her gown. The lacing of her stays. Once these were undone, she shrugged off the garments. Removed her boots, which she set beside each other at the foot of the bed. Unrolled her stockings and pulled the pins from her coiled hair, which fell in a luxurious hiss of dark softness.

Along her shoulders. Down her creamy back.

She stood and turned toward Seb, wearing only her chemise, which was a humble lawn garment that didn't suggest the complexity or beauty of its wearer. He could make out the pink nubs of her nipples pressing against the thin fabric. The curve of her belly. The dark curls covering her innermost secrets.

She appeared nervous yet defiant. Eager yet vulnerable. Just as he felt.

She pulled the chemise over her head, revealing her entirety to his eyes.

She was glorious. A Venus. All he'd ever imagined. All he'd ever desired.

Seb's breath caught at the back of his throat.

"So beautiful," he murmured. "Come closer."

She joined him anew on the bed, her body beside his. Side by side. Eye to eye. Chest to chest. Her nipples pressed against him, taut. Aroused . . . just as he was.

"It's cold in here," she whispered, snuggling closer, "but you're so warm."

"As are you, darling." He'd never called her this before; somehow the endearment sprang to his lips. "Here. Is this better?"

He set the blankets over them. As he did so, he brushed his lips along her shoulders. Her breasts. And then he sucked her right nipple into his mouth. Laving it. Taunting it until it pebbled beneath his tongue, before turning to her other breast. Her breasts were just as he'd envisioned that first night when she'd come to him, asking him to pretend she was Felicity Vita. The perfect shape and size for his palms. For his mouth.

"Oh," she moaned as his attentions grew. "I don't think I can bear this much longer . . . " a deep breath ". . . but I shall endeavor."

Seb felt a chuckle rise from his chest. "I hope you will more than endeavor, darling."

"And what about you?" She caressed his erection. "Surely there's more I can do here."

"Not yet. Soon . . ."

He reached beneath the covers toward the thick curls cresting her cleft. Gently tucked a finger inside her warmth.

So wet. She desired him. Well, he desired her more than he'd known to be possible.

Another low moan. She pressed against him, offering him all the encouragement needed to insert a second finger. She was so tight. So eager. Well, there were other things they could do that didn't involve deflowering her or risk leaving her with child.

And so he did.

As he slid his fingers in and out of her, her thighs spread to allow him greater access. Her hips buckled and rose to meet him especially once he stroked his thumb against her clit. She gasped, she moaned. He watched her eyes shut, her mouth curl into a rosebud of yearning. How desirable she was. How enticing. It took all his control not to roll on top of her and press into her tight chasm. To take his pleasure. He'd never felt so drawn to someone in this manner before . . . but then again, he'd never loved another as he loved her.

"Sweet heaven," she whispered, shuddering and tightening as he slowed and then sped. Teasing her. Leading her. "I-I can't bear it . . ."

"You can," he breathed against her ear.

"More," she gasped.

All of a sudden she buckled against the mattress, her legs taut and shaking. He felt her spasm against his hand. Release. And then she sighed. Laughed. And with this, he came too—he couldn't have stopped himself even if he wanted to. He'd barely time to turn from her to spill against the sheets.

Once their hearts calmed, he embraced her and tenderly pressed his lips against her forehead. But this wasn't enough for her. She leaned over and gave him the most enthusiastic kiss he'd ever received in his life.

Once they broke away, she said, "That . . . was . . . astonishing. Amazing."

"I know," he agreed. "Because you're amazing in so many ways."

And I love you.

Already he was starting to harden again. Such was her effect on him. She must have noticed, for she settled on top of him anew, just north of his hips. Her moist pink loveliness against his stomach, where his erection strained for her.

She leaned against him, her mouth hot against his ear, her breasts pressed against his chest.

"I want you to take me, Seb. Now."

This Seb had not expected. With this, all of his scruples returned in a rush. His guilt.

"You do know what you're saying, Musa."

"I do." A wide smile, so trusting. So eager. How it tore at his heart. "I don't expect anything of you, Seb—I know I'm a Bartham, and Barthams don't wed . . . well, it's unlikely though I know Angela will in time. Or I hope so." She drew a deep breath. "But I *do* want you. Badly. And not out of carnal curiosity—well, maybe a little—but because I-I—"

She broke off, confusion clouding her expression. Emotion. Desire. Yearning.

And then Seb knew without a doubt she loved him just as he loved her. Which made what he'd done in selling her letters all the more awful.

"Will you?" she asked.

With this, everything he'd done returned to Seb a hundred-fold, along with her vow. *"If I ever find out who stole those letters . . . If it's anyone I know, I'll never speak to them again . . ."*

It took Seb all of his self-control to extract himself from beneath her warm eager body. To resist accepting her offer, which was all he'd ever dreamed of since first writing to Felicity Vita over a year earlier.

He tried to say the words he knew he should. He formulated

them in his brain. Pushed them toward his tongue. But what came out of his mouth was this:

"You, Musa Bartham, are the most amazing woman I've ever met. Talented. Courageous. Beautiful. Loyal. Clever. Even if I live to be a hundred years old, I will never ever forget this day with you." He forced a smile. "Or any other encounter I've had with you, whether it be you showing up dressed in pink lace in the middle of the night, dropping my art in a puddle, writing your god-forsaken children's book, or nursing my fever."

"Someone had to take care of you," she jested in a half-hearted manner.

"And I'm grateful you did, Musa. So very much. But—" he brushed a tendril of hair from her forehead "—we both know what's best."

She laughed, disbelieving. "Best for who?"

He forced himself to say the words. "Best for you."

Her eyes pooled ever so briefly. Vulnerable, that's how she felt. Rejected. And it was all his fault.

"You're turning me away then?"

"No, I'm refusing the circumstances, Musa. I'm about to leave the country for heaven knows how long—I have no idea how many months I'll be in Nice. I'm not going to make love to you, then abandon you . . . and there are things you don't know about me." Emotion clotted his voice. "Things I've done."

Things I should confess though you'll hate me.

"I'm certain whatever you did couldn't be that bad," she countered, her gaze meeting his. Questioning. An uneasy laugh. "It's not as though you pretended to be Felicity Vita or something."

Seb didn't trust himself to speak.

A moment passed. Another.

"What have you done? You're frightening me, Seb."

"Nothing I can talk of now." How ineffectual his words sounded.

"Have you wife somewhere? A sweetheart?"

"Lord, no! I told you there's no one else. Only you, darling."

"Did you tell someone I'm was Felicity Vita?"

"No." A slender truth. He'd only informed Luke of his suspicion, not her confession.

"Yet you don't trust me enough to tell me your secret."

"It's not that . . ."

Just tell her. She'd hate him, but at least she'd know the truth, which would bring her some reassurance. But how to begin? He considered various openings that never found their way to his tongue. The possibilities ranged from "I've been writing you as Henry all these months, sorry I failed to mention it" to "I sold the letters you wrote me as Felicity Vita, but don't worry it will all work out."

But none of these would lead to what he most desired: Musa unscathed. Musa forgiving him. Musa still loving him.

Coward.

"I feel a fool," she choked out, shifting away from him. "One minute we were making love, or about to. The next, well, I don't understand what happened." She pulled her clothes off the bed. On went the chemise, cloaking her lovely body from his view. Her stockings, her boots, which she shoved onto her feet. "I should go home."

He drew a deep breath to calm himself. "No matter what, I'm grateful you came here today, Musa—truly I am! But before you go, I've something I need to tell you."

She whirled to face him, her hazel eyes pooling with emotion. "What would that be?"

"Believe it or not, I'm desperately in love with you."

CHAPTER 32

"So he told you he loved you? And then let you leave without confessing what his bloody secret was?" Mary Nicholson whispered, her head curled in toward Musa's. "I don't believe him!"

"Well, we didn't leave immediately," Musa answered, her voice just as low. "And not just loved me. *Desperately* loved me."

It had taken Musa three days after her visit to Kent to bring Seb's illustrations to Persephone Press—three long days she'd spent alone in her room, astonished by the depth of her distress over what had occurred between them. To her family, she claimed exhaustion after finishing *Poems of Morality and Goodness for Children to Abide*. To herself, she claimed she was furious with Seb.

Not sorrowful.

Not vulnerable.

Not heartsick.

Even then, she knew she was lying. Try as she might, she couldn't banish the memory of his deep blue eyes darkening with desire. The sight of his aroused body. The intimacies they'd shared . . . until it all turned so awkward and awful and he told her he desperately loved her.

But now there was something else weighing Musa besides Seb

and his mysterious secret and his travels to Nice with his sisters. Something she'd tried to set out of her mind as much as she could.

Musa glanced toward the closed door of the back office of Persephone Press, fearing someone overhearing their conversation. In particular, the American heiress who had taken over running the publishing house with an iron fist. Amanda Seeley of the Seeleys of Boston.

Thus far, Musa had only caught glimpses of Miss Seeley. She appeared very formidable in her smartly tailored day suits, which were sewn of a twill fabric such as a gentleman would wear. Even Mary's father seemed intimidated; Musa had come upon Mr. Nicholson uncharacteristically bumbling about the office one morning. Rumor held Miss Seeley had a sweetheart in London, which was why she'd been so eager to leave Boston behind.

"Don't worry, no one's going to interrupt us," Mary assured. "The American is away for lunch, along with everyone else. No one will return for at least another half-hour. Though I should warn you she asked about you. She noticed you the last time you stopped by."

"What sort of questions did she ask?" In a strange way, Musa was grateful for something else to fret about.

"Who you were, how I know you. I told her you were one of our authors." Mary shrugged. "I suppose I should have introduced you, but I didn't want to subject you to her nosiness."

Musa's stomach tightened. "She doesn't suspect I'm Felicity?"

Mary shook her head. "She's a suspicious sort, that's all." She bit into a square lemon biscuit after offering one to Musa. Musa inhaled the sharp citrus scent but refused.

"So if you didn't leave immediately, what happened after this, Musa? Did you take tea or something?"

It figured Mary would think of food. "No tea, though my stomach was growling. We dressed ourselves and walked to the train station and waited for the train." Reluctantly: "I refused to let him sit with me because I felt so hurt. So rejected. It was very awkward, especially since I had his portfolio with the book illustrations. It was like I was still connected to him, yet not."

Awkward is an understatement. Heartbreaking would be more accurate.

But she'd never admit this, not even to Mary. She could barely admit it to herself.

So this is what it feels like to be heartbroken.

Musa shifted in her seat. Even now, days after she and Sebastian Atkinson ravished each other in his family home, her body still felt exquisitely attended. Adored. She wished she didn't, for it reminded her too much of what happened between them.

Or rather, what *didn't* happen, but nearly had. Especially now that she knew he loved her.

But do you love him?

To her shock, Musa felt her eyes sting at the question. *It no longer matters,* she firmly told herself. Anyway, he'd refused to confide whatever was bothering him—that alone was reason to avoid Seb. She prayed it had nothing to do with his friend, Luke Ward, who'd interviewed them about their children's book. The journalist seemed eager but honorable. Still, it would have been wiser to refuse, given her parents' history with the press.

"I'm sorry it came to this, my friend," Mary soothed, finishing off her biscuit and taking another for her lunch. "I can tell you're sad. And I don't think it's about his secret—"

"I'm fine, really!" Musa protested too eagerly. "Sebastian Atkinson was just a dalliance. Truly. In time, I'll look back and laugh."

"Just as well really. You don't want to marry. Nor have I ever heard you mention wanting a lover."

Musa's voice caught to her shame. "It's not that I don't want to love someone. It's improbable. After all, I'm a Bartham, though I suspect Angela's fate will work out."

That morning, Angela reported two more bouquets of flowers had arrived, encouraged by Aunt Minerva's meddling and the Countess of Sunderland's anxiety. Poor Sunny had taken to showing up at the Barthams every few days to inquire about Musa's book's progress; Musa understood he was really fishing to find out who was courting Angela.

Mary shrugged, biscuit in hand. "You know what I think about marriage. A form of unpaid employment that has little to do with the heart." She tilted her head toward Seb's portfolio containing the ink drawings for *Poems of Morality and Goodness for Children to Abide.* "I must admit his illustrations are stunning. They'll be easy to engrave. Clear lines, compositions not too complicated. They'll print well."

"Yes, damn it. He's a talented conundrum," Musa agreed. "The important thing is the book is finished and will be printed and all will be well for my family and Angela. As for Sebastian Atkinson, I doubt I'll ever see him again. He told me he won't be at my great-aunt's ball. He'll be on the continent for at least the next few months with his sisters."

Mary's brow crinkled. "Here's a thought. After you confessed to Atkinson you were Felicity Vita, did you tell him about Henry? Perhaps Atkinson was jealous. That's why he acted so strangely."

"I wondered that myself. But I did tell him I'd broken things off with Henry . . . which is for the best, considering those letters."

Letters that had yet to appear in the newspaper, thankfully. No one could prove the provenance of them, according to the last article Musa read in *The Greater London Gazette.* There'd been a rumor someone found a poetry draft of Felicity's, but it hadn't been enough evidence. Musa prayed this continued to be so, especially since a week earlier a newspaper editor had approached Persephone Press requesting a sample of Felicity's handwriting. Mary promptly refused with a few choice phrases.

"I'm still convinced Henry sold those letters," Mary said.

"But Henry did write to warn me someone meant Felicity harm. That proves otherwise, don't you think?"

Musa tried to hold on to the logic of this response. Oh, none of it made any sense! She'd adored Henry—well, as much as you can adore someone you only know through a pile of letters. And now he was gone, along with Seb. Her eyes prickled with heat.

That'll teach me to give way to emotion. And a pair of sea-blue eyes.

To distract herself from her recriminations, Musa finally accepted a biscuit from Mary. She bit into it. The sharp lemon tang was bracing. Exactly what she needed.

"You're too trusting, Musa. You put yourself at risk by writing Henry."

"I know, I know—you've said this before." Another bite of lemon shortbread. "However, there's something I realized last night. In some ways, Seb reminds me of Henry, though this makes no sense. There's something about those letters Henry wrote me, an eagerness and emotionalism. A vulnerability. Like Seb." Musa pursed her lips. "Again, this is illogical."

Mary laughed. "Could you imagine if Seb was Henry? Maybe that's his secret."

"Impossible. Far-fetched. That's the stuff of romance novels, not life."

"Well, both were obsessed with Felicity."

Musa rolled her eyes. "A lot of people are obsessed with Felicity—that's what got me into this mess in the first place."

"I suppose. Where are Henry's letters now?"

"Burned. For the best."

As Musa said this, her heart panged with more than disappointment. Grief, that's what she felt. Henry's letters had opened her heart in a way she'd never expected. As for Seb . . .

Admit it: you loved him. That's why you're so devastated.

Musa considered her parents, how their all-consuming passion undermined every corner of their lives. It propelled them to thumb their noses at society, scandalize London, and ruin their children's prospects. As a result, her father had most likely lost his life in his quest to repair their family's reputation, which led to her mother lying in her bed for months—no, *years*—in mourning with her rumpled negligees and herbal remedies.

It's for the best Seb is gone, she told herself. *Soon I will be as I once was. Logical, practical, in control.* As for Henry, Musa strangely felt no desire to write him. She knew she should send a last letter requesting he destroy any remaining correspondence. But how safe was this even?

Mary said in a bright tone designed to distract, "By the way I received my ball invitation this morning! I hadn't realized the date is just over six weeks away—February's gone so fast. Your great-aunt is really making a splash. Engraved type, gold foil. Fancy. I forgot it's a costume ball. What are you dressing as?"

Musa rolled her eyes. "Certainly not Felicity Vita."

"I shall go as a bluestocking. All I have to do is borrow your spectacles," Mary replied cheekily. "We should sell a lot of books that night. I've already had to increase the first printing, thanks to Mr. Ward's articles. Even the American is pleased."

Musa breathed, "That is good news!"

"Yes, though I question where to send Mr. Atkinson's share of the proceeds, now that he's gone. Ah well!"

The sound of footsteps outside the office door. Sharp, high-heeled, and staccato.

"The American," Mary whispered. "She's back. I can always tell by her step. She walks so quickly! It's unnatural."

The door to the back office opened without preamble. A petite woman of no more than thirty years of age offered a tight smile from the threshold. She wore an enormous turquoise hat with more feathers and flowers than appeared possible; Musa couldn't imagine how it remained on her head without slipping. Beneath the hat, the woman's face had fine features but a sharp nose. She was scented with strong French perfume. Expensive, just as her hat and twill day suit seemed to be. She was accompanied by a well-dressed gentleman of distinguished appearance, who hung behind in the hallway before bidding a sheepish farewell. Her sweetheart, Musa supposed.

"Miss Nicholson!" Amanda Seeley said in a strange nasal

accent that sounded pleasant but really wasn't. "I thought you to be in the front office during lunch."

Mary brushed biscuit crumbs from her lap. "I've an author here, Miss Seeley. Miss Musa Bartham, who wrote the children's book *Poems of Morality and Goodness for Children to Abide*. We were going over the illustrations, which are ready for the engraver. I think you'll be delighted with them."

Miss Seeley offered her gloved hand to shake Musa's. "At last we meet! I've seen you about the office."

Mary interjected, "My apologies for not introducing you earlier."

Musa rose for the door. "A pleasure, Miss Seeley. I'm sure we'll speak again."

Miss Seeley gave Musa an appraising look. "You're a decidedly better class of author than that Felicity Vita hoyden." She slammed down a *Greater London Gazette* onto Mary's desk. "Have you seen this yet? It just came out this afternoon—it's a matter of hours before *The Times* follows suit. I trust you've destroyed whatever books of hers remained in the warehouse."

This time the newspaper article was above the fold, but the font size wasn't large. However, the headline was far, far worse than Musa anticipated.

LUST! LONGING! LETTERS!
Love Poetess's Secret Life Revealed

Musa blinked. *It cannot be.*

It was.

"I thought they weren't able to authenticate the letters?" Mary asked in a faint voice.

Miss Seeley's eyes widened beneath her huge hat. "You won't believe this. Someone managed to obtain Felicity Vita's manuscript fair copies from the printer up north—it's all in the article. It's most shocking!"

"*Merde*," Musa whispered.

CHAPTER 33

"Shit," Seb muttered, glaring at that morning's *The Greater London Gazette*, where a headline proclaiming *LUST! LONGING! LETTERS!* shouted from the front page. He'd stopped by Chassen & Sons to obtain his last paycheck before leaving for France to meet his sisters. The day's newspapers were displayed on a long oak table outside the accountant's office as though it were any other day.

But it wasn't any other day. It was a day in which Seb's worst fears had come to pass.

There, for all the world to see, were the words Musa had mailed him under the *nom de plume* of Felicity Vita. Kind words he'd cherished for so many months in the privacy of his studio. Loving words. Taken out of context, there was nothing damning in those letters. Nothing to titillate. But the newspaper had provided plenty of tawdry insinuations to serve as food for those ravenous for scandal.

Seb tried to read on, but couldn't without feeling sick to his stomach. Anyway, what he'd seen confirmed his suspicions: Luke hadn't kept his word. So much for his vows of loyalty and friendship over ambition. Seb shouldn't have trusted him—but what choice did he have?

Luke promised only the letters would be revealed, not this ugly editorializing that teased sordid suppositions. On top of that, Seb had taken hope the letters wouldn't be published after all—the last article he read stated Luke's scrap of poetry wasn't enough to authenticate their author.

As for now, Seb couldn't imagine how Musa would respond to the article. He wished he could run to her, assure her all would be well, but there was no time—his train to Dover was in just over two hours. Daphne's last letter urged him to come as soon as possible. If he didn't make the train, he'd miss the ferry to Calais he'd booked. Anyway, what good would it do?

As for Luke, Seb knew what he had to do—and there was just enough time for that.

Newspaper still in hand, Seb strode down the long halls of Chassen & Sons toward the pressroom, not even waiting for the accountant to return with his pay. He shoved the double doors open.

The pressroom was filled with the usual clatter of conversation and activity. Seb pressed his way into it, feeling possessed. There was Luke, laughing with one of their friends at a worktable. Was that a new hat he was wearing? It was a deep peacock blue with a matching feather tucked in its band. No doubt it had been bought with whatever additional resources Luke earned betraying Musa.

"You! Blackguard!" Seb shouted. "Liar!"

And then he slammed his fist into Luke's cheerful face before his erstwhile friend could sputter even a word of greeting.

Luke's eyes widened with shock. He shoved him away.

"What the hell are you doing, Sebastian?"

"You know what and why. You lied to me!" Seb threw the newspaper at Luke. "You betrayed her!"

"Calm down, Seb! I did no such thing!"

Seb grabbed Luke by his collar. "Liar!"

"Ow! Stop! Let me explain!"

A circle of workers collected about the two men, shouting out encouragement. "Fight! Fight! Fight!" As though from a distance,

Seb even heard someone offer to take stakes. "I'll raise you half a crown on Ward!" "I think they're fighting over a woman," another shouted. "Oooh! I'd bet on Atkinson!"

Instead of cooling Seb's temper, their attention only inflamed it. He felt overcome by a fury he hadn't known himself capable of, one that seemed to encompass every regret and disappointment and insult he'd ever experienced. This anger flowed through his veins, intoxicating him. It made everything appear sharp, sparkling, as though viewed through a light-flooded magnifying glass. And in that moment, everything wrong in his life seemed to be caused by Luke—Luke who lied when he promised to protect Musa after Seb agreed to sell her letters. *"I'm your friend,"* Luke claimed. *"I only have your best interests at heart."* Seb had entrusted him to value friendship over ambition, truth over sensationalism. He'd been wrong—but not as wrong as Luke proved himself to be.

Seb raised another fist to pummel him. But before he could inflict further violence on Luke, someone pulled Seb away. Tall Bob, the strongest pressman on the floor. "Atkinson, what the hell is wrong with you?" And then Seb was on his back, looking up toward the pressed tin ceiling, Luke's face towering over him; a trail of blood trickled from his friend's nose. Part of Seb felt horrified at the damage he'd done, the other part of him deeply assuaged.

"Apologize, Atkinson!" Tall Bob demanded. "Now!"

"No," Seb muttered. "He lied."

"You asshole." Luke sniffed, holding his handkerchief to his seeping nose. "I didn't lie to you." To Tall Bob and the other pressmen, who were milling about in various stages of confusion: "It's fine. I'll talk sense into him. Get back to work."

Luke offered Seb his hand. Before Seb could refuse, Luke pulled him to his feet and dragged him into a private office. He locked the door and shoved his friend into a chair.

"What the hell got into you?" Luke asked, searching his handkerchief for a clean corner. "I thought you were in France, not lurking about here."

"I was on my way," Seb replied. "You deserve worse! You

promised me she wouldn't be raked through the mud! How could you let this happen?"

Luke threw the newspaper at Seb's chest. "I had nothing to do with this article. Nothing! Yes, things got out of control with the Felicity Vita situation, but it wasn't because of me. I may be a rogue at times, but I'm not dishonest."

"Who else could have authenticated those letters?"

"Not me! If you were to read the entire article instead of pummeling me like a bareknuckle pugilist, you'd know someone managed to obtain Felicity Vita's fair copies from her printer in Hampstead—that's how they authenticated those letters. I didn't write that article. Hell, I didn't even know about it until it was printed."

"Really?" Seb rubbed his hands, which had bruised along the knuckles.

"Really. I refused to let the *Gazette* use that poem to verify her letters—I gave them some nonsense I wrote myself. Yes, I took a risk they'd demand their payment returned. But I figured they'd be too eager for a story to bother."

Seb blinked. "You did that?"

"Indeed I did." Luke wiped at his nose anew; the blood had finally slowed. "But that's when the newspaper hired someone else to step in."

Seb demanded, "Who? Tall Bob? Joseph?"

Luke shrugged. "I've no idea. I may be hungry for a story, but I'm not about to ruin a woman's life even if she's a Bartham."

"That's a change of pace!" Seb threw up his hands. "Before you were all 'Oh she's a Bartham, she's used to scandal, who cares?' Tell me, what made you change your mind? Suddenly you acquired morals? Or perhaps you found a better way to score some tin?"

Luke's words came slowly. "I've had time to think the past few days."

"About other ways to make money? To lie to friends?"

"Believe it or not, I really did have your best interests in mind."

Luke's voice dropped. "I could tell you were in love with her. It was plain as day."

Seb flinched as though he'd been slapped. "That's not important."

"Isn't it though? You'll be shocked to learn your mooning over her actually moved my stony heart. It inspired me to find out more about the Barthams beyond the usual gossip."

"Really?"

Luke nodded as solemnly as he could considering he'd a bloody nose. "Thought it could make a good article. A responsible article, not the rubbish you just read. I knew the father was missing, but not the circumstances. I sent inquiries out to a journalist I know in Jerusalem. So far, no luck. But soon, I hope."

Seb was shocked into silence.

"I'm going to leave now," Luke said, unlocking the door, "before you decide to punch me again. Or I decide to punch you."

"Sorry about that," Seb grunted. "Truly. I was wrong."

"Yes, you were wrong. It's a good thing I'm your friend because if I was your foe, you'd really be in trouble." Luke pointed to the newspaper. "If you love Musa Bartham as I believe you do, why don't you grant her peace of mind? Tell her the truth before you flee the country. Send her a letter. Let her know you didn't completely sell her down the river."

Seb choked out, "She'll hate me forever."

"Perhaps that's what you deserve then." Luke opened the desk drawer. "Everything you need is in there, Mr. Henry Whitney. Get writing."

Luke slammed the door behind him without a farewell, leaving Seb alone with his bruised hands and his remorse.

He's right, damn it. She deserves the truth.

Seb glanced up at the clock on the wall.

Just over an hour and a half until my train.

Seb looked down at the desk drawer, which contained pen, ink, and paper.

His letter spilled out quickly, more words than Seb ever imagined possible in so short a period—after all, he was an artist, not a writer. He hadn't time to labor over each sentence or phrase, as he would when writing her under the guise of Henry. Not if he wanted to reach her before he left the country.

He began:

> *My dearest darling Musa,*
>
> *I suspect you will recognize the hand penning this letter . . .*

CHAPTER 34

My dearest darling Musa,

I suspect you will recognize the hand penning this letter—a hand belonging to your correspondent Henry Whitney. It is also a hand that belongs to me, Seb Atkinson. For you, my beloved darling, are not the only one with a secret nom de plume.

Now that I have stunned you, I will reveal everything as best I can. It's the least I can do after the mess I've made.

When I first wrote to you as Felicity Vita over a year ago, I chose to use a nom de plume for reasons I still don't understand. Perhaps it was a desire to separate the life of my heart from the acclaim I desired as a painter. Or perhaps it was that I felt vulnerable baring my tenderest emotions to a poetess I only knew through her books. However, after much thought, I realized the truth was far more complex: I already was in love with you.

At first, you'd won my love because of your poems. Later, after we'd exchanged numerous letters, I discovered I loved you for your kindness, intelligence, and passion. You, under the guise of Felicity, offered me compassion at a time when I most needed it—this alone would have won my devotion. But as our correspondence turned more frequent, our letters grew ever more intimate. Sensual, though always within the realm of propriety.

To my shame, I became obsessed with meeting you, to uncover the woman behind the poet. And here is where I first encountered you as Musa Bartham.

You are correct: the first time we met at Persephone Press, I was indeed hungover—I'm not proud of this. You see, I'd just received your letter refusing to meet with me. You, of course, refused—and wisely so. I can still quote exactly what you wrote, for it is engraved in my mind: "Let us enjoy the communion of our Souls through our Words, not our Bodies. True Love is an Ideal only spoiled by the intrusion of Life—this is a Truth I know from personal experience." As you can probably surmise, I was devastated by your rejection. Heartbroken. Mad with yearning.

You no doubt recall what happened next. I burst into Persephone Press, using my portfolio of drawings as subterfuge for my lovelorn quest.

And there you were, my darling Musa.

I still remember the first time I saw you that rainy day. You were seated across from Miss Nicholson, wearing an oh-so-proper navy blue day suit. Your lustrous chestnut hair was scraped back tightly from your rather wide forehead. Those adorable wire spectacles you always wear were balanced on the tip of your nose, as though you were so engrossed in conversation you didn't notice they were about to fall off. At first glance, you appeared sharp, intimidating in your intelligence and wit. Prim yet with a strange wily spirit barely held in check.

Musa, your presence frightened me as much as it called to me— but in retrospect, I understand why. Upon meeting you, I sensed my life would change irrevocably.

I was right. And here we are.

Now here comes the hardest part of my confession: I'm the one responsible for selling six of your letters to The Greater London Gazette. *Me, alone. No one else, though Luke Ward had initially stolen them from me in an attempt to uncover Felicity Vita's identity.*

I sold the letters because I was desperate to save my sister's life.

Besides needing to send her to Nice to convalesce, there were urgent medical bills to be addressed . . . which is why I brought you to my family home: so you could understand the duress of our situation.

I sold your letters only after trying every other possibility I could think of: loans, pay advances, and selling art. I even considered letting Bexley Manor, but it would have taken too long. Alas, I came up skint even when I took into consideration the generous advance Miss Nicholson paid for my illustrations for our book. (If it makes my actions any less reprehensible, I will not claim any future payments. I shall instead ask Miss Nicholson to forward these to your family.)

I was careful only to sell the letters that seemed the least damaging and embarrassing to your precious self. To further protect your reputation, I arranged for Luke to sell these letters on my behalf, so no one would ever guess my connection to your family—I had no desire to expose you to further scandal after all you'd suffered with your father's disappearance.

As a condition for the sale, I obtained a promise from the Gazette via Luke not to publish anything untrue about the letters or Felicity Vita. However, I was naive not to expect them to lead with insinuation and slander—for this I am especially sorry. I cannot imagine the shock you experienced when you encountered that salacious headline.

Musa, let me assure that, during all of my interactions, I never once revealed the secret of your identity. However, I must admit I guessed you were Felicity Vita several days before you confessed such to me. Before then, I'd made the mistake of confiding my suspicions to Luke. Though I told him I was wrong about your identity, the die was cast when he discovered one of your poem drafts outside your home. To be fair, Luke decided not to participate in the publication of your letters. He assures me he has no idea who provided the newspaper with the fair copies to authenticate them.

And that's the entire mess, my darling, beloved Musa. I've confessed all this to assure you needn't worry about any further letters being sold. As long as I have air to breathe, I will do every-

thing within my power to make sure no one ever learns the truth behind your nom de plume.

I don't expect a response to this letter. Nor do I expect forgiveness. However, I pray you'll understand in time. As for myself, I wish more than anything I'd accepted all you'd offered me that afternoon when we were alone in my family home, but now you understand how wrong this would have been. It would have been an even greater theft than the liberties I've already taken.

Musa, I love you beyond reason and fear I always shall. But that is my burden, not yours. If we never see each other again, I wish for you a happy life where you experience no further pain or betrayal.

Yours forever,
Seb/Henry

CHAPTER 35

THE LETTER AWAITED Musa that afternoon when she returned from Persephone Press after delivering Seb's book illustrations. She hadn't walked home directly. Instead, she'd taken a long detour through Green Park, recalling that Sunday when Seb tried to kiss her in the snow. Was that when she began to fall in love with him? Or later? Looking back, it all seemed so obvious. She loved him—whatever she felt for Henry had been a chimera. She loved him. And now Seb was gone, and she was alone. How could it have it gone so very wrong? She forced herself to relive every moment of their time together in the same way in which a scientist breaks down the results of an unsuccessful experiment.

And then she arrived home and found his letter waiting for her in the last post of the day.

Henry and Seb. Seb and Henry. One and the same. It can't be.

When Musa first spied the letter, she immediately recognized the handwriting on the envelope and her stomach had flipped before settling into a low hum. She told herself Henry had written regarding the publication of their correspondence in *The Greater London Gazette*; somehow the letter made its way to her home, instead of Persephone Press. But once Musa realized the envelope did bear her name and home address, that low hum of anxiety grew deafening.

And then after she read the letter . . . well, it was fortunate her family was in the dining room taking tea. Musa actually gasped like a ninny. She sank to her knees after shoving the letter that Henry—no, *Seb*—had written into her pocket.

He'd sold her letters. Thrown Felicity Vita to the wolves. Betrayed her. Seb could invoke Luke Ward all he wished, but Seb had accepted the money from the newspaper, ill sister or no.

Musa rubbed the bridge of her nose. Drew deep breaths.

I won't cry. I won't cry. That would be illogical—and logic was definitely called for. Not emotion. Not love. Not now.

Musa's mind rushed as she strained to comprehend it all. No wonder she'd felt such an unexplainable attraction to Seb, the feeling she somehow already knew him. She did—and that made it too easy to love him. Too easy to desire him. Looking back, she should have suspected he was Henry, but it seemed impossible. Far-fetched, as she'd told Mary. Yet hadn't she sensed something? Not logically, but intuitively. Instead, she'd convinced herself all she felt was attraction, like when her mother met her father—intuition was something Musa didn't dare trust.

More fool me.

The air spotted gray as her head grew light. To steady herself, she stared at the sitting room, taking in the sagging Morris wallpaper with the water stain in the corner, the tattered upholstery that hadn't been replaced since her father's glory days at the Royal Academy. The walls covered with his art. The pastels he'd drawn of her siblings, her mother. The landscapes of their holidays in the Cotswolds in happier times. The oil studies for his famed canvas of *Mariana in the Grange*. The Ophelias gaping down. The Juliets. All those women with broken hearts from lost love and betrayal.

And now she was just like them.

To think I actually let myself fall in love with him! But oh, those letters . . .

She'd cherished Henry's letters—Seb's letters, now that she

knew he wrote them. She'd read them over and over when she was in need of strength and affection during her most solitary moments. It had been so *so* hard to burn them, but she forced herself for Angela's sake. And now six of those letters she'd written him as Felicity would be published for anyone to read.

And it was all Seb's fault.

Well, she learned her lesson. From here on, she'd be practical Musa. Logical Musa. The Musa she'd been once upon a time, prior to the creation of Felicity Vita. Not the Musa who did unwise things like shamelessly prance around naked in bed with an artist who was too damn handsome for anyone's good.

A Musa who didn't fall in love.

Which was the worst thing that could have happened to her. Love had made her weak. Vulnerable. Foolish.

How shall I deal with this? What should I do?

No answer came, though her brain circled and twirled and clicked in its usual way. This time, logic couldn't save her. Nor could her practicality.

And then it happened, the event setting off everything. Somehow she'd leaned against a table bearing a small clay figurine of *La Dame sans Merci* made by her father during his brief foray into sculpture. The figurine fell onto the carpet. Thankfully, it didn't break.

Musa cradled the figurine in her palm. How delicate it was, how lovely! She recalled her father based the figurine upon her mother, who'd posed for it. *"When I met your mother, I thought of her as La Dame avec Merci,"* Neil Bartham would relate when describing their courtship. *"The compassion she held in her eyes immediately called to me, children. She seemed the opposite of the Keats poem . . ."* Her father had also written of this in those love letters Musa used for Felicity's first poems.

And then she thought of her parents, of their actions, and how she'd proven no different. How alone she felt. But she wouldn't break down. Not now. There was too much to do.

Step one, she told herself, *go to Mary and tell her what Seb did.*

Step two, confront Luke Ward to limit the damage.

Step three . . . well, I'll figure that out later.

Still clutching the figurine of La Dame sans Merci, Musa forced herself to her feet. First, to see Mary. She'd ready herself to go out anew.

Then she looked out the window. The sky was gray. Stormy. It made the task ahead seem all the more intimidating.

There's nothing that can be done. Not really. And, for some reason, this invited a surge of frustration akin to a child's.

Before she could stop herself, Musa threw the figurine of La Dame sans Merci against the wall, where it shattered in a hail of clay.

Clio rushed into the room, followed closely by Angela, who'd stopped by to update her mother on her latest news. Clio cried, "What's happened? I nearly jumped out of my skin!"

"I-I dropped Papa's figurine," Musa forced out. "That's all."

Angela carefully gathered the pieces. "It sounded like you threw it."

"I didn't mean to! I'm sorry, I don't know what got into me."

The twins rushed in, Lyra after Theo, teacups still clutched in their hands. "What's wrong?"

"Nothing, really!" Musa tried to smile, clenching her mouth, her lips, her jaw. "I'll be fine."

I won't cry. I won't cry . . .

Musa must not have been as convincing as she hoped, for her mother gathered Musa in her arms and kissed her brow. Musa didn't resist as Clio led her toward the threadbare sofa. Her mother smelled of castile soap and the stewed apples she'd eaten for lunch.

"There, there, sweetheart," she cooed, smoothing Musa's hair. "Tell me what's happened. Surely it can't be that bad."

Musa drew a deep breath, swiping away the tears falling from her traitorous eyes. She looked at her family, all who were gathered around her. Angela appeared alarmed, Clio worried, and Lyra and Theo simply puzzled.

"I have a confession to make," Musa began in a tremulous voice.

"I never wanted any of you to know this . . . well, Angela knew some of it. Not that it matters—it's too late. But I can no longer hold this to myself alone."

Angela took her sister's hand. "Not alone."

Clio grasped Musa's other hand. "Not anymore. Tell us."

And so Musa spilled out everything that had happened since she'd taken on the mask of Felicity Vita to provide for the Barthams: the poems, the books, the infamy. The desperation leading her to write that children's book after Persephone Press changed ownership with the American heiress. The letters from Henry that turned out to be written by Seb, who'd known more about her *nom de plume* than she realized.

She told her family everything, all the way to the *"LUST! LONGING! LETTERS!"* article, spurred by Seb selling a selection of Felicity's correspondence with the aid of Luke Ward. She even confessed of the peculiar attraction she'd felt for Seb that became an obsession akin to love. Though Musa spared her family the details of their physical intimacies, her mother's sidelong glance suggested she guessed enough.

By the time Musa finished her saga of scandal and poetry and art, the mantel clock had struck past the hour.

"And that's everything," she concluded, her voice low and weary. "Well, everything I can think of now."

She glanced at her mother, awaiting her censure. Her shock, now that she knew Musa had supported their family as Felicity Vita.

"My poor baby," Clio breathed, patting Musa's hand. Yet Musa sensed there was something bothering her mother. Something she'd yet to admit. The air felt tense, as though a storm was about to break.

"You read my private love letters from your father?"

Musa nodded.

"And you used them to write your poems?"

Clio's voice was very small. But there was a sharpness in it Musa had never experienced before.

"Only at first, Mama."

"At first?" Clio rose from the settee, her jaw tight. "I thought I knew you. Trusted you. I understand you were desperate and I was wrong to leave you responsible, but I never expected this. What else have you done, Musa? Tell me!"

"Nothing beyond this. I never wanted you to know. Never wanted to worry you."

Clio's eyes gleamed with unshed tears. "Those letters are immeasurably precious to me. They're all I have left of your father." Her voice caught. "To think thousands of people read our private communications published under the name of Felicity Vita." To Angela: "Were you aware your sister did this?"

Angela swallowed hard. "Only about Felicity Vita. Not about your letters."

"I only used small parts for the poems," Musa assured. "For inspiration, that's all."

"Inspiration?" Clio's tone cut like a knife. "My love for your father has been the defining force of my life. Not inspiration for a common book of poetry." A deep breath. "I know things were dire, but—"

"No one could tell they were yours, Mama," Musa interrupted. "I promise! I was every so careful. I had no choice. It was to save us—"

Musa gasped, for then she understood. She was no different from Seb.

What a hypocrite I am!

And then she recalled her words to him in the South Kensington Museum. *"If I ever find out who stole those letters, I'll never forgive them . . . If it's anyone I know, I'll never speak to them again!"* No wonder he'd remained silent.

Musa sank into a chair, overcome. She could no longer judge Seb for selling her letters, though she could judge him plenty for deceiving her about Henry. As for her mother, she had amends to make.

Musa bowed her head. "Mama, I'm so very sorry! I truly am—"

Before Musa could complete her apology, the doorbell jangled impatiently.

"If it's a journalist, turn them away!" Angela cried.

"They'll only come back," Clio sighed, turning from Musa.

Theo and Lyra ran for the door, prepared for battle. But it was someone far fiercer than a journalist: Aunt Minerva. She bustled into the sitting room, her arms overflowing with a new bouquet of flowers for Angela. Today's were ivory-hued Easter lilies surrounded by fronds of green.

"What's all this? You all look as though you've come from a funeral," Aunt Minerva huffed as she spilled the flowers onto the sideboard. "I'm here for Angela. I'm not alone—you'd best perk up!"

Following Aunt Minerva came Sunny, who was dressed in black mourning himself. His auburn hair was wild, his eyes reddened. However, a hint of a smile tugged at the corners of his lips, along with a resolute attitude Musa had never before witnessed in him.

He collapsed to his knees before Angela.

"Marry me, Angela! My father passed away last night. Unexpected. A heart attack."

"Sunny now has his title!" Aunt Minerva crowed, nudging Clio's shoulder with her elbow. "It's good news."

"I'd hardly call someone's death good news," Clio interrupted, her eyes locked on Angela's face—Angela, who'd turned as pale as the Easter lilies on the sideboard. "I'm so sorry for your loss, Sunny. Your father was a most loyal friend to my husband. Our deepest sympathies, dear."

Sunny stammered out, "Of course I'm devastated about Papa's death—sorry, I didn't consider how this would appear! But the sad event leaves me master of my life. Mama can't stop me from doing as I wish, now that I'm the Earl of Sunderland." He squared his shoulders. "What say you, Angela? We'd wait an appropriate amount of time. You know I adore you! I always have."

Angela's tone was as gentle as the palm she set on Sunny's shoulder. "I can't do that, my friend."

To everyone's astonishment, Angela swept out of the sitting room and rushed upstairs. A flight up, a door slammed.

"I'll speak to her," Musa told her mother.

"Angela?" Musa called from the hallway outside their bedroom. "Open the door! I know you're in there." She knocked anew. "Let me in! Please!"

Angela opened the door a crack. "Go away, Musa!"

"Not until you let me speak to you."

"There's nothing to say. I'm fine."

"Then why are you weeping?"

A pause. Angela wiped at her pretty blue eyes.

"I'm not weeping. I'm just tired."

"If you're just tired, I'm Queen Victoria." Musa pressed her shoulder against the door. "Do I have to force my way in?"

Angela glanced down the staircase, where Clio, Sunny, and Aunt Minerva stood, their heads craned collectively her way.

"Very well," Angela said, sniffing. "But only as long as you don't let them in."

Once the door was bolted, Angela perched on the edge of the bed. She folded her arms across her chest. "Don't try to convince me to marry him."

Musa settled on the bed beside her sister. "I thought you always wanted to be with Sunny. We all did, Mama especially. Isn't that what this is all about? Finding a husband, having a family, and so on?"

Angela burst out, "You don't understand. Sunny truly loves me."

"That's entirely appropriate for a husband."

"Oh, stop being so damn practical, Musa! Sunny's a dear

friend. I care deeply about him. I love him. But—oh! what a mess this is!"

Angela hung her head in her hands, sobbing.

Now Musa understood.

"You don't love him *that* way."

Angela shook her head. "I can't bear to lose Sunny as my friend. Can you imagine how awful it would be for him to be married to me? Me only caring for him like a brother, not a husband? It would be a disaster."

Well, Musa knew plenty about disasters.

"Is there someone else you love then?" Musa tried to recall all of Angela's various suitors. Wasn't there Mr. Carles with the tulips, another one with daisies?

Angela's tone turned odd. "Yes, there's someone I love . . ."

"Who then?"

Angela met her sister's eyes boldly. "Mama. Lyra and Theo. Our family. That's who I love. Especially you, Musa—you're not just a sister. You're my champion. My protector."

Musa flinched. "I only did what was necessary."

"You did more than that." Angela took her sister's hands. "I saw how hard you worked to take care of us after Papa disappeared. The late nights, the fretting over money, the worries Felicity would be unmasked, Mama's health. I saw how alone you were."

"But it was my responsibility, Angela! I'm the eldest."

"And it's been your responsibility for too long." Angela's blue eyes turned flinty. "Now it's my turn. I'm the beauty in the family, the only one with a chance of rehabilitating our family's reputation and reversing our fortunes. I'll marry someone who can take care of us."

"Yet you won't marry Sunny."

Angela shook her head vehemently. "He'd resent me in time—I know it. There are other gentlemen equally settled who'll do nicely. Gentlemen I'll respect and trust, ones who'll treat me kindly and give me a family. Gentlemen who haven't loved me for all their life and will be devastated if I don't consider them my soulmate."

"But will you love them *that* way?"

"Musa, it's not that I don't want a husband I love, but this isn't the point. Not anymore." Angela's jaw squared. "What just happened with Sebastian Atkinson and those letters only proves I'm right." A pause. "Are you going to respond to his letter? You could write him *poste restante* in Nice. He deserves a good telling off!"

Two hours earlier, Musa would have agreed in a heartbeat. But now everything was different; she recalled Clio's tearful face.

"No," Musa said at last. "Not yet."

A sharp rap on their bedroom door. The two sisters jumped.

"Musa? Angela?" Clio called out from the hallway. "Everyone's gone. It's safe to come out!"

Yet Musa couldn't seem to move, for all she could think of was Sebastian Atkinson selling her love letters for the sake of his family. Seb, who was more like her than not.

CHAPTER 36

FIRST LOOK AT
BARTHAM CHILDREN'S BOOK

The Times, Foreign Edition, 5 April 1872: Persephone Press has turned over a new leaf with the publication of Poems of Morality and Goodness for Children to Abide, *an illustrated book penned by Miss Musa Bartham. Persephone Press was formerly the publisher of the infamous love poet Felicity Vita, whose personal correspondence was recently published in* The Greater London Gazette. *To the disappointment of those with prurient minds, the reclusive poetess's letters proved as scintillating as a laundry list.*

While Poems of Morality and Goodness for Children to Abide *is written with wit and charm, the illustrations accompanying Miss Bartham's debut book are equally delightful. They were drawn by Mr. Sebastian Atkinson, a young painter new to London.*

The publication of Poems of Morality and Goodness for Children to Abide *will be officially marked by a masked ball sponsored by Lady Minerva Hadley later this month. Much of society is rumored to be angling for invitations to the exclusive, unusual event. However, those eager to make Mr. Atkinson's acquaintance will find disappointment.*

"Mr. Atkinson won't be present. He did not want his presence to distract from the family affair," Miss Mary Nicholson explained at the bequest of her father, Mr. James Nicholson, who founded the press two decades earlier. "After all, Miss Bartham is the great-niece of Lady Hadley." In addition, Miss Bartham's sister Angela has been witnessed of late in the better drawing rooms of London due to Lady Hadley's sponsorship.

As for Mr. Atkinson, it is believed he is away on the continent studying art.

"It's for the best I not see Miss Bartham," Seb said, avoiding Daphne's gaze as he folded away the latest edition of *The Times*. "Even if I wasn't here with you, I shouldn't attend the ball. Now you know why."

Just over a month since he'd joined his sisters in Nice, Seb finally confessed how he'd paid for their travels—a confession spurred when Daphne noticed the article about *Poems of Morality and Goodness for Children to Abide* in a café popular with British expats. Under Daphne's gentle questioning, Seb found himself unable to avoid telling the entire truth in an attempt to gain solace and sympathy.

It hadn't worked.

"For the best . . ." Daphne's voice was a low reproach in the dusk. "I'm upset with you, but I'm furious with Luke for stealing those letters. I thought him better than that. What was he thinking?"

"He really was trying to help in his crazy way, or so he thought." An inhale of breath. "But I'm more at fault! I agreed to sell them, Daphne. I deceived Miss Bartham about Henry—we exchanged intimate letters for over a year. There's no way she'll ever forgive me."

Now that Seb's confession was complete, brother and sister were seated on the balcony adjoining their second-story rooms they'd let. It was a balmy evening for early April, one suggesting the promise of early summer rather than the start of spring. Though their rooms weren't on the Promenade des Anglais—they didn't possess such funds—they were close enough to the sea that the clean tang of salt hung on the air along with a hint of roses; the trellis leading up toward their balcony wrapped around the iron-work like a swollen promise. In the distance, orange trees blos-somed, a voluptuous scent. Temperate air, sunshine, and sweet flowers were precisely why they'd traveled to Nice: to give Jessica's heart a chance to heal.

And her heart *did* seem better, or so the doctors they'd consulted assured . . . though Seb couldn't resist throwing an anxious look in Jess's direction, where she was quietly drawing in bed. She had a way with art and embroidery, taking after her older siblings.

As for Seb's heart . . . best not to think of that.

Daphne pressed, "Are you in love with Miss Bartham?"

Seb didn't answer. There was no need to. Evidence of his devo-tion was displayed on the French easel by the window. Though he'd left the canvas of *La Dame Sans Merci* behind in Spitalfields in his rush to depart, he brought those pencil sketches he'd drawn of Musa. He'd used them as studies for a series of watercolor portraits, which Daphne considered his best work. She said there was a tenderness about them that was very affecting.

"Don't ignore my question," Daphne continued. "Do you love her?"

"I didn't ignore your question. I chose not to answer it."

"That tells me all I need to know." She pursed her lips. "I sensed something was wrong with you besides worry over Jess. You seemed so removed. Unemotional."

Seb didn't feel unemotional. No, he felt numb, which was a different sort of emotion. One he welcomed. How else could one deal with a broken heart?

"What of Miss Bartham?" Daphne continued. "Does she love you?"

Seb's throat tightened. Musa *had* loved him—he could tell that last day in his home. That's what made all of this the worse.

"If she ever loved me, I'm certain she no longer does," he said at last. "Hopefully she'll understand my decision in time. To desire anything more would be impractical."

Damn it, he sounded like Musa with her prattle about practicality and logic. To his dismay, his voice caught. Stupid emotions.

Daphne took her brother's hand. "I wish you'd told me earlier—I'd assumed the children's book paid for our travels. What a shock it must have been for Miss Bartham to learn you were her secret correspondent!"

"I'm ashamed of myself, but what choice did I have?"

Though now, with the distance of travel and a month's time, he was uncertain of anything save his regret for his behavior, his love for Musa.

Best not to feel anything, he reminded himself. He wrapped his arms around his chest. The breeze had turned cold, that's all.

Daphne countered, "You should have spoken to me first. We could have borrowed money, I could have looked for more commissions. Something. Anything."

"It wasn't feasible. Not on such short notice." Seb rose from his chair to bring their conversation to a close. "We should check on Jess."

Daphne wasn't done. "You ran away from Miss Bartham without giving her the chance to confront you. To hear from your lips what you'd done and why."

"I wrote her a letter. A very good and apologetic letter! I did my best to protect her. As long as she remains silent, no one will learn the truth behind Felicity's letters."

Daphne shook her head. "Letters, that's all the two of you do. Write letters. Deflect emotion on to the page instead of into life, where it belongs."

"I'll remind you those letters made it possible for us to come here. Anyway, she hasn't responded."

Initially Seb checked the post office every day for forwarded correspondence, hoping against hope for some sign from Musa. Soon his visits slowed to twice a week, then once. During this period, the only mail that arrived from England was an embossed invitation for Lady Hadley's ball in honor of *Poems of Morality and Goodness for Children to Abide*. He set it aside without responding.

Daphne shook her head. "You didn't trust Miss Bartham to understand. Or forgive. And now—"

"Now I'm alone, as I deserve to be."

"Deserve to be?" Daphne countered, unusually confrontational. "Have you such low regard for yourself? Yes, what you did was awful, but you're still a good person. The best. I know this. Jess knows this. Even Luke knows this, which is why he had to steal those letters in the first place to convince you to sell them. You would have never thought of it unless he'd dangled the money in front of you!"

Before Seb could respond, the door to the terrace opened. Jessica clutching a sheet of paper. She stood there clad in her white nightdress, her long dishwater blonde hair in plaits.

"Is something the matter?" The child's expression was more puzzled than distressed.

Seb picked up his little sister. She felt heavier than even a week ago—the warm sunshine and air were definitely helping. He forced a lightness into his words he didn't feel.

"Nothing's the matter, elfling. Shall I help you with your picture?"

Jess smiled. "I'd like that. I'm trying to draw a kitten, the one we saw this morning on the beach."

"Ah, the tabby! I can help with that. Come with me . . ."

As Seb led Jessica inside from the terrace, he ignored Daphne's soft retort.

"If you truly loved her, you'd fight for her."

～

All night Seb lay awake in his narrow bed, Daphne's words resounding in him. *"If you truly loved her, you'd fight for her."* Well, he and Musa had fought plenty, from their first meeting at Persephone Press to their last encounter at Bexley Manor. But fight *for* her? That seemed a very different proposition. It had shocked him to hear those words come from Daphne's mouth—Daphne, who was the gentlest person he knew, with her serene ways and artful embroidery.

And then Seb recalled the euphoria of finding Musa awaiting him on that lavender-scented bed at Bexley Manor. The brave glance she'd thrown his way before she'd asked him to unbutton her bodice, baring herself to his gaze. How silky her skin felt as he'd wrapped his arms around her, yearning to never let her go. Beautiful. Beloved.

It had taken every iota of self-control he owned to refuse her offer of love—and it *had* been love he'd witnessed in her warm amber eyes.

A love he hadn't fought for.

A love he couldn't accept. Not after selling those letters.

A love he didn't deserve. Not after deceiving her about Henry.

A love that had felt like a thread tying them together—a thread leading all the way to his future even before he learned she was Felicity Vita.

As Seb imagined this thread, he saw Musa seated beside him in Bexley Manor while he drew illustrations for the books they could create together. He saw Musa curled over her desk as she wrote new poems and stories too charming to be resisted. He saw parents with their children reading these books, which Seb would oversee the printing of from a sanctuary of creativity he and Musa would forge together. Most of all, he saw Musa's body pressed against his as they laid together in their soft bed after a long day of art and companionship.

And then he'd gone and broken the thread tying them. All those scenes of love, passion, and art scattering like beads from a broken necklace.

With this realization, Seb finally felt *something*, though it wasn't the dazzling heat of desire or the chill of remorse. He just felt hopeless. But perhaps that's just how life was once you reached a certain age. You learned life required choices you'd rather not make, that it was woven of threads spun from loss as well as love. Life became logical.

Since the death of his parents, Seb had tried his best to be so strong, so self-sacrificing . . . and in the process, he'd sacrificed the woman he loved most outside his sisters. But even before meeting Musa, he'd forced himself to work long hours at Chassen & Sons, chosen to live in a frigid attic in a neighborhood where he feared for his safety, and made himself paint hour after hour in an attempt to find fortune beyond the confines of his salaried job.

He stared out the window facing his bed. The sun was starting to rise, a thin line of orange fire on the horizon. It suggested so much possibility, so much beauty, that it felt a tangible reminder of the promise lost when he betrayed Musa.

Well, if he wasn't able to sleep, he should at least accomplish something.

Seb pushed the bed linens from his exhausted body, determined to clear the mess he'd made with Jessica while they'd sketched the previous evening. They'd left papers, scissors and all manner of art supplies on the small table used for their meals.

A shuffle of steps sounded behind Seb. Jessica yawning; she really did look healthier.

"Go back to bed," he whispered. "It's early."

"I'm wide awake, Sebbie. What are you doing?"

"Cleaning your mess, elfling," he teased.

"I'll help."

Somehow her presence helped his sour mood. He found himself grinning as he took in their drawings. There was the tabby cat, a bouquet of flowers, a princess and her knight. He set Jessica's drawings to one side, gathered the remaining papers into a pile as she happily chattered to him.

And then he found it. The invitation to Lady Hadley's ball in honor of *Poems of Morality and Goodness for Children to Abide.* It must have gotten mixed in with other papers.

Seb drew a breath as though he had a blow.

"Are you okay, Sebbie?"

"I'm fine, elfling. Just something I'd forgotten about."

Now, in the dim light of dawn, Seb forced himself to read the invitation as though he was examining a tender wound.

Your Company is Respectfully Solicited
by Lady Minerva Hadley
for a
GRAND MASKED BALL
in honor of the publication of
Poems of Morality and Goodness
for Children to Abide
by Miss Musa Bartham
with illustrations by Mr. Sebastian Atkinson

Saturday Evening, 13th of April
Dancing to Commence at 7 o'clock

Well-Behaved Children Welcome
Refreshments Will Be Served

The invitation was typeset in script on heavy paper stock with gold decorations. Expensive to print. Tasteful too; Seb had to give Lady Hadley credit.

Suddenly he envisioned the children at the ball, the costumes they'd wear, their laughter mingling amid the music. How would they react to his and Musa's book? Who else would be at the ball? Certainly Angela Bartham; Seb imagined a line of suitors eager for her favor. The twins would probably dress to resemble each other, with matching masks. As for Clio Bartham, perhaps she'd attend incognito. The prospect of this pleased Seb very much.

And then it was Musa Seb imagined.

He saw Musa dressed in a ball gown holding a quill. Or better yet, wearing a crown of laurels. He couldn't imagine her costume beyond that. Though she'd certainly be masked, he'd recognize her immediately. He'd know her warm eyes, the piquant beauty mark at the side of her mouth. Would she be smiling? Or weighed by sorrow?

"What's that?" Jessica asked, her brow crinkling as she pointed.

"An invitation."

"To a party?"

"Something like that. It's a ball for the children's book I illustrated." Seb began to pace. *Fight for her.* A peculiar surge of joy began to rise, one he couldn't explain logically or practically.

"The book I posed for. You'll go to the ball?"

"It's in London. I shouldn't leave you, elfling."

"But I'm better now, aren't I?"

"Getting better," he answered. But even as Seb said this, a plan began to circulate in his mind, one that was wildly impractical but plausible. *Fight for her.*

He gently woke up Daphne, who was still in bed.

"I need to go to London," he whispered. "I promise to return as soon as I can."

<h1 style="text-align:center">CHAPTER 37</h1>

"Why aren't you ready, Musa?" Angela asked. "There's a ballroom full of people waiting for you!"

"Because I've never been so nervous in my life," Musa admitted, fastening the last button on her gown.

Musa was sequestered behind the dressing screen in Aunt Minerva's boudoir, fiddling with the costume she'd reluctantly agreed to wear. Her hands were shaking to her embarrassment, though there truly was no reason for her to be so anxious. *All is well*, she told herself. And it was: everything had gone as best as could be expected despite the shock of that letter Seb-Henry had sent just over a month earlier. Musa behaved exactly as he'd directed, though it had been difficult not to react when Felicity Vita's letters were published in *The Greater London Gazette*. It wasn't the content of the letters as much as the snide articles accompanying them—Seb really had chosen the least sensational letters, just as he'd promised. *LOVESTRUCK POETESS PENS SWEET NOTHINGS* read one headline. Another proclaimed *SECRET LETTERS REVEALS SECRETS OF FELICITY!*

But there was another reason Musa was nervous. Before she'd left for the ball, she'd finally written Seb a letter. A letter that bore only three words; she'd spent hours thinking what to write before settling on them. She placed the letter inside her reticule, feeling too vulnerable to mail it just yet.

However, she told herself all this was secondary to other concerns: *Poems of Morality and Goodness for Children to Abide* was published, a book she was convinced gained attention due to her family name as much as Seb's art. All the reviews said so, though they were careful to compliment Musa's prose as well. "Miss Bartham is a gifted authoress whose words are filled with wit," the critic in *The Times* opined. A less kind newspaper wrote, "To our surprise, the new generation of Barthams possesses talents beyond one for scandal—and beauty, if one is to judge by the presence of Miss Angela Bartham in society's better homes."

But tonight isn't about Felicity or me, Musa reminded herself. *Tonight is about Angela.*

Angela was being wooed by three different men in earnest. Aunt Minerva was convinced at least one of them would offer for her hand during the ball. Musa didn't know how she felt about this.

"Do you need help with your costume?" Angela pressed again. "It's quarter past seven!"

Indeed, the string octet Aunt Minerva engaged was tuning up. They sounded more akin to cats howling than anything orchestral.

"No," Musa answered. "I'm ready."

She stepped out from behind the dressing screen only to be met by a concerned look from Angela, who was dressed as Giselle from the ballet, complete with a set of delicate net wings. It had taken some persuasion to convince her not to wear toe shoes, which would be far too slippery for the marble ballroom floor.

"Well? What is it?" Musa stared at herself in Aunt Minerva's tall dressing mirror. "I'm trussed up like a peacock, aren't I? Wasn't that the plan?"

Even Musa had to admit her gown was more suitable for a goddess than a children's book author. It was designed by a modiste personally chosen by Aunt Minerva. Instead of being sewn with a full flounced skirt, like most fashionable ball gowns, Musa's bore a narrow silhouette akin to the styles of a half-century earlier. The silk taffeta glittered gold from its capped sleeves all the way down to its hem. The warm hue shimmered against Musa's tightly curled chestnut hair, all the better to set off the gold laurel headdress Clio loaned to complete Musa's costume.

The offer surprised Musa. Despite Musa's apology, Clio was still distant with her eldest daughter since discovering she'd used her love letters for Felicity's poems. Nor would Clio be at the ball tonight . . . nor would Seb. Though this was to be expected, Musa still felt a tangible loss.

Again, she thought of the letter in her reticule. Those three words she'd written.

"Do I pass muster?" Musa prodded her sister, stomach swimming.

Angela replied, "You look stunning. But why on earth are you wearing spectacles? It's a masked ball!"

"I can't wear a mask with spectacles."

"Everyone has to wear one, even you." Angela offered Musa a gold mask trailing red ribbons. "The plan was for you to reveal your identity at nine o'clock when you give your speech about the book."

Musa shook her head at the mask. "I'm peculiar, Angela. I like to see where I'm going."

"You don't need to see! You only need to be gorgeous and accept compliments."

Musa replied in a jittery voice, "You assume there will be compliments."

"Oh, there will be, lovely! You shine like the sun—no one will be able to look away. The modiste truly outdid herself."

"Maybe I don't want to be the sun," Musa countered. "Is so much attention wise?"

Angela resolutely nodded. "Wise. And deserved. You're the main attraction, after all."

"That's not true, Angela." Musa's voice dropped. "Are you prepared to face your suitors tonight?"

Angela nodded resolutely. "I'm ready."

"Have you a preference?"

What Musa really wanted to ask was, "*Is there someone you love?*"

Angela answered, "All three are charming and handsome . . . though I must admit Mr. Carles is rather appealing. I've always wanted to live in Surrey."

I suppose this is the best we can hope for, Musa thought.

Though Carles clearly adored Angela, Musa found him kind but a bit dim. She'd tried speaking further with Angela about the wisdom of not rushing into matrimony, but had gotten nowhere. Again, she wished with all her heart Angela loved Sunny in the way necessary to accept his hand, though she supposed there was an advantage to not having Lady Sunderland as a mother-in-law.

The boudoir door opened without a knock. Aunt Minerva poked her head in, a glass of champagne in her hand. "Where is our lady of the hour? Everyone's clamoring!"

"Here, Aunt." Now Musa's heart was really hammering.

Aunt Minerva took in Musa's costume with a long gaze. "You'll do very nicely, miss! For once I shan't have to be ashamed of Neil Bartham and his stiff—"

"I know, I know," Musa interrupted. Her great-aunt would never change.

"But do you have to appear quite so terrified?" Aunt Minerva thrust the glass of champagne into Musa's right hand. "Here, drink this."

Angela plucked Musa's spectacles off her nose and pressed the gold mask into her left hand. "And wear this—I'll tie the ribbons for you."

In the ballroom, everything appeared a blur before Musa's nearsighted eyes, especially when viewed behind the confines of her mask. Colors merged, bright and swirling and cheerful, surrounded by the warm glow of golden candlelight. The inability to see clearly made the clatter of conversation feel equally indistinct. Words rose and fell, accompanied by laughter. The string octet was deep into a mazurka, sounding far more harmonious than they had while tuning up. Couples danced in the center of the ballroom surrounded by what Musa suspected to be a circle of children, judging by their petite stature and high-pitched voices. Several solitary masked figures dashed by. They reminded her of people she knew: her mother, Seb, even Luke Ward.

Wishful thinking, Musa decided. Well, save for Luke Ward—for all of Seb's reassurances, she would not be pleased to find the journalist present. After all, he'd pressed Seb to sell her letters in the first place.

"Come here, lovely," Angela said, guiding Musa by her wrist. "See that table? There's your books! Many are already claimed, or so it appears. Aren't they gorgeous?"

Musa said wryly, "I'll have to trust you on that."

She squinted. A tall pile of books laid across a long table. If she strained her eyes, she could make out Seb's drawing printed in gold on the blue cloth binding. The table was surrounded by children with their parents. Were they reading her book? *They must be,* Musa decided. *Oohs* and *ahhs* and other compliments rose, along with laughter.

Angela said in a satisfied voice, "I think it's fair to say your book is a success, Musa."

Musa felt a grin settle across her lips. It wasn't due to the half-glass of champagne she'd imbibed. "You think so?"

"I know so." Angela pointed toward a distant corner of the ball-room. "I think that's Miss Nicholson with Miss—what did you say her name was? The American lady? I can always recognize her by her hats."

"Miss Amanda Seeley of Boston." It figured Miss Seeley would wear a hat to a ball. "Does she look pleased?"

Angela laughed. "Very pleased."

Musa admitted, "I do wish Mama was here to see this."

Along with Seb. Every time she caught a blurred glimpse of a tall dark-haired man, her heart gave a little lurch.

"I wish she was too," Angela replied. "I tried to convince her to attend. After all, it's a costume ball! No one would have recognized her. She could have been in society for the first time since she became a Bartham."

"It's my fault," Musa said. "I still feel so awful about her letters." Hopefully in time Musa would find some way to make it up to her mother beyond apologies—how blindly presumptuous she'd been! Yes, she'd been desperate, but she wished she could have found another solution.

"I think she understands, Musa," Angela consoled. "Just give her time."

A rise of applause sounded as the octet finished the mazurka. Angela gave her sister's elbow an affectionate squeeze before releasing it to grab two flutes of champagne from a silver tray proffered by a passing waiter.

"Drink up!" Angela ordered. "No sorrow tonight. Only joy."

She clinked glasses with Musa as a gentleman approached dressed in some sort of dark purple robe—it was hard for Musa to tell who without spectacles. Not Sunny, who'd avoided the Barthams since Angela's refusal of his proposal, though the Countess of Sunderland had surprisingly sent word she'd emerge from mourning to attend the ball out of gratitude to Angela for refusing her son's suit. "The girl has some sense after all," she opined loudly to anyone who'd listen.

This gentleman was tall with dark hair. He grew close enough that Musa was able to make out he was costumed as an artist, replete with a paint-splattered palette and brushes. His black mask hid most of his face.

It can't be Seb. Still, Musa's heart rose.

Alas, he approached Angela, not her.

"Miss Angela?" The artist gentleman offered a deep bow as the string octet tendered the opening notes of a spritely galop.

Angela trilled with coy laughter as he brushed her lips against her hand. "I know you! Mr. Carles, isn't it?"

"I am found out!" he answered in a genial tone. "How did you know it was me?"

"You're clutching an invitation with your name on it," Angela simpered. "Plus you're ever so tall!" Indeed, Carles towered over nearly everyone else in sight.

"And I recognized you because you're wearing the gardenias I sent. I also recall you saying *Giselle* is your favorite ballet." Mr. Carles offered his arm, smiling broadly. "Might I have the next dance?"

Angela smiled. "You may, sir."

Before Angela jetéd away in her long white tutu with her lanky suitor, she kissed Musa on her cheek. "Enjoy yourself, lovely! This is your night. Don't worry about Mama—she'll be fine. Look, there's Lyra and Theo! They'll stay with you—they're dressed as black cats. See, they're wearing cat ears."

"Where?" Musa turned around searching for the twins, unmoored between her lack of spectacles and the crowded candle-lit room.

Then she was no longer alone. A petite woman dressed in a calf-length medieval-looking smock and dark blue stockings approached. She was accompanied by a lady wearing a bright red ballgown improbably crowned by an oversized hat above her mask. Her heels clicked staccato on the marble floor.

"Musa? Is that you? It's me, Mary, with Miss Seeley." Mary indicated her ankles. "I'm a bluestocking!"

"Mary!" Musa gave her dearest friend an embrace.

"Papa sends his congratulations," Mary related, kissing Musa's cheek. "I'd hoped he'd attend tonight. As usual, he's off to Essex again."

"I'm so relieved to find you, Mary! I can't see a thing without my spectacles and Angela just abandoned me to dance with a suitor and—."

"Everything is going far better than I ever hoped," Mary interrupted, squealing with excitement. "Everyone is so enthusiastic about *Poems of Morality and Goodness for Children to Abide.* We'll need to do another printing immediately! Don't you agree, Miss Seeley?"

"I suppose," Miss Seeley responded in her nasal American accent. "I still can't believe Mr. Atkinson won't be here tonight—it is his book too. I understand he's quite handsome, which would surely help sales." A pout beneath her mask and that enormous hat.

Musa's smile faded. "Is all well, Miss Seeley?" She took another sip of champagne to steady her nerves, the bubbles prickling the back of her throat. Out of the corner of her eye, a masked blonde woman dressed in the graceful robes of a muse slipped by. For a second Musa's throat constricted from more than champagne bubbles.

Not Mama.

For a moment, Musa wished for her mother's presence with all her might. That their relationship would be as it was before Clio learned of Felicity Vita.

The American responded, "Oh, all's well with your children's book despite Atkinson's absence." She waved her hands as though she was conducting the string octet herself. "It's another book that troubles. Actually *books*."

Mary laughed nervously. "Let's not dwell on unpleasantness. Tonight is about Miss Bartham's children's book, is it not?"

Miss Seeley pouted again. "I shouldn't confess this, but I fear I've done something unwise."

She drew out a copy of *The Poetics of Passion* from a satchel. Even without spectacles, Musa could make out its florid purple binding.

Merde. Musa drained the rest of champagne, nearly choking on it.

"What is it you've done?" Mary asked in a low voice. "Is this something I should be aware of?"

Miss Seeley shook her head. The ostrich plumes on her enormous scarlet hat trembled as though in a wind. "I shan't speak of it. I can't. But it's most distressing!"

"What is?" Musa had to ask. Had to know.

"Very well, but you must keep this to yourselves . . ." Miss Seeley leaned in and whispered, "You won't believe this, but I have a suspicion Felicity Vita will be here tonight. Incognito! Can you imagine?"

Musa felt as though her knees had gone weak. "And what makes you think this, Miss Seeley?" Her voice felt very far away.

"It's unimportant, Miss Bartham. All that matters is I find Miss Vita to speak to her!"

Miss Seeley strode off, still clutching *The Poetics of Passion* against her bosom. Musa could hear her heels clattering away despite the music and the dancing.

As soon as the American was out of ear range, Musa collapsed against Mary's shoulders.

"My heart is pounding like it's going to burst out of my chest! What was that about?"

"I've no idea," Mary whispered, giving Musa's hand a quick tug. "She's been in a mood all day. This morning she received a letter—"

"A letter from who?" Musa grew queasy, and it wasn't from imbibing two glasses of champagne quickly. Was that the Countess of Sunderland near the orchestra? Could she be pointing at them?

"Miss Seeley has a sweetheart in London—you recall him from that time at Persephone Press. He travels quite a bit for business. All I know is she read his letter, and the next thing I knew, she'd pulled out that copy of *The Poetics of Passion* and was acting ever so peculiar. Asked me if I knew Felicity Vita's true identity, whether she'd be attending tonight. I told her no, of course."

"I really believed this was behind us," Musa whispered in turn. "She destroyed all of Felicity's books!"

"If it's any consolation, she truly has no idea who Felicity Vita is," Mary soothed as she reached for a slice of cake. "I'm more convinced of it than ever. She's a peculiar one."

Miss Seeley approached anew.

"I must go," Mary said, waving goodbye. "Business awaits. Don't worry! The book is a huge success. You're brilliant!"

Felicity Vita. It would never end.

"I don't feel brilliant," Musa muttered. "I just feel alone."

"You're not alone," a husky male voice said behind her.

Musa whirled. A tall gentleman stood, dressed in a black wool cloak and a silvery Venetian mask that glowed like the moon, or so it appeared. Everything was so blurred.

Drat you, Angela, she thought, wishing for her spectacles.

"How would you know?" she countered. Were the gentleman's eyes blue beneath his hood?

Wishful thinking. Anyway, he sounded nothing like Seb.

"Because you're the author, are you not? Miss Bartham, I enjoyed your children's book very much. The art from it, not so much."

"This is a masked ball, sir," she said, her eyes straining. She made out a shadowy hint of stubble beneath his mask. "It's ungentlemanly to guess a lady's identity before the appointed hour."

"Then I must trust you not to guess mine," the gentleman parried in that strange deep voice. "We'll encounter each other as strangers."

"Are we strangers, sir? Or friends?"

"I hope not enemies."

Musa inhaled sharply. His scent. Linseed oil. Lemon verbena. Was she imagining it? Perhaps he'd disguised his voice to speak to her.

It can't be Seb. He's in Nice with his sisters.

He was gone. For months, if not longer. Hadn't he written as much? Still, her body grew warm with unexpected longing.

"Who are you, sir?"

Any reply he might have given was interrupted by applause; the octet finally concluded the galop. The first notes of a waltz sounded.

"Dance with me?" he asked. "This one time."

"I don't know how to dance," Musa admitted, her gaze raking

his masked face, his hood. It was impossible to even make out the color of his hair.

"You needn't worry. I'll lead." The masked gentleman offered a hand gloved in fine black kid. "Please?"

Before Musa could refuse, he swept her into the waltz.

CHAPTER 38

Seb hadn't been able to resist when he'd pulled Musa into that waltz, which felt the most vulnerable thing he could have done. When he'd arrived at Lady Hadley's ball, his intentions were quite different. He'd planned to observe Musa until after the ball, then find a way to speak to her in private. To apologize and grovel. To woo her—no, fight for her—before returning to his family with either a refusal or an acceptance of his love. But then he'd spied her standing there in her gold gown, her shimmering mask, those gold laurels tucked in her chestnut curls. How could he ever have considered her fox like? No, she was a goddess draped in light—a goddess he loved with every cell of his being.

Unable to resist, he eased closer until he could sense the scent of her hair, the warmth of her flesh.

"I don't feel brilliant. I just feel alone," she'd said.

Once he overheard this, Seb knew he was lost. Utterly lost. He had no choice: he had to find some way to offer comfort before speaking to her in private. To embrace her using the only socially sanctioned way to do so in public: the waltz.

To avoid discovery, he'd deepened his voice like a boy playing at being a man—a man desperately in love. He sensed no flicker of recognition in Musa's eyes. No warmth save the polite regard she'd offer any stranger.

As the waltz swirled about them, Seb dizzied as the tempo increased, but it wasn't from the music. He was a good dancer. His parents had improbably insisted he and Daphne learn for the sake of polite society. It was Musa who made him dizzy. Her presence was intoxicating as she swayed within his arms, her white-gloved hand clasped in his. The sandalwood perfume wafting from her hair. Her dear face so close, yet so distant.

He felt a subtle tremor radiated from her palm set on his shoulder. Nervous, that's what she was. Well, he felt nervous too . . . along with an exquisite longing that made his breath catch.

It took all his fortitude not to kiss her despite the ridiculous moon mask covering most of his face. To not pull her aside and say all the sweet words springing to his tongue, the apologies, the compliments, the pledge of eternal devotion. But he knew this would be presumptuous of him. Not before her moment of glory.

If I'm to never hold her again, this waltz shall have to suffice.

"I cannot believe you've never danced before," he murmured, careful to keep his voice gruff. "You feel . . ."

Glorious. Celestial. Like you belong in my arms for all of eternity.

"Graceful," he finished.

Musa glanced up from the marble floor; she'd been counting steps. "Your eyes are blue, are they not? Like the Adriatic Sea."

"More gray than blue," he countered, his pulse speeding. "Their color is hard to discern under candlelight."

"I suppose."

He sensed an edge of disappointment in her tone, which confused him. Perhaps she'd believed him someone else. Someone she'd welcome. Someone who wasn't Seb.

Another swirl around the ballroom floor. Had not Seb held them back, they would have collided into a group of daisy-chained children. It was then Seb realized that Musa without her spectacles was truly shortsighted. He hadn't noticed this that day at Bexley

Manor . . . but then again, he hadn't noticed anything save his arousal as they'd raced up the stairs toward the bedroom.

Once she was righted, he asked gently, "You'd said you were alone. Are you really?"

She blinked. "It would be forward to admit such to a stranger."

Oh Musa. Prim as ever in public, though he knew the truth about her in private. His heart surged with tenderness, the desire to soothe her. To make amends for the way he'd broken her heart.

He answered, "You may feel alone, but you won't be for long. You're the most stunning woman in this ballroom. Everyone is staring at you."

Musa's cheeks flushed below her mask. "I appreciate your kind words, but that honor belongs to my sister, who is here tonight." She gave a little nod toward the edge of the ballroom. "Can you tell me if you spy a blonde lady dressed as a ballerina with fairy wings?"

Seb glanced over his shoulder. "I do. She's in the arms of an Egyptian prince."

"Ah. Another suitor," Musa breathed. "I wonder which one that is. She's three gentlemen courting her. An abundance. It's quite the change for my family!"

"Does this please you?"

She bit her lower lip just above that beauty mark he'd always adored. Remorse flooded him. Behind his mask, Seb blinked back emotion, thinking how much he loved her. How he regretted selling those letters.

"I suppose it pleases me," Musa answered at last. Her eyes fluttered as though she was thinking; Seb imagined the clicking of her brain calculating away. "I sense I know you, sir. We've met before."

"Then perhaps we're not strangers after all," Seb countered. "As for your sister, she's lovely, but she's not you." To his dismay, a low growl of yearning infused his words.

Contain yourself, Seb.

A sharp laugh. "You're a flatterer, aren't you?"

"If we're to only have this dance, I'd like for it to be as enjoyable as possible for you. Then you'll never forget it." His voice caught with emotion. "Perhaps you'll understand you're not so alone."

"Alone . . ." Her words trailed off. "I once admitted I felt alone to someone I cared for. Alas, he proved untrustworthy."

Seb stumbled for a step, but regained his rhythm. "I'm sure he regrets it very much."

"I have no idea what he thinks. I haven't seen him in some weeks. He did send me a letter though."

Her eyes dipped toward the ground anew. *Please don't let her be weeping.* Seb didn't trust himself not to break the masquerade if she was.

"However, I've since realized something important." She boldly met his eyes. "I was wrong to judge him."

Seb felt a bead of sweat along his neck. "How so?"

Musa's voice dropped so low that Seb strained to understand. "I learned a truth about myself . . . and about the gentleman in question."

His heart began to pound. "What was it?"

She halted mid-step in the center of the ballroom, bringing their waltz to an abrupt standstill. Around them couples swirled unaware, or so it seemed, for all Seb could see was Musa's willowy figure in that gold gown sewn of sunlight. No one else mattered. No one else existed.

"It's a bitter truth," she said. "One I hold myself responsible for."

Seb grasped the soft of Musa's arm. "What is this truth? Tell me!"

Her answer was drowned out by applause. The waltz had arrived at its final exuberant chords. She reached toward Seb's neck; Seb was too startled to resist.

He felt her pull something soft from below his collar. Something that, all too late, he realized what it was.

Jessica's scarf. He'd tucked it beneath his cloak for luck.

The red wool scarf fell onto the white marble floor of the ballroom.

Shit, Seb thought. *Too soon.*

Once Musa picked the scarf off the floor, she reached for his hand. The next thing Seb knew, she'd pulled him toward the nearest door. He was too startled to protest.

Seb found himself inside what appeared to be a library—he'd half-expected her to be tossing her out on the street before he could offer the speech he'd prepared. He looked about the library. Tall bookcases, long tables, Persian rugs.

She locked the thick oak door behind them with a firm slide of the bolt.

"It was you!" she breathed, throwing his red scarf at him. He caught it neatly.

"Musa, I only wanted to see you—"

She stamped her foot. "Take off your mask, Sebastian Atkinson. Now." A glance toward the door. "We haven't much time."

Seb obeyed, girding himself for her fury. *Fight for her*, he reminded himself. He set his mask on a table.

"Musa, I never wanted you to know it was me. Well, I did, but not yet. That is, I wanted you to know later, after the ball—that was my plan. Never meant you harm. Truly. I only wanted reassurance you were well." A long breath. "I can't imagine you want to see me. Nor can I imagine you want to listen to me. But I'm begging you to give me exactly sixty seconds. Only that. Nothing more. Just enough time to tell you how much I love you, how sorry I am, how wrong I was, what an idiot I am. The usual . . ."

Seb took out his pocket watch. He dropped to his knees before her. Waiting. Begging, if he was to be honest.

"We don't need sixty seconds," Musa said at last.

A slow grin spread across her mouth as she untied her gold mask from her face. Then, to Seb's complete and utter surprise, she dipped her mouth toward his.

The last thing he recalled was the room spinning like a top.

CHAPTER 39

MERDE, he'd fainted.

Musa watched Seb's tall form tip against the floor. Fortunately, the floor was carpeted in a thick red Persian rug, which cushioned his collapse—she supposed it was the shock. As for herself, her heart was speeding like a train leaving Paddington, her breath catching and blood rushing, and it had nothing to do with the champagne she'd imbibed. Joy, that's what she felt when she recognized him. A joy so bright it startled her. Well, along with a hint of horror. For a moment, she feared he'd hit his head on a coal bin.

"Seb, are you okay?" Musa patted his cheeks, which were drained of color. "Should I fetch a doctor? Smelling salts? Water?"

His blue eyes fluttered open, shadowed by his thick dark lashes.

"If I'm dreaming, don't wake me," he muttered, offering a wide smile. He sat upright. "Hello, darling."

And then he pulled her down onto the rug next to him. He embraced her, weeping and laughing like a madman.

"You're so emotional," she teased, brushing his dark curls from his brow. "Same as you ever were."

And then she handed him the letter she'd tucked in her reticule. Those three words she'd yet to mail.

She'd written:

Understanding and forgiveness.

She'd chosen these words hoping he'd understand her intention: that she'd forgiven him for his betrayal; that she understood what he'd done and why. She'd granted him this because she yearned for the same from Clio. That she grown to understand that she was much like him: complicated, compromised, desperate.

Seb looked up from the letter. Met her gaze.

The letter dropped from his hand.

And then his lips were on hers, and hers were on his, and she lost all rational thought. Were they in a library? It appeared to be— the shelves were blurry, as were the gas sconces lining the wall. She didn't even know her great-aunt had a library. It would do for their needs in that moment and felt entirely appropriate: there they were, surrounded by words and books, the same force that had brought them into each other's lives. Better yet, locked door, thick walls; she could barely hear the string octet.

Musa considered the ball taking place on the other side of the room. She imagined Mary and Amanda Seeley seeking Felicity Vita, and even Angela with her suitors, or the possibility of journalists and scandals. But none of them would deter her. Not now.

Seb had returned. Sebastian Atkinson was back from the south of France. She, Musa Bartham, had waltzed with him, a dance that brought him so near that she could smell his scent, see his pulse in the hollow beneath his jaw. His gloved hands caressing the small of her waist, expertly guiding her around the ballroom. During the entire time she was swirling in his arms, she thought she'd swoon from yearning despite everything that had come between them.

You're imagining him to be Seb, she'd told herself, thinking of the letter with those three words. *You only wish.*

Once she'd made out the telltale flash of red wool around his neck, the leap of her heart confirmed the truth she'd tried so hard to contain: she still loved him. It had taken all her control not to push him against the wall and brazenly set her mouth against his, like Felicity Vita might have.

But now that they were alone in a room filled with books with a locked door far from the crowd . . .

"I love you," he said again once they broke away. "Desperately. That's why I had to return to see you."

"I know. I'm so glad you're here. I love you too. Desperately."

"And you truly understand all I did?" His eyes searched her face. "You weren't being polite in your letter to make me feel better?"

She thought of Clio and her love letters, and how very wrong she'd been. One day she'd tell him. "I do."

"I'm so grateful. And relieved." He rained gentle butterfly kisses all over her face. "I know how very wrong I was, Musa." A kiss on the tip of her nose. "Despicably, miserably wrong. I've hated myself ever since."

"I can't bear to think of you hating yourself," she said, clutching his hands. "I forgive you, Seb. I really do. You did what was necessary for your family." She swallowed away the lump in her throat. "I would have done the same."

And have done the same.

But she wouldn't think of this now. No, there would be plenty of time for that later—the remainder of their lives, she hoped.

As for now, there was only one thing on Musa's mind and it didn't involve letters or apologies or remorse or fretting about what was happening on the other side of the door.

She peeled her long white opera gloves from her hands, then his black kid ones from his.

"What time is it? I can't see a blasted thing beyond your handsome face."

Seb glanced at his pocket watch. "Nearly half-past eight."

"I suspect we've fifteen minutes before someone comes looking for me. Twenty, if we're lucky. We'll need to be quick."

She yanked his cloak off him and unbuttoned the fall of his trousers. His erection sprang forth, aroused and red. Welcoming. She hadn't had enough of him that day at his family home.

She quirked an eyebrow. "Am I too forward?"

"Not at all. I'm delighted," he said, grinning broadly. "I appreciate your practicality. If we've only fifteen minutes, do with me what you will."

She wrapped her palm around the length of his arousal. How warm and smooth it felt! Hard. A drop of pearly moisture appeared at the tip. Her breath caught. She felt her nether regions grow moist with anticipation. Desire. She wanted him. All of him.

Any shyness she might have held banished. Instead, she felt brazen. Eager. Emotional. But she was no longer pretending to be Felicity—she was all Musa.

And Musa knew what she wanted.

"You should know I'm not leaving this room a virgin," she announced, lifting her gold gown up to expose the pale expanse of her thighs above her stockings, the delta of dark curls. She silently blessed the modiste for a costume design that didn't involve yards of flounces and petticoats to get in their way.

"I'm happy to oblige," Seb replied, his voice husky with desire. "You should know I'm never letting you go, Musa." He brushed his lips along the column of her neck. "I've learned my lesson. Now how can I assist you?"

And then there were no more words, for there was no time. Musa pushed Seb back against the rug and climbed on top of him, much as she had that day in his family home before everything turned so horribly wrong.

"I think I'm ready for you," she said. "Hurry, please."

"Ah, but for a first time . . ." He met her eyes. "Trust me?"

She nodded.

Ever so slowly he inserted one finger, his eyes never leaving hers. Another. She inhaled deeply. It took all her control not to rub against him, especially with his arousal so close to the warmth of her cleft.

And then a third finger. A fourth. She felt filled to breaking. But she didn't.

She closed her eyes, wanting him more than she'd ever wanted anything in her life. And then his thumb was on her clit, stroking her so gently but surely she thought her bones would melt. Pleasure. Only pleasure. She gasped and moaned as her body dissolved into light.

Before she recovered from her climax, he set his erection against her warm portal and pressed against her gently. Slowly. Gradually. She inhaled as she felt herself adjust. Stretch to accommodate him.

"Don't move, darling," he breathed against her ear. "Not yet."

He kissed her deeply before he broke away to nip at her earlobe.

A sharp burst of pain from the center of her being.

And then there was no more pain, only soreness—but she welcomed the soreness for it was proof of what she'd left behind and what she'd gained.

She opened her eyes to find Seb's hungry gaze awaiting hers.

"Better?" he asked, brushing her hair from her brow. He kissed her tenderly.

She laughed. "Definitely better."

"Glad to hear." Another kiss, this one below her lips near her beauty mark. "I'll make certain to pull out to protect you."

"I expect no less of you." She glanced at the door, imagining the ball on the other side, the ticking clock before they were found missing. "But hurry!"

A broad smile. "If that's what you want, Musa Felicity Bartham Vita."

She bit his chin gently. "That's exactly what I want, Sebastian Henry Atkinson Whitney. This may be my first time with you. But it won't be my last."

With a growl of desire, they rolled together until he was on top. And then he was moving inside her and her hips were rising to meet his and it was more than better. It was exactly what she wanted. No, *needed.*

Their coupling was fast and voracious and filled with all the yearning they'd suppressed for so long, like a summer storm arriving in the midst of a sunny day. As Seb took her, he murmured her name over and over in all its variations and possibilities, and she cried his name too. Musa felt her body open to his, welcoming and eager and curious.

"Only our first time," Seb promised once they'd collapsed together, smiling and spent.

"But not our last," she answered, setting her head against his shoulder. "What time is it?"

"Ten to nine," he said, kissing her hand as though he was a knight and she his La Dame avec Merci.

"Nine! I'm expected to speak about our book then!"

She let him help her to her feet. She adjusted her gown, examining it for any sign that might reveal their intimacies.

"How do I look?"

Seb smoothed her hair where her pins had loosened. "Glorious. Beautiful." A kiss on her forehead. "Mine."

She laughed. "And here I was fretting my gown looked wrinkled! Where are our masks?"

Before they could don their masks, a demanding knock sounded on the library door.

"I suppose they've found us," Seb said, teasing. "Or someone is in need of a book."

Musa's laughter caught in her throat. All of a sudden she recalled Miss Seeley searching for Felicity Vita, her suspicion the poet would be at the ball tonight, how the news made Musa's stomach twist with anxiety. Oh, and there was Angela and her suitors who might even propose.

For Angela's sake, there must be no scandal. None at all.

CHAPTER 40

Seb had no time to linger in the euphoria of being reunited with his beloved Musa. Nor did he have a chance to replace his moon mask or the red scarf or fasten his black cloak (though he'd thankfully buttoned his trousers). Musa appeared too jarred for his comfort at whoever was pounding on the library door.

"What is it, darling?" he asked, taking her hand.

Musa replied in a low voice, "Miss Seeley—that's Persephone Press's new owner—believes Felicity is here tonight. I have no idea why Miss Seeley wants to confront her. All she said was she'd made a mistake about some books."

"Shit." Perhaps Luke hadn't deflected attention from Musa as promised. Earlier that evening, Seb had thought he'd spied Luke's familiar yellow bowler outside Lady Hadley's in Grosvenor Square, but decided he'd imagined him.

"*Merde* indeed," Musa agreed, her jaw tight.

The knock sounded again, louder and more demanding than the first. This time, it was followed by the scuttle of conversation from the other side.

"Musa? Are you in there?" A high-pitched female voice. "Open up!"

"My sister, Angela," Musa explained, her smile returning.

"She's probably looking for me to present our book. And now that you're here, we can do it together!"

As Musa unbolted the library door, she threw him the most beautiful smile he'd ever seen. Seb felt as though he was glowing like the sun and moon combined.

All of a sudden the library was invaded by Angela Bartham costumed as a ballerina, a ridiculously tall gentleman wearing an artist's smock, a petite lady Seb recognized as Mary Nicholson in spite of her mask, the twins dressed as black cats, and Luke Ward without a mask. Seb hadn't imagined spying him in Grosvenor Square after all.

The library suddenly felt too small for the ensuing melee of conversation. Seb struggled to comprehend everything.

Angela to everyone: "I'm engaged!"

Tall gentleman to Musa, bowing: "I'm Mr. Carles, Miss Bartham. Forgive me, I forgot I should have asked Mrs. Bartham for Miss Angela's hand first—"

Angela, scoffing: "Oh, Mama won't mind! She's not here tonight anyway. You can ask Musa instead!"

Lyra and Theo in chorus: "Will we live with Mr. Carles in Surrey?"

Musa to Angela: "That's all well, but can you give me my spectacles? I can't see a damn thing, let alone congratulate Mr. Carles."

Miss Nicholson to Seb, smiling wryly: "Mr. Atkinson, how fortunate you're here! And unexpected—I'd thought you to be in the south of France."

"I was," Seb managed to inject, his head spinning. "But—"

Miss Nicholson to Musa, winking: "*Now* I know where you two went. I hope you got the job done this time!"

Angela primly, after offering Musa her spectacles: "I refuse to understand your insinuation, Miss Nicholson. This is not a conversation my fiancé and I should be party to."

Finally, Luke Ward came forth—Luke, who appeared near to bursting with whatever he'd come to say. Seb's nerves prickled. What happened?

"I must speak to you both," he mouthed. "Immediately."

Musa's eyes widened. But then she drew herself up to her full height, again appearing like the sun goddess who'd demanded Seb take her virginity earlier that evening.

"Everyone out!" she ordered, gesturing toward the door. "Save for Mr. Ward."

Once the library was cleared and door shut, Luke's words spilled.

"It was Amanda Seeley who sent your fair copies to the *Gazette* to authenticate Felicity's letters, Miss Bartham," he said in a rush. "I only wish it hadn't taken me so long to uncover the truth. I've been trying to speak to you all night, but you were masked. I had no idea where you were. Nor did I dare send a note."

"Why would Miss Seeley do that?" Seb asked.

Luke flung out his arms. "I have no idea. Perhaps to gain publicity for Persephone Press. Perhaps to ensure Felicity can't publish again."

Musa appeared to wobble ever so briefly before she snapped upright.

"Bitch," she muttered. "Not only did she put Felicity out of print, she nearly ruined my sister's chances for marriage!"

Without another word, Musa adjusted her spectacles on her nose and stomped from the library.

Where was Miss Seeley? Musa had to tell Mary, warn her. Whatever the American had planned for Felicity Vita, Musa would stop it.

Now that she finally had her spectacles, Musa felt overwhelmed by colors and light. The entirety of the masked ball seemed brighter than ever, more crowded, the music louder and even more out of tune. Alas, the string octet had only grown in enthusiasm as the night progressed.

Musa's eyes darted about the ballroom. There was the lanky

Mr. Carles in one corner holding court with Angela as they received congratulations, her great-aunt speaking to the blonde lady adorned in white robes suitable for a muse—Musa's heart again constricted with yearning for her mother—and a cluster of excited parents with adorable children. The Countess of Sunderland reclined on a chaise, her identity revealed by her mourning gown and lack of mask. She appeared simultaneously bored yet pleased; Musa supposed she'd learned of Angela's engagement. In another corner, Mary stood beside the table holding all those copies of *Poems of Morality and Goodness for Children to Abide*, her blue stockings glowing beneath her woolen smock as she ate a slice of chocolate cake.

Musa squinted into the distance. *No Miss Seeley.* Hadn't the American been wearing a bright red ballgown and an overly large hat?

But in the midst of her search, Musa realized she'd lost the most important person of all . . . and it wasn't Amanda Seeley.

Seb. Where had he gone?

Her heart gave a stutter. She'd left him behind when she'd run from the library. As usual, she'd gone off on her own, not inviting anyone to accompany her. No, worse: not trusting anyone to help her. She had to be the practical Musa. The solitary Musa. The Musa responsible for everything and everyone.

She whirled around the ballroom, her breath catching. Again, she saw Angela, Mary, and the entire ballroom, colors and light and chatter.

Alone. That's what I am.

Well, she'd chosen this, hadn't she, when she'd rushed off without Seb? It was her own damn fault. But it wasn't too late, was it?

Musa felt a hand grasp her wrist. Seb. He'd chased after her.

He turned her to face him. "You rushed off so quickly! I was worried."

"First I was furious. Then I panicked," she admitted. "It suddenly all seemed too much to bear."

"Oh, Musa . . ." He set his forehead against hers. "Whatever happens, you're not alone. Not anymore."

Not alone. She let out a little cry of relief, of joy. She collapsed against Seb's broad chest, all of her anger and anxiety fleeing. As they embraced, she felt malleable and emotional, and it wasn't only due to the physical intimacies they'd just shared on the library floor. For some reason Seb's warm voice—no, his words—provoked this unexpected response. This awareness. It felt a gift.

Seb cupped her face in his palms as though Musa were the most precious jewel in the world. She had the sense the entire ballroom had paused in their dance to stare their way. She didn't care.

"Musa, whatever happens, I'll never leave you."

She laughed, a hiccupping sound. "Even if all of London condemns me as Felicity Vita?"

A gasp rang out. Musa and Seb turned.

Amanda Seeley stood behind them. She pointed at Musa, her mouth agape and her eyes wide and oversized scarlet hat askew.

"You!" she squealed. *"You're* Felicity Vita! I knew it!"

"She didn't mean it," Seb protested. "A jest."

"I heard what Miss Bartham said, Mr. Atkinson—and now it all makes sense!" To Musa: "I'd thought it peculiar how secretive you were with Miss Nicholson. I'd hoped the ball would draw Felicity out from hiding—and it has!"

And then, to Musa's astonishment, the American curtseyed low enough to kiss the marble floor.

CHAPTER 41

Musa felt as though the marble floor had cracked beneath her feet—and it wasn't only because Amanda Seeley appeared prepared to press her lips against it. On top of that, the American's be-plumed red hat was so huge that it drew every set of eyes their way. Worse, the string octet staggered to a halt—perhaps they'd only been engaged to play until nine—so anyone could hear every word they said.

"I've been searching all over for you, Miss Vita!" Miss Seeley screeched. "Your poems! We need to speak. I was so very wrong!"

Yes, very wrong, Musa wanted to snap. But this was not the time or place for a confrontation. Not with over a hundred people clutching their children, Angela smiling tersely beside her Mr. Carles, Aunt Minerva and Lady Sunderland whispering, and heaven knew who else from society.

"It's not what you think, Miss Seeley," Musa whispered, her head light. "I'm not you-know-who."

Miss Seeley retorted from the floor, "I just heard you confess as much, Miss Bartham. Why would you fear being condemned as Felicity Vita unless you were? I'd suspected such all along, but hadn't any proof."

"You're wrong," Musa hissed. "So very wrong!"

"You don't understand! I *want* to publish your poems—well, Felicity's poems, that is. I was wrong to destroy those books."

Well, this was a turn of events.

Seb protectively gathered Musa into his arms. "Miss Seeley, I thought you hated Felicity Vita."

"I did, Mr. Atkinson! Well, I *had* hated her, but I've been enlightened. My one true love—" here Miss Seeley colored prettily beneath her large hat "—rather, the gentleman courting me." Another flush. "I didn't know he'd been sending Miss Bartham's poems to woo me."

"Woo you?" Musa frowned, distrusting her senses. "How so?"

"Letters, Miss Bartham! Glorious ones too—that's what brought me to London. Well, along with buying Persephone Press."

"Oh lord." Musa knew this story. Too well.

Miss Seeley continued, "This morning I discovered he'd quoted Felicity Vita's poems after the *Gazette* returned those fair copies of your poems—"

"You mean *Felicity's* poems, not mine," Musa protested.

"Oh, come, Miss Bartham—I overheard your confession! There's no shame in writing love poems!"

It wasn't shame Musa felt. It was panic. Even with Seb beside her, his arm draped across her shoulders, her stomach churned.

"You see, I'd assumed they were—" Miss Seeley's voice dropped "—scandalous. I feel such a fool for not reading them first."

"Yes, you're a fool," Seb agreed. "Now get up from the floor!"

Miss Seeley growled, "Not until Miss Bartham accepts my apology and promises to let me republish Felicity's books."

Musa cried, "I can't do that! I'm not Felicity Vita!"

Too late: Musa's protest went unacknowledged as Miss Seeley's accusation spread from one set of lips to the next through the soirée. They echoed around Lady Hadley's ballroom like a howling wind sweeping across a ripe wheat field:

"Did you hear? Felicity Vita is here! In this ballroom!"

"Miss Bartham is Felicity Vita?"

"She's Felicity Vita!"

"Can you believe it?"

"Oh, I believe it! She's a Bartham after all . . ."

Musa met Seb's eyes.

But I'm not alone. Not anymore.

"I'll take care of this," Seb said, squeezing her hand. "I promise."

"How?" Musa's tone was more puzzled than panicked. Such was his effect on her.

"Trust me, darling."

Seb offered Musa a kiss on her forehead before pulling away. She watched him stride toward the podium, which had been set up for Musa to introduce *Poems of Morality and Goodness for Children to Abide.* His approach was purposeful, eager. The sort to inspire confidence. Trust.

"Excuse me!" he called out, tapping a wine glass with a spoon. "Hello! May I have your attention? I've an announcement to make!"

The ballroom quieted as all turned his way as one. Musa's heart pounded. What was Seb up to?

"Sorry to interrupt your festivities! I'm Sebastian Atkinson, the illustrator of *Poems of Morality and Goodness for Children to Abide* —yes, I know I wasn't expected here tonight because I was in France. I won't speak further of this save to say life can be surprising." He glanced at Musa, offering a lopsided grin; her heart swelled. "For example, four months ago, I had no idea I would work with Miss Bartham on a children's book. Nor did I expect I'd end up falling desperately and hopelessly in love with her—"

A loud tsk rang out. "Spare us your sentimentalities!"

Aunt Minerva. Musa couldn't tell whether she was impatient or appalled.

Seb continued, "Anyway, as I was saying, I love Miss Bartham . . . and when you love someone, you want to protect them, especially when you overhear gossip that's destructive. Unkind. Untrue."

He paused to take a deep breath.

"Over the course of the evening, a rumor circulated that Miss Bartham secretly writes poetry under the *nom de plume* of Felicity Vita. I'm here to assure you it's completely false."

Seb met Musa's eyes. A smile curled his delicious mouth.

"You see, I'm Felicity Vita."

A gasp. A cry. A woman screamed. Someone even called out, "A man can't be Felicity Vita!"

Seb shook his head vehemently. "Anyone could be Felicity Vita—and that somebody is me! Me, me, me! I wrote those poems, every single last one of them. Me, Sebastian Henry Atkinson of Folgate Street in Spitalfields, previously of Bexley, Kent. No one else." He pointed at Luke, who stood near the podium. "Make sure you publish this in the *Gazette* so everyone knows the truth!"

"Hogwash!" the Countess of Sunderland shouted. "Rubbish! Musa Bartham wrote those poems. I know such."

"My lady, you're wrong!" Seb replied. "Dare you slander an innocent woman's reputation? Why, if you were a gentleman, I'd call for pistols at dawn!"

How defiant he looks, Musa thought. If she wasn't so anxious, she'd find it arousing.

Seb turned back to the audience. "As I was saying before I was interrupted, I alone wrote *The Poetics of Passion, Verses of Love Lost and Love Found,* and *The Triumph of Eros,* and the rest of those books, every single one. Sestinas, sonnets, limericks! All of them—I'm the author!"

"Oh posh!" The Countess of Sunderland rose from her chaise. As she hobbled toward the podium, she cried out, "Threaten me all you like, but I knew Musa Bartham was Felicity Vita all along. As long as she kept it a secret, I chose to say naught—well, I would have said something had it become necessary, say, if a Bartham were to marry my son. But! I cannot bear to hear you, young man —" she smacked her folded fan against Seb's shoulder "—spread falsehoods among the Ton. No, no, no! Now take your pistols at dawn and—"

"Stop! I know who Felicity Vita is!"

A lady's voice rang from the back of the ballroom—a voice Musa knew very well. It was a musical voice, one that had sung lullabies to Musa as a child and soothed her hurts after she'd grown into adulthood. A voice belonging to the woman who'd taught Musa what it meant to love deeply and fully, even if it meant losing yourself in mourning . . . or being betrayed by your eldest daughter.

Musa's heart skipped a beat.

It cannot be. But oh, how I hope!

Every head in the ballroom turned as a graceful older woman costumed in white robes emerged from the crowd—the same muse Musa had witnessed earlier. Now that Musa had her spectacles, she could see the muse was conjured of silver and moonlight and beauty and love.

Better yet, understanding and forgiveness.

Once the white-robed muse removed her silver mask, Musa held no question as to the lady's identity.

"Mama!" Musa rushed to her mother's side. "You came after all!"

Clio Bartham enveloped Musa in her arms. "Of course, sweetheart!"

Musa felt her brow crinkle. "But why? How?"

Clio laughed, shaking her head. "I'd never miss your moment of glory! I didn't dare tell anyone I was here, for I feared drawing attention to myself . . . but perhaps that's what's called for." She winked at Musa. "Shall we, sweetheart?"

And then, hand-in-hand, mother and daughter turned to face the crowd.

CHAPTER 42

LOVE POETESS UNMASKED AT BALL!

THE TIMES, Morning Edition, 14 April 1872: *Last night in a sensational scene not to be forgotten, the poet Felicity Vita was revealed to be none other than London's very own 'Muse of Scandal', Mrs. Clio Bartham, née Hadley. Mrs. Bartham made her shocking confession at a masked ball sponsored by Lady Minerva Hadley of Grosvenor Square. The ball was to mark the publication of* Poems of Morality and Goodness for Children to Abide, *a children's book written by Mrs. Bartham's eldest daughter Musa and illustrated by her fiancé Mr. Sebastian Atkinson.*

Mrs. Bartham confessed her secret identity after Miss Bartham was mistakenly identified as Felicity Vita by Miss Amanda Seeley, Persephone Press's new American publisher. In an exclusive to The Times, *Mrs. Bartham explained, "I decided to publish as Felicity Vita after my beloved husband was reported perished in the Holy Land. These poems were inspired by our private correspondence. Though I relied on my daughter to make fair copies for publication, their authorship remains mine alone."*

As a result of Mrs. Bartham's unmasking, Persephone Press

plans to issue new editions of Felicity Vita's books, proof scandal is good for business.

In a happier development, Persephone Press stated that Poems of Morality and Goodness for Children to Abide *won't be the press's last children's book collaboration with Miss Bartham and Mr. Atkinson. The couple plan to begin work on* Tales of Clever Animals and Witty Birds *in the coming year.*

"We plan to take our time writing and illustrating it," Miss Bartham said. "Mr. Atkinson and I so enjoyed working together on our first book that we've no desire to rush our second."

Coincidentally, Miss Angela Bartham's engagement to Mr. John Carles of Surrey was also announced at last night's masked ball. "Why wouldn't I marry Miss Angela?" Mr. Carles replied to our reporter's inquiry. "Love is more important than scandal."

A Christmas wedding is planned.

EPILOGUE
THE FUTURE

Six months later

THE MORNING LIGHT in Venice was particularly spectacular in October, Seb decided. But then again, all light was spectacular when it revealed the alluring form of his wife sleeping in their bed. Musa's long chestnut hair was tousled against the white crisp linens, her rosy lips parted as she let out a decidedly unladylike snore.

"Darling," Seb whispered, gently tapping Musa on her bared shoulder. He settled beside her on the edge of their bed. "Tea?"

She shifted and muttered and made all the sweet sounds Seb had grown to know since their reunion after the masked ball—a ball that marked so many changes in the Barthams' lives.

"What time is it?" Musa muttered, yawning as she accepted her tea. Milk with a little sugar, no lemon.

As she sat up to sip the hot beverage, the sheet slipped down from her body to Seb's appreciative view. As tempting as the prospect of morning lovemaking was, he was already dressed for the day. Not only was he ready to go out, he wore his best suit, a custom tailored one sewn of the finest linen that great-aunt Minerva could unearth. The dowager had insisted on it upon the newlyweds' arrival in Venice for their honeymoon. "He may be only an artist, but he should be a well-dressed one if he's going to marry into *my* family," she'd said.

Today was the sort of day that deserved a best suit.

"Eleven o'clock." He offered her a *fritoe*, a sugary Venetian pastry she'd grown nearly as fond of as she had his landlady's Chelsea buns from Seb's Spitalfields days—days now behind them thanks to the success of *Poems of Morality and Goodness for Children to Abide.*

She glanced up from her tea, alarmed. "Eleven! You should have woken me hours ago! We're due there at noon."

"You needed the rest. No need for both of us to be anxious."

"You're very good at settling my mind." She offered him a sly grin as she set down her tea on the nightstand. She opened her arms. He slid into her embrace, the gesture comfortable. Familiar.

Mine, he thought.

"Good morning—well, nearly afternoon." She offered her husband a lingering kiss. "I panicked when I learned the time. I'm too nervous."

"And good morning," Seb rejoined once they'd pulled away. "I'm more excited for you than nervous."

He inhaled her skin, which bore the faint scent of lovemaking and floral soap and her customary sandalwood perfume. Despite his intentions to remain focused on the day ahead, he recalled her face flushed with passion beneath candlelight during the previous night's festivities. Her soft cries of devotion. The sound combining with the murmurs of the sea beyond their window made for a heady combination.

If today wasn't so important, he'd gladly take her right now. But there'd be time for that later.

Before they left, Seb tucked a small magnifying glass into his pocket.

~

Musa discovered her mother already waiting for them when they arrived inside the Ca' d'Arte. The art gallery was but a short walk from their rooms along the Fondamenta Zattere, which wasn't far from Aunt Minerva's small palazzo on the Grand Canal—she'd continued letting it all those years. It turned out to be convenient. Clio, Daphne, and Jessica used it as their home while visiting Venice, while Angela remained behind in London with the twins to better plan her Christmas wedding. After all, it wouldn't do to share lodgings with newlyweds—especially since Clio had gained a fair amount of attention after announcing she was Felicity Vita. She was working on a new volume of poems in honor of Musa's father, using Venice as inspiration.

"Mama!" Musa called out, Seb by her side. "I'm sorry we're a little late."

"Actually you're on time, sweetheart."

Clio had been pacing back and forth in front of Seb's painting of *La Dame avec Merci*, which he'd completed shortly before they'd departed London for their honeymoon. It had been tricky traveling with a large canvas, but Seb and Musa managed. After all, it wasn't every day an artist received an invitation to exhibit in Venice—an opportunity that offered them sanctuary while Bexley Manor was made habitable so they could begin work on *Tales of Clever Animals and Witty Birds* upon their return.

Poems of Morality and Goodness for Children to Abide affected their lives beyond Musa's plan to write a new children's book. Due to Seb's illustrations, Luke Ward was able to persuade *The London Illustrated Daily* to publish an article about his friend's oil paintings —an article that had gained widespread attention for both Seb and Luke. As a result, Luke was sent to Paris to report about art and culture, an unexpected shift in his journalistic career. As for Seb, while *La Dame avec Merci* had little to do with children's book illustrations, the stars had aligned in his favor . . . though there was another reason they were at the Ca' d'Arte that afternoon. A reason Musa still couldn't believe could be true. If so, it was decidedly the best wedding present they could ever hope to receive.

The person responsible for uncovering that reason rushed toward Seb and Musa, circumventing Musa's ability to offer her mother a welcoming hug.

"Mr. Ward," Musa greeted. Her nerves were evident in her voice, she decided, along with a joy she didn't fully trust. Nor did her mother apparently; Clio's cheeks were closer to ecru than pink.

"My colleague will be here in a moment," Luke said. He was dressed even more outlandishly than usual. Perhaps it was the Parisian style. "I must warn you he's concerned he's wrong—he understands how important this is to your family."

"Whether he's wrong or not, we need to know the truth," Clio said, her silvery voice catching with emotion. She fingered the pearls surrounding her neck, the ivory-hued gardenia tucked into her lace collar.

Musa took her mother's hand in hers. "Whatever happens, we'll manage. After all, we're Barthams."

"And Atkinsons," Seb added.

Luke offered the three of them a wry smile. "A formidable combination." He rose to his feet. "Ah, there he is!"

They were approached by a stout middle-aged blond gentleman dressed in a brown suit and floppy felt hat. As he drew near, Musa made out faint wrinkles around his dark brown eyes as though he'd spent too much time staring into bright sunlight.

"Signore Antonio Donati of the *Corriere Adriatico*," Luke introduced. "Yes, I know he's a poor dresser for an Italian . . . and a journalist."

"*Buon giorno*, Signora Atkinson, Signora Bartham," Signore Donati greeted, his expression as heavy as his accent. "Ward, charming as ever."

"Get on with it!" Luke pressed. "I haven't come all this way from Paris for you to play coy."

Signore Donati's brow creased. "I fear upsetting you, Signora Bartham—Ward has explained of your losses. I hope I'm not—how you say?—*non sbagliarmi.*"

"Mistaken," Luke translated for Clio, Musa, and Seb. "We'll be the judge of that, Donati."

"Just show us what you found," Clio demanded. "I can no longer bear it!"

Signore Donati pulled out a small photograph from inside his jacket. This was Seb's cue to provide the magnifying glass he'd brought, which Clio promptly grabbed.

All five bent over the photograph as though it was a holy relic. Which in a way it was, for if the photograph was what Donati believed it to be, it would provide proof of Neil Bartham's survival in Jerusalem.

Musa adjusted her spectacles.

The photograph revealed six men dressed in military uniform standing around a wooden cart set beneath a cluster of tall palm trees. A lanky man laid inside the cart—a man whose face was oh-so-familiar, though his features appeared affected by pain and shadowed by shaggy hair streaked with gray. He wore a heavy beard and shabby clothes. One of his legs was wrapped in thick bandages beneath the hip as though it had been amputated.

His dazed hazel eyes were open. Wide.

Alive.

"My husband," Clio breathed. She looked up from the magnifying glass. "It's him. I know it!"

"Are you certain, Mama?" Musa asked. It looked like Papa, but the photograph was so grainy.

"I've no doubt, sweetheart! See, he's wearing the signet ring I gave him when we wed."

Seb asked, "Where did you take this photograph, Signore Donati?"

"Outside Cairo. I took the photograph ten months ago when I was traveling toward Suez. I'd no idea what it signified until Ward wrote me of your situation."

Luke smirked. "And it was a good thing I did, was it not?"

"A very good thing," Clio agreed, her eyes bright. "I will find my husband. I must."

With a cry that sounded halfway between a gasp and a laugh, Clio wrapped Musa and Seb in a joyful embrace, which was returned with as much enthusiasm as it had been offered. Oh, how Clio hugged them! Musa had the sense her mother would never let them go; that the photograph of her father had become a thread tying their family's past to their future and beyond to the new century. Seb squeezed Musa's hand, brushing his lips against her cheeks.

And then Musa realized she'd gained everything she'd dreamed of. After all, a happy life was all she ever wanted.

AUTHOR'S NOTE

Thank you so much, dear reader, for spending time with *The Poetics of Passion*. I hope Musa and Seb's tangled tale of family, romance, and love letters amused and moved you. Though the act of writing a novel appears a solitary task, it's a group endeavor in many ways. However, before I acknowledge the individuals responsible for helping me bring this book into the light, I'd like to share a few words about the inspiration that led to my writing it.

The story of Neil and Clio Bartham's love-at-first-sight infatuation and subsequent elopement may be familiar to readers acquainted with the Pre-Raphaelite art movement. Like Neil and Clio, the painter John Millais's marriage was born of scandal: he fell madly in love with Effie Ruskin, the unhappily wed wife of famed art critic John Ruskin, author of *The Stones of Venice*. The dissolution of the Ruskins' troubled marriage led to a high profile annulment that scandalized Victorian England—and left Effie permanently outcast from polite society. However, once wed, the Millaises spent the rest of their lives deeply devoted to each other and their many children. Elements of Neil Bartham's artistic travails were also inspired by the spotted career of William Holman Hunt, whose travels to the Holy Land enabled the creation of his religious-themed paintings; *The Scapegoat* and *The Light of the World* are perhaps the best-known of these.

As for the writing of *The Poetics of Passion* itself, Musa and Seb's story incubated in my brain during the long months of the pandemic, when romance novels provided me with much needed comfort and escape from a stressful world. During this period, I was extremely fortunate to have access to online writing workshops with Sarah Maclean, Sherry Thomas, Olivia Waite, and other romance world luminaries. These workshops gave me the push to finally set words to page after years of "one day I'll write a romance" procrastination. On a related note, I'm deeply grateful to Eliza Knight for her insightful editorial feedback and support, Harper St. George and Mimi Matthews for their generous endorsements, and Rachel McMillan for her sage market feedback.

Beyond the romance community, a huge thank you to Heather Webb, Michelle Brower, Natalie Edwards, Jennifer Johnson, Karen Zuegner, Terry Lynn Thomas, and Crystal King, all who read and commented on various drafts. Much gratitude to the good people at Muse Publications, who took on my fledgling romance novel with enthusiastic aplomb. Finally, much love to my family and my sister who always have my back no matter what I'm writing.

—Delphine Ross

Turn the page to read an excerpt from
The Dance of Desire,
the next Muses of Scandal novel
by Delphine Ross.

PROLOGUE
AUGUST 1859

On the sultriest day London had seen all year, Virgil Sydenham, Viscount of Sunderland, was locked in an artist's closet.

This hadn't been Virgil's intention. He'd only gone inside the closet to steal a moment of solitude before rejoining his father and mother, who'd been arguing again. Hiding had become a habit since Virgil's tenth birthday some months earlier: go someplace quiet where no one could find him, preferably with a thick wood door. Breathe deeply until he felt able to confront the world anew, before anyone noticed his absence.

Never before had the door locked behind him.

Prior to this occurrence, Virgil and his parents had been visiting the artist who owned the closet, a certain Neil Bartham. Virgil's father, the Earl of Sunderland, had engaged Bartham to paint Virgil and his mother as a surprise for her birthday. Bartham immediately dazzled Virgil with his looks, charm, and talent—all elements Virgil believed he lacked. (Even at the age of ten, Virgil held few illusions about himself.) As for Bartham, he was a tall man of perhaps five and thirty years. He wore a cobalt blue jacket that had little similarity to the Savile Row tailoring Virgil's father favored. Bartham bore thick chestnut hair, a broad smile, and an easy, engaging manner. (Also unlike Virgil's father.) Bartham possessed a large family—Virgil overheard several children playing in the lush garden outside the studio, which was in a wing of the artist's home —and a fair-haired wife, who doted on the artist as though he was the sun and she the moon. Clearly, Neil Bartham was someone fortune favored.

However, his mother had not at *all* been pleased when the earl's birthday gift was unfurled. Her mouth pursed, her eyes widened. Virgil sussed there was something uncouth about Neil Bartham for all his pleasantness. Something disreputable.

"You do know his wife is an adulteress?" his mother hissed once Bartham stepped away to request refreshments for them. "The newspapers call her the Muse of Scandal. She was married to some art critic when she ran off with Bartham—"

"Her first marriage was annulled years ago, Eliza," his father interrupted in a tight voice. "Consider Bartham's talent, darling. He'll paint a masterpiece worthy of you."

"Talent is no substitute for moral rectitude, Richard." She stamped her silk-clad foot. "I do wish you'd warned me before we ambulated here on such a hot day…"

Once his mother's voice began to rise, Virgil slipped from the studio toward the hallway. Toward the artist's closet, which turned out to be the first door on the left.

No one noticed.

The closet was filled with several tall canvases and a folded easel. Enough room for a boy to hide. But once the door locked behind Virgil, he understood the worst: he was trapped. Yet he didn't panic despite the smoldering heat and the pervasive stench of turpentine. Instead, he felt an odd gratitude. A locked closet was an excuse for him to escape the arguing. The strife. The sense of being perpetually underwhelming to his parents.

I suppose I should yell for help, he thought. He didn't.

A moment passed. Another.

Outside the closet, Virgil heard a scuttle of voices. Not his parents, thankfully—perhaps they thought he'd gone to play with the artists' children. Speaking of which, Virgil heard a young boy lisp in a high-pitched tone, "One, two, three, four…"

A game of Hide and Seek. Well, hopefully no one would find Virgil until he was ready.

But then the closet door opened and shut—and he was no longer alone.

A slender body slammed against him in the dark. A girl, judging by the flounces of her diaphanous skirts, which made his skin itch. Some sort of fluffed up netting.

"Musa, is that you?" the girl hissed under her breath. "I called the closet!"

"Not Musa," Virgil answered, trying not to stammer. He'd never been so close to a girl before. Not like this. She smelled of floral soap and newly mowed grass.

The girl pulled away though her skirts still brushed his legs; the closet wasn't meant for two. "So sorry! Zeus, you must think me rude. I didn't know the closet was occupied."

"It is rather."

The girl let out an odd laugh. Embarrassed, that's what she was —this was an emotion Virgil knew too well. Perhaps to compensate, she released a soft torrent of words. "You must be the boy posing for Papa. He mentioned you and your family were scheduled for today. A large oil painting. Told us to behave—" another odd laugh "—well, not like *this*, mind. That's why we were playing in the garden, but it got so hot. It is rather crowded in here, isn't it? Anyway, I'll leave—"

"You can't leave," Virgil managed to interject. "Door's locked."

"I forgot about that." The girl let out a sigh, skirts rustling. "Yes, the lock is fussy. I suppose Papa hasn't repaired it yet. No reason to panic—someone will find us soon." More brightly, "Hopefully only after I win the game."

Some distance outside the closet, Virgil heard the young boy shriek, "Ready or not, here I come!"

"Shush!" the girl whispered.

Virgil whispered in turn, "Who are you?"

After several moments of silence, she murmured, "I'm Allegra Jane Bartham. But everyone calls me Angela."

"Do you look like an angel?" Virgil couldn't resist asking. He'd hadn't even caught a glimpse of Angela when she dashed into the closet. She'd been so swift.

In the distance, a shriek of laughter. Someone's hiding place must have been discovered.

"I wouldn't know."

Her bashful tone offered all the confirmation Virgil needed.

Several yards outside the closet door, slow footsteps drew near. Angela grabbed Virgil's wrist.

"They're coming!" she mouthed against his ear.

"Who is?"

"My sisters and brother."

Virgil felt an unexpected pang. He had a brother once—well, he couldn't think of him now. "Aren't they hiding too?"

"I suspect they've all been found. But I want to see how long it takes them to find me. Shush!"

A moment later, the footsteps turned away; Angela released his hand after letting out a long breath.

"That was close! I suspect it was Musa," she whispered. "She knows I'm here, but won't betray me."

"Musa's your sister?"

He sensed Angela's vigorous nod in the dark. "She's the eldest. Bossy."

Virgil knew all about that. His brother had been seven years older. He'd been the dominant one, but not in a bad way. Virgil had admired Robert so much; all of life's gifts seemed centered in him.

But again, Virgil didn't want to think of this. Not now. Not during this unexpected encounter with this peculiar yet enticing angel girl.

"What of your other siblings?" he asked.

"They're twins."

"Identical?"

"No, though they resemble Papa. Their names are Lyra and

Theo. They're only four. Babies really." A pause. "Anyway, who are you?"

Virgil held back a stutter, as he often did when anxious. "It doesn't matter."

And here was the sorry truth. He, Virgil Sydenham, Viscount of Sunderland, didn't matter to the world save for the title he'd inherit when his father passed to his eternal reward (though Virgil prayed this wouldn't be for many, *many* years). He never wanted to become earl—that honor was meant for Robert, not him. Virgil would have been content in a humble country estate filled with fragrant flowers and gentle animals, far from anyone who might find him lacking.

"Surely you have a name," Angela prodded.

"Virgil Sydenham," he finally answered. "Viscount of Sunderland."

"Oh."

Angela exhaled the syllable. Virgil cringed, imagining her thoughts. *You're an aristocrat. Above my station.* What if she fawned over him to gain social advantage? Such insincerity was all too common among the *ton* and beyond.

Before Angela could say another word, the closet door burst opened. Virgil's mother at her most distressed.

"There you are, Virgil!" she cried. "I had no idea where you'd gone I was worried something happened!" Her eyes narrowed as she took in Angela. "Who are *you*."

His mother's words were a demand, not a question.

"Angela. Well, Miss Allegra Jane Bartham, ma'am. I'm the artist's daughter."

Virgil cringed as he recalled his mother's earlier tirade. *"You do know Bartham's wife is an adulteress? The newspapers call her the Muse of Scandal."* He prayed Angela hadn't overheard.

"'You are to address me as *my lady*," his mother corrected. "I'm the Countess of Sunderland, not your governess."

Out of the corner of his eye, Virgil made out Angela's graceful curtsey. "Forgive me, my lady."

"And why are you and my son in a closet, Miss Allegra Bartham? You led him astray?"

"No, my lady."

To Virgil's surprise, Angela didn't appear cowed by his mother's displeasure. He supposed she was used to judgment, given the gossip about her parents. Still, he recognized his mother's temper rising like the heat outside in the garden.

Perhaps Angela sensed this too, for she quickly added, "Don't be angry with the viscount, my lady. The closet locked behind us. An accident, that's all."

His mother's mouth pursed. "Enough. Both of you, come."

"Yes, my lady."

Angela offered a hand to help Virgil out—he'd been wedged in a corner of the closet against the easel—and at last he saw her in the full light of day.

Angela Bartham had long pale hair, like her mother. A lithe figure. About his age, maybe a little younger. Blue eyes. She wore what appeared to be an enormous lavender tutu and ballet slippers. A costume glittering with sparkles. Was she a dancer then? Or just dressed like one?

She took him in similarly, her soft pink lips curving.

"I had no idea what you looked like in the dark," she said.

With this, Virgil's stomach dropped. He knew he was plump. Ruddy-cheeked. Rude red hair. Freckled. In other words, everything Angela Bartham wasn't. For she was exquisite. Yes, that was the only way to describe her; he imagined his father using the word in the same way he would for a work of art.

Virgil waited for Angela's smile to slip into dismay over his awkwardness. But, to his amazement, her expression appeared decidedly sympathetic. He knew she somehow understood all his sorrows and disappointments…and, even more miraculously, she cared.

And in that moment, Virgil's heart expanded in a manner that felt decidedly new.

Still smiling, Angela set her forefinger against her chin. "I know this is forward, but you don't look like a Virgil to me."

"His proper address is *my lord*, Miss Allegra Bartham," his mother called out over her shoulder. "Virgil is a fine name."

"That's true, my lady," she conceded. To Virgil: "But I'd rather call you Sunny, if I may. Your hair is like the sun before it sets. Warm. Kind. Like you."

Virgil swore he heard his heart knock against his ribs.

"Sunny then," he agreed. "Thank you, Miss Allegra."

"Angela," she corrected. "Because we're friends now, aren't we?" A last curtsey in his mother's direction. "Well, I should let you go pose for my father. I've already taken much of your time."

And then she skipped away to join her siblings, taking Sunny's heart with her.

As the years passed and they grew into adulthood, Angela proved to be a worthy guardian of his heart. She and Sunny became the best of friends; his heart grew in devotion despite his mother's disapproval. As children, they'd spend spring mornings walking about the rose gardens of Green Park, winter afternoons reading novels aloud in her sitting room. His heart expanded further when he escorted her to the ballet, where he watched her rapturous face drink in *Giselle*, her favorite. After he learned to play the piano, he became her only audience when she danced alone in Neil's studio and, on several memorable occasions, under the full moon on summer evenings, when he thought his heart would burst from bliss.

Alas, some things cannot last. Thirteen years after their first meeting in a closet, Angela would break Sunny's heart.

He would not take it well.

CHAPTER 1
THIRTEEN YEARS LATER

BARTHAM DAUGHTER TO WED TRADESMAN

The Times, 27 December 1872. Lady Minerva Hadley of Grosvenor Square is pleased to announce the imminent marriage of her great-niece Miss Angela Bartham to Mr. John Carles of Surrey, a noted sherry importer. The nuptials will take place on the morning of December 30th at Holy Trinity Brompton.

Miss Bartham, a noted beauty, is the middle daughter of artist Neil Bartham, whose elopement decades earlier with the former Mrs. Clio Sutton née Hadley—aka 'the Muse of Scandal'—drew much censor. In 1866, Mr. Bartham disappeared whilst traveling to Jerusalem to paint religious subjects. His unexplained absence left his family on the edge of financial and social ruin. Fortunately, the artist was recently located alive in Egypt.

Many will recall that Lady Hadley sponsored Miss Bartham's brilliant introduction to society earlier this year. Miss Bartham's grace and silver-blonde hair drew much attention despite her notorious parents.

On the loveliest winter morning in the sweetest church one could imagine in all of London, Angela Bartham possessed only one question before her wedding.

"You're certain Sunny's here?"

The person Angela addressed was her elder sister, Musa, her matron of honor—Musa, who'd unexpectedly married that spring to an up-and-coming artist named Sebastian Atkinson. Their union had gained much attention thanks to a popular children's book they'd collaborated on.

"Completely certain," Musa answered, glancing up from the train of Angela's gown, which she'd been arranging. Sewn of a delicate silk brocade, the train was easily wrinkled, something Angela hadn't taken into consideration when she conferred with the modiste.

Musa added, "That solves one mystery, though there's still no word about where he'd been all this time."

Six months earlier Sunny had asked for Angela's hand in marriage, a proposal Angela promptly refused for reasons only Musa understood. Afterward, he'd disappeared from London to heaven knew where. Rumors flew high and low. Some said Sunny purchased a commission in the military, which seemed ridiculous— after all, Sunny was an earl, not a second son without prospects. Others said he'd simply gone off on a Grand Tour to soothe his broken heart. Even his mother was uninformed as to his location. She'd taken the surprising task of approaching Angela to see if she knew where her son had gone.

Now Sunny was back in London without notice…and a guest at her wedding.

How? Why? Angela fretted, her usual cheerfulness muted. She knew she should be relieved. Perhaps Sunny's presence meant he'd forgiven her, though she doubted it. They'd been the best of friends until his proposal. He'd since refused to speak to her.

She wondered who could have invited him. Certainly not her mother, Clio, who'd been disappointed when Angela refused

Sunny's hand. Nor her great-aunt Minerva, who was relieved when Angela promptly agreed to marry a sherry merchant named John Carles soon after Sunny's proposal. (Not the same as an earl, but definitely a step up for the Barthams.) Carles even had a home in Surrey. Angela had always wanted to live in the countryside surrounded by animals and flowers. More importantly, he adored Angela…or so she told herself.

As for Angela's feelings for Carles, those were more complicated.

You're very fond of him, she told herself. *That's enough for a happy marriage.* John Carles ticked all the boxes off her list of Gentleman Worth Marrying. He was well-off, kind, and handsome enough. Her great-aunt Minerva assured Angela he was a wonderful match, with a good reputation and honorable family name. Anyway, Angela didn't believe in true love, the sort of passion that brought flutters to your stomach and heady kisses. Not anymore.

She'd experienced such a love once. It nearly destroyed her.

She'd learned her lesson. Now Angela was determined to be happy no matter what—she'd take her joy where she could find it. She understood there were more important considerations when it came to choosing a husband. There was respectability, the possibility of children, financial stability, even futures for her sixteen-year-old siblings, Theo and Lyra, who yearned to become musicians.

Anyway, passionate affairs of the heart rarely lasted…save for a few lucky couples.

Angela stole a glance at her mother and her sister, Musa, who were adjusting each other's floral garlands.

Mama and Papa are the exception. So are Musa and Seb.

Everyone who encountered the couples could tell they were meant for each other. Musa and Seb spent their days finishing each other's sentences as though they were of one mind and heart. As for Clio, such was her devotion to their father that she hadn't been the same since his departure for Jerusalem. Now that Neil Bartham been found in Egypt, she was scheduled to leave in three days to help bring him home; he'd been seriously injured there.

Angela told herself she didn't envy her mother's and sister's marriages. At the age of three and twenty, she already understood life was filled with inequities. All things considered, she really was fortunate. Carles would be a good husband. She was delighted to become his wife. Really.

As for Sunny…that was an entirely different matter.

"I'm surprised Sunny's here," Angela forced out. His presence in the church was an uncomfortable reminder of the romantic love she'd given up on. Soulmate love. The kind of love that doomed lovers in ballets.

For Sunny *did* believe in such a love…but Angela couldn't love him that way. She cared enough not to wed him without reciprocating his affections. Unlike Carles.

On that front, Angela tried to suppress the guilt roiling her stomach.

"I invited his mother," Clio admitted sheepishly. "I should have told you, but I never expected she'd attend, and with Sunny, no less. I thought she'd still be in mourning for the previous earl."

Angela couldn't think how to respond. On one hand, her heart leapt to see her old friend had returned for her wedding—perhaps he'd gotten over her refusal. On the other hand, it was all so awkward.

"Well, this is a surprise," Musa said dryly, adjusting her spectacles. "Sunny looks so different. I hadn't recognized him until I heard his mother bleating in her usual way."

Angela was saved from her uneasy ruminations by the arrival of her great-aunt Minerva, who was overdressed for a wedding. She appeared to have decked herself in every diamond she owned.

"Posh, the Earl of Sunderland is old news," she clucked to Angela. "Look at this article, miss! I'd hoped someone would write about your wedding."

Aunt Minerva held out a newspaper folded to the society

section. BARTHAM DAUGHTER TO WED TRADESMAN, the headline declared. The article lasted for all of three brief paragraphs, flattering to Angela but touching on her spotted family history. Angela supposed it couldn't be avoided.

"There's three journalists here," Aunt Minerva added. "They came right up to me, the rascals! I hoped this article would be enough to satisfy them. Well, one must accept such hardships when one is a famed beauty such as yourself, miss."

"I suppose," Angela said.

"I'll see you inside the church! Soon your family will be received at the most elite addresses in London—and it's all because of my sponsorship." Another cluck of pleasure. "Oh, no need to thank me, Angela. Not yet. There's time for that later."

Once her aunt bustled out, Angela peeked out the rectory doors, taking care to remain hidden.

The church was full on the Barthams' side, but scant on Carles'; he claimed it was too far for his family to come from Surrey. He'd considered applying for a special license, so they could be wed near them, but settled for a common license to avoid declaring banns for their wedding. ("That's for plebeians who can't afford privacy," he said.) Still, a common license required them to be wed in the parish church closest to Angela's home.

Carles awaited her at the head of the aisle with the vicar. As for everyone else in the church, Angela made out the dowager countess —well, she remained the Countess of Sunderland until Sunny chose a bride. She appeared as always, with her receding chin and haughty demeanor, only more annoyed, if such a thing was possible. She was seated near a man Angela didn't recognize.

Then she did.

Angela's stomach dropped as though she were about to tumble down a hill. She must have let out a gasp, for Musa said, "I should have warned you."

Lyra, Angela's youngest sister, added, "Wherever Sunny went—"

"He came back quite..." Angela's words faded away.

"Altered," Clio finished.

Angela stole another glance at the man who'd replaced her old friend. It couldn't be. But there he was.

Virgil Sydenham, the former Viscount, now Earl of Sunderland. Sunny, her dearest companion from childhood. If not for his bright auburn hair, she wouldn't have recognized him.

Angela's heart panged. Given the scandals surrounding her parents, his friendship had been especially precious—he saw Angela as who she was, not as people gossiped. Sunny was kind, good, and compassionate. For a moment, she recalled picnicking with him in Green Park as children. The two of them laughing as they chased rabbits at his country estate in Berkshire. Reading books together. His piano and her dancing to his playing. Days of innocence that could never be regained or revisited.

Sunny was seated directly on the aisle—Angela would have no choice but to pass him directly on her way to the altar. His hair had grown markedly longer since they'd last met. The length subdued his unruly curls into something sleeker, vaguely scandalous even. His hair nearly reached his shoulders, like one of Papa's bohemian friends.

His clothes were different too. Though Sunny always dressed in accordance with his station in well-tailored clothes from the finest Saville Row tailors, today he was completely dressed in a black morning suit save for a dark red necktie. He looked leaner. Powerful.

But it was more than this that made him appeared so changed. There were new creases across his brow, a hard set to his jaw. His brown eyes colder. The sweetness she'd loved about him was gone, along with the gentle, wondering way he approached the world that made him appear stumbling and awkward at times. Angela had known differently.

To Angela's shock, her old friend looked angry. Defiant. A bit dangerous. Not at all like himself.

Even more surprising was the fashionable young lady seated

beside him. Her chestnut-hued hair was arranged in tight ringlets to her shoulders beneath her be-plumed bonnet. She appeared several years older than Angela. No one could deny the lady was beautiful in a showy way. She reminded Angela of a peacock, all display and dazzle. The lady stared down at her navy-blue lace mitts, her lips pursed with ennui.

As for the Countess of Sunderland, every so often she threw an alarmed glance in Sunny's direction and fluttered her purple fan.

"I can't believe it," Angela whispered.

Lyra replied, "You can believe it. I even spoke to him when he arrived, to make sure I wasn't imagining things."

"What did he say?"

Lyra shrugged. "Just hello and fine morning, did I think it was going to snow, that sort of thing. But he spoke French to the lady. I understood enough."

"Aren't you going to tell me what he said to her?" Angela asked, her mouth dry.

Lyra's voice dropped to a breath. "That he'd buy her a new gown once this was over."

Angela pulled back from the door. If Sunny was courting the lady, it was decidedly forward to take her shopping. This proved that either they were engaged or she was his mistress. Worst of all, she was French—or so Aunt Minerva would say.

"It seems he's been on the continent after all," Musa said. "Like the rumors claimed."

As though sensing Angela's presence, Sunny's head pivoted toward the door. Angela scuttled away. The church doors slammed so hard that the sound reverberated.

"He saw me!" Angela cried.

"And what if he did?" Musa soothed, taking Angela's hand. "You're trembling. Has this really upset you so?"

"I'm only trembling because I'm so happy," Angela claimed. "That's all."

"Happy people don't look as though they're about to faint."

Musa whispered, "If you've doubts, you needn't marry Carles. I hope you know this."

"I want to marry him," Angela replied.

That, at least, was the truth. Wasn't it?

Clio swept Angela into an embrace just as the church bells struck ten. "Come, beautiful. It's time."

"Indeed it is," Seb added; he'd come in from the church to escort Angela down the aisle. He offered Angela his arm. "Are you ready?"

"As ready as I'll ever be," Angela answered, grateful for her brother-in-law's steady warmth. She forced a smile. All was well, really. "I'm going to be married!"

It was enough she was fond of Carles. Love of a sort would come in time. Anyway, love made you vulnerable; marriage made security—and security would hopefully lead to love. And if love didn't come, Angela would survive. There'd be children to adore, a home to create. There were worse things than a loveless marriage…though right now she felt queasy enough to vomit.

I swear I will be happy no matter what. There is beauty, there is goodness in this world. I'll make it so.

"The music's starting!" Lyra squealed, clapping in anticipation.

Inside the church, the organ swelled with the majestic chords of the wedding march from *Lohengrin*. Angela gathered her bouquet, a generous spray of exquisite pink roses with soft yellow stamens. Clio settled Angela's veil over her eyes, transforming the vestry into a blur of white. Seb led her toward the door, with Lyra and Musa following as her bridal attendants.

Before they entered the church, Angela stole a last look through her veil at her family, all whom she adored beyond measure. Clio was wiping away tears of pride. Musa and Lyra looked beautiful dressed in pink gowns, Seb regal in his best suit, and Theo grown up beyond measure. Once her mother brought Papa back from Egypt, the Barthams would all be together again. Even better, her family would gain security and respectability thanks to Angela's marriage. That would have to be enough.

Suddenly Angela realized she was marrying for love after all.

For the love of her family.

And with this, joy filled her heart.

I will be happy no matter what.

CHAPTER 2

ONCE THE ORGAN began to play the wedding march, Sunny, or more properly Virgil Sydenham, Earl of Sunderland, decided the worst day of his life wasn't the day he'd lost his brother Robert, as awful as it was. Nor was it the day his father died, which happened to be the same day that Angela Bartham refused his proposal. No, it was today, but not for the reason one would expect.

His head was splitting like the devil's anvil was smashing into it.

Sunny rarely drank, not anymore. One would have thought he'd learned his lesson after his previous experiences. Last night he hadn't been able to resist, knowing Angela's wedding was this morning.

Damn it. I shouldn't have attended. But he'd forced himself to come. Forced himself in order to prove to himself, his mother, and the world that he cared nothing for Angela Bartham. Not anymore. That he was doing better than ever and even had a beautiful woman by his side.

As for that beautiful woman, her name was Hélène Charlotte de Castel-d'Albret, an appropriately grand name befitting her aristocratic lineage. Hélène, seated between Sunny and his mother, sniffed dismissively. She whispered to him in French, "She's beautiful, but rather ordinary."

He replied in a low tone, "What of it?"

He'd brought Hélène to prove he wasn't at a loss for feminine companionship. Wasn't someone to pity. Hélène's arrival had horrified his mother, even after he assured her Hélène was the daughter of a former French noble from the Second Empire. Sunny didn't dare tell her the extent of their relationship.

"And she's wearing white," Hélène added. "*Trés bourgeois, non?*"

He nodded wearily. Yes, wearing white as a bride was very middle class. White had always been his least favorite color…especially on Angela.

To his horror, she looked lovelier than ever. Glowing, as she approached her future husband, that tradesman. Joy-filled. This was one of the qualities he'd always loved about her—no matter what, Angela found good in the world. This extended to the people surrounding her. He'd been a desperately awkward, lonely child; she'd seen the good in him.

But not enough to wed him.

"We shouldn't have attended, Sunderland," the countess muttered to her son. "If this is your idea of revenge, you've wasted my morning."

The Countess of Sunderland had long despised the Barthams for reasons too copious to enumerate. Which was surprising, considering that Sunny's father, rest his soul, had esteemed the art of Neil Bartham and ignored the family's reputation. Then there was the matter of Neil and Clio's four children, three girls and one boy, of which Angela was the middle daughter.

As well as the kindest, most beautiful and grace-filled woman in England. Angela was sunshine and kittens and bright smiles. Mozart on a summer night and roses in a summer garden. Or so he'd once believed.

"I wish this was over," his mother whined beneath the swelling organ music. "I feel degraded."

"*Je suis d'accord*," Hélène agreed, tapping her fan against her thigh.

"That's exactly why we're here," he muttered, grumpier than usual. "To prove we're above them."

All too soon Angela drew close, her brother-in-law Sebastian clasping her arm. She progressed down the aisle as though she were floating in a sea of silk, revealing her years of ballet dancing. Her face was soft beneath her long ivory veil, her eyes trained on the huge bouquet of luscious pink roses clutched in her arms. Her lips curved in a gentle smile.

His head gave another pound.

To his dismay, Angela didn't meet his gaze as she passed Sunny on the aisle; he could have been dressed as a chimney sweep for all it mattered. Her lacy skirts brushed his hand, which he'd rested against the pew to steady himself. He flinched at the unexpected contact. Yet he didn't remove his hand.

Worse, his fingers flexed to caress her skirts.

The pale cream silk was crisp against her petticoats, the lace trim soft. Just like that day long ago, when they'd been trapped together in that closet as children.

This is as close as you'll ever get to holding her.

He unwillingly recalled the future he'd envisioned when he proposed to Angela six months earlier, before she'd broken his heart. He'd imagined summers in his ancestral home in Berkshire, countess of all she surveyed as they walked along the lush woods and gardens. Winters in London in his townhouse in North Kensington, where they'd attend ballets and she'd visit her family. Private soirées where he'd play Mozart, and she'd dance for their friends.

Most of all, he imagined clasping Angela in his arms in their nuptial bed, her pale gold hair falling across the bed linens as they made love. Warm sunlight gilding her shoulders, birds chirping outside their window. Dandelion clocks and rose petals and teacakes dusted with sugar.

Suddenly Sunny wanted to bolt for the door. Run. Though that would undermine the point of his attending the wedding: to prove Angela had made a mistake in refusing his proposal. He glanced at Hélène. Thank goodness she was there, though what sort of revenge could it be if it went unacknowledged?

At last, Angela arrived at the altar, where Carles awaited. He really did look like a weasel, Sunny decided. Too tall. Thin. Lanky brown hair draped across his forehead. Darting eyes.

The vicar cleared his throat in preparation for the ceremony. Angela raised her eyes from her roses. Sunny made out a subtle flush cross her face as she gazed up toward her future husband; Carles was much taller than Angela. He took her hand in his, returning her warm gaze. He beamed—that was the only word for it.

Sunny resisted the urge to gag.

"Dearly beloved, we are gathered here to witness the union of Allegra and John…"

The vicar's drone circled Sunny's ears like a mosquito. How many times had he witnessed the service of marriage? As a boy, he'd found it enthralling, the hope that one would meet your true love and live happily ever after like a fairy tale. Today, the ceremony irked him more than he'd ever expected to be possible.

He jiggled his foot against the pew. His eyes smarted from lack of sleep.

Revenge only hurts the bearer.

This was a saying Sunny's father trotted out regularly after the death of Sunny's brother. Sunny hadn't wanted to believe him, for he had plenty of fodder for revenge. When another boy at Eton shoved him into a pile of horse manure. When his mother criticized his waistcoat straining at the buttons. When someone at his club ridiculed the stammer that emerged when he was stressed. Most of all, when Angela refused his suit to choose Carles.

But now he knew his father was right. When this was over, Angela would live happily ever after. He'd take to his bed until his headache subsided—Hélène could shop on her own. As for his mother, who appeared to be dozing, he'd follow her lead.

"Wake me when it's over," he whispered to Hélène as he shut his eyes.

She offered a warm chuckle. "*Exactement.*"

He didn't look up when the church doors creaked open. A late arrival.

The vicar continued despite the interruption. "Do you, John Francis, take Allegra Jane as your lawful wedded wife?"

"I do," Carles finished. To Angela: "Your turn, darling."

Despite everything, Sunny's heart thudded in anticipation. He forced himself to look at Angela. To his surprise, Angela looked pale beneath her veil, queasy even. Her gentle smile had become a rigid seam.

The vicar began, "Allegra Jane, do you take—"

A baby's cry interrupted the vicar. Angela's mouth grew tighter. Carles' gaze darted toward the door.

How loud the baby was! Angela's heart gave a thud, especially after the vicar's words came to a halt. Her cheerfulness drooped like an unstarched collar as she glanced over her shoulder.

Through the haze of her white veil, Angela made out a lady, someone she hadn't met before, enter the church. The lady wore respectable navy blue broadcloth, her dress fuller than the current fashion. She stood in front of the church doors, cradling a swaddled infant. A little girl about three years clutched her skirts. The lady was pretty in a delicate way, like Angela, though her hair was dark, not blonde, beneath her straw bonnet.

It must be someone from Carles's side—that was good. Angela had been distressed by how few showed for their nuptials from his family, though Carles had prepared her. Still, Angela wished the lady hadn't interrupted the ceremony. For a moment, when those church doors creaked open, she imagined someone interrupting their wedding, like Bertha Mason's brother in *Jane Eyre*. She and Sunny had read the book together long ago.

Her heart gave another thud at the thought of Sunny's presence. She'd never seen him so fashionably dressed. The French lady by his side really was stunningly beautiful.

It's good he's here. It proves he bears you no ill will.

The vicar cleared his throat and began anew.

"Allegra Jane, do you take John Francis as your lawful wedded husband?"

This was it. The moment that would tie them together forever. No turning back.

A deep breath. "I-I..."

I do. Two syllables. That's all. It should be easy. But Angela couldn't seem to get the words out. That lady's arrival had rattled her.

As for the lady herself, she let out a cough. But it wasn't the sort of cough one would make if ill. It was more the sort to gain attention if one was too polite to make a scene.

Angela's skin prickled as whispers rose in the church.

"Answer the vicar, darling," Carles said, his smile tight.

"Who's the woman?" Angela whispered, her stomach clenching anew.

"No one important," Carles said. To the vicar: "We've a train to catch."

They were to honeymoon in Wales, which wasn't Angela's choice. Wales felt so far away with her mother leaving for Egypt— what if something arose with the twins? Anyway, their train wasn't until much later that afternoon. First there was the ceremony to complete, the registry to sign. Then the wedding breakfast, which her great-aunt would host in her townhouse in Mayfair. All markers of church and state—markers that would finally return Angela and the Barthams to social respectability.

The vicar's brow creased. "Is there something we should discuss in private, Mr. Carles?"

Though his tone was low, the implication was clear.

No scandal, Angela prayed, all of her cheerfulness gone. *Please, no scandal.*

Another murmur ran through the church. Angela couldn't resist peeking over her shoulder. The dowager countess's brow arched. Sunny sat upright as though his spine had turned to steel.

Something bad is going to happen. They know it. Everyone knows it.

"All is well," Carles snapped. "Continue."

"If you please," the dark-haired lady called out in a broad West Country accent; her baby wailed anew. "We should speak in private, John—"

"You're not to call me by my christian name," Carles scolded.

The lady ambulated down the aisle with her children in their direction. As she drew near, Angela smelled something damp and rank seep from her cloak. Travel. Horses. Mud.

"Mr. Carles then. Regardless, we should speak." She shrugged in Angela's direction. "Sorry, love."

"Sorry for what?" Angela asked, suspecting the answer she was about to receive would make her *very* unhappy. "Who are you?"

The young lady answered, "Perhaps you should ask John—I mean, Mr. Carles—that question."

Angela's gaze darted between Carles, this rather shabby looking lady, her children, and the vicar.

"I'd rather hear it from you, madame," Angela replied.

"He's the father of my children. My husband."

Angela would have told herself she'd misheard had not a collective gasp rise in the church.

"Your husband?" Angela said weakly. Perspiration beaded on her forehead beneath her veil.

A nod. "My name is Mary Elizabeth Carles. Mrs. John Carles, yes. We wed in Surrey four years ago as of last May. I've papers, certificates, whatever proof you require. I'd suspected Mr. Carles had a pretty piece on the side, but had no proof until I read this."

She brandished a clipping of a newspaper article from her reticule—the same article Aunt Minerva had been so proud of moments earlier.

This can't be happening to me.

"Papa!" the little girl cried, her arms straining for Carles. "I missed you!"

"Liar!" Carles grabbed Angela's hands; his palms were unpleasantly moist. "Angela, say you believe me! That woman is not my wife." Carles's voice dropped to a whisper. "She's Catholic. We all know papist ceremonies don't count."

A long moment passed, a moment in which Angela sensed her family's future melt like snow in summer. Musa and Seb's books avoided by anyone respectable. Lyra left without prospects for marriage or as a musician, Theo laughed out of school. Worst of all, her mother wouldn't leave to help her father return home from Egypt because she'd be too busy fretting about Angela.

"That's not exactly a denial," Angela said at last.

Another lady stood up. Well, staggered really—she'd been seated in the back on Carles's side of the aisle apart from everyone else. Angela noticed her earlier; she'd appeared so out of place in her magenta evening gown, like she'd come directly from a ball. However, the bump rounding her stomach was impossible to ignore despite the generous flounces on her skirt.

"He's my husband too!" the pregnant lady called out in a heavy Cockney accent. "We wed in Gretna Green two years ago. I wasn't going to say anything unless I had to—" she nodded at the first wife "—but then I realized I'd been a coward." To Angela, "You're better off without him, duckling."

A hiss swept around the church. Angela's face burned, her knees trembled beneath that lovely silk and lace gown she'd been so proud of that morning. Her head buzzed with light. She wasn't going to faint, was she?

Instead, her mother fainted; Seb caught her before she hit the stone floor of the church. Musa dashed to Clio, waving smelling salts over her face. Angela couldn't bear to look anywhere else, knowing what she'd witness. Lyra's mouth would be agape, her great-aunt flailing, Theo slinking in the pew as though to disappear.

And then Angela knew. She wouldn't be getting married that day, or any day for that matter. Once word got out, she'd be the laughingstock of all of London. Worse, England. It didn't matter she was a famed beauty, or how noble her intents had been in agreeing to wed Carles and his supposedly good family name. All that mattered was that Angela Bartham, daughter of Clio Bartham, the Muse of Scandal, had been abandoned at the altar after nearly wedding a bigamist.

She'd join her mother in infamy…and so would the rest of her family.

A sharp cackle broke the horrified silence of the church. The Countess of Sunderland—Angela would know her laugh anywhere.

She muttered, "It figures a Bartham daughter would choose such a husband."

With this, what felt like all hell broke loose. The middle class woman thrust the baby into Carles's arms—"Take your child, sir!"—and the little girl coiled her arms around his knees like an attacking octopus. Tiny as she was, the child's weight threw Carles off. He crumpled to the red-carpeted aisle, nearly hitting his head against the altar.

Next, the pregnant woman kicked Carles in his thigh. Angela sensed she'd intended to aim for parts further north.

"Bastard!" she hissed. "I suspected as much about you, but didn't want to believe it!"

Then Aunt Minerva fainted next to Clio, Lyra's eyes bugged out, and Musa caught their aunt while her ever-active brain clicked away in search of How To Fix This.

But no one could fix this; this Angela knew without a doubt.

It's all true, Angela thought in an oddly detached manner. Now it all made sense: Carles's anxious manner after she'd accepted his proposal, his refusal to show her his estate in Surrey. Even the common license so they wouldn't have to post banns, and how few showed from his side for the wedding.

This is the worst day of my life.

With this, Angela's emotions returned in full force. A rush of embarrassment—how could she have misjudged Carles so?—along with a bright blade of fury.

He ruined her life. Well, now she'd ruin his.

"I'll kill you," she hissed.

She stared around for a weapon. Something. Anything. Meanwhile Seb strode forth, his fists raised—he had a temper when provoked—but that wouldn't provide enough satisfaction for Angela's liking. The prayer books were too small to wreck any damage save for a bruise or two. The brass candlesticks too far away. Her eyes finally settled on the generous bouquet of pink roses in her arms.

Roses had thorns. Thorns were sharp. They would do just fine.

Just as Angela was about to smash her roses into Carles's face, another burst of laughter from the Countess of Sunderland. She cackled like a seal drunk on gin.

"Shut up, Mother," Sunny snapped.

"Oh come, it's hilarious, Sunderland!"

In lieu of an answer, he majestically rose from the pew, looking more self-possessed than Angela had ever witnessed. Was he going to leave? That would be a kindness. How humiliating this all was!

No, instead he approached Angela.

Sunderland, no," his mother called out, any amusement banished from her tone. "Don't!"

Don't what? Angela thought.

Sunny dropped to his knees before Angela.

"Angela Bartham," he said, "I'd like to offer for your hand in marriage."

And then it truly was the worst day of her life.

In 1873 Paris, a marriage of convenience between a ballet-dancing beauty and a beastly earl is about to get messy.

WHEN ANGELA BARTHAM of the notorious Bartham family is stranded at the altar on her wedding day, she's saved from ruin by her old friend Sunny, the Earl of Sunderland. He offers a startlingly generous proposition: a marriage of convenience that will last exactly one year. Long enough for society to stop gossiping. Long enough for the press to lose interest. Then they'll quietly annul their unconsummated union.

Left without choices, Angela agrees. But Sunny is no longer the sweet but awkward boy she grew up with—and who once loved her. A mysterious trip abroad has transformed him into a surly, secretive beast of a rake who can't seem to stand the sight of her. Nor is

Angela the romantic girl who once danced all night under the moon. She's a heartbroken beauty trapped in a fake marriage that can't end soon enough.

To avoid the chattering crowds, Angela and Sunny flee London to spend their year of marriage in Paris. But what they don't take into consideration is that emotions aren't particularly rational . . . especially when there's only one bed in the gothic kitten-laden chateau they're stuck inside near the Bois de Boulogne. Forced proximity reveals hidden depths, turning their marriage of convenience into a messy affair of the heart. Will Angela and Sunny's dance of desire come to an end, destroying everything they hold dear—including their friendship?

Now available on all platforms and in print.

ABOUT THE AUTHOR

Delphine Ross writes lush, witty, and angsty historical romances set during the nineteenth century. In her spare time, she loves traveling to places where she can imagine other lives in earlier times. Under another name, Delphine writes critically acclaimed and bestselling fiction and nonfiction. Learn more at DelphineRoss.com.

 instagram.com/delphinerossbooks

Books *that make you think.*

Books *that make you feel.*

Books *that inspire.*

Thank you for reading *The Poetics of Passion* by Delphine Ross. We truly hope you enjoyed it! As a small independent publisher, we rely on supportive readers such as yourself to get the word out. Here's three ways you can help.

1. REVIEW. Take a moment to leave a review on Goodreads, Bookbub, and other review sites and retailers.

2. REQUEST. Mention this book to your local library or favorite independent bookstore. Request they stock it. (Wholesale discounts are available via Ingram Books and Baker and Taylor.)

3. BOOK CLUB. Suggest this book for your book club. Reach out to us at ReadMuse.com to set up a virtual author visit.

Any other thoughts? Suggestions? We'd love to hear from you! Contact us at ReadMuse.com.

With much gratitude,
   MUSE PUBLICATIONS